Spectres in the Smoke

SPECTRES IN THE SMOKE

Tony Broadbent

All the characters and events portrayed in this work are fictitious.

SPECTRES IN THE SMOKE

A Felony & Mayhem mystery

PRINTING HISTORY
First edition: (St. Martin's Press/Thomas Dunne): 2005
Felony & Mayhem edition: 2006

ISBN 1-933397-51-9

Manufactured in the United States of America

We all have our heroes.

In memory of my dad, and Kirk's dad,
and John Czaja, and Joan Haigh,
and Johanna "Jo-Jo" Bradley.
And one or two other extraordinary people.

"Inspirations, all."

Acknowledgments

Thanks to Dan Cruickshank for first opening my eyes to the magic and mystery of London town so very long ago. "Thanks for the keys to the city, Dan."

Thanks to Nina Fishman, historian, *femme du monde,* for throwing light onto the political and social history of post-war Great Britain, any shadowy misinterpretations of which are entirely my own.

Thanks to David Thomson, that most perceptive and erudite of film biographers, for his thoughts and reflections on the influence and effects that the cinema and the film stars of the day had on post-war British society.

I'd like to acknowledge James Morton's many books on British criminals and crime, especially *East End Gangland;* also, Peter Ackroyd, the city's undisputed Boswell, for his hugely enjoyable books on London and Londoners, especially *London: The Biography.* As to elements within the plot I'd like to acknowledge my debt to Richard Griffiths's *Patriotism Perverted;* Martin Allen's *Hidden Agenda;* Nicholas Mosley's *Beyond The Pale;* Peter Wright's *Spycatcher;* and Alan F. Bartlett's *C.* I'd be remiss, too, if I didn't also acknowledge the writings of special heroes John Buchan, Ian Fleming, and David Niven.

Heartfelt thanks to family and friends for their unstinting support, especially to my wife, Christine, and my brother, Seth.

And to Barry and Mary Tomalin; Andrew Tonkin; Andrew Hyett and his mother, Jean Simpson; Dr. Hank Cross; Kirk Russell; and, of course, the inimitable Chris Haigh.

Thanks to my agent, Jill Grosjean, for her unwavering spirit, and to my editor, Pete Wolverton, for his patience and perspicacity.

Thanks, again, to "the Angel in the Hawaiian shirt." And to the many wonderful mystery booksellers—especially those at Partners & Crime, Rue Morgue, The Poisoned Pen, "M" is for Mystery, and Book Passage—who ventured with such unabashed vigour into *The Smoke*.

Glossary of London Underworld Slang

Banged up: locked in a cell

Beak: magistrate

Bees and Honey: rhyming slang = money

Bent: crooked

Berk: idiot, or worse (Berkeley Hunt)

Blag: robbery with violence

Blitz: the Blitz. WWII period of Nazi bombing of London

Blow: blowing a safe open with explosives

Blower: telephone

Bob's your uncle: everything will now turn out fine

Bogey: a policeman

Bones: form of skeleton key

Bottle: (bottle and glass) arse; having the courage to do a deed

Brassard: a taxi-driver's licence, worn on sleeve; or a disk

Butcher's: to look (butcher's hook)

Cane: a jemmy; short crowbar

Case: to survey, or check out premises prior to burglary

China: close friend; mate (old china plate)

Chiv: a knife or razor for cutting and slashing, not for stabbing

Climb/er: usually refers to the act of cat-burgling; a cat burglar

Clock, clocked: to take a look-see

Cocoa: rhy. sl. = "say so"

Collar: trad.—a policeman arrested a criminal by taking hold of his collar, i.e. "have one's collar felt"

Copper: a policeman

Cozzer: a policeman

Crack: to open a safe

Creep: entering a dwelling by night, quietly and without noise

Creeper: cat burglar

Doddle: anything easy to achieve

Dog and bone: telephone

Drag: motor car; to draw on a cigarette

Drum: a house or an apartment

Face: a crook of some repute

Fence: receiver of and/or trader in stolen property

Fiver: five quid; £5

Frummer: Orthodox Jew

GBH: grievous bodily harm

Germans: (German bands) hands

Ginger: (ginger beer) queer

Glim: a torch

Grand: a thousand pounds sterling

Grass: an informer; to inform

Groin: a ring with gemstones

Guv'nor: gang boss or senior policeman

Half-inch: to pinch; to steal

How's-yer-father: nonsense; rubbish

Iron: (iron hoof = poof) homosexual

Jelly: gelignite

Jack: "on my Jack Jones" = alone

King Lears: rhy. sl. = ears

Kip: sleep

Linens: newspapers (linen drapers)

Manor: the territory of a particular policeman or criminal

Minder: bodyguard, trouble-shooter

Nancy: homosexual

Nark: an informer

Narked: to be very irritated

Nod: "land of nod"; to be asleep

Nosh: food

Old Bill: the police; policeman

Petercane: small crowbar

Peterman: safe-breaker

Ponce: pimp

Porridge: time spent in prison

Quid: one pound sterling

Rip-rap: to tap; to borrow money

Sarky: sarcastic

Screwsman: burglar or safe-breaker

Shufty: to take a quick look

Skels: form of skeleton key

Skint: without money

Smoke: London ("the Smoke")

Snout: informer; or tobacco

Spiv: (back slang = VIPs; "very important persons") Black Market street trader

Stoppo: an escape; a getaway

Strides: trousers

Stumm: to stay silent

Swallow: to accept a situation

Sweeney: rhy. sl. *Sweeney Todd* = the Flying Squad

Tealeaf: rhy. sl. = thief

Team: a gang of people that regularly work together

Tearaway: small-time criminal, known to be reckless and violent

Tod: on own; alone (Tod Sloane)

Tom; Tomfoolery: jewellery

Top: to kill

Trouble and strife: wife

Turtles, turtledoves: rhy. sl. = gloves

Twirl: key, skeleton key

Villain: a crook of some standing

Whistle and flute: rhy. sl. = suit

Wide: "wide boy"; streetwise

But First, a Quiet Word
in Your King Lears

It'd promised to be a very different world after the War ended. But now, nearly three years later, we were all of us still waiting for the dust to settle and clear. At times, in between the curtains of soot-laden fog, it seemed as if London was one huge wasteland. There were bombsites everywhere. Dark toothy gaps a dozen houses long in streets otherwise untouched or whole streets and neighbourhoods gone, with solitary buildings left here and there like pinched, blackened stubs in an ashtray. And even those rows still standing bore the marks of doodlebug, incendiary bomb, and fire.

And with so many things busted, broken, or blown to smithereens no one knew quite where to begin. Was it better to start by clearing away all the mess and confusion? Or better to soldier on, build what you could on top of the rubble, and simply hope for the best?

Most families had suffered a tragic loss of some kind. A dad, a son, an uncle, a brother, who'd once waved a "cheerio" by the front door and gone off to war, then never returned. Or a sister, a granny, an auntie, a mother, who'd watched and waited, and then had perished to blazes in the Blitz. And all of them now gone forever, leaving gaping holes that could never be filled. True, a lucky few did manage to come through the War unscathed, and some did very well out of it. And more than one or two had lined themselves up to prosper whichever way the War went. Not that you could pick them out in a crowd, mind you, but they were there. They always are.

As there was still no end in sight to the Government's austerity measures, most everyone had gaps of a more pressing if no less dispiriting sort to contend with. Empty shelves and empty shopping-baskets were the rule, more often than not. And with officially-allotted allowances going up and down like a see-saw most weeks, people stood in queues for hours on end, never knowing what they'd get for their troubles. All basic everyday foods were on ration points, all clothing was on coupons, and as soap was rationed, too, it left people feeling pretty lousy about things. And what with it having been another especially hard winter, it was a miserable old time for most Londoners. Continuing fuel and electricity shortages meant that even the bright lights of Piccadilly Circus stayed forever dark. With no tinsel to be had anywhere, but down the picture house, life seemed forever grey.

To give them their due, Clement Attlee's Labour Government were still struggling to get to grips with the five giants of *want, sickness, squalor, ignorance,* and *idleness,* and were slowly starting to make good on their promise to provide everyone "comfort and care, from cradle to the grave." And despite bitter opposition from conservatives of every stripe, they forged ahead and introduced the National Health Service that meant free spectacles and false teeth for anyone that needed them and a doctor or a hospital bed when you were ill. They promised better state pensions for the old and poor; new housing for slum dwellers; and secure employment for the men that'd fought the War. Add a new Education Bill, so kids could stay in school longer and go on to grammar school or even university if they had the talent, and you had the makings of something very different to what'd gone before. Even, perhaps, a new and better Britain.

To be honest, though, a lot of people—me included—had thought the Labour Party a right load of duffers when they'd first started nationalising everything in sight, and things had gone from bad to worse. And although many in Britain regarded the Welfare State as the promised light in the wilderness, a good few saw it as the first flicker of the all-consuming fires of Communism. The middle and upper classes felt uneasy, under siege, and resentful. To them, Socialism promised nothing but the end of the Britain they knew and loved; they were terrified of power passing over into the wrong hands. Fears made all the more real when Communist trade union leaders down the London Docks voted repeatedly to go on strike, crippling imports and exports. And so it was, as night follows day, that the spectre of Fascism began to rise from out of the ashes again and draw people to its "Britain First" banner.

Was it any wonder then that the very idea of *"a new Jerusalem"* gave rise to such bitter disagreement in England's green and pleasant land? Or that for one dark moment Britain stood at a crossroads, as if spellbound, with no one knowing whether the morrow would bring a glorious social revolution or mobs roaming the streets looking to put heads on sticks.

"Crikey," I can hear you saying. "What's all this politics malarkey got to do with an honest-to-goodness London cat burglar, when he's at home?" Well, you'd be surprised what people will try and steal from you when you're not looking, really you would. But I have to admit I had to keep asking myself that same question over and over again during this caper; what with all its "who's who's" and "what's what's" and all its strange comings and goings. I tell you, it's not easy being a pawn in someone else's game, especially when the clock's ticking and you're being played as a promoted knight out to lay an old ghost and save a king. And all the while, you're worrying yourself sick about one old mate who's in dead trouble and you're fighting to help keep another old china's dream alive.

The icon above says you're holding a copy of a book in the Felony & Mayhem "Historical" category, which ranges from the ancient world up through the 1940s. If you enjoy this book, you may well like other "Historical" titles from Felony & Mayhem Press, including:

Man's Illegal Life, by Keith Heller
City of the Horizon, by Anton Gill
City of Dreams, by Anton Gill
The Smoke, by Tony Broadbent
The Blackheath Poisonings, by Julian Symons
Bertie and the Seven Bodies, by Peter Lovesey

For more about these books, and other Felony & Mayhem titles, or to place an order, please visit our website at:

www.FelonyAndMayhem.com

or contact us at:

Felony and Mayhem Press
156 Waverly Place
New York, NY 10014

Spectres in the Smoke

CHAPTER

1

Noises Off

So there I was... lying on the lids again, not yet the dead of night, but almost the witching-hour and the chill on me already enough to keep a corpse from smelling, and me barely breathing, all wrapped-up in my listening, just waiting for London finally to succumb to sleep.

You could tell the nightingales had got the night off; there hadn't been a single chirp from down in the Square let alone a song. And the only real noise I'd heard was the quiet tread of the beat copper proceeding at his regulation two miles-per-hour up towards Mount Street. There'd been a couple of happy drunks serenading the chimes of midnight an hour or so earlier and the inevitable screech of brakes as black cabs scurried round the top of Berkeley Square back to the West End clubs in search of another "double fare." And I suppose if you'd lumped it all together it wouldn't have been loud enough to set anyone's heart racing, yet every single sound had me as still as the brick walls around me and my senses thrust deep into the void that followed.

And every silence during that first long, slow hour of the creep seemed to be even emptier than the one before it, and bit by bit I got the feeling I was in the wrong place at the wrong time.

Normally, I'd have heeded my sixth sense and abandoned the creep on the spot, but that night the decision wasn't mine to make, it'd been made for me. Not that I'm pretending to be anything other than what I am; a cat burglar and jewel thief, and one of the very best if you're interested. It's just that this time I'd been prodded and pushed out onto London's slippery soot-covered tiles by a cold-blooded master of the game. And all, as he'd so silkily put it, "in Defence of the Realm." Though why he'd needed me out on the rooftops again, so soon, I don't know, especially as he must've known I wasn't fully recovered from the last caper he'd sent me on. One minute, it'd been a private hospital room and pretty nurses, and bunches of grapes and postcards telling me to "get-well-soon." The next, ka-bosh, I was being lifted off a busy Soho street and bundled into the back of a big black motor car, and back on the other side of the looking-glass.

On top of which, he hadn't even given me time to plan the creep properly, and I hated a rush job; that was always a sure way for things to go wrong in a hurry. I heard a sound and sent my senses flying out across the rooftops again. But, just as before, it was nothing. So I melted back into the walls and let the Smoke swirl around me like a wet army blanket to dampen down all thoughts of irritation. There's never any place for ruffled fur on a creep, and even waiting is work in my business.

Colonel Walsingham of "I'm somebody quite high up in Military Intelligence" and his Savile Row–suited partner-in-crime Simon Bosanquet of some very special branch of Special Branch had silently side-stepped into my life the previous year and made me the sort of proposal that only ever has one answer. They'd asked me to do a creep for King and Country, while making it very plain I had no choice at all in the matter. And having not been born yesterday, I'd done what they'd asked and had very nearly died for their sins. After which, I'd thought that in gratitude Walsingham would've left me and mine alone to get on with our lives. But, oh, deary me, no, up he'd popped again, all brushed bowler hat, George Trumper haircut, and tightly furled umbrella, with news that he had yet another nasty little itch and that mine were the hands he'd chosen to scratch at it with. "I can assure you, Jethro," he said, "that if it wasn't of the utmost importance to national security, I wouldn't have bothered you again, so soon. But as it is, with all my resources seriously compromised, I needed to call on someone I could trust absolutely."

Trust absolutely? That's a bit rich, I thought. But I was what he called "a gifted irregular." I possessed certain skills that he'd deemed he and his department could and should put to better use. And as the tricky bugger had also gone and got me to sign the Official Secrets Act, I couldn't exactly go and complain about it. Not that anybody would've believed me. Sometimes, I could hardly believe it myself. And what's more, as I didn't appear on any official list he could deny all knowledge of me should I ever find myself in the middle of some really nasty mess.

So I'd sat there in his secret office that was hidden in plain sight on Regent Street, the sounds of Soho still ringing in my ears, him and Bosanquet on one side of the big meeting room table, me on the other. "So good of you to drop by," he'd said, pleasantly, tapping on a buff-coloured file folder with his briar pipe. I knew from the letter *J* on the red card stapled to the cover, that it was the "unofficial" file Bosanquet had compiled on me. The very sight of the bloody thing was enough to bring on a fear of heights. If any of the stuff inside was ever given to Scotland Yard or, worse, the Tax Man, I'd be hauled away in irons, and my sister Joanie and her old man, Barry, out on the street. Very soon after which, they'd have had me and my one and only fence, Ray Karmin—a lot more about him later— banged up in some damp distant clink far, far away from any recourse to legal counsel. And the both of us gone from the Smoke forever.

As usual, Walsingham was all business. "It'll be a snap, Jethro," he said. "Simplicity itself, for someone of your nefarious skills. The owner will be away for the weekend, staying at the country estate of a friend. His manservant is sure to accompany him, so the house will be empty. You can be in and out in a trice." Easy enough for him to say; it wasn't going to be him hanging from a drain-pipe, five storeys up in the air. He slid a piece of paper across the table to me. It had an address on it. Then Bosanquet leaned over and took the paper and set a light to it with his gold lighter and let the burning ashes drop into one of the ashtrays. Walsingham pointed at me with his pipe. "It must appear to be just another run-of-the-mill job; no subtlety, no finesse; nothing that might prompt difficult questions later." And I thought, Bugger it, then, I'll go in through an upstairs back window, just like any other self-respecting Mayfair cat burglar. I asked him if he thought a striped jersey and a mask were in order, but he didn't even bother to respond to that. "Do understand, Jethro, it has to be done quickly and without fuss. As I said, old chap, it'll be a snap." Yeh, I'd heard him the first time. I only hoped it wasn't my neck he was referring to.

It was a nice, respectable-looking Georgian house; perhaps not as nice as some of the others along that part of Berkeley Square, but nothing for anyone to be too ashamed of. It was certainly better than the huge, shapeless office blocks and motor car showrooms over on the far side. At the rear of the house, a few lights were still showing from the line of cottages that fronted onto Hay's Mews. There was a faint glow coming from the upper rooms of the house next door but one. Light showed from the caretaker's flat in the basement of the eight-storey office building to my right. But there was nothing but darkness below me. Then all of a sudden the night changed and it was curtain up. And in the blink of an eye, I was over the side of the house and hanging from a black silk rope, ready to enter downstage-left, the classic first steps for villains and villainy.

I felt for and counted the knots tied every eighteen inches along the working-end of the rope, and followed them down. I didn't have far to go, just a bend in a stack-pipe that angled up to just below the main bathroom window on the third floor. And I hung there for a moment, a shadow against the brick wall. I'd studied the rear windows the night before, with a big pair of German Afrikakorps binoculars, so I knew there were no iron bars for me to deal with. But as people are so untrusting, I'd taken it for granted the place was wired and had come prepared to loop the alarm. The sole reason I'd gone down from the roof and not climbed up from below being that I wanted the extra purchase the rope gave me. And with it coiled around my left shoulder, I wedged myself on the ledge and studied the casement window. I felt along the underside of the upper window frame, probed gently with the flat blade of a putty knife, but felt nothing out of the ordinary. And I was just about to push against the catch when I heard my old dad's voice: "Measure twice, cut once." And in a spit, I had a little rubber suction cap moistened and was drawing a hole in a windowpane with a diamond-tipped pencil. I stuck my hand in and felt around inside, the soft buttery leather of my turtles brushing the paint-work, but there were no telltale bumps or pimples; everything was as smooth as a baby's arse. The brass catch was as clean as a whistle, too. I slid the catch, and with a gentle heave, I was in and through and down onto the black-and-white chequered bathroom tiles. I closed the window, felt for the circle of glass, removed the rubber suction cup, pocketed it, and turned and crouched down in the darkness. I put the glass on the floor, and sent my senses flying through the apartment. But there was nothing out of the ordinary.

Then out of nowhere, there was a whistling in my ears, like a badly-tuned radio set and my forehead beaded with sweat and I began to sway. And I was tempted, even in the dark, to look down at my feet to check that I was really stand-ing on solid ground. That's a bit odd, I thought. And for some reason, I felt for my watch like a blind man groping for a hand and felt strangely comforted to find my timepiece still on my wrist. Then I shivered violently. And the very next second, I was down, crouching on the bathroom floor, the hairs on the back of my neck waving like reeds in a cold Norfolk wind. "What the . . ."

Funny, how you suddenly know you're coming down with something. I shivered again. It was all I bloody needed, but there was no turning back; the quickest way out was forward. And I shook my head and crept towards the bathroom door. I opened it and stepped straight into a corridor as dark as a cupboard. The silence echoed back, mocking me, but at least, the whistling in my ears had stopped. I wiped my forehead and reached for the glim. The thin beam of light cut the dark like a butcher's knife and I slipped into the gap and crept slowly along the top corridor.

I turned the handle of the first door I came to. It was a large bedroom with all the usual furniture and effects. Bed, night-tables, tallboy, dresser, writing-desk and chair, leather club armchair, side-table, standard lamp, bookshelves; Oriental carpets on the floor, oil paintings on the walls; and everything antique or very expensive. I skimmed the glim over the tops of the desk, tables, and bookcase. There were small groupings of statues and figurines, busts and heads; in stone, metal, and pottery; Egyptian, Greek, Roman, that sort of things you see down the British Museum. I crossed to a door on the far side; it was a dressing room. I skimmed the glim over the top of the tallboy and saw a metal bust, eight or so inches high, and a leather tray full of wrist-watches. And like a magpie, I swooped in for a closer look. There was a Jaeger-Le Coutre *Reverso,* a Girard-Perregaux chronograph, and a Breguet chronograph; in gold, rose-gold, and silver; two square-faced, one round; all very nice, and each worth a working man's annual wage, at the very least. Now, a nice watch is catnip where I'm concerned, time, of course, being of the essence in my line of work; so in seconds I had all three timepieces safe inside my satchel.

I slipped out of the room and padded along the corridor to the next room. I wiped my forehead on the back of my sleeve, opened the door, and flashed the glim. Silvery things twinkled and sparkled as the finger of light touched them; solid silver candlesticks; dozens of them; a bloody fortune. But there was no way I could carry off a single one on this creep. I could always come back another time, under my own lights, I said to myself.

I stepped forward and stopped dead in my tracks. Someone had moved over on the far side of the room. I thumbed off the glim, took three steps to the right, slid my Commando knife from its leather sheath and crouched down and listened. But all I heard was me. I crouched, ready to spring, held the glim away from my body and thumbed it back on. It took me a moment or two to realise that what I'd seen was me reflected in a wall of mirrors, in front and behind me. It looked as if I was trapped in a tunnel with many exits, but no end. It was very disorienting.

"Come on, Jethro, pull yourself together," I whispered. I was giving myself the willies and no mistake. The place was empty; it was just my imagination that wasn't. Then I heard myself whistle and that just about stopped my heart dead. I never whistled while I worked, never. Not when creeping, it'd be like setting off an alarm bell; and never in the theatre, either, where I worked occasionally as a stage-hand. It was dead unlucky for anyone to whistle anywhere on stage; almost as bad as mentioning the name of the Scottish play, and that you never did. The theatre wasn't my real job, you understand, it was just my way of hiding in plain sight so the rest of London's criminal fraternity would think I'd lost my bottle and leave me be. But, still, I'd whistled on a creep, and that I never did. I mean, the whole point of being dressed from head to toe in black and swathed in a cloak of silence was to help render me invisible. It was all very odd.

I swept my glim round the room. There were two walls covered in mirrors and two walls covered in heavy black drapes. It looked like a fitting room in a mortuary. I sniffed up the cold in my nose and went downstairs to slide-shut the top and bottom bolts of the front door, so if the house's owner or his faithful manservant suddenly appeared on the doorstep, I'd have time to get away. Then I searched the rest of the house.

There were four floors, plus the basement, all beautifully furnished and appointed. And one good thing; they hadn't closed the curtains on the lower floors and the faint glow coming from the lamp-posts outside gave more than enough light to work by, so I pocketed the glim. And I stood in the doorway of the big drawing-room, on the second floor, and let my eyes adjust. The door on the far side of the room led to the library, where Walsingham had assured me I'd find an old Milner safe. And true enough, there it sat, in the corner by the window, all squat and black ugly, just waiting for me to go up and stroke it.

There are only two kinds of safes in the world: beauties and beasts; and it's my good fortune I was born with the gift of being able to tell the character of a safe merely by stroking my fingertips across its front and down its sides. And if you find that a bit hard to believe, I do too. So let's just say that, having studied them as much as I have, I find it easy to imagine what's going on with the lock, and I sometimes even "see" what's locked away inside the safe. But that night, although the knack had worked a thousand times before, I couldn't sense a bloody thing from that old Milner, not a thing. And I stood there, in the semi-darkness, scratching my head. Then I remembered I wasn't even supposed to be acting like me, so it didn't bloody well matter. I rippled and flexed my fingers inside my leather turtles, more out of nerves than out of habit, and I was just about to get started, when I sneezed, a bloody great big sneeze, all but blowing my head off. "Bloody hell," I croaked, "I'll be glad when I've had enough of this."

Seeing Things

Walsingham was so adamant that it all come off looking like a regular bit of safe-breaking, I had little choice but to introduce gelignite into the equation. Bosanquet, always the one for the finer details, even suggested the jelly and detonators come from quarries in the Midlands or Wales, where London's villains always went to acquire their dynamite. And he promised that on the night of the caper everything I needed would be in the boot of an unmarked police car parked in Farm Street, just off Berkeley Square. It felt odd having a copper tell you that to your face. Being found with gelignite in your possession got you five to seven years, no questions asked. I was just very grateful they hadn't asked me to steal the stuff.

Blowing safes was never really my line. Some people reckoned jelly gave them the keys to the kingdom, but I never did. In my heart of hearts, I was always a climber and a creeper; and first, last and always, a key-man; never a safe-breaker. I'd had a few run-ins with that side of the business, of course, and I knew which end was up. But there was an episode once, very early on, near Gray's Inn Road, that'd nearly put paid to me and my career before it'd even started, and I'd hated explosives ever since. Same with pistols, revolvers, and shotguns; there's a very nasty tendency for people to get killed whenever any of that stuff starts going off, "bang."

Safe-breaking was simple enough, though. It was basically a question of filling the keyhole up with gelignite and blowing the front of the safe off, although not too many ever even managed to do that properly. Most people tended to use too much jelly and a successful result was usually more by luck than judgement. So a lot of safes went to meet their makers taking their hidden treasures with them. But, as in all things, there were always one or two artists whose touch was legendary, and before the War I'd had lessons from the very best of them, Eddie Chapman. He kept meticulous records as to the varied effects of various grades and amounts of gelignite on different sizes and makes of safe. And he devised many artful touches such as hanging a handy typewriter from the handle of the safe so that when the blast weakened the lock, the extra weight would pull the door of the safe open before too much damage could occur inside. He'd even shown me the trick of squeezing jelly into "a rubber Johnny" and topping it off with water, then knotting it, so one end could be gently pushed inside the lock. All of which kept the gelignite from dropping down inside the safe and rendering itself useless to man or burglar. Another thing he did was use a wodge of chewing gum to hold the jelly and detonator in place. And it was when traces of the gum kept on being found on blown safes, that a specially formed police squad brilliantly surmised that an American gelignite gang had invaded the country. The quality linens went so far as to suggest it was all the work of the IRA, who were leaving a false trail on purpose. We often had a chuckle over that little titbit. So I always used a well-chewed bit of gum, as a nod to Eddie.

I fixed the detonator in place with chewing gum and attached the two end-wires to a reel of electrical flex, which I ran off into the next room. I searched around for a handy typewriter, but couldn't find one. Then I remembered the small metal bust on the tallboy in the master dressing room, and dashed back upstairs. I picked it up, the weight was perfect, and I was carrying it back through the bedroom, when I stopped dead. A pair of dark hypnotic eyes was following my every move. I blinked, and realised that the beam from my glim had alighted on the face of the figure in an oil painting on the wall. Curiosity sometimes being an unfortunate part of my nature, I went over for a closer look. Then I really did start to imagine I was seeing things, for floating in midair was Adolf Hitler himself. I blinked again and saw it was a life-sized portrait of the Führer; the very last thing you'd expect to come across, anywhere in London. And the dark hypnotic eyes stared at me, and I stared right back at them. "And you can fuck off, too," I said, wiping my nose.

Back in the library, I looked at the metal bust more closely and, of course, I realised who it was then. "I've wanted to do this for years," I whispered, and I twisted the wire around Adolf's neck and hung it from the handle of the safe. I pulled an Oriental rug from off the floor and piled it on top to dampen the blast, then remembered the heavy black drapes on the walls upstairs. And I raced back up the stairs again and back along the corridor. I tugged at a velvet drape, but it just slid silently along the wall and wouldn't come off the curtain rod. I flashed the glim back and forth, and was surprised to see odd-looking symbols painted all over the wall. They were like nothing I was familiar with, more like bits of an electrical diagram. Thing was though, at the centre of it all, was a symbol that looked a lot like a swastika. Bloody hell. Hitler and swastikas in Mayfair, three years after the War, what was that all about? I stepped back, and my glim lit up part of the floor and bugger me if there weren't dozens of symbols painted down there, as well. I moved the finger of light around and saw the symbols were in a huge circle, and that I was standing in the middle of it. I sneezed, violently, and cursed. I wiped my runny nose on the back of a sleeve and hurried back downstairs again.

I couldn't have the windowpanes blowing out, so I had to chance closing the curtains. And I sidled up to each window, took a sly butcher's down into the Square to make sure nobody was happening by, and in one fluid movement walked the curtains closed. Then I retreated back into the drawing-room, settled down on the floor behind a big leather chesterfield, pulled a nine-volt battery from my satchel, and holding the glim between my teeth, attached the first detonator lead. I wound the nut down tight to get a good contact, took a deep breath, ducked my head down, muttered something about it all being for God, King, and Country, and probed the second contact wire into place.

The explosion made little noise; my sneezing had been worse; and I held my breath and listened. But there were no sounds of alarm. I dashed into the next room, my hand over my mouth to stop from choking in all the dust, and pulled the rug away and thumbed the glim and just stared. The safe looked as if there wasn't a scratch on it. I hadn't used enough gelignite. Bugger. I should've paid more attention to Eddie's charts. I stepped over the rugs with a heavy heart, and bent down and tried turning the handle of the safe just for luck. The door swung open. I'd popped it, perfectly, just like Eddie would've done. And I stood there, taking it all in, my spirits lifting by the second. There were enough dark-blue velvet-covered boxes and posh red leather-covered books or ledgers to need a liveried servant to carry them all. I started with the biggest jewellery box.

Inside it was a solid gold ceremonial chain made up of five-petalled gold-and-red roses with gold knots alternating in between. A lovely piece. I let it slide like a dead snake into a chamois-lined pocket in my black canvas satchel, but something caught on my leather turtles. A tiny, jewel-studded figurine was hanging from one of the gold rose links. I couldn't make out who it was meant to be, though, so I just rippled my fingers and let it drop.

Next, there was an oversize, diamond-studded brooch shaped like an eight-pointed star. And even in the darkness, its sparkle was all but mesmerising. I thumbed the glim and was dazzled by over a hundred small stones. At the centre, was a red cross of rubies, surrounded by diamonds set in white gold, the whole lot encircled by a dark-blue enamel band with letters, chased in silver. The sort of thing you'd see pinned on a red silk sash when some foreign dignitary in white tie and tails set out to impress the rest of the world or as the finishing touch to a Field Marshal's full-dress uniform. I slid the lovely piece into my satchel and shook my head in appreciative wonder. Then, hardly daring to breathe, I attacked the rest of the boxes and found two more diamond-studded stars of similar design, only a lot less ostentatious. I bagged them, anyway, as well as two sets of gold regimental buttons and various monogrammed cufflinks and gold signet rings. I left the boxes of medals and campaign ribbons, though; I'd already won that war. I also kept what I took to be an Edwardian fancy choker studded with diamonds and decorated with silver filigree, no doubt spelling out words of undying love.

Walsingham had said to take everything inside the safe. So I'd come prepared with an extra satchel. And I reached for the stack of red books and slipped two into one satchel and the third into the other. They were of the finest leather and came with solid brass clasps and must've cost a pretty penny; they weren't the sort of things that you got, two for half-a-crown, in Woolworths. I hurried back into the drawing-room and ran the glim over my watch-face. The big hand said it was time to be gone. And that was the exact moment I heard someone rattling the street door downstairs. I froze, the pencil-thin light of my glim suddenly as blindingly bright as a beam from a Hyde Park searchlight battery in the Blitz. But experience had taught me not to move or cause a change to light or shadow. It's the difference between movements people catch sight of, never anything solid. I just prayed I didn't sneeze.

Though, if someone had heard the explosion and telephoned West End Central, there would've been half a dozen Railtons lined up outside, their engines still running, the front door already smashed in, and size twelve daisy-roots thundering up the stairs. The rattling sounds continued. So it had to be the beat copper checking the front doors, along that side of the Square. The noise gradually faded away, and I slowly moved my hand over the glim and thumbed it off. Then as much as it went against my better instincts, I decided to give the copper ten minutes to clear the area. And I just plonked myself down on the chesterfield and waited in the darkness. As I said before, it's all part of the job.

I sat there and twiddled my thumbs. And it was okay for a bit. Then all the stuff in the satchels seemed to be digging into me in all the wrong places, and I reached inside to rearrange everything. And I can't exactly say how, but suddenly I had one of the books in my hands. Now, I'm not nosy by nature; well, no more than the next man; but as I had a few minutes to kill, and had signed the Official Secrets Act, I thought it wouldn't hurt to have a quick peek. It was a thing of moments to open up the little brass clasp with a pick. And I think I was a bit surprised to find it was a photo album and not a ledger or a set of company accounts. Or, God forbid, a code-book or a list of spies or something; I'd already had enough of that nonsense to last me a lifetime. But I'll tell you this, for nothing, I was bloody astonished at the pictures stuck inside it.

I waved my glim back and forth over the images as if it was a magic wand revealing things from a different world. And I was a different man afterwards; I felt unclean, as if I'd peered through a keyhole and stayed long enough to get a black stain around my eyeball. I know people get up to all sorts of things, but blimey. When I'd worked the big passenger liners before the War I'd seen a fair bit in some of the most infamous port cities in the world. On board every ship I'd ever sailed on, there'd been men who were more like women than a lot of women, if you get my drift. Not that it was my cup of tea. But there was always some good steel amongst the irons. And during the War with everyone fighting for their lives, it didn't seem that important, really. Apart from which, there's always been millions of gingers in the acting profession. And live and let live I say. It takes all sorts and all walks. And what I think is this, having been forced to almost meet my maker on far too many occasions, I'm for most anything that's going in life—in people or politics, it makes no difference—just as long as no one tries to make any of it compulsory.

Up to that point, I suppose, I'd always thought there were limits, but the sharp-edged black-and-white photos in the album clearly showed there weren't. And even though a lot of the people were wearing opera masks or cloaks with hoods, there were an awful lot that weren't and whose faces you could clearly see. Upper-class faces, mainly, with aristocratic profiles, stiff upper lips and missing chins galore. There were also a lot of old bags who should've known better, and men that hadn't done much more in the way of exercise than wrestle with *The Telegraph* or *The Times* or drink too many glasses of vintage port. But there were men who looked like they could have commanded a cavalry brigade or just stepped off a yacht or a polo field. And women who were as glamorous as any Hollywood movie star or as exotic as the leggiest fan dancers the Club Pigalle had ever stuck a spotlight on. And it struck me then, that a good few of the faces seemed familiar; not that I knew them personally or anything, just faces I was sure I'd seen in the linens or on the newsreels. But the whole bloody lot of them were going at it, in one way or other; and doing things to each other, the women as well as the men; that was an education even for me.

I closed the book, snapped the clasp shut, stuffed it back inside the satchel, and sat there pondering what I'd just seen. And maybe I leaned back for a moment or two and closed my eyes, I don't know. But suddenly, I noticed it felt much colder, freezing almost, and my breath was steaming out in front of me in long streams. And I shivered, then pushed myself to my feet, my head like concrete, sweat pouring off me. And that was it, I'd had a bellyful of the place. Silver candlesticks; walls of mirrors; Adolf bloody Hitler and Nazi swastikas; filthy pictures, and all. "Sod this for a game of soldiers," I said. And was gone.

CHAPTER 3

Coming Down with Something

I was on someone else's clock the moment I exited the bathroom window. And with Simon Bosanquet's head for planning, I had to believe he'd have someone up on a nearby rooftop watching the back of the house through binoculars. I also didn't put it past him having someone at street level waiting to shadow me back to the little chapel on South Audley Street, where two of his men were waiting for me in a black Humber Snipe. But I needed a few moments to myself before I stepped back into Walsingham's little shadow play. So I took a different route down from the one planned and came out at the other end of the mews and made straight for a little, dark green, two-seater MG TC that I'd left parked in Charles Street the day before, when I'd been free from prying eyes.

It was a right-hand-drive export model, and all legitimate and paid for. But as the Government had cancelled the petrol ration again, all but putting an end to "private pleasure" motoring, I only ever used the MG when I was disguised as a Canadian businessman setting up offices in London. Because then, as a rep for a foreign company, I had full use of a "for business use only" petrol allowance. It didn't render me as invisible as the old London cabby I sometimes became, but it was great for visiting a safe manufacturer's showrooms or offices; and just far enough out of the ordinary to be totally believable. I'd tried being a Yank, but soon gave it up; it's the one accent I could never do convincingly. As a Canadian, all I had to do was flatten my vowels, throw in a little Scottish burr on words like "about" and "boat", smile a lot, and I was away and running. I also left a few empty Parliament cigarette packets on the passenger seat and a folded copy of *The Globe and Mail* in a side-pocket, for stage dressing.

Anyway, there I was hot-footing it through the dark, deserted streets of Mayfair, making for the MG, looking to offload the diamond brooches and all the rest of the loot that didn't figure in Walsingham's plans. I knew I'd be searched and there'd be hell to pay if they found anything on me that wasn't kosher. On top of which there was always the risk of being stopped by a motorised police patrol. So, as per Bosanquet's instructions, I'd abandoned most of my burglary kit back inside the house and left the black silk rope dangling down the outside. But I still had my little leather case of diamond-tipped twirls and my little diamond-tipped glass-cutter. I'd said at the outset I'd never leave those behind.

I padded up to the little MG and slid inside. I'd fitted a steel box in the space between the back of the seats and the upright petrol tank, and hidden it underneath a false floor. Not, perhaps, what Morris Garages originally had in mind, but an additional feature that gave me miles of satisfaction. And in a flash, and a twist of a little barrel key, I had the lid up. I pulled the book of photographs out, stuffed the jewel satchel down inside the hidden compartment, threw the Fairbairn-Sykes Commando knife and black knitted balaclava in on top, and closed up. Then I squeezed the photo album into the other satchel, alongside the other two, and did up the straps. Walsingham would have sore eyes looking at that little lot; but for the life of me, I couldn't think what he wanted them for.

I pulled a flat tweed cap from out of the glove compartment, checked the mirrors, and got out. I patted the MG on the boot. "Safety fast," I whispered. The motor car company's clever slogan could've been one of my dad's creeping mottoes, but me, I stole ideas from anyone. Then again, so as no one stole anything from me, I'd taken the precaution of removing the rotor arm when I'd parked the MG, so I knew it wouldn't be going anywhere fast anytime soon. I blinked. Spits of rain started appearing all over the MG's bodywork and all over me, not that you could've told the raindrops from the beads of sweat on my forehead. I looked up and down the empty street. Even though I only had six blocks to cover to the pick-up point, the way I was feeling, and with the temperature I was starting to run, it might as well have been six miles.

It really started coming down as I cut up Chesterfield Hill and I quickened my pace as I turned into South Street, and by the time I reached South Audley Street I was all but sprinting, which is never the best way to stay unnoticed. Up by Grosvenor Chapel, the sidelights of a big black Humber winked on and off, and I padded up to it, opened a rear door and got in. Nobody said a word. Nobody turned round to ask if I was alright. The driver just turned the key in the ignition, switched on the headlights, and roared off down the street. But that's people for you, if they think they've got you by the short and curlies, they take you for granted.

We hit Park Lane with a screech of tyres, which set my teeth even more on edge and I sat back and wiped my forehead with my sleeve and looked out the window into the dark, and almost shouted out. The face reflected back at me was as pale as bleached bone in moonlight. I sneezed, loudly, and suddenly out of the shadowy darkness there was a hand offering me a hip-flask. "Here. Mr. Bosanquet said you might like a nip, once we'd picked you up." It was the big bloke in the front passenger seat. "You look as if you might need it, too, you look as white as a bloody sheet."

I nodded and took the flask and only then noticed he'd already taken the black canvas satchel in trade. "Yes," I said, between sips, "It's been a bit of a funny old night."

We skidded around Hyde Park Corner and made for the road that led down to the Palace, and left Piccadilly to disappear back into the night. I didn't think the King was going to come down in his dressing gown to thank me for committing burglary for him and his Realm, so I was fairly sure I wasn't being taken to Buckingham Palace. And when we hurtled past the entrance to the Mall and Queen Victoria's statue, and headed down Birdcage Walk, I wondered if Horse Guards Parade, the back way into government, was where I was to meet Walsingham and Bosanquet. But no, we rattled on into Parliament Square. I glanced over at the Houses of Parliament, which were covered in scaffolding. The Luftwaffe had bombed the Commons to bits during the Blitz and it was being rebuilt so MPs could have a proper place to sit in. After all, we'd won the War, hadn't we, and there were appearances to keep up. The House of Lords, on the other hand, had hardly been scratched. But then it's just like the nobs and toffs to have got off scot-free. Privilege, I think it's called.

We took a left, down towards Downing Street, and I

twigged it then, Walsingham never missed a chance to stir my patriotic spirit, and this was my sixpenny Empire-tour. And as if on cue Big Ben struck the hour and the sounds of the giant bell bounced off the walls of all the buildings and raced us along Whitehall. I nodded my respects to the Cenotaph as we went by. How many wars and how many dead were we remembering in granite and marble, now? I'd lost count. And for what? God? King? Country? Patriotism? Pig-headed pride? It was hard to know, sometimes.

I wiped my nose on the back of a glove and looked out the window, just staring at the raindrops as they streaked across the glass. And suddenly we were barrelling round Piccadilly Circus and I knew then where we were heading. The driver skidded to a stop, throwing me forward, and I tried not to throw up all over the leather seats. Then someone rapped on the window, the door opened and I was told to get out, and I'm not saying I slipped or anything, but all of a sudden I was seized by men in Trilby hats and belted raincoats. And I found myself being carried across the pavement towards flat sheets of wet ice that only slowly rearranged themselves into the plate-glass windows of a posh export-only crystal and porcelain shop. To the left, highly polished, double-wooden doors led into a small wood-panelled entrance foyer for the businesses that had offices on the floors above. I thought at first they were going to use my head as a battering ram and I began to struggle. "Easy, sunshine, looks like you've had a bit of a turn," said one of the blokes holding me. Then the old bugger in a Commissionaire's uniform stuck his nose in, "Is he alright? Do you need any help?" I wanted to yell at them all, tell them all to get stuffed, but I found I just didn't have the energy.

Next, I was in a lift with everyone helping me stand upright and we started going up as slowly as a judge's head at a sentencing. Again, I tried not to throw up. Then door after door opened and closed and what with the incessant clack-clacking of typewriters, I must've gone dizzy, because everything went black. And when I came to I was heaving away on my hands and knees in the Gents' toilets. Then after a year or so of staring at nothing, I was helped to my feet again. Next thing, I was sitting on a chair, in an empty room, and on the table in front me was my now very crumpled tweed flat cap, my little silver pencil-shaped glass-cutter, and my tiny leather case full of twirls. I'd been given an expert going over in the lift. But at least now they knew I had nothing untoward on me, like a deadly Commando knife or a suite of star-shaped diamond brooches. I tried to smile at my cunning, but sneezed loudly instead. Someone handed me a glass of water. "Flu, is it? You poor bugger. There's a lot of it going about." Then the door opened and Walsingham and Bosanquet walked in.

"Get him a hot cup of tea, someone, and a Beecham's Powder, too, if we have any. Failing that, get him a shot of brandy or something."

I looked up into Colonel Walsingham's face; Stewart Granger played by James Mason. I gave him my best impression of a sardonic look, then went back to my shivering. "This won't take long, Jethro," he said. I heard a thump and looked round. Bosanquet had dropped my black satchel and the three red leather-covered books down on the table. Funny thing was, though, they both seemed more interested in the empty satchel than the red books. I noticed the books had all been opened, since they'd been out of my hands, and by a real amateur, too. There were telltale scratch marks all over the little brass locks. Walsingham looked at me. "I'm told this is the only satchel you had with you at the rendezvous. I was under the impression you'd planned to take a second bag in with you."

I nodded. "Yes, I did, but what with the explosion and the dust and everything, and with me feeling groggy, I must've just left it behind."

"What did you have in the other satchel?" It was Bosanquet, the sly sod. Smooth as silk, just like his appearance.

I forced out a sneeze for some cover. "Excuse me . . . this bloody flu will be the death of . . . er, nothing, it was empty once I'd taken the jelly, the wire, and the sticks out. It must still be back there." I made as if to sneeze again and, without a moment's hesitation, Walsingham pulled out a large white handkerchief and handed it to me, which was very decent of him, really. The loss of a good cotton handkerchief was nothing to sneeze at, what with everything being on coupons.

I blew my nose until my ears rang. Then Walsingham said, "Let's start again from the very beginning, shall we?" So I did, with me blowing a trumpet voluntary every now and then to clear my head. Then Bosanquet piped in, again, prodding and probing, trying to get blood out of a stone. "Tell us, again, Jethro, about the symbols on the wall."

And I tried drawing what I'd seen on a piece of paper, but it still looked like so much gibberish. "Well, there was a swastika-like thing at the centre, but I couldn't make head or tail of the rest of it." Then I told them again about the metal bust and the life-size oil painting of Hitler.

"You're quite sure it was Adolf Hitler, and not, say, Joseph Stalin?"

I gave them both a look. "I know my left elbow from my right elbow, if that's what you mean, Mr. Walsingham? No, it was definitely Adolf."

Then I went over it all, again. I didn't tell them about the diamond brooches, of course, or the velvet choker, or the heavy gold chain. But I felt so tired, a number of times I almost admitted I'd peeked inside one of the red books, but just caught myself. I knew, though, that if things went on for much longer, sooner or later, I'd end up dropping myself in the cart.

Walsingham looked at me sternly, like a copper that suspects you've been half-inching things from off a barrow. "So there were just these three red leather-covered books in the safe?" He tapped the table in front of each one. "You came across no other files, papers, or letters of any kind?"

I looked him straight in the eye, always a good thing when truth's on your side. "No, no letters or files." They seemed really disappointed with the night's haul and I wondered then, whether they'd actually looked inside the red books or not. But maybe the photographs were nothing out of the ordinary to them, just more of the usual things the upper classes got up to at private masked balls and weekend parties in the country. As I said, it takes all sorts; there are all sorts of skeletons in all sorts of cupboards. "No, just those..."—I nearly said, dirty photographs—"just those diaries or ledgers, or whatever they are." I sneezed again violently.

"Bless you," Bosanquet said. "Thank you," I said through my fingers. But he still tried to slip one in. "Why did you go via Charles Street, afterwards, Jethro, and not directly to the rendezvous?"

I sneezed. "Excuse me," I said. "I...er...thought I saw someone in Farm Street. And at that time of night it could've been anyone, even the local beat copper. So I went the long way round to be safe, that's not a crime is it?" I said, blowing my nose very loudly. "Look, don't blame me because you're dissatisfied with tonight's haul, you're the ones that planned the caper, you know." I stuffed the handkerchief down inside my pocket. Regardless of the truth, I still didn't like not being trusted. And if they weren't careful, the Realm could just go and defend itself in the future.

They looked at one another; then Walsingham cleared his throat. "Thank you for your assistance, Jethro. I'm sure I don't have to remind you that everything is bound by the Official Secrets Act and, therefore, may not be discussed with anyone. Is that clearly understood?" I nodded. "In which case," he said, "I'll have someone take you home."

I felt like telling Walsingham where he could stick his motor car. But as I felt as weak as a day-old kitten and nothing at all like a cat burglar, and all I wanted was to get home and get some kip, I just nodded, meekly.

Then later, as the cold flat light of morning found me once again in the back of a big black motor car, this time hurtling along the Euston Road, I remembered what my sister, Joanie, had so often told me. She said, I was a better drunk than I was a patient. Even drunk as a skunk, I was all nice and mellow and could never be stopped from singing my head off. But when I was sick, I turned into a right old misery-guts, a bear with a sore arse, and after caterwauling at the world and blaming it for all my troubles and woes, all I ever wanted to do was crawl into a hole somewhere and die.

As per usual, she was right.

CHAPTER

4

Food for Thought

The smell of fried food wafted up from the Victory and my nose twitched like it hadn't smelled food for a month of Sundays. It's handy having your sister be in charge of your favourite cafe, especially when it's downstairs from where you live. Joanie and her old man, Barry, who ran his own taxi-cab, lived in the flat above the cafe, and I lived above them, on the top floor, in the flat with the windows that opened out onto the rooftops of London. As it happened, I owned the whole building, but none of the nosy sods on Church Street knew that; they all thought Joanie and me just had a very understanding landlord. Well, you should always do something charitable with your ill-gotten gains, and as charity begins at home, it was the first place I bought when I'd had enough put by.

I'm not saying I was fighting fit, but the fever seemed to have broken and the thumping in my head was about bearable, and hunger is always a very good sign if you know there's enough food to be had. I stepped over a couple of empty whisky bottles on the floor and tried to remember how they'd got there, and went into the bathroom and looked in the mirror. This bleary-eyed bloke who looked like death warmed up stared back at me. I blinked and tried to focus on the clock on the window ledge and saw it was almost lunchtime. Blimey, I had slept in late. But after the night I'd had, that was only understandable. I took a quick soak in some Epsom salts, shaved, got dressed and slipped down the stairs as silently as if it was night. I opened the front door expecting the market to be in full swing, but other than a few stalls selling fruit and vegetables, and another selling women's knickers, there was hardly anyone about. I shook my head and tacked to port and pushed open the door to the cafe. The little brass bell on top of the door clappered away, and I stuck a smile on my face; always the best thing to do if you're intent on getting a bigger share of whatever's going.

The smell of fried food made my nose twitch something rotten, and my stomach grumbled its impatience. "Morning, Joanie; morning, all. A mug of tea and a breakfast as big as King George's, if you please." I didn't expect applause or anything, but the silence that followed would've woken the dead. "Nice weather we're having." I looked back out the window to check if there was anything other than the usual grey clouds, like a red sky, for instance. Then I felt Joanie take hold of my arm and push me to the table she kept special at the back of the cafe.

"Bloody hell, Jethro, what do you think you look like?"

"And very nice to see you, too, Joanie. I see business is booming."

She turned and looked at the half-empty tables, then back at me, questions already gathering behind her eyes. "You look like something the cat dragged in, Jethro. You in trouble again?"

"Me? No, I'm fine." My own questions started gathering

then. "Business a bit off for a Saturday, isn't it? Buggy must be right put out; he'll be lucky if he sells a single tub of bug powder. Been in, has he?"

Joanie gave me a look. "Jesus, Jethro, what you been up to this time?" She shook her head, beckoned to Mavis behind the serving counter and, nodding at me, waved her cupped hand close to her mouth and within seconds Mavis was over with a steaming hot mug of tea. "Ta, Mave," I said. Joanie just nodded and said, "Bring him a special and tell Pauline, lots of black pudding, he looks like he could do with the iron."

"Still looking for someone to, er, replace our Vi?" I almost couldn't get the name out. Old Vi had been the Victory's cook for dogs' years, but she'd died in bad circumstances. I wasn't the one that'd knocked her flying and run over her with a motor car, but I still reckoned it'd all happened because of me. It was hard to live with sometimes. I stared at the sweet jar over on the counter. It had a picture of a rose cut from a seed packet stuck on the front of it and was half-full of copper and silver coins and the odd ten-bob note; and all of it for Rosie, Vi's little girl. Not that she really needed it, but people wanted to help. I'd decided soon after her mum was murdered she'd never want for anything as long as I lived, and I'd called in a favour, and Rosie was away at a posh boarding school down near the coast.

Joanie leaned over and gently pulled my face towards her. "We all still miss Vi, Jethro, but life goes on, eh?" She looked at me. "And listen, I know you're not trying to be funny, love, but it's not Saturday or Sunday, it's Monday. Buggy doesn't work the markets today, you know that."

You could've knocked me down with a teaspoon. Monday? But the look on her face told me she wasn't kidding and I reached for the tea and gulped it down in one go. I'd been out of it for two days straight. Bugger me, but that touch of flu had really wiped the floor with me. At least that explained the empty whisky bottles; I must've taken the old cure; whisky and lemon and brown sugar in hot water, followed by lots more whisky.

"You should've let us know you were feeling poorly, Jethro, I'd have brought some soup up. Barry said he thought he heard you come in. But with us both working all Saturday and Sunday, and not seeing you, we reckoned you were away again, on one of your jaunts."

"No, I was in, Joanie, only I must've been out like a light. Better make that two breakfasts, I've got two whole days to make up for."

Afterwards, I walked straight round Buggy's house, tugged at the bell pull, and stood back so I could be seen from an upstairs window. I knew it'd take him a while to answer the door, because as it was a Monday, he'd be living over in his other house. Buggy Billy—*Undisputed King of Bug Powder, from Church Street to Petticoat Lane and the Kingsland Waste*—was at home Fridays, Saturdays, and Sundays. However, every Monday through Thursday, Buggy turned into a different bloke altogether; someone that lived in a house in the next street. Stand the two characters side-by-side and you'd have been hard-pressed to see any similarity. The one, a Cockney costermonger of fearsome voice and reputation, always dressed in scraggy fur-collared long black coat, spotted silk scarf, and bowler hat. The other, a quietly spoken, scholarly Jewish gentleman of impeccable taste, known to frequent the Reading Room at the British Museum, and thought to have interests in the diamond trade. One Raymond L. Karmin, Esq. No one round Edgware Road and Lisson Grove had ever twigged they were one and the same person. And there wasn't much you could put over on them.

Ray was also my fence, and very few people ever knew about that, either. I trusted him as I trusted no one else; he was my oldest friend, and in some ways after my dad died he helped fill that gap, too. So for obvious reasons, whereas Buggy and me were known to be as thick as thieves, Ray and me tried never to be seen out in public together; out of disguise that is. His neighbours had long put down my weekly visits to an old, flyblown postcard still on display in a local newsagent's window: *Keen chess player hoping to find same for ongoing chess game.* A torn bit of paper scrawled with the words *Game in progress* had been pinned on the card almost from the day it went up, so no one else had ever bothered to respond to it. But as Ray said, it's always best to let people find things out for themselves; they're far more likely to believe them, then.

It was from Ray I'd first got the idea of living a double life. Hiding in plain sight, he called it. And under his expert guidance I'd learned how to pass unseen by day and by night, and improved my creeping in leaps and bounds. And I was soon able to put enough away to pay for a place at the Seamen's College, in Southampton, and from there at last fulfilling my dream of getting away from the Smoke and off and out to sea. Who'd ever suspect a young Cunard deck-officer—me, if you haven't twigged yet—of being a cat burglar? At least, no one ever did in any of the ports I sailed into. And I did very nicely for a few years, pinching diamonds from New York to Hong Kong, until Adolf marched into Poland and his U-boats torpedoed my plans. Then, after surviving the War, I just told everyone around town I'd given up the creeping lark for good and taken up as a jobbing stage-hand round London's theatres and music halls. Most people put it down to me having lost my nerve. It was well known I'd had a couple of convoy ships sunk from under me, so no one thought I was soft or anything, simply that I'd lost my bottle for clambering over rooftops and balancing on window-ledges. Truth was, all the work on the theatre fly-floor with knots and ropes and pulleys and weights kept me fit, and my eye in for going up and down walls in inventive ways. And, of course, being able to watch England's finest actors, night after night, helped me no end when I needed to pretend to be someone else.

I didn't see the curtains move, but he's a bit fly, himself, is our Ray. The front door opened a crack. "Get yer arse in here, quick. Buggy Billy's supposed to be off doing business out of the Smoke." The voice was low, but the growl was unmistakable. I slipped inside, closed the door and let my eyes adjust to the dark. There was no kettle on, no radio blaring, no fire in the gate; the house felt empty and cold, despite it being filled to the rafters with bric-a-brac and other bits and pieces that Ray—excuse me, Buggy Billy—had collected round the markets over the years. It was like a junk shop out of Dickens; everything from stuffed animals and brass hunting horns, to chipped Toby jugs and button chairs that needed reupholstering. I'd fallen in love with the place on my very first visit and had always thought of it as Ali Baba's cave. I still did.

Ray disappeared into the wardrobe in the upstairs back bedroom, and I pushed aside the moth-eaten clothes and followed him through. I slid the panel at the back of the wardrobe back into place, then did the same with the wallpaper-covered screen. Then I slid the big metal door across, locked it, pulled another wallpapered screen into position, slid the back of the second wardrobe into place, and—gingerly pushing aside Ray's bespoke suits—stepped out into another room and another world. I closed the wardrobe door and went downstairs. I'd just reached the foot of the stairs when Ray called out from the kitchen. "Cup of tea, is it? And so, stranger, to what do I owe this premature, but not entirely unexpected pleasure?"

"Wotcher, Ray. Excuse me coming round early, I did try the dog and bone, but it was busy. Only, I was wondering if some of your boys could go pick up my drag. I'd go myself, but I've got a funny feeling and I'd rather stay clear of the area."

"Funny feelings that go unheeded oft herald tragedy." He called back. "Go sit in the front room, I'll bring the tea through."

I went through. There were books everywhere, on every subject under the sun, all arrayed on shelves that stretched from floor to ceiling. It was a marvellous place; cosy, but orderly; a red leather armchair by the fireplace, a rosewood writing table against one wall, a mahogany library table by the window piled high with the books. And all of it nicely complemented by a couple of fine oil paintings and the best rugs, so he'd told me, outside the Turkish Legation.

"So, some help with one of the motor cars, is it? I was only saying to your Joanie on Saturday, how . . . Blimey, Jethro, you look like you've been right through the wringer. Here, take my cup, it's got tons of sugar in it." I gulped down the tea and he disappeared off into the kitchen. "Okay," he said, when he came back. "So, you did a creep over the weekend, yes?" I nodded. "And as you didn't share with me you were setting one up, I can only presume it was a little caper for our friend, Mr. W?" I nodded again. "Well, at least this time the sod didn't think to hold me as ransom for you." We both pondered that for a moment. "Only, I got a sense something was up, from the way his man down the Reading Room has been acting, lately. He's been seeing Communists and fifth-columnists hiding behind every fluted column and been nagging at me, constantly."

"So, you still sending Walsingham bits of gossip you hear

from all those foreign émigrés you come across in the diamond trade?" I asked.

He nodded. "Anything at all, that helps put a flea in Joe Stalin's ear, but never any names, just the odd juicy titbit for Mr. W to gobble up as he pleases. But if it keeps your neck and mine out of the Tax Man's noose or both of us from ending up in the clink, then all to the good."

I smiled again. "Still out-poaching a poacher, eh, Ray?"

He gave me a look as if to say, was there any other way? "So, tell me, sunshine, what needs moving; the MG, your van, or your taxi-cab?"

So I told him. And he went into the hallway and got on the blower, rustled up a couple of the lads that worked for "Buggy Billy" and said he needed a favour. It was funny to hear Ray slip into Buggy's raspy voice, but changing voice and manner to suit the different characters we sometimes became, out in the world, had become second nature to both of us.

"Right, that's sorted; spare rotor arm and all. They'll have it parked outside Paddington Green Children's Hospital in a couple of hours." It was a good call; with the hospital being all but sacred ground, the MG would be taken for a doctor's motor car and left untouched by all the local tealeafs. Ray looked at the clock. "How about a little game of chess while we're waiting? Then you can tell me about your latest caper." I nodded and tried to compose myself as he went through his usual ceremony of carefully placing a record onto the turntable on the gramophone. It's not that I don't fancy classical music, but there was this piece he played over and over again that gave me the willies, each time I heard it. "Do I hear the herald of someone's coming defeat," he said, cupping his hand to his ear and doing the things with his eyebrows that Groucho Marx always did with his.

He put his hands behind his back, then held his arms out, crossed at the wrists, both fists closed. And as per usual, the hand I picked contained the black pawn. We set up the pieces on the board, and I told him all about Berkeley Square, and the room of mirrors, the symbols painted on the walls and floor, and the oil painting and bust of Hitler.

"What number Berkeley Square?" he said, giving me an odd look. So I told him. "I thought maybe you'd burgled Maggs Bros. the antiquarian booksellers. I buy from them occasionally; they're good people. Only, that place of theirs is said to be the most haunted house in London."

"Haunted houses in Mayfair? Give over."

"Truly. Lots of people went mad or died after seeing ghosts there. A couple of sailors broke in, once, and kipped in one of the upper rooms. The police report said one dashed outside and ended up insane, the other fell out the window and impaled himself on the spiked railings below. Another top up?"

"You're not serious?" I said, shaking my head.

"Never more so, old son. Then, of course, there's Count Cagliostro, Freemason, occultist, and friend of Anton Mesmer, the hypnotist. He lived in the house during his exile from France. Legend says that when he was there he saw visions predicting the French Revolution and the overthrow of the French monarchy. Though, some think he didn't really see the future, at all, but was simply helping to plan it, him being a Rosecrucian and a founding member of the Illuminati, the secret society that, it's said, orchestrated the Revolution from the shadows."

"Sounds fascinating, Ray," I said, trying to keep a straight face. "But I didn't do the booksellers, did I? I did a house up the street."

He swirled the whisky around in his glass. "Nevertheless, it's all very intriguing; especially with all your talk of pictures of

Hitler and swastikas, and candles and occult symbols in circles on the floor."

I'm not saying I wasn't listening, but that bit about the sailor falling out the window and impaling himself on the railings had made me come over all queasy, again. "I don't believe in ghosts," I said, shaking my head.

"It's not ghosts, I'm talking about Jethro," he said quietly, "it's secret societies and black magic covens; London's been chock-a-block with them for years, and any house or locality with a dark history is prized above all others as a secret meeting place."

Guts for Garters

Ray's back parlour was as safe a harbour as any ex-seaman could hope for, warm and snug, and with a glass-fronted antique cabinet full of bottles capable of buoying anyone's spirit. The moment he opened those etched-glass doors and poured us both a tumbler of The Glenlivet was a sure sign we were about to get down to business. The weekly business of him examining whatever pieces I'd managed to acquire in my unceasing efforts to help redistribute the wealth of the upper classes. Our very own Welfare System; with him and me always the most deserving poor. But whether I had any loot to fence off or not, over the years those Monday evenings had become as valuable to me as any jewels or pearls. "So, let us talk of cabbages and kings," he'd say, trickling water into his lead crystal whisky glass. Then with his malt nicely opened, I'd open up my satchel and we'd begin. First the jewels, then a game or two of chess.

After he'd finished cackling over checkmating me twice in a row, Ray looked at the clock and said, "Your motor car should be outside the hospital by now. I'll make some cheese sandwiches while you're gone."

I borrowed a hat and coat, walked round to the Children's Hospital, slid inside the MG, did the necessary with the barrel key, retrieved the satchel, got out, and patted the little sports car on the bonnet. "Be good while I'm gone." Then back at Ray's house I unbuckled the satchel straps, and as he served up the cheese sandwiches I laid out the chamois leather jewel-pouches all in a row. "So, Jethro, let's see what the cat's brought in this time," he said. And I opened the first pouch and held up the three wrist-watches, in turn. He nodded and I put them back in the satchel. Then as if I was holding a large white rabbit by the ears, I lifted out the biggest of the star-shaped diamond-encrusted brooches. "Ta-ra," I trumpeted.

Ray's hands started trembling as soon as he touched it. They got worse when I produced the other two star-shaped brooches, the velvet choker, and the gold chain. And I'd never seen that happen before, ever. For one awful moment I thought he was coming down with the same thing I'd gone down with. Then I thought, No, this must be the big one we'd so often talked about; the job you could retire on, because you could never top it again, not as long as you lived. I began to smirk. But the look on his face said that wasn't it, either. He just tore off his glasses, not even bothering to reach for his loupe, which was another first; then he shook his head slowly and all but exploded; yet another first for a Monday night.

"God's Holy Trousers, Jethro, out of the frying pan, into

the friggin' fire. Last year it was things hot enough to get you sent to the Bloody Tower. Now you've nicked things that could get you your head chopped off and stuck up on a spike at Traitors' Gate. You've only stolen someone's Order of the Garter insignia; the highest order in the land that only ever gets given to the most powerful nobs or to royalty itself. God damn it, Jethro, it's like stealing the Crown Jewels. They could have you hung, drawn and quartered for this. At the very least, Walsingham will have our guts for garters or he'll lock us up forever and throw away the friggin' keys."

I could tell he was upset. And while I pondered on that and wondered what in hell garters had to do with it all, he disappeared off amongst his bookcases, muttering. I quietly ate my sandwich. And after a while he came back and laid an open book on the top of the table. Then he picked up one of the diamond-encrusted stars, placed it next to an almost identical illustration in the book, and stabbed his finger back and forth between the two. And once he was sure that little fact had penetrated my thick skull, he pointed to each of the other pieces in turn.

"It's as I suspected, Jethro, it's all to do with the Order of the Garter." He adjusted his spectacles and read aloud. "The oldest and most senior British Order of Chivalry. Founded by Edward III—the Black Prince—in 1348. The patron saint of the Order is St. George, patron saint of England, from whom the Order takes the Red Cross as its main symbol." He held up the heavy gold chain and pointed to the little jewel-studded figurine of St. George hanging from one of the knot-shaped gold links.

I looked at him daft. If this Garter thing was all tied up with St. George and England and loyal, upper-class Englishmen, then what was Hitler still doing in the picture? It didn't add up; not after the War we'd had. I reached for The Glenlivet, as Ray read on. "The origin of the emblem of the Order, a dark blue garter, is obscure. It is thought, however, to have been inspired by an incident which took place whilst the King danced with the Countess of Salisbury, who, court gossip said, practised dark and arcane arts. The Countess's garter fell to the floor and the King retrieved it, and tied it to his own leg; an act that scandalised the watching courtiers. But the King admonished them, saying, *'Honi soit qui mal y pense.'* The phrase was subsequently adopted as the Order's motto."

I looked at him, blankly, and he looked at me over his glasses. "It means, 'Evil be to he who evil thinks.' It's been used as a simple warding against evil, ever since." He held up what I'd taken to be an Edwardian-style choker of diamonds arrayed on velvet and moved his finger slowly along the edge. "See, the diamonds spell out all the words in Latin, *'Honi soit qui mal y pense.'* The odd thing is, though, until tonight, I'd always thought it was Henry VIII that said it. But history's funny that way, you never know what you know until you check it; and even then not everyone agrees." He closed the book on heraldry and placed the diamond-laced Garter on top of it.

"You're not suggesting the King's got something to do with all this?" I whispered, not really wanting to know the answer.

He picked up the white king from the chess-board. "No, I don't think so, Jethro. There may be entire regiments of skeletons hidden away in the royal closets, but I honestly can't see him or the Queen being knowingly mixed up in anything like this. It doesn't sit right."

That's when I told Ray about the photographs. He'd also had to sign the Official Secrets Act when Walsingham had had him in "safe" custody the year before; so what was the harm? But Ray's response really startled me. He slammed the chess piece down on the board. "The Garter Star under the same roof as Hitler and swastikas stuck up all over the place is bad enough. But magic symbols in a circle, painted on the floor, and dirty photos of England's finest all going at it like rabbits, says there's real devilry afoot." He pushed back his chair and went over and stoked the fire; then he turned, his face clouded. "There was a huge surge of interest in the occult between the two World Wars. People were desperate to explain away all the death and chaos of the First War, and strange times make for strange bedfellows and even stranger ideas, and a lot of people took to spiritualism and other esoteric teachings. But a good few turned to black magic and witchcraft. So, I don't think those symbols are there just for show."

"But what's it all mean, Ray?" I said, biting into a pickled onion. "And what's Walsingham's interest? Chasing Communists and spies is more his line." I wiped my fingers on my napkin. "I can't really see them getting their knickers in a twist over dirty pictures or witches in Mayfair."

"Neither can I, Jethro. But there are only two ways I can add it up. It's either devilry, plain and simple, and there's a coven that meets at the house that practices sex-magic rituals, in which case good riddance to them. Or the owner has a taste for the pornographic and what you saw is for his private use. It's also possible he deals in the stuff. The sort of books you describe; leather binding, gilt-edging, marbled end-papers; are the rich man's equivalent of a plain-brown wrapper. And as you must well know from your travels, there's an insatiable demand for that sort of material in every city in the world." He stretched his arms; a sure sign our session was at an end. "But what we're both forgetting is you said Mr. W wasn't at all interested in the photos. So the real mystery in all this, sunshine, is what's MI5 really after?"

I nodded, but I had no ideas. And as with most puzzles, I wondered if the answer was staring me in the face and I couldn't see it for looking.

Ray stretched again and put all the chess pieces back in their wooden box and put all the pieces from the creep into an old Lock and Co. hatbox that he kept under the table. "Let's just agree then, Jethro, that all these Garter bits and pieces just disappear until we know more. They're hot enough to start a fire, so I don't want them anywhere near the Smoke."

When I got home, Joanie was still up, waiting for me on the stairs outside the door to her and Barry's flat. She looked tired and had on the face she wore whenever there was trouble of a personal nature.

"It's your mate, Seth," she said, quietly. "I had his wife, Dilys, on the phone, asking for you; she says he's been hurt real bad. He was beaten up by a gang and is in hospital. She wants to know if you'd go down to Slough to see him? I said that you hadn't been too well yourself, lately, but knowing you, you'd crawl there if you had to. She left a telephone number for someone that'll take a message."

"Can I use the phone?" I said. She nodded and went inside to get the keys to the cafe, and with my heart growing heavier by the minute I went back down the stairs and into the darkness below.

CHAPTER 6

Mess Up the Mess They Call a Town

I took the Great West Road out past the new London airport at Heath Row, and carried on towards Slough. I had the top down. I run hottest when bad things happen to anyone I call "family" and I needed to feel the cut of the wind. And not knowing where the day might lead me, I had to be sure and let the steam out beforehand. As I'd learned in the War, it's always best to approach the unknown with a cool head and cold heart. And once I'd set my mind on helping Seth, I all but forgot Walsingham and the Berkeley Square caper and just concentrated on driving the MG, taking pleasure in smoothly double-declutching, up and down, through the gears. I drove through Slough, over the crossroads that led down to Eton and Windsor, and accelerated out onto the Bath Road, keeping my eyes peeled for the Three Tuns pub. I took a right turn towards the Farnham Road and was soon up and onto the railway-bridge. I pulled over by the side of the road. I needed a cigarette and another look at the directions I'd been given. I got out of the motor car. The town's vast modern trading estate stretched off to the left and right, factory after factory after factory. It was quite a sight.

I watched a passenger train steam up the track on its way to Paddington Station and let the smoke of my cigarette get swept up in the huge white plumes of steam that engulfed me. And I stood there blinking away the soot and thought about Seth. He'd saved my bacon twice in the short time I'd known him. The first time, when he'd literally bumped into me backstage at the London Palladium. He was one of the aspiring amateur performers trying out for one of the ENSA Armed Forces tribute-shows, and I was there working the fly-floor. Then as chance would have it, not an hour after that, we bumped into each other again in the pub, round the corner. We chatted, had a couple of beers, shared a few laughs, and I'd left, expecting never to see him again. Five minutes later, round by the Palladium's stage-door, without the slightest hesitation, he'd waded into a gang of London heavies intent on slicing me up for breakfast. A few weeks later, round Christmas time, he saved me from being burnt to a crisp by a bunch of nasty foreign crooks out to cook my goose. And that added up to two things in my book, he was "family" and I owed him big time. Now here I was, looking for his wife Dilys's sister's house, before going to visit the hospital. Only this time it wasn't me lying half dead, it was Seth, and I'd come to Slough to find out what'd happened and to settle the score.

It's the smell that gets you first, a mix of carbolic soap and boiled cabbage. I walked into the ward, Dilys leading the way. The beds were all lined up against the walls as if awaiting kit inspection and I couldn't see where he was at first, for the crowds of visitors all milling around. Then there he was, all propped up, his one good eye locked on Dilys, the other hidden behind a white bandage wrapped around his head. Then he turned and I could see he was surprised at seeing me. He looked pretty bad, and maybe it was all the bandages, but whoever had done him over had really gone to town. He grinned, but couldn't hide the grimace as he slowly held out an iodine-stained bandaged hand for me to shake.

"This is another fine mess you've got us into," I said, pulling a face. It wasn't the best Oliver Hardy, but ever the ham, Seth slipped straight into Stan Laurel's look of pathetic befuddlement. I could see it hurt when he tried to point both ways at once, but I laughed along and if I'd been wearing a tie I'd have waggled it in greeting. "It only hurts when I laugh," he croaked. And I chuckled and put the bag of fruit I'd brought on the bedside cabinet. "I hear you've been trying to save the world again," I said.

Dilys had told me in the motor car, tears streaming down her face, that Seth had a fractured skull, broken arm, broken wrist, broken ribs, and was in danger of losing an eye. But what really had her worried was the doctors thought there might be other internal injuries; they just couldn't say yet. "But he's a good man, Jethro, why did those men do that to him?" she'd said, wiping her eyes. "That's what I'm here to find out, Dilys," I'd said, squeezing her shoulder. "Because he is such a good man; I know from experience, he's one of the best."

Seth looked up at me and smiled a tired smile, "Silly me, sticking my nose in. I should get my head tested, as well, while I'm in here." He tried to sit up and we both gingerly reached in to try to help him. "It's good of you to come, my old pal. I suppose you'll be wanting a song, will you?"

"No," I said, slipping right into step. "I'll tell you a joke. After all, laughter's the best medicine. So just hold your sides ready." I pulled up a chair and did my best, but I'm no Max Miller, and I could see how quickly he tired. So I said we'd better be off. And after smoothing down his blanket and rearranging the flowers by his bedside for the millionth time, Dilys leaned in and gave him a kiss. And I pushed the chair back to leave them to it, and with impeccable timing, one of the senior housemen approached the bed. He was tall for a doctor, and I just hoped for everyone's sake he didn't look down his nose at Seth and Dilys, or me. Or there'd be trouble.

"Immediate family only, I'm afraid," he said. "I'm going to have to ask you to leave while I talk to the patient."

"We were just going," I said, getting up. "I'm his cousin, from Canada." He looked at me, at Seth, and at Dilys, who having caught on quick was nodding her head like mad. "I wonder if I might have a quiet word with you," I said, leading him off to one side. "I'd like to make sure my cousin gets the very best attention; private room; any tests or specialists you consider necessary." He looked at me properly for the first time, then. It might've been the cut of my jacket or the Breitling on my wrist, but I think it was more the check-book I produced; a bank account said substance. "It's on my London bank, if that's acceptable?"

Anyway, soon they couldn't do enough for Seth. And I was escorted to the admissions office, where I wrote a check large enough for them to say, "Thank you, very much, sir." Then I went back, bid Seth adieu, and told him he'd be moving to a private room. He protested, of course, so I said if it'd been good enough for me, he should have one, too, and told him he should have his head examined, now it could be done in private. He laughed, and Dilys laughed and kissed him goodbye, and I gave him the thumbs-up and told him to get better. Then I drove Dilys back to her sister Betty's house. And after tea, I took Betty's husband, John, out for a drink at the pub on the Farnham Road where Seth had been beaten up.

John and a bunch of his mates had rushed outside the George pub and piled in, and even though they'd taken a bit of a beating themselves they'd saved Seth from being murdered or, at the very least, crippled for life. He was a nice lad; Polish; curly fair hair; blue eyes that were a lot older than his face. But the War did that to people. "So what happened, John?" I asked, peering at him over the rim of my beer glass.

He'd picked up English along the way, but that didn't stop his passion any; his words came out in a torrent. "The bleddy swines. Two of them came into the pub and started trouble, they pushed people, smashed glasses, then left, and Seth went after them. I followed outside with some mates from work, and we saw three or four other men attack Seth with pickaxe handles, from behind. The bleddy swines hit him in the legs and head. Then when Seth fell to the ground, they began kicking him."

"Take your time," I said. "Have a sip of your drink. I get the picture. And you say these men were all from London? Offering people protection against bad things happening, is that it?"

His eyes clouded. "Some men went into the greengrocers where Seth works and threatened the manager. Seth was out on his break, but he came back and saw them pushing things onto the floor, and so he threw them out." I smiled, I couldn't help it, I'd seen Seth in action, and I knew he would've wiped the floor with the sods. I nodded. John took a sip of beer. "That night, they came back with a Molotov cocktail," he said, quietly.

"They fire-bombed the place?" He nodded, but I had the

funny feeling he was holding something back. "Anything else, John?"

He swallowed and nodded again, very slowly. "Seth told me that one of the men shouted at him that he knew him from somewhere."

I went icy calm. "Did Seth, by any chance, say where he might've met this man?"

"He said it was the time he went up to London with his guitar."

"That time he came up to the London Palladium, was it, John?"

"Yes. Seth said the man yelled at him, 'You skinny bastard, you're a dead man.' But Seth hasn't told Dilys, or Betty, only me. He said it wasn't a good idea to worry the ladies."

Worry was right; it set my bloody alarm bells going like the clappers. If one of the men that'd attacked Seth had been part of the gang he and I had tangled with that night, round the back of the Palladium, it was odds on Darby Messima was involved, somewhere. Messima, the most feared gangster in all London; a real nasty piece of work; and someone I'd been trying to steer clear of ever since I'd got out of hospital, seeing how he was one of the reasons I'd found myself there, in the first place. Then, as fate would have it, not thirty seconds later a couple of well-dressed faces I knew worked for Messima swaggered into the pub. I watched them in the mirror behind the bar, but they didn't see me, they were too busy looking tough. And once they'd pushed their way through to the private bar at the back, and the noise level in the public bar had come up again, I said quietly, "Are those two of the men you saw, John?" He nodded into his drink. I blinked and caught sight of my reflection in the mirror. I seemed to have gone very pale again. But I knew even then, I couldn't sort it all out on my own, I needed help; it called for fighting fire with fire. And with my course set, I turned back to John. "Seth's lucky having a plucky young brother-in-law, like you, John. Fancy another drink, maybe somewhere quieter?"

As I drove back to the Smoke, the top up, a cigarette for company, I stared out at the MG's headlight beams pushing back the darkness; but my thoughts were fixed on Messima. He had all the West End and Mayfair as his manor; enough to keep anyone rolling in dough for a lifetime; so what in hell was the Emperor of Soho doing, messing about in Slough?

Then, honest to God, it was just like you see in those Yank gangster movies; I saw one newspaper headline after another coming at me, as if projected onto the windscreen. "SOHO'S KING OF SLIME." "LONDON GANGS FIGHT FOR CONTROL OF VICE EMPIRE." "THE FILTH BEHIND LONDON'S WEST END GLITTER." The *News of the World* and *The People* and the other Sunday linens had a field day with Mr. Darby Messima and so did the coppers from Scotland Yard. So the little Maltese bastard had had little choice but to keep his head down and his arse out of sight. Everything dropping on him, like that, would've been like pressing down on a sponge cake; all the jam in the middle just got squeezed out the sides. And that told me the slippery sod Messima had just spread himself out farther afield, until things in the Smoke got back to normal. He was ever the pragmatist.

I drove on through a deserted Slough High Street, but still had to stop at the town's only traffic lights. And as the throb of the MG's exhaust echoed back from the darkened shop fronts, the world was suddenly all limned in red. And I saw myself lying in a hospital bed in Windsor, not three months before, just back from the dead; dried blood still on the bandages, burns barely starting to heal. And Walsingham, standing there, calmly telling Bosanquet to plant stories about Messima's evil empire in the Sunday linens, and to instruct the Flying Squad to keep on harassing him until he got the message not to do deals with foreign villains. Yet, in the end, what had it all come down to? In pulling strings to get at Messima, Walsingham had only managed to get Seth badly beaten up and me up to me neck in it again. But that's the trouble with people who pull strings for a living, they never have to worry about the consequences of their actions. They're never the ones that have to clear up all the mess, afterwards. But someone like Walsingham should've known that no deed is ever without its repercussions.

I'd already worked out how I was going to get back at Darby Messima. But suddenly I got it into my head it was high time someone got back at Colonel bloody Walsingham. I'd promised myself, lying in my hospital bed, I'd do his drum; I'd climb up into his ivory tower and mess up his private little world; see how he liked it. But he wouldn't like it, would he; he'd bloody well hate it. It'd break all the rules. It wouldn't be cricket. After all, an Englishman's home is supposed to be his castle, isn't it? And soon I couldn't think of anything else; it was like catching the flu again. I was full of it and my head all but throbbed with what needed to be done. First, I had to set about setting dog against dog. Then I was going to creep into the lion's den, tweak its nose and pull its bloody tail. The red light turned to green, and I let out the clutch and roared off into the darkness. I was Jethro, the righter of wrongs. Jethro, the revenger.

CHAPTER 7

Ahead by a Whisker

The next morning I was up and about with the larks. I knew what had to be done and I was eager to get on with it. So, first thing I did was nip across the newsagents and pick up a *Mirror,* a *Mail,* a *News Chronicle,* and an *Express.* Then I sat at the back table in the Victory, had a fry-up, and read the linens from back to front. And by the time I'd finished I'd gone through so many mugs of tea, Joanie had switched me on to coffee. She'd asked how Seth was, the moment I'd sat down. Then she'd gone away shaking her head, probably as much from the look on my face, as about the condition I'd found Seth in. But then Joanie knew better than anyone the way my mind worked and what was now likely going to happen.

Breakfast done, I dashed back upstairs, went to the toilet, washed my hands and brushed my teeth. Then suitably armed with what the linens had reported was going on in the world, I went round the barbershop in the Edgware Road tube station to get myself a nice close shave. It was only a ten-minute walk, but with it being another cold, grey, miserable London day, I slipped on a hat and overcoat. And I was lying back in the chair with a toasty hot towel on my face just as Jack Spot walked in bang on the dot of ten, just like he did every morning. Jack was Guv'nor of the Manor everywhere north of the water, bar Soho and the West End. And the great thing about Jack was, he hated Messima even more than I did. Sharp as a razor, he knew it was me lying there even before his regular barber gave him the bent eye or a whispered word.

"Morning, Jethro, nice pair of shoes," he said very cheerily. "You can always tell a man by his shoes."

He exchanged pleasantries with all the staff, but even I knew it was never wise to talk when a man had an open razor at your throat, whether that man was your barber or your friend. Jack leaned in close, so only I could hear. "If you will insist on trespassing on my morning ablutions, this better be something I want to hear." I gave a muffled grunt of assurance. Then after chatting about football, the horses, the state of the railways since nationalisation, and of course the weather—and with Jack's whiskers and mine safely gone to meet their maker—I walked with him down the Edgware Road towards the Cumberland Hotel. The hotel's coffee shop was where he set up court each morning, but as I'd already had enough coffee to reawaken the dead, I got us under starters orders as soon as I could.

"It's about Messima, Jack."

Jack sniffed in some soot-laden air and smiled. "Lovely business, those pieces in *The People,* by that Duncan wotsisname fellow. All that stuff about Soho vice rackets and gang feuds has given our friend Darby Messima a right old headache. And with the Sweeney running around like elephants, ready to stomp on his toes if he puts a single foot wrong, he's walking on eggshells, he is. Why, something new about to break, is it?" He slid his eyes in my direction; then slid them forward, again. "Only, I did hear he had some very iffy dealings with some foreigners in the diamond business; but happily, it all blew up in his face, apparently. Can't be about that, though, can it? That happened a good few months back."

I shook my head like a nervous horse. Spottsy always seemed to know more than was good for me, and the sooner I got us both into the starting gate, the better. "No, Jack, it's about what Messima's been getting up to out of the Smoke. His mob's started muscling for business in a town out west of London, just the other side of Heath Row."

Spottsy stopped dead. "Heath Row?" he said, a sudden dangerous edge to his voice. "Not messing about around there, is he?"

I didn't know what that was all about, but I didn't let it throw me. "No, Jack, farther out; town called Slough; big land development back in the Thirties; huge trading estate with hundreds of factories."

He started walking. "So the Malt's setting up in the old bread and butter business, again, is he? He must really be hurting."

"That's right, Jack, promising everyone protection for a price." I got into step. "His mob's working their way through the shops, pubs, the clubs, everything. They've already done the dog track and a couple of cinemas." I paused. "Though, I reckon, it's the factories he's really got his eyes on." I kept my voice flat and myself reigned in. "Just waiting to set up a really big one, probably; that's more his style." I waited for the flag to go up.

"Lots of big payrolls then, are there?" Jack said softly.

I leaned in. "Thousands of workers, Jack; wages paid weekly and in cash, and come Fridays, all the banks and security vans are loaded with it."

I knew we were off to the races by the way he scratched his chin. He slid his eyes towards me again. "So, what's in it for you, Jethro? Robbery with violence or blagging payroll safes isn't exactly up your alley, is it?"

I nodded and looked at him straight. "I'm out of the game, Jack, you know that. I need a special favour, is all, but not for me, though; a good mate; someone I owe, big time."

Spottsy smiled a knowing smile that said he'd really like to believe I'd given up villainy. Then he stopped dead in his tracks and looked at me hard. "You okay, are you? Only now I look at you in daylight, you look a bit peaky. You're not coming down with anything, are you?"

"Er, no Jack, I did have a touch of the flu, as it happens. But I'm much better now, the old hot towel did me a world of good."

He nodded. "Yes, good barbers, them. And as to that little favour, consider it done, whatever it is." He didn't add, "Only, remember now, you owe me," but he didn't need to, I knew the score.

"Thanks, Jack," I said. Then I told him about Seth, and how Messima's men still had Seth's cards marked for when he got out of hospital and so I needed his help in redressing the balance a little.

Spottsy didn't turn a hair. "If you say he's your old china, Jethro, that's good enough for me. As I said, consider it done." And we walked on in silence; Jack nodding to people as they passed; my stock round the neighbourhood going up by the minute. He sniffed. I held my breath. "But you do surprise me, Jethro, you haven't asked after our Billy. Not once."

Billy Hill was a London face with a growing reputation, and if not yet a top villain, he was very definitely a comer. "Er, how is, er, Billy Hill doing, Jack?" I said, trying to keep my voice level.

He raised an eyebrow. "Enjoying his porridge like a good boy."

This time I stopped dead on the pavement, but Spottsy just carried on walking. I caught up, quick. "Billy in prison, Jack? You're kidding?" He didn't even bother to shake his head. "Blimey, I have been out of touch."

His eyes swivelled back in my direction. "I did also hear as you'd been away a while. Holiday, was it?"

"Er, yes, sort of a surprise holiday." I thought it best to change the subject. "What did Billy get sent up for, Jack?"

"Gave himself up of his own accord." He gave me another sideways look. "Come to think of it, that last time we had you in the motor car; him and Big Tom had just come back from doing a Manchester bookies' safe, for nine grand; very nice little job, too. Anyway, Billy and me have been talking about teaming up for a while; my planning, his connections; give Messima an even bigger headache. Only, it turned out he was still wanted for an old job he'd pulled. So what with the nasty new Criminal Act coming in, we both did the arithmetic and it was simple. If the cozzers felt his collar for anything after the first of January, it would've been a certain three-to-five stretch, on top of whatever the judge gave him fresh. So Billy gave himself up just after Christmas. With remission for good behaviour, he'll be out in a year; he can do the porridge standing on his head."

"Smart of Billy," I said, nodding. "Smart of you, too, Jack. You and Billy, together, you could really clean Messima's clock, you time it right."

He blinked slowly. "My thoughts exactly, Jethro. Planning, that's what it's all about, now, planning and patience."

For once, Spottsy and me were in total agreement. "Thanks again, Jack. My regards to Billy come visiting day. I'll, er, be seeing you then."

"Not if I see you first, you won't." He had the smile of a wolf eyeing a lost sheep. I did my best not to shiver. "Bye, Jethro," he said chuckling. "Be good, now. Expect a call from Big Tom."

Tommy Nutkins, "Big Tom," arrived in a dark blue Jaguar Mark V saloon, sporting trade-plates. I got in. It was brand new and smelt of newly tanned leather, polished-walnut veneer, and fresh motor-oil. A rare delight in itself as most drags were earmarked for export. It turned out the Jag was a display model on semi-permanent loan from a grateful garage owner whose wife had had all her jewellery nicked. But a whispered word in Spottsy's ear, over a morning coffee, was all it had taken to ensure their immediate and safe return. Oiling the wheels of commerce it's called.

Tommy nodded, and purred the Jag down the Edgware Road, before turning onto the Harrow Road and the A40 to Oxford. I knew he fancied himself as a driver and he'd take real delight in putting the Jag through its paces, so neither of us said a word and I spent the time looking out at the swiftly passing countryside. But when we reached Beaconsfield and he turned left, down towards Slough, it was like he'd turned a switch on the dashboard and it was time to get down to business. But then Tommy always liked entering a new town from the north; it was all part of his theory that successful conquests always come from that direction.

"Bit far out for the Malt, isn't it, Jethro? Anything south of the water or beyond Shepherd's Bush is foreign country to him."

"Messima's always talking of building empires, though, isn't he, Tommy?" I said. "And if he does manage to get himself dug in there, I tell you, the poor sods in Slough aren't going to know what's hit them. It'll be 'I came, I saw, and I conquered,' all over again."

Tommy nodded. "Benevolence, that's what they're going to need, some warm-hearted benevolence. And we know who's going to give it to them, don't we?" He chuckled and threw me a look. " 'Er, you alright, Jethro? Only you look like you've got things on your mind."

I shook my head. Keeping my eyes front and forward. "Me? No, I'm okay, Tommy. Just this Messima business, is all."

He turned back to his driving. "Not prying, old son, just making sure we're clear, you and me."

"Clear as an horizon line," I said. Then it started to pour with rain.

Tommy switched on the windshield wipers, and broke into another throaty chuckle; his gloved finger waving at a pub we were passing. I gave it a look. It was called The Jolly Butcher. "A man should always enjoy his work, I say," he said, pressing his foot down even harder on the accelerator.

I nodded, and watched the scenery go from green trees to red brick.

Tommy was an old mate from my time on the passenger liners, and a grand bloke. Though that wouldn't have counted for much if ever we found ourselves on opposite sides of a serious argument. Hard as nails and with fists like rivet hammers, he was ferocious in a fight and not surprisingly he'd worked his way up to be one of Jack Spot's top minders. My job was to help him recce the area and supply as much local detail as I could remember. So we toured the Farnham Road with me pointing out the places I'd been told were paying protection and the places that hadn't and still bore the scorch marks. I pointed out The George pub where Messima's mob camped out during opening hours and the billiard hall they used as their headquarters the rest of the time. Then we did a quick tour of the trading estate, so Tommy could get the full lay of the land, and with what happened later he must've already had his eyes out for an empty factory, but he didn't say anything at the time. We had egg and chips in a cafe and waited until nightfall. Then we sat in the Jag in a side street across from The George and smoked our way through a packet of twenty. I'd brought my Afrikakorps binoculars with me, and by passing them back and forth between us, we managed to put names to all of Messima's faces.

"That's it, we've clocked them all," said Tommy. "Eight in the pub, three back in the billiard hall. So those twins you saw must be the bag men that drive the takings back up to the Smoke each evening."

I counted up on my fingers and toes. "Unlucky for some," I said.

"It will be," Tommy said quietly. "Especially now we know that big ugly one was one of the mob that did for your mate Seth."

I'd recognised the bloke's ugly mug the moment he'd sailed into view. His face looked a bit puffier than it had that night behind the Palladium, but you could see by the way he carried himself, he still fancied himself as someone to be reckoned with. But then so did all of Messima's thugs, even the muscle-ridden twin brothers I'd once christened Tweedle-dum and Tweedle-dee, one very dark night, in Soho. None of that mattered anymore, though, it was out of my hands from that point on; it was Spottsy's call as to what happened next. But knowing Jack, I knew it'd be planned and executed like a military operation and that once it started, Messima's boys wouldn't know what hit them, and only fitting, really, as that's what they'd done to Seth. And I know they say revenge is best served cold. But me, I think it should always be served at body temperature and with the aid of a well-honed knife.

CHAPTER

8

False Fronts

I left Messima and Slough in Spottsy's capable hands and turned my attention back to Walsingham. And I took myself up West and staked out his "secret" MI5 office, and became one of the faceless masses on Regent Street; walking up and down, up and down, for hours on end, hoping to catch sight of him. He'd have soon seen me, had he looked, but I wasn't worried, it would've been hard to miss anyone with half-a-dozen sausage-shaped balloons tied to his arm. Add an old army greatcoat and a row of campaign medals, forage cap, putty nose, wig and glasses, and shoes doctored to give me a limp and I became just another ex-soldier reduced to selling matches or nick-nacks from a tray. I'd seen some scroungers pretend to be blind, or fake a lost arm or leg, but that wasn't me. True, my voice didn't sound much like me either, "Bal-looons. Pretty coloured bal-looons for a bob." But at least the singsong Welsh accent was pleasing to my ears. And by the second day, I might as well have been a London landmark,

I was that invisible. But even after another full day of it, there was still no sign of Walsingham or Bosanquet. I moved on to Plan B.

I knew Walsingham and his department worked all hours, so there was no question of me doing a midnight creep. So the next morning I telephoned the building manager's office, and a few hours later I pushed through the all-too-familiar double doors and stepped into the wood-panelled entrance foyer that I'd all but been carried into not ten days before. Only now I was a smartly dressed Canadian businessman looking to set up offices in London. "Can I help you, sir?" barked the Commissionaire. It was a bloke I'd never seen before. "Yes," I said, with just enough of a pause to show a well-practised ease when dealing with lower ranks, "Mr. Jeffrey Hardcastle, Toronto Global Timber. I have an appointment with the building manager. I'm a trifle early, but I do hope that's not going to be too much of a bother." The man retreated back behind his uniform. "Very good, sir, thank you, sir, if you'll just wait a minute, sir. I'll telephone his office." And once he'd confirmed I was expected, he escorted me to the lift. "The building manager is still in a meeting, sir, but if you'd like to go on up to the sixth floor, he'll be with you as soon as he can," he said, saluting. I nodded and was on my way up in the world again.

My plan had been to arrive early; say I needed to use the Gents; then find my way, unescorted, to the fourth floor. This was even better; I'd just get out two floors early. So I did. And I thought, at first, I was on the wrong floor. The secret hush-hush offices of Messrs. Walsingham and Bosanquet, otherwise the Universal Group of Companies, had vanished into thin air like so much Scotch mist. Not only had all the furniture disappeared, but everything else had gone, too: doors, walls, corridors; whole rows of offices. The big meeting room with the two-way mirror had gone, and so had the secret room on the other side of it. There was nothing to say that Walsingham's department had ever been there; someone had even cleaned the tea stains from off the floor. Gone without a trace. I took the backstairs to the fifth floor and found a team of painters hard at it, drinking tea. I went back down to the third floor; then the second and the first. Nothing, but import and export companies, foreign airlines, and a posh theatrical management agency. I talked to any number of receptionists, without result, then returned to the ground floor, to discover the building manager talking earnestly to the Commissionaire. The doorman's eyes slid in my direction; and the manager turned, his welcoming smile again firmly in place. It quickly disappeared, though, when I shook my head and said the building wasn't quite what I was looking for. And before he could say anything, I'd already disappeared out into Regent Street.

The next day I took the balloon man for a walk down Whitehall to try and catch sight of Walsingham there. But not ten minutes had gone by before a young copper, straight out of the new intake at Scotland Yard, asked to see my street-seller's permit and sent me packing. Something about no fancy dress or unofficial uniform being permitted within a mile of the Palace of Westminster, without it being a public holiday or official state occasion. I looked down at the medals I'd bought down the Portobello Road and threw the name of an appropriate regiment at him, but he wouldn't budge. "I fought the war for people like you," I sniffed. "And which war would that be, granddad?" he countered. I pointed to all the schoolkids milling around outside "the mother of all parliaments." "What about them uniforms, then, constable?" He smiled and pointed with his pointy-helmeted head for me to get off back in the direction of Trafalgar Square. "All right, Taffy, off you go, now." And muttering loudly, I turned to go and saw Walsingham on the other side of the street. I thrust all my balloons at a young kid in school blazer and cap, and even his mum was startled when I wouldn't even stop long enough to take threepence for them. "Here, I say, you, mister. What's the catch, then?" she called after me, but I was already racing up the street as fast as two legs of different lengths could carry me. But Walsingham had disappeared.

The next day I returned to Whitehall, only this time in the guise of a London cabby complete with old Austin Seven "growler." I drove up and down, past the Ministry of Defence, the Foreign Office, Downing Street, and all the rest of it. Then I just continued circling round and round, through Admiralty Arch, along the Mall, down Horse Guards Road, back by Parliament Square and up Whitehall again. I pulled in and waited whenever I could and kept my eyes glued on the building near where I'd last seen Walsingham. And despite repeated helpful enquiries from ever-eager and seemingly ever-younger coppers whenever I was parked for too long, I managed to keep up my surveillance.

I'd just about completed another circuit, ready to give up and go visit the taxi-shelter at the other end of Lambeth Bridge for a cup of tea and a cheese bun, when I caught sight of Walsingham and Bosanquet marching across Horse Guards Parade. I put the "growler" into a U-turn and sped off after them, passed them, and pulled over and sat and waited, eyeing them in the mirror. They were both in classic Guards mufti; dark grey suits, Eton ties, bowler hats, and tightly furled umbrellas. They crossed over the Mall in the direction of

Carlton House Terrace and marched up the stone steps in perfect unison. Off to one of their bloody gentlemen's clubs, I said to myself, feeling as proud as Sherlock at the brilliance of my deduction. I let go the handbrake and set off round Cockspur Street so I could catch them as they came out of Carlton Gardens, and was parked on the other side of Pall Mall when they emerged. I followed them round to St. James Street and saw them enter one of the clubs. I wasn't sure which one it was, so I pulled over into the cab rank on the opposite side of the street, and with the flag down and light off, pulled out a newspaper and waited.

My stomach started growling after a bit and all I could think about was the two of them, stuffing their faces in their club's restaurant. Sod this for a game of soldiers, I said, reaching for a cigarette, and as I drew the smoke down deep into my lungs I went over all the things I was going to do to Walsingham once I found out where he lived. And I must've really been lost in thought, because when I looked up someone was waving at me in a none-too-friendly manner. It was the club's doorman, yet another puffed-up ex–sergeant major in a Commissionaire's uniform, all spit and polish, shiny buttons, peaked cap, and campaign ribbons. I waved back, indicating I wasn't available and mouthed that he should hail another cab, rather proud of myself I'd refrained from giving him a V-sign. But the doorman kept on waving and I kept on waving back. Then suddenly Walsingham was standing there and the doorman turned to him and said something and then marched very purposefully in my direction.

He stuck his head inside the cab and growled at me from across the luggage compartment. "Listen, you malingering bastard, I don't know what your bloody game is, but get this cab and your arse in gear in double-quick time or I'll stuff that brassard of yours right up your hole and have this old heap sold off for scrap in Warren Street. Got it?" And before I could say anything, he'd turned back towards Walsingham and was saying, in that voice lower ranks always used to impress an officer, "He won't be but a minute, sir, a little starter trouble is all, but it appears to be fixed now."

I rolled forward and saw Walsingham pass a tip into the doorman's hand as if both men were unaware of the exchange, and the doorman tipped his hat and threw me a look that said, "I've got your bloody number now, sunshine, so watch it!" Walsingham got into the cab and called out the address he wished to be taken to, and I tried to keep my head down and my eyes off the mirror so he wouldn't recognise me. Then I thought, That's daft, even I couldn't recognise me in this get-up. And then it hit me, I just might've cracked it, he hadn't asked to be taken back to Whitehall, but to somewhere over in South Kensington, which might even turn out to be where he lived. I flipped the flag up and down again to start the meter going, shifted into first gear, and we were off to the races. Only this time it was him that was heading for the high jump, not me.

I flew round Hyde Park Corner and along Knightsbridge, and could hardly stop myself from cackling, it was suddenly all going so well. And I sped us up the Kensington Road, past Kensington Gore and the Albert Hall, turned down into Palace Gate, and took a right. I didn't want to overplay my hand so I didn't try chatting about the weather or anything, and neither did he. Then he called for me to pull over. And I yelled out what was on the meter, but kept my head down when he handed me the fare and tipped my hat when he handed me a tip. "Ta, Guv," I said, making sure my eyes were well hidden by the peak of my cap. As he turned away I had a quick butcher's at the tip. He'd been very generous. But then appearances were always so deceptive where Walsingham was concerned.

He lived on one of those nice-looking terraces that always seem to pop up from out of nowhere around South Kensington, but I still wasn't sure which house his was. I released the handbrake and set off slowly and kept an eye on him in the mirror. And when at last I saw him go in, I quickly pulled into the curb and got out the cab. I hurried back waving a ten-bob note in my hand, as if there'd been some mix-up over the fare, and climbed the steps to his front door. Then under the cover of pressing the doorbell which I didn't press, and trying the knocker which I didn't knock, quick as a flash, I had a tin key-blank out and inserted into the keyhole. I gave it a sharp turn so the first pin in the lock left a mark on the tin. I'd cut that bit out with a pair of tin-shears later, and be back to do the rest of the pins, by-and-by. And with a quick shufty at the door, the fanlight, and the front windows to see if there were any obvious signs of burglar alarms, I took my leave, shaking my head, as well as the ten-bob note for added effect. I'd got his number now and all done in two shakes of a cat's tail, too.

I cased the house for a week, in various disguises, so I could get a full set of key marks. I went as a London County Council surveyor, checking the siting of everything from the lamp-posts to the drains. I sketched my way around the area in a natty pencil moustache, black beret, corduroy jacket, and faded Slade art-school scarf. It wasn't the right area for the balloon man, as other than all the uniformed nannies pushing prams to and from Kensington Gardens there were few if any children about; the older ones probably all having been packed off to boarding school. But burglars shouldn't be seen or heard, either, so each to his own, I suppose.

I did the "wrong box from Harrods" routine so I could do the final bit of filing on the ghost-key I'd made up from the tin-blank and got the fright of my life when an elderly woman that turned out to be Walsingham's housekeeper unexpectedly opened the door. But she was a nice Scottish lady and I slipped easily into a Lowlands' burr and we were soon two Scots together in the land of the Sassenachs. And, very helpfully, she just happened to mention that the coming weekend she was away back home to Edinburgh, to see her sister. I wished her a safe journey. And the next day, when I was sure she'd gone out shopping, I was a postman with a special-delivery letter that needed signing for, and a key that needed a final test in the lock. And with a quick bit of filing I was all but home free.

I'd noted the times Walsingham left for Whitehall each morning and returned home at night. But when I saw him come home early on the Friday afternoon and leave soon after in a big Wolseley with a gun-case and a couple of weekend bags, then saw his housekeeper leave for the station suitcase in hand, I knew I had my opening. And that night around seven I did a last reconnoitre, found everything nice and normal, and drove back to the lock-up to make my final preparations for the creep.

Thus far, Walsingham's string pulling had nearly got me killed twice, and all but cost Seth his life. And all of it without any thought to the consequences. So it was high time I did some string pulling of my own. High time Walsingham started suffering for his actions. He'd started the game. Now it was my turn to make a move.

Pawn to King four.

CHAPTER

9

Pawn to King Four

Around ten o'clock, I drove back down to South Kensington in my little black Austin van; like my taxi-cab it'd seen better days, but that just meant it blended in all the more with the rest of London. I parked in a nearby street and did a final walk-past. I had on a bowler hat, overcoat, spotted silk scarf, and carried a briefcase and rolled umbrella. I swayed a little, as if I'd stopped off at my local after a long day at the office and had had one too many. Again, all to blend in. I reached Kensington Road, changed my gait, then circled back to the van. I unlocked the door and got in, exchanged the bowler for a deliveryman's peaked cap, and hunched down in the driver's seat. I sipped from a thermos of hot coffee Joanie had made up for me and stared off into nothing, the wisps of steam making me blink, repeatedly. Faces flickered through my mind; family and friends; the living and the dead; I focussed on Walsingham until the image curled and burned like film stuck in a projector. I blinked again. Got him. I donned the bowler, got out, and slipped back through the dark empty streets; a fleeting shadow cast for a moment across parked cars, iron railings, brick walls. And as I got closer to Walsingham's house, I became solid and took on his walk and gait and I went up the steps to his front door as if I owned the place. I inserted the ghost-key in the lock and with a twist of the wrist I was in.

I have to say, I'd expected a bit more from Colonel high and bloody mighty Walsingham. His burglar alarm wasn't worth spit; a kid in wet nappies could've done it. The arming switch was in an open panel, behind the front door; one click, and the whole place was laid bare. I switched on the hall lights. Three telephones, black, red and green, stood on a stand. I stared at them. Perhaps the sod had been doubly tricky after all, and had the alarm circuit linked by telephone to the local cop-shop, as was occurring increasingly round the posher parts of London. I picked up each handset in turn. But there was no sound of a gramophone endlessly repeating its message that the house had been broken into, just the tinny silence and hollow click before the operator from the local exchange answered.

I felt the house waiting, poised, as if still uncertain of my purpose. "What are you staring at?" I said to a nearby aspidistra, and got about my business. Usually, I'd send my sixth sense flying out. "Bat's ears," my dad used to call it. "Bat's ears and cat's eyes; signs of a born burglar." But I thought, Why bother? I'd seen Walsingham go off for the weekend. And as deadly serious as I was about doing the creep, it wasn't a matter of life or death. I dropped the umbrella in the umbrella stand, put the briefcase on the floor, removed bowler hat, coat, and scarf, but kept my turtles on. I looked around. All the doors in the hallway were closed; a simple enough precaution against the spread of fire we'd all learned to do during the Blitz, but it was just like

Walsingham to still be doing it. I knew then that the rest of the place would be all ship-shape and Bristol-fashion, just like my own drum. Perfect, for what I had in mind.

I soft-shoed along the passage and through the kitchen to the back door, which I unbolted, but more out of habit, really, than any thought of setting up a possible exit. I peered out into the little garden, and even in the light spilling from the kitchen I could see it was all neat and tidy; the flowers all regimented, the bushes tied to sticks. But how else would it be? I rearranged some flowerpots, then returned along the passage-way and fairly danced up the stairs to the top of the house and worked down from there; moving a chair here, a vase or an ornament there; opening a drawer half an inch; leaving a cup-board door ajar. And having opened all the doors to all the rooms on all the upper floors, I slipped back down the stairs, tapping out a paradiddle on the banisters, because I'd done it, hadn't I? I'd banged on Walsingham's drum. And if that was-n't worth a drink, I didn't know what was. He was bound to have a few bottles hidden away somewhere, and maybe a box or two of handmade cigarettes.

Now, it might not seem like I was doing much. I mean, I'd even wiped my feet coming in from the garden, and I certainly didn't intend to steal anything; well, nothing you could carry away in your hands. But I knew from experience, the simple fact I'd been there would be enough for Walsingham's cool, calm, well-schooled demeanour to crumble. With some people, it's only ever the small things that get to them. And I was thumbing my nose at everything he held dear: his home, his cas-tle, his sense of order, his profession. No spy likes to be spied upon; no thief likes to be thieved from; rubbish someone's pas-sion and you rubbish everything they hold important in life. It's a consequence of being who we are.

I rippled my fingers inside my leather turtles and opened the last unopened door in the house. I felt for the light switch and stepped into a drawing room of dark-red walls and ebony-coloured bookshelves, black leather chesterfields and armchairs dotted with red silk cushions and bolsters, and standard lamps with red silk lampshades. There was a beautifully lit oil painting of a striking-looking woman on the wall opposite, Margaret Lockwood to the life. And I remember thinking; She's lovely, I wonder who she is, when she's at home? Then I said aloud to the empty room, "Right, you bugger, where do you hide your drink?"

There was a moment's silence—no longer than the breath between words—and a voice that wasn't mine said very quietly, "A glass of sherry, Jethro, which would you prefer, sweet or dry?" A clock ticked; a floorboard creaked; the coal in the unlit fire settled in the grate. "Or considering the time of night, perhaps you'd prefer a single malt?"

Dumbstruck, I stared at Walsingham sitting motionless in a high-backed, leather armchair. What the bloody hell was he doing there? He was supposed to be off in the country, somewhere, shooting at little furry animals or things made of feathers or clay, not pointing what looked to be a fully-cocked, well-oiled, .455 calibre, six-inch barrelled, Webley service revolver, "officers, for the use of," at me. I took a step forward and the barrel of the gun raised just enough for it to stay pointed at my heart. I stopped dead, and the clock ticked slowly on into a suddenly unknown future.

"This is not at all what I expected from you, Jethro. And although I will admit to being somewhat intrigued, I'm a trifle confused as to why you've chosen to expend your not inconsiderable energies on me." He leaned forward, into the light, but all I could see was the dull sheen along the barrel of the gun, and the mouth of the muzzle. "So, do be a good chap, and explain yourself," he said, calmly, and very much in command.

"I think I've just been castled," I said, swallowing.

"So it would seem," he said, both he and his gun, unmoved.

"It was only a game, Mr. Walsingham; no harm intended. You took me very much for granted when you pushed me into that Berkeley Square creep, so I wanted to pull your strings, for once; see how you liked it."

"Well, I don't like it," he said, a dangerous edge to his voice.

"I didn't expect you to," I said. "It was done to me, once. Someone breaks into your place; moves things out of line, takes a few personal odds and ends, but otherwise leaves everything else untouched. It leaves a very nasty feeling behind, it says you can be got at, any time they choose."

"I take it, you're referring to that time Von Bentink burgled you?" he said. I nodded. "And all you've done is move a few things around?"

I nodded again. "A few drawers opened and all your doors left ajar."

"I couldn't tell what you were doing," he said.

"Is that thing loaded?" I said, pointing with my chin.

He gave the very slightest of nods. "Of course."

"You weren't really thinking of using it, were you?" I asked.

"I don't know, Jethro, that rather depended on you."

"You don't really think I came here to top you, do you?"

"It's possible you might've convinced yourself you had reason enough to try. Or you might've broken in to steal secret papers; things of that sort." The clock chimed the hour. "A man in my position develops many enemies; I stumbled across you, others might've done the same."

"What, me work for someone else?" I said, feeling oddly offended.

"Well, are you?" he said, like a barrister pressing home a point.

"No, Mr. Walsingham, that'd never happen. I only ever work for me; even the things I've done for you, were only done to keep me and mine out of prison or off the streets."

"Others might well have succeeded in persuading you, Jethro," he said flatly. "After all, I did. What makes you so sure of yourself?"

"They wouldn't have your charm, Mr. Walsingham. And unless you've been leaving that red file you have on me lying around for all to see, there's no reason for me to be on anyone else's radar. Even round Soho, I'm considered a face of the past."

The front door bell rang and I stared at Walsingham as a mongoose must stare at a cobra. I heard a key turn in the lock, the front door open and close, then Simon Bosanquet walked in, in black bow-tie and matching Walther PPK automatic. And to add insult to injury, from the look on his face, it appeared he fully expected to find me there.

"Good evening, sir," he said. Then he nodded in my direction. "Jethro." But he didn't offer to shake hands.

Guns levelled at me have a funny way of holding my attention, and all I could do was stare at a point midway between the two handguns. And we all remained motionless, like actors when the curtain drops at the end of Act One.

CHAPTER

10

Goodbye Mr. Chips

I stood, stock-still, waiting on the reviews of the critics, with no idea as to whether I had any future as a player or not.

As usual Walsingham didn't mince words. "It's as you thought, Simon; sheer bloody-mindedness," he said, his eyes not leaving mine for a second. "It seems Jethro has a chip on his shoulder about our working arrangement. He told me he wanted to pull my strings, for once." A ghost of a smile played across Bosanquet's lips, but I noticed his gun never wavered. "Have a quick look around, will you, Simon. We'll wait."

Bosanquet left the room and Walsingham kept his revolver levelled at my heart. I moved a hand, but Walsingham shook his head. "Don't move a muscle or I'll shoot you where you stand." And so I stood there, in stunned silence, the only noise the tick-tocking of the clock. And just when I thought the bloody thing was going to drive me up the wall, Bosanquet slipped back into the room, gun still very much in hand.

"Nothing much to report, sir. A few doors opened; the safe untouched, the oil painting in front of it, just as you left it. There's nothing stacked in the hallway and nothing at all in his briefcase."

Walsingham gave me a look straight out of *Goodbye, Mr. Chips*. "What are we to do with you, Jethro?"

"Well, for a start, Mr. Walsingham," I said, rolling my shoulders as if I was getting rid of all the tension in them, "you could pour me that whisky you promised me, a moment ago." And he gave the very briefest of nods, and I heard him un-cock his revolver and Bosanquet reset the hammer on his automatic, and in the blink of an eye I had the Fairbairn-Sykes out of its leather sheath and hurled across the room. There was a brief moment of silence, as the three of us stared at the handle of the knife sticking out of one of the blood-red cushions on the black-leather chesterfield next to Walsingham's chair.

"Just in case you thought there was no other possible end-game, Mr. Walsingham, sir. But I'll settle for a draw, if that's agreeable with you?"

I know it was dead cheeky of me, but I had to show them, as well as myself, that even if I had lost my marbles, I hadn't entirely lost my edge. And I don't know whether it shook Walsingham or not, because he simply stared at the knife-hilt, then back at me and said, "And, yes, Jethro, I was perfectly capable of shooting you, too. A drop of Knockando, for you?"

"Yes, please," I said, and I looked over at Bosanquet and he looked at me, but with no smile on his face now. And I nodded and held my arms up and he came over and patted me down, and then very pointedly clicked the safety on his Walther PPK. Then Walsingham poured us each a generous measure of Scotch, and my gambit all but played out, I sat there, glass in hand, savouring the hot, peppery nose of the malt whisky, feeling oddly at ease for perhaps the first time in months. And just as well, really, as they both then took turns in cutting me down to size.

Walsingham slid the knife in, first. "It was your bogus Harrods parcel delivery that first alerted us," he said. And that did make me wince. Borrowing a Harrods van—a fiver to the driver, for a lunchtime's use, was the going rate—had always been a winner for me and I'd always thought myself very convincing. I must've looked puzzled. "Let's just say," he said, flatly, "that my housekeeper, May, is a very canny woman."

"You can say that, again," I said, reminding myself to steer well clear of elderly Scottish ladies in the future.

"We had you under observation from your very first appearance as a postman," he said. And that did cut me to the quick, for it was now all too clear the sods had been expecting me, almost from the start.

Bosanquet gave the blade a twist. "The artist in the beret was very convincing, Jethro; as was your inebriated performance earlier tonight."

Blimey, I really had been playing to the gallery. I wondered where he and his Watchers had hidden themselves. Then Walsingham cut in, again. "We could've lifted you off the street, on any number of occasions, Jethro. But we had to be absolutely sure you were acting alone, and not with or for a third party." And I must've looked puzzled, because he added, "It's happened before, Jethro. Given the right inducements or pressures, a great many people have been turned against their own country."

The penny finally dropped then, and the very idea I could've been marked down as a turncoat or traitor narked me no end. "So people have been turned against their own countries, have they, Mr. Walsingham? What, like you and the

Double-X Section did to those Nazi spies during the War? Capturing the whole bloody lot, then using them to send back false information?" And that brought him up short; it was still all very hush-hush and "Top Secret," and he looked at me with a very stern look on his face. Good; I'd hit home. "I mean to say; I may've been a bit slippery in the past, but I was never a double-crosser."

"How the hell do you know about Twenty Committee?" he barked.

"It was just me and Eddie Chapman, one creeper to another," I said. "He's an old friend from way back. And we've both had to sign the Official Secrets Act, so it's still all in the family." He wasn't too amused by me or my explanation, but throwing one of his precious secrets in his face like that, and my little knife-throwing act, meant I was treading on very thin ice. It was time for a little back-pedalling. "I'm not trying to get your goat, Mr. Walsingham, but you saying you suspected me of doing the dirty, after what I've done for you and the Realm; well, it's bloody offensive."

Funnily enough, my little outburst seemed to mollify him. Though looking back on it, afterwards, the simple fact he hadn't shot me on the spot should've told me he already had something else in mind for me. He squeezed the bridge of his nose. "I should've expected no less, from two such incorrigible rogues as you and Chapman, but, I assure you, Jethro, I'm deadly serious. We live in unsettled and dangerous times; the corridors of Westminster and Whitehall are rife with suspicion and intrigue; with all manner of groups prepared to do whatever's necessary to succeed. It was imperative I know whether you'd been compromised in any way."

I'd almost been cited as a co-respondent in a couple of divorce cases; but, compromised, what did he mean by that?

The second penny dropped. "Do you mean, was I got at?" He nodded. It was my turn to shake my head. "Given the number of hooks you've got in me, Mr. Walsingham, there's no room for anybody else's strings. Believe me, it could never happen."

He squeezed the bridge of his nose again, then excused himself and left the room. And I sat there in silence, and looked over at the oil painting of the beautiful woman with purple-blue eyes. I asked Bosanquet who the woman in the painting was. A shadow crossed his face. "Don't ever say I told you, Jethro, but it's of his late wife, painted just before the War. She insisted on staying on in London, and doing her bit for King and Country, even though she could have easily sat out the entire conflict in safety. She volunteered as an ambulance driver for St. Thomas' Hospital and was killed in the Blitz."

I stared into the bottom of my glass. I'd lost my mum and dad in the Blitz and I knew the wounds never really closed up, you simply rebuilt the roads as best you could and marched on. "Mum's the word," I said, softly. And even though we both had serious questions about one another, I felt closer to Walsingham at that moment than I'd ever thought possible. We'd both been orphaned by the War; both of us scarred and marked forever. And he might've noticed a difference in me when he came back into the room, I don't know, but in my mind it was already a different world. But something must've definitely changed in him, because he came up to me and held out a knife in a black-leather scabbard, hilt first; and no ordinary knife, either. It was an all-black Fairbairn-Sykes, the same pattern as my knife, and about an inch shorter, but no less deadly.

"I want you to leave your knife exactly where it is," he said. "It'll serve as an alarm clock; a permanent wake-up call for me to bloody well stay awake. So, I'm giving you mine, in trade." I looked at my old knife sticking out of the red cushion, then at him, then over at Bosanquet, who looked about as surprised as I was about the proceedings. "And as to what occurred here tonight," Walsingham said, "it never happened." He looked at Bosanquet, who nodded, then at me, and I nodded and touched my forehead with my new Commando knife. "I do need to talk to you again, Jethro," he said, "and soon, but this is not the time or place. Simon will contact you to arrange our next meeting. But as for now, a good night to you, and please just bugger off." He picked up his whisky from the side-table and downed it, in one. Then he turned and led us out into the hallway. "And if you ever try doing anything like that again, Jethro, I'll have you out of the game, and for good. Is that clearly understood?"

And with that he closed the door on the whole episode. It felt oddly comforting, though, to have Walsingham back to his old charming self; it said that at least something was right with the world.

Knowing the Score

W in, draw, or game abandoned, there's always a bit of a come-down after a caper; the lows balancing out the highs, and for weeks on end, sometimes. But there wasn't much chance of that happening this time, as I was all but committed to doing another job for Walsingham and knowing him, probably sooner rather than later. And I told Bosanquet, as he escorted me back to my van, I needed a week or two before I could even think of gallivanting anywhere, and that if he popped his head up any sooner, I'd snap it off. Nothing personal, I said, but if I was to be any use to them at all, I needed to get myself into some sort of shape. He had the grace to chuckle, and said that a week from the following Monday would be quite soon enough.

I'd only been out of the game for three months or so, but the physical side of the Berkeley Square caper had been a lot more difficult than I'd expected. My grip was weak and my muscles had softened so much they'd ached like nobody's business. But more than that, I needed to get my head on straight. I'd felt far too much like a victim since I'd got out of hospital, and that was just asking for trouble.

Then there was all the personal business I had to attend to. I had to pop down to Slough to see how well Seth was mending. I needed a quiet word with Tommy Nutkins to get the latest on Spottsy and Messima. On top of that, I needed to spend some time smoothing out Joanie's feathers, as they tended to get a bit ruffled when she knew I had a job on. Not that she had any moral quibbles about it, it was just that she didn't ever want to hear I'd been nicked or that I'd fallen off some roof somewhere. She'd dig me up and kill me again, if that ever happened. So a night out on the town with her and Barry, just being my old silly self again, would soon put that to rights. Add to all that, me getting myself all spruced up for a few nights out with a girlfriend, and it was quite a to-do.

Deep down, though, I knew I needed to find out if I still had the bottle for top-class creeping or not. And the only way to know if that part of you was still alive and kicking was when you were hanging from a drain-pipe, sixty feet up in the air; that's what always sorted the cat burglars from the dogsbodies. So I visited a few local gyms, though never the same one two days in a row, I didn't want to give rise to too much idle gossip. And I worked out on the heavy bag, did some rope skipping and shadowboxing, then quietly moved on.

I had no tom for Ray to examine, so Monday evening was given over to chess, The Glenlivet, and sorting and polishing whatever was on our minds. "The more I've pondered it, Jethro," Ray said, putting me in check, "the more I think all that paraphernalia to do with Hitler is the key to that Berkeley Square job. It all points to politics. And for the life of me, I can't see how a black magic coven or a book of dirty photos could seriously endanger national security, and that's the only thing that ever brings MI5 out of the woodwork. So you go careful." I asked him how he knew I was about to do another caper for Walsingham. "Don't be daft," he said, "of course you are. That's why I'm telling you to beware." I said that sounded like something out of *Julius Caesar* and asked whether "the ides of March" had come or gone yet. He gave me one of his looks. "I think you should just be extra careful, Jethro, that's all." So, of course, right away, I knew he knew something, so I gave him the bent eye. And he told me his colleague down the British Museum Library, the one that passed titbits of émigré gossip on to Walsingham, had been pressing extra hard for whispers of anything at all to do with any recent Communist or Fascist activity, anywhere in London.

"I can understand them going after the Communists, Ray," I said. "They're all but running the Docks and they're in most of the big trade unions, too. But I can't see anyone trying to push Fascism again, not after the War we had. Though, that Franco is still at it, in Spain, isn't he?"

"Ideas die hard, Jethro. You can try and stamp them out, but they always pop up again, somewhere, in a new guise. The Fascists weren't all killed in the War or hung at Nuremberg; a lot of them are still out there. There're rumours all around the markets that the Sheikh's been seen in the Smoke again, and, of course, there's that iffy New Britain mob. And if it smells like a fish, it's a fish." He sniffed. "Walsingham sends you out on a creep for important papers and you just happen to stumble across a bloke who idolises Hitler. All a coincidence? I don't think so." He waggled his empty glass at me. "Incidentally," he said, cackling, "that's checkmate."

The following day I nipped down the barbershop in the Edgware Road tube station and caught up on all the local gossip. Spottsy was away up North, on business, and hadn't been in for a shave for over a week; and no one had seen hide or hair of Tommy Nutkins for almost twice that. It was, everyone agreed, all quiet on the West End front. I dropped tips all round, then hoofed it over to Paddington Station and took a train to Slough, and then a taxi from the station to the local hospital. Dilys was already there, of course, and looking a lot better than the last time I'd seen her, which I put down to the marked improvement there'd been in Seth. The spleen wasn't ruptured; the kidneys were working fine; the bones all mending nicely; the eye, too; and the good news was they were sending him home, soon. "You shouldn't waste your money, coming to see me," Seth said. "It's my money and I'll waste it how I please, thank you very much," I said. "Strewth, you'd think I had friends coming out my ears, listening to you."

When Dilys went off to fill his water jug, I took a brown paper envelope out of my pocket and handed it to him. "Here, Seth, this is so you and Dilys can get away for a few weeks' holiday, somewhere. Maybe pay a visit to that sister of yours up in Halifax. I'm sure you could do with a break after being in here for so long; do you a world of good." I gave him a look. And he gave it me back. But we both pretended not to know the score. "I couldn't," he said. "Gertcha, you stubborn Yorkshireman," I said. "Go off somewhere nice and get yourself fighting fit, or I'll use an Halifax Persuader on you." And he laughed. And I laughed. It was all harmless banter between friends. But we both knew I had to find out whether or not Messima's men would be waiting for Seth when he popped his head up. Because if they did try to do him over again, it was odds on someone would end up dead. And that wasn't at all the result I'd planned for.

We said our goodbyes and I took Dilys home by taxi. Then bang on opening time I paid a visit to The George. There was no sign of young John, Betty's husband; he was probably on late shift at the biscuit factory; but then there was no sign of any of Messima's tearaways, either. I bought myself a pint, and had just begun to engage the barman in conversation, when someone came up and introduced himself. He stood at a respectful distance; just beyond the length of a broken bottle, held at arm's length.

"Mr. Nutkins's respects, Mr. Jethro," the bloke said. "He said you might call in some evening. All drinks were to go on his slate."

"I know your face," I said. "You're one of Spottsy's accountants from the Saint Bartolph's Club. Long way from the East End?"

He bowed. "Maurice Goldring," he said. "I do have that pleasure. And as you can see," he said, sweeping his arm out like a headwaiter in a posh hotel restaurant, "thanks to Mr. Spot taking an interest, things have quietened down considerably." And it was true, there was no muscle on display anywhere; it all looked deceptively normal; just like Mr. Maurice Goldring. Like many men of smallish stature, he was very dapper, and wore a dark suit, highly polished shoes, and a signet ring as if to the manner born. He was no more than five-five, and just over nine stone, but you could tell he was very confident of his place on the ladder. But it's always the small, quiet ones you have to watch out for. I raised an eyebrow.

"I myself am only in Slough for a short time, Mr. Jethro, simply to help the landlord appreciate the full possibilities of his establishment."

I nodded. Everyone has to pay sometime and Spottsy was a past master at finding ways of coming out ahead. Beer watered down a little more than usual; measures from the optics not what they seem; a penny here, sixpence there, it soon all mounted up. Add to that a nice, respectable front for black market spirits that'd fallen off a lorry on its way down from the North, and Bob's your uncle. I looked round at the punters in the saloon bar, they seemed happy enough to have their pub back to some sort of normal. But a quiet place to have a drink in, to play dominoes or darts in, to have an occasional knees-up in, was all most people ever asked for.

"Another drink, Mr. Jethro?"

"Nice of Tommy, but no thanks," I said, finishing my pint. "But next time you see him, Mr. Goldring, please tell him I was in."

He nodded, and insisted on calling me a taxi. I got the message; the fewer eyes that clocked me, the better it was, all round. And I was driven to the station and got a slow train back to Paddington, mostly pleased with the way things had turned out, but still lost in thought most of the way.

The following day I telephoned and left a message for Seth saying that even though the weather down South looked as if it was going to turn out fine, a few weeks holiday, up North somewhere, would definitely do him the world of good. It was true, things looked pretty stable in Slough, but you learned never to count chickens where Spottsy or Messima were concerned; they both tended to take the long view when hatching plans, including plans of revenge or retribution. And better safe than sorry.

Later on in the week, Joanie and Barry and me took in a night at the Metropolitan Music Hall, just round the corner from the Victory. Max Miller headed the bill and, as ever, was as blue as the Chancellor's office would allow and then some, if you had a dirty mind to begin with, that was. Saturday night, Natalie, one of my best girlfriends, and me, did the Café Royal and a few of the night-clubs and had a lovely old time. And, come Sunday, I felt like a new man in more ways than one. On the Monday, I did an early-morning workout at a gym up in Kilburn, nipped back to the Victory for breakfast and a read of the linens, then got myself a shave and paid a visit to the Turkish baths on the Harrow Road. I felt real good afterwards, so I took a brisk walk down to Paddington Station and bought a cup of tea in the buffet and took some time to catch up with myself. Then I strolled out into Praed Street and immediately caught sight of Simon Bosanquet hiding behind a newspaper on the other side of the road. He had on a Trilby and a mackintosh. And if he hadn't also been wearing very expensive brown suede shoes, even the blind newspaper seller on the corner would've marked him as a plainclothes copper.

He didn't give any sign of having seen me, but walked off slowly in the direction of the Edgware Road, banging his now rolled-up newspaper absent-mindedly against his leg. It was his signal that I was to follow him. I looked both ways, up and down the street, waggled my right ear between my thumb and index finger, then crossed over the road and followed him along the street and down towards Sussex Gardens. There was a black Humber Snipe waiting near the corner of Star Street. I stopped to light a cigarette, but seemed to have a bit of trouble with my Zippo, so I shook it a few times, demonstrating to all the world that it must be out of lighter fluid. Then as if noticing the motor car for the first time, I walked over and knocked on the window and enquired of the driver whether I could possibly borrow a match. It was the Special Branch driver from the Berkeley Square caper. "All right, Laurence Olivier," he said. "Get in." So I did. It's always nice to know people appreciate talent when they see it.

CHAPTER

12

New Orders

Bosanquet and his driver took me to a big ugly building, down by the river, in Victoria. We entered at the rear and I was taken up in a service lift, well out of sight of people important enough to come in through the big front doors. I suppose it was pretty typical for a government office: acid-green-painted corridors stretched off in every direction, and by the third turning I was all but lost; the maze at Hampton Court had nothing on the place.

They left me in a room with an old table; five badly scuffed wooden chairs; and a framed picture of the King. I'd just sat down when the door burst open, and banged back against the wall hard enough to make the picture frame tilt. I sprang to my feet just as a fully laden tea trolley was pushed in through the doorway.

"There's no need to stand for the likes of me, dear, I'm no one important." The tiny grey-haired old lady in flower-patterned pinafore brought her tea trolley to a halt in a rattle of cups, and looked at me over her eyeglasses. "Though, you must be. His nibs ordering tea and biscuits, this time of the afternoon; it's only VIP or department heads, normally." She poured a cup of tea from the tea-urn. "One lump or two, dearie?"

"Er, two lumps, please. Ta, very much."

"Here you are, ducks," she said, handing me a cup. She opened a big square tin and counted three digestive biscuits out onto a plate. I drank the tea, ate all but one of the biscuits, and I was just thinking I'd love another cup, when the door banged open again and in walked Walsingham carrying a cup with a saucer balanced on top. He nodded, sat down, placed the teacup in the saucer, and sipped his tea. Then he pointed to the last digestive biscuit and took it and bit into it before I could tell him I was saving it for later. Then Simon Bosanquet walked in carrying a cup in one hand and a bunch of cardboard files in the other; one, buff coloured, with a red card stapled to the front of it, and two others in duck-egg blue. I tell you, it was a regular Mad Hatter's tea party.

Walsingham raised an eyebrow. "We had a report of a Canadian gentleman, a Mr. Jeffrey Hardcastle, that paid a visit to Regent Street. Was that you, by any chance?"

"Mr. Hardcastle, of Toronto Global Timber? Yes, that was me."

"I thought it might be the Cousins trying to keep tabs on us," he said, peering at me over the rim of his teacup. "Good, that clears that up, then."

"You're not kidding," I said, "there wasn't a stick of furniture left."

Walsingham leaned forward so as not to spill his tea on his trousers. "I thought it wise everything be moved," he said.

"Military Intelligence gone down in the world, has it?" I said, looking around the cramped little room. "So who am I defending the Realm for now then; these cousins of yours, or the Ministry of Housing?"

Bosanquet choked as his tea went down the wrong hole, and as he tried to cough himself back to normal, Walsingham looked at me and smiled, but his eyes didn't. "It's still my little show, Jethro. Let's just say, I find it prudent to pick up sticks, now and then; squeeze in somewhere, pro tem. People tend to overlook us, then; leave me to get on with things."

Hiding in plain sight, right under people's noses. It was typical Walsingham. He glanced over to see whether Bosanquet was still in the land of the living and without any sense of irony, he said, "Simon tells me you'll soon be fighting fit." I sat there wondering if Bosanquet would last out the night or not, but Walsingham fixed me with a look. "I wanted to hear it from you, myself, this time."

I nodded and went over and slapped Bosanquet hard on the back until he stopped choking. "The way I see it, Mr. Walsingham, the sooner I get on with whatever it is you have in mind for me, the sooner I can get back on with my own life." I gave a little cough. "That buff-coloured file you have on me notwithstanding, of course."

"Quite," he said. "Let's to business then, shall we? I want you to break into the London headquarters of the New Order of Britain Party and pinch a few things for me," he said as calmly as if he was ordering a five-shilling meal at his favourite Soho restaurant.

So there it was, my next caper, and boy, could he pick them, because if it involved NOB in any way, all things considered I'd have rather ridden a cocked-horse to Banbury Cross, thank you very much. The NOBs were nutcases, fanatics, throwbacks to before the War, or at least the ones you saw out on the street were. Political parties were banned from wearing military-style uniforms, but NOB marched up to the line and stuck their highly polished boots and shoes right on it. And the sight of them striding along the pavement in their black Trilby hats, stone-coloured trench coats, starched white shirts, and Windsor-knotted black ties, was enough to make your toes curl. They didn't come right out and say they were Fascists, but that's what oozed out of every pore.

So, Ray had been right; Fascism did play a role. Funny, how well he could read the tea-leaves, sometimes. I looked up and Walsingham's eyes measured me, even as he pushed his teacup aside. How much could he tell me, how much could I take in? He steepled his fingers and launched straight in. "The New Order of Britain Party is but a new face of political extremism. In the Thirties, there were groups such as the British Union of Fascists, the January Club, the White Knights of Britain, the New Pioneers, the Right Club." I nodded. Ray had mentioned many of them, way back when, though I hadn't taken much notice at the time. I waited while Walsingham patted his pockets for his tobacco pouch, a little ritual he always did when marshalling his thoughts. "In the run-up to the War, there was a widespread belief the Jews were responsible for the coming conflict. And even those people that saw themselves as the most patriotic of Englishmen and women saw anti-Semitism and pro-Nazism as but two sides of the same coin. So, come the outbreak of hostilities, they found themselves in a considerable dilemma. Should they do their duty and fight? Or should they oppose a war they believed was a Jewish-Bolshevik plot to push Britain into an unnecessary war against Germany?"

Walsingham found his tobacco pouch, but he'd lost me on that bit about it all being a plot. It was Bosanquet that filled me in. "As many of the prime architects of Bolshevism were Jewish, some people saw it as a direct outgrowth of Zionism and regarded the two ideologies as one huge conspiracy to overthrow Christian civilisation and gain world power."

Walsingham looked up from closely examining the bowl of his pipe. "The most charitable view one can have of the members of these extremist British groups is that they were loyal, but foully misguided."

Bosanquet produced a piece of paper from a duck-egg-blue-coloured file. "On 1 March, 1940, six months after Britain declared war on Germany, Sir Oswald Mosley gave a speech at a well attended luncheon at the Criterion Restaurant, here in London. In his speech, he said: 'The real reason why the British Government have declared war on Germany is because Britain is controlled by Jews, and they desire to see the end of the present German government so that they can assume their exploitation of the German people.' Mosley was loudly applauded."

Walsingham, at last, puffed his pipe into life. "Mosley is little changed. And now, no doubt spurred to action by NOB's growing political presence, he's formed the British Union Movement." He pointed at me with the stem of his pipe. "He's set up shop in Dalston and has every intention of moving on to his old stomping grounds in Hackney, Shoreditch, and Bethnal Green. All stepping-stones to him establishing a power base in local government bi-elections."

He let that sink in. I was born in Hackney, and even though the house and street I'd grown up in had been blown to bits in the Blitz, both me and my sister, Joanie, still regarded it as home. Now here was Mosley stirring up old hatreds in the East End again, and just like before, all for his own ends. And as Walsingham had no doubt intended, things began to stir in me, too. True, a lot of East-Enders had supported Mosley before the War, and even though most would now say they were simply looking for a strong man to lead them out of all the miseries of the Depression, it still didn't sit too well. But it wasn't just about laying old ghosts to rest, anymore, or waving the flag; the problem was on my doorstep, and it was my fight, too, if I wanted. But as Ray always said, "It can't hit you, if you're not already there." And there I was, with my chin firmly stuck out.

As per usual, Bosanquet hit home with the telling details. "NOB and BUM aim to contest local government seats, ward by ward, and build their influence from the ground up. They're effectively hiding in plain sight behind ballot-box curtains."

"Cloaking themselves in legitimacy," Walsingham said quietly.

There was silence in the room, after that, with nothing to relieve it; not even the sound of Walsingham sucking on his pipe. The thought that so many had fought and died in the War, only to find the same old demons alive and well again, left a strange taste in the mouth. I eyed my empty teacup and wondered if I tried rattling it, whether it'd frighten away the spectre of Fascism that suddenly seemed to be looming over everything again. Walsingham lit another match and I moved towards it as if it was a beacon on some distant headland. "We believe that whoever is behind NOB is also funding Mosley, as well as most of the other extreme right-wing groups. The only conclusion we can draw is that someone is making a determined and concerted effort to affect the balance of power within the country. It's my job to find out how and why." He fixed me with his eyes. "We've been told that there's a master file that lays out the entire interlocking framework of all extremist right-wing groups, dating back to 1930. It also lists all those individuals that have secretly financed the groups."

Blimey, even I knew that'd be political dynamite. Half the nobs and toffs in the country would want to let those sleeping dogs lie dead and buried. A thought suddenly hit me. "Don't tell me. This master file is a red-leather-covered book, about so size, complete with a little brass lock."

Walsingham leaned back and steepled his fingers and tapped them together, repeatedly. "It may very well be, Jethro, we simply don't know."

I understood, then, why he'd been so disappointed with the three red books I'd come up with. It wasn't the dirty photos he'd been after; it was this so-called master file; the key to everything. "So, is that what I'm supposed to be looking for this time, Mr. Walsingham, some sort of file?"

He nodded. "Any sort of diary or ledger, whatever its size or colour; especially if it contains names and addresses, dates, marginalia, columns of figures, as well as any dossiers, documents or letters you come across."

"Right," I said. "I'll need a couple of weeks to suss the place out and set up the caper. Then another week, at least, for . . ."

Walsingham shook his head. "No, Jethro. The job has to be undertaken much sooner than that." And before I could even howl a protest, he turned and said, "Simon, I think it's high time you introduced Jethro to Mr. Daniel Cruickshank." From the funny looks they exchanged I had no idea what they had in store for me. But, I tell you, when I found out, you could've knocked me down with an empty teacup.

CHAPTER

13

Keys to the Kingdom

They had some smashing-looking girls working at the hush-hush, top-secret building that Bosanquet took me to the next day. So, right away, I knew I'd be rubbing shoulders with VIPs. All the girls looked like debutantes, and they usually don't let high-class young skirt like that out anywhere, without there being good prospects for a good marriage close by. The powers-that-be at MI5 probably thought blue blood was far more secure than any other security measures they could dream up. Selective breeding, I think it's called in some circles.

Bosanquet called the place the Registry. And maybe it was. Anyway, he'd asked me to come as the Canadian businessman; I think, wanting to see for himself the get-up that'd eluded his teams of Watchers. In my Harris-tweed jacket, Tattershall-check shirt, club tie, and brown brogue shoes, I looked like someone from the New World trying to pass for an Englishman. But the military policeman who studied the green security card that Bosanquet had had knocked up for me overnight, didn't even give me a second look. He just nodded us both through with a curt rejoinder that my pass was restricted to corridors F1, F2, and F4 on the ground floor, and Department K in the basement. Then there I was, on the other side of the looking-glass, inside the very heart of Military Intelligence; though for the life of me, I still hadn't a clue why I was there, unless Bosanquet wanted to show how well MI5 could keep secrets.

I followed him down more endless corridors, and once we'd shown our passes a second and third time to increasingly squinty-eyed MPs, Bosanquet pushed hard against a security door and we descended a narrow concrete staircase. At the bottom he pushed open another door and we stepped out into a long wide corridor with big red fire doors studded at forty-foot intervals along both sides. From the sound of all the muffled shrieks and bangs echoing up and down the corridor they could've fitted a pistol firing range, a gymnasium, a metal shop, as well as a work's canteen and torture chamber down there, and still had room for a madhouse.

"What's down here, then, the dungeons?" I whispered loudly.

"Yes, that's exactly what we call our little collection of special workshops and storerooms; there's a firing range, too, at the far end."

I raised my eyebrows; the taxes I hadn't paid were paying for all of this. "Why the Grand Tour? It's not as if you needed to impress me any."

He turned to me with an enigmatic smile. "Nevertheless, I think even you might be impressed by this, Jethro."

He stopped outside a big red door with the letters *K132* stencilled on it in black and pressed a little button on the wall.

After a minute or two there was the sound of a lock being opened and I stepped into what can only pass for heaven to a creeper like me; outside of an unattended diamond vault, that is. There were walls and walls of keys; a vast array of them; thousands of them, all hung in rows along each wall. And if that wasn't enough, there were long wooden benches lined with all kinds of safes, and wooden frames displaying safe and door-lock mechanisms like so many specimens in a manufacturer's showroom. My eyes feasted themselves sick in seconds. The metal workshop wouldn't have been out of place at Rolls-Royce, up in Crewe; it was that immaculate. I thought my lock-up was pretty good, but this was a Shangri-la. I turned to Bosanquet, only to find myself staring up into the bluest eyes I'd ever seen in a man.

He was six-three, if he was an inch; big-boned, but slight; and dressed in an undertaker's black suit. His hair was black, too, and wiry like a chimneysweep's brush gone awry. He had ten years on Bosanquet and me, and I couldn't tell which branch of the Armed Forces he was from, but from the way he moved he hadn't just polished chairs with his bum. Bosanquet did the introductions. "Jethro, let me introduce you to Mr. Daniel Cruickshank, or 'Keys' as he's better known, down here."

The hand of a concert pianist reached out and I took it and shook it and I could tell I was in the presence of greatness; you didn't get hands as subtle and strong as that without years of practice. I tried to remember the name Bosanquet had chosen for the MI ID-pass he'd told me was mine for the day. "Pleased to meet you, Mr. Keys ... I mean ... Mr. Cruickshank. The name's Hitchcock, Jeffery Hitchcock."

"The pleasure's mine, Mr. Hitchcock." He continued looking directly at me, but spoke to Bosanquet. "One of

Walsingham's new boys, is he, Simon? Canadian, too, by the sound of him. Interesting."

Interesting wasn't the half of it. It was hardly likely I'd be the first one sent to the Dungeons by Walsingham; but I still had no idea what I was in for; maybe it was some kind of test. I thought I better play along with what it said I was on my green security card. "Toronto. RCMP."

"Ah-ha, the Royal Canadian Mounted Police?" Keys rippled his fingers. "Better show me your pass, so we can dispense with the trivialities of paper security and get down to real business." He took my security card, glanced at it, and handed it back. "If W and our good friend, Simon, here, have gone to all the trouble of having such a high-class forgery run up for you, who am I to question their motives." He smiled his best conspiratorial smile. "Welcome to my humble abode, and please do call me Dan."

Bosanquet handed him an official-looking envelope and "Keys" took a long-bladed knife from off a nearby desk and deftly slit it open. He removed a single sheet of paper, studied it for a moment, then looked up at me. "The motive is now clear. So let me see what I can do to help the Mounties get their man." He produced a box of matches from out of his pocket and set alight to the paper, holding onto it until the last possible moment before finally dropping the still flaming ashes into an ashtray. He prodded at the remains with the end of a pencil, reducing them to dust. "Old habits, like new secrets, die hard," he said smiling, and then he excused himself and went over to a cabinet full of filing-card drawers, like you see in any public library. He spent a few minutes locating and consulting different cards, wrote things down on a little notepad, then walked over to the nearest wall of keys. That's when I noticed a huge grid pattern painted on the wall in red. Letters, A to Z and AA to ZZ, ran alphabetically along the top; the numbers, 1 to 36, down the side. The next grid was a different colour; and so on, around three walls. "Keys" ran his eyes along the double-letter groupings, came to a stop, then ran his finger down to a numbered square; in which two keys hung on tiny hooks. He pulled off each key in turn, confirmed that its ID number matched his notes, and then placed it into a small brown paper packet. He returned, tore off the top page of his notepad like a doctor handing out a prescription and gave it to Bosanquet. "If you'd be so good as to do the honours with the slide drawer, Simon, I'll prepare the keys. We'll be with you shortly." Then he turned to me and said, "If you'll come this way, Mr. Hitchcock, I'll give your first lesson in the dark and arcane art of locks and lockpicking."

The penny dropped then. On this side of the looking-glass things went in reverse and lawful ends justified unlawful means. I sat opposite "Keys" as he put each key in turn into the key-copying jig and made me a new set. At least I knew how I was expected to get into the headquarters of the New Order of Britain. I was going in through the front door.

"Call me Jethro," I shouted over the screeching of the metal key cutter. "Tell me, Dan, do you always make copies? As a precaution, like?"

"No, old sport, standard procedure for certain missions, only. Yours is coded VD." He raised his bushy black eyebrows at me. "Not to worry, it's not in reference to any necessary visit to the pox doctor."

"Oh, what's VD stand for in my case, then?" I said, scratching.

"Stands for 'very dangerous.' As in, likelihood of violence up to and including the use of firearms," he said, all matter-of-factly.

"Charming, that really fills me with a lot of confidence," I said.

"At least it wasn't coded ED, Jethro, old bean." He paused with all the timing of a music hall comedian. "Stands for 'extremely dangerous.' As in, the probable demise of all mission operatives." I don't know what my face looked like, but he had a big grin plastered all over his. "We simply can't afford to lose these," he said, holding up a bright, shiny key. "You never know when we might need to use one of the little darlings again."

Yes, it was people like me that came ten-a-penny, I suppose.

Anyway, once he'd stopped chuckling to himself and had finished cutting and filing the new keys, he ushered me towards the workbenches at the far end of the room, where all the safe and key mechanisms were on display. Then he proceeded to demonstrate how to attack different kinds of locks. He picked up a lock mounted on a wooden frame. "The Chubb, here, although widely advertised as being unpickable can be overcome with but a modicum of patience." He picked up a couple of twirls from a metal box on the workbench, and without even looking at what he was doing, proceeded to pick the Chubb lock clean. "The ins and outs of which, I hope," he said, "I have now made apparent." He glanced at me to see if I was paying attention, only this time, it was me that was trying to hide a big grin. He gave me an odd look, then looked over my shoulder. "Ah, Simon, so good of you to join us. Come back for a little refresher, have we?"

Bosanquet nodded, put the slide tray onto a nearby table, and took a stool next to me. Then "Keys" picked up a demonstration Yale mechanism. "This is the little beauty you'll come across most often," he said, and then described how a series of pins were set in different positions inside the barrel of the lock.

He drew a large diagram on a blackboard and pointed out how the bites in the Yale key pushed up the pins and allowed the key to be turned in the barrel. His explanation was simple and concise, and it made the lock's hidden inner workings appear as clear as day. It was a joy listening to him. He picked a bone with a tumbler hook at one end and a tiny flat metal torsion bar, and inserted both twirls into the keyhole and began to stroke the inside of the lock in a steady, rhythmical motion. "You simply stroke the first pin," he said, "until it goes up a notch, then you know you've got one up into line." His hands flexed and stretched like a concert pianist's, tensing and relaxing as each pin was pushed in turn. "Then you just keep applying pressure until you get all the little darlings up into place." He turned the tiny torsion bar and the Yale sprang open. "And you're inside." He beamed at us. "What you do then, of course, is your own business." We all laughed at that, especially me.

He moved to another safe. "Now this one's a right bugger. It's a Burmah; used for diamond safes, mostly; and by far the most difficult thing you're ever likely to encounter outside of having to blow a safe open with gelignite." He pointed to the lock mechanism. "You see, in this model the pins move horizontally through the lock, not vertically, which makes it impossible to pick in the usual way."

Well, that was like a red rag to a bull. And I decided it was high time I hoisted my true colours. "Can I have a go?" I said.

"Indeed, old fruit, consider the bench yours." He waved his long, bony hand across a whole display of Chubbs and Yales, but me being me, I stepped right up to the Burmah and closed it. Then I quickly selected four different twirls from his tray, and just like I'd learned how to do in Chinatowns all round the world, I held them like chop-sticks and gentled them into the keyhole and set about picking it. It took about five minutes to get each horizontal tumbler pushed aside, and the truth is I was greatly helped by having another dismantled Burmah mechanism right there in front of me, but I eventually did it. One thing I hadn't seen, though, was that "Keys" had produced a stopwatch out of thin air, and timed me.

"That was a truly spectacular display, Jethro, old thing. May I?"

He handed Bosanquet the stop-watch, stepped up to the Burmah and copied what I'd done exactly; only, he did it while also explaining aloud what it was I'd accomplished. When he finished, he turned to Bosanquet and said, "Time, Simon, if you please?" And Bosanquet clicked the stop-watch, looked at it, and held it out and showed it to us. A dead heat. "Keys" couldn't stop beaming. He marched up and down, flapping his arms like a giant jackdaw about to take off; obviously as pleased as Punch. "Simon," he said, "thank you for bringing this paragon of dexterity, this Rachmaninoff of the tumblers. The very best, you've ever brought me, the absolute best; four skeleton keys, at once; beautiful, simply beautiful. If I hadn't seen it for myself, I would never have attempted it."

It was my turn to be open-mouthed then. "Your first time using four? Dan, you're kidding?" He beamed, "It's how I learned to play the piano, old love. I hear something once and I've got it forever; the same with picking locks; I watched your hands; as beautiful a display of finger-work as ever I've seen, quite wonderful." He looked at me, his blue eyes as bright as sapphires in an Asprey's display case, and held out a twirl he'd used on the locks. "Please do me the honour and accept this, Jethro, I know it'd be going to a very good home." He beamed at Bosanquet. "Priceless, old sport, bloody priceless." Then he turned back to me. "Do just remember, old thing, always carry your RCMP pass, as technically you're breaking the law, anytime you have a lock-picking tool upon your person. And we wouldn't want anyone thinking you a common burglar, now would we?"

I tried to stop myself from laughing like a hyena with hiccups, and started to choke instead. And Bosanquet began slapping me up and down on the back. For some reason he had a huge grin plastered over his face.

CHAPTER

14

Just Desserts

W ho was it said, April is the cruellest month? Well, that one was; it was the wettest April for a hundred years. And if it wasn't bucketing it down one minute, it threatened to the next. It was a real damper on spir-its. But like everyone else I just had to step around whatever puddles I came to, and lump it. I continued to work out at local gyms, visited the Turkish baths, took massages, and within a very short time, even I noticed the difference in me; as did the girls in the Victory, if their whistles and catcalls were anything to go by. I could see that Joanie was wrestling with her emotions; she was very glad I looked more like the Jethro of old, but she was also very worried about what old tricks I might be getting up to again.

I took the old cabby out, to get a closer look at NOB head-quarters, up north of Camden Town. It was a big, detached mock-Georgian house, set back from the road and hidden behind a high brick wall, with gated entrances leading in-to and out-of a gravel forecourt. I hated gravel; you could wake the dead creeping on that stuff. But I already knew about that little problem from the slide show "Keys" had put on; photos of the house, front and back; original floor plans; that sort of thing. He'd followed that up with his analysis of NOB's likely security measures, and the pros and cons of the safe they had in their main office. And not too bad really, considering it was everything I usually had to find out for myself.

It was then a question of putting it all out of mind and letting it steep, like tea in a teapot. I'd learned over the years that ideas will come pouring out if you give them half a chance to draw together. So, a change being as good as a rest, I took myself up West. And I put my head round a few stage doors, got word on the new shows getting in, and let it be known I was open for work; always making sure to drop a few packets of fags, here and there, as a "thank you." Fishermen call it "breading the water," but it's common sense; you've always got to give out, before you get back. And the truth was, I needed to put some feelers out. I'd been off the patch for months, and I had to keep my hand in as a stage-hand or people might start to think I'd reverted to my old ways. And that would never do.

Most everyone in Soho had a favourite bar or cafe they'd frequent at the same times everyday, knowing people could find them there if they wanted to. And once it was known you weren't on the rip-rap or a nark for the police, everyone was pretty friendly. So once I'd done all the theatres, I stopped in, here and there, out of the rain, to say "hello." It was never time wasted; it was like holding up a wet finger to catch the way the wind was blowing; and more than once it'd helped me navigate the hidden shallows and unseen reefs of Soho. But even my smile starts to wear a bit thin after a bit, so when it started to rain, I knocked it on the head and slipped into Moroni's to pick up an *Evening Standard* and have a quick shufty at the pictures in the foreign magazines. Then I popped next door into Patisserie Valerie for a cup of coffee and a pastry, and a quick read of the linens. Three cups later, the rain had stopped, and I was back out on Old Compton Street. I adjusted my hat, peered into the fading light, slowly drifted round the corner into Dean Street, and started walking quickly in the direction of Oxford Street. I'd just turned the corner into Soho Square, when out of the corner of my eye I saw someone step out of the shadow of a doorway and slip up behind me. The big bloke stuck what felt like a gun into the small of my back. "Tom Mix?" I said, raising my hands.

"Nah, Jimmy Cagney," the voice growled.

I kept my hands held high. "Which one, the gangster or Yankee Doodle Dandy?"

"Give over," the voice said. "I dance for no man."

"That's what everyone says till someone's got them by the short and curlies or they get paid so much they no longer care."

"Wotcher, Jethro," the voice said, with a deep chuckle.

"Hello, Tommy," I said, "I wondered when I'd bump into you."

"Hope you're hungry?" he said. "There's this little place I know."

We crossed Oxford Street, went up Rathbone Place, and Tommy filled me in on events in Slough. "It's all sorted," he said. "Messima must still be scratching his head, wondering what the fuck happened. But you knew that; Mo Goldring said you'd popped your head in The George." He stopped, to cup his hands and light a cigarette. "But that's Spottsy for you; he planned it all out, from the start. First, he pays his respects to the local firm and does a deal. It all looks like business as usual then; like the locals were just protecting their turf and we were the hired help. And as no one could say it was a war between rival London firms, there was no Scotland Yard 'Heavy Mob' hurtling down from the hills. Spottsy gets his cut of profits on the go-forward, *plus* he's lined himself up nicely with the local firm, *plus* he's got a big favour to call in, sometime. Dead clever." Tommy flicked the cigarette end into the gutter. "I don't know what your deal with Spottsy was, Jethro, but he wanted it done fast and tidy." I nodded and tried to look gratified, but I knew Jack was keeping book and that some day I'd have to pay, and dearly. I pulled my collar up to keep out the sudden chill. Tommy offered me a fag, but I shook my head. He shook his head then. "A quick flash of the shooters, a few good smacks from the Fullertons, and Messima's team folded like a house of cards, the whole lot of them."

Jesus aitch Christ. If Spottsy had brought in the Fullerton brothers, the scourges of Bethnal Green, it must've ended very badly. It wasn't the size of them that made people shit themselves, they weren't really that big; it was the flat, dead look they got in their eyes when it was all about to go off. Then the only way to stop them was to shoot them dead. But I'd known going in Spottsy was never one for half-measures; with him, the only way to fight fire was with a blowtorch or a flame-thrower. And I'd counted on that, because, in the end, all it came down to was, who was going down for the count, Messima's thugs or Seth? I hadn't been the one to start it; it'd just fallen to me to help bring it to a finish.

The sign on the restaurant door said CLOSED, but Tommy was never one for rules when he had his eyes fixed on a result; he tapped on the glass door. I thought, at first, it must be a business paying Spottsy protection money, but it didn't seem like that at all, from the warm welcome he got. And I didn't ask and Tommy didn't say anything, beyond the fact he'd done the owner a favour. We were ushered to a corner table, away from the window, and we ordered spaghetti. The owner, a little thin bloke, with a smile almost as wide as he was, insisted we enjoy a little something he'd been saving, special, and poured us some red wine out of a bottle wrapped in its own straw basket. We'd both got a taste for wine when we'd worked the passenger liners, before the War. Nothing fancy, but both of us could tell good from bad. "Not bad," Tommy said, smacking his lips. "No, not bad at all," I said, reaching for some bread. And anyone looking in would've thought we were two old mates marching down memory lane, without a care in the world. I tell you, appearances can be so deceptive.

They served up the spaghetti with a thick tomato sauce.

"How bad was it?" I asked, twisting my fork round and around in the spaghetti, trying to see the blood-red sauce for what it was.

"Good grub here, isn't it?" he said, his mouth full.

I nodded, and said how they'd done bloody marvels, considering how every other restaurant in Soho was busy complaining there wasn't any olive oil, garlic, or Parmesan cheese to be had anywhere for love or money. Tommy just tapped his nose and kept on slurping up his food.

He finally came up for air. "Not too bad," he said, stabbing at his spaghetti, "considering how many bones usually get broken when the Fullertons start wielding their red-painted crowbars." He sipped from his glass of wine. "No one got topped, though, if that's what you mean?"

I sat there looking over his shoulder at the darkness outside, and wondered at the precariousness of life. I wondered, too, who might be out there, in the wings, waiting for me with a crowbar in his hands. "They wouldn't have known what hit them," I said, almost wistfully.

"Found out, soon enough," he said, saluting with his glass. The owner hurried over, poured us some more red wine, then he cleared away the plates and returned to wipe down the table. He chatted with Tommy for a bit and asked whether we'd like some rice pudding, then disappeared.

"So, that's all there was to it, then?" I asked, very quietly.

"More or less," he said.

I raised my eyebrows. He ran his tongue over his teeth.

"We took them to an empty factory and had them all sitting, bare-arsed on the concrete. And I told them, No grassing to the Old Bill or anyone about what'd gone down or they'd end up as pigs' swill; the choice was theirs. Then we backed an old army ambulance in through the loading doors, loaded them up, and dropped them outside Slough hospital. One of the Fullertons even stuck a crisp, white fiver in each of their top pockets to show he bore them no ill. I tell you, there wasn't a dry eye in the house."

So it'd all ended with Messima's mob being carted away like rubbish in a corporation dustcart. I pulled out a ten-bob note to cover dinner, but Tommy wouldn't hear of it. Then when he tried to pay, the owner of the place wouldn't hear of it, either. Tommy nodded, but when the bloke went back in his kitchen, he slid a ten-shilling note under the saucer as a tip.

"Was there anything else you wanted to tell me, Tommy?" I said. "Only, I sensed there might be something."

He ran his tongue slowly over his teeth. "Might not be a bad idea if you were to disappear for a few weeks." He twisted round and looked out the window; he turned back, his voice flat. "Or even a few months. Out of sight and well out of mind."

He scratched his chin. "Look, I'm only telling you this, Jethro, because I owe you. And knowing you, as I do, if you ever got sent up for a long stretch, you'd probably go and top yourself, just to put yourself out of your misery. And I don't want it on my conscience." He swirled the last of the wine around in his glass. "Spottsy's putting up a big one, a really big one; one that's not been done before, not ever."

Blimey, I thought. Tommy was giving me the exact same advice I'd recently given Seth. "Bugger off out of it, for a bit, for the good of your health." I just hoped Seth had more sense than I did. I looked at Tommy and nodded. I knew there was more yet to come.

"There's a real big result in the offing with what Spottsy's setting up. There's also a real big risk. There'll be shooters; GBH merchants; and whoever lays on the drags will to have to be top-notch." He finished his wine and ran his tongue slowly across his lips. "The point is, Jethro, it also calls for a first-class creeper and key-man. And after these past events in Slough, it's a dead cert, it's going to be you Spottsy wants." He put his empty wineglass down on the table, and gave me a flat, dead look that seemed to drain all the light out of the restaurant. "Not that you're supposed to be doing any creeping, anymore, Jethro. But if it ever came to it, and you were on the team, and it was a go, and we all had our balls on the line, and you bottled out of it so as not to get yourself nicked, and you went and fucked it all up. Then even I'd mark your cards. And I'd come looking for you with a gun in one hand and a shovel in the other."

CHAPTER

15

Cabal

What is it they say down Petticoat Lane? "If you want to hear God laugh; make plans." Tells you, be very careful who you listen to.

The very next morning, right out of the blue, I got a message from the Hippodrome asking if I could fill in for the early- and late-evening performances of *Starlight Roof*. And although I had the caper to do for Walsingham, the following night, I thought it wouldn't hurt to go fly a few flats, push a few sets around; check my gyroscopes; make sure the old muscles were working properly. So I used the phone in the Victory and called back, said I'd pop over and see them lunchtime. I think I just wanted to do something for myself; however small, however mad. Funny, that.

I took a tube to Leicester Square and came up onto Charing Cross Road. I had thoughts of a quick one in The Shaftesbury, but then thought better of it and did a quick dash for the stage door and stepped right into a puddle. And standing there like a demented stork, shaking my wet foot in the air, I was all but sent flying when the stage door burst open. I looked at this bearded, long-haired, young bloke standing there with a broken chair-back in his hand, and he looked at me; and we both burst out laughing.

"Hello, Jethro, doing a balancing act, now, are we?"

"No, Mike, it's my impression of a one-legged footballer. What's that you got on your face, a dead rat?"

He let out a demented cackle and pulled me inside. "It's my bold new look," he said, stroking his beard and ruffling up his shaggy haircut to impossible heights "Like it? My wife thinks it makes me look much older."

"Makes you look like a bomb-throwing anarchist," I said. "You still blowing them away with your broken chair-back routine?"

He laughed. "Crazy, isn't it? But the audiences still seem to lap it up, thank God."

"So they should, Mike, so they should. Whatever they're paying you, isn't enough; the act's completely original."

He grinned from ear to ear and pumped my hand up and down. "Don't owe you money, do I? But thanks, Jethro, very nice of you to say so. Come to help out in the wings, have you?" He looked at me for a moment and the manic grin disappeared from off his face as suddenly as if he'd whisked away a mask of laughter and replaced it with one of sorrow. And it may just have been the lighting in that backstage corridor, but it seemed he looked at me in that odd way Ray did sometimes. "Jethro," he said quietly, "don't take this wrong, but go careful. I've got the strangest feeling you're in some sort of deadly danger."

And I stood there, one foot still sopping wet, the other dry, as if caught between two worlds; and the sounds of London fading so fast, it fair made me dizzy. "Jesus, Mike, what on earth made you say that?"

"Call it a sixth sense; my Pop, my Ma, my brother, and me, we all have it to some degree. With me, it's what they call clairvoyance; I see coming events in my mind's eye." From the look on my face he could see he'd struck a nerve and from the look on his face I knew he wasn't joking. "Didn't mean to startle you," he said. "But the sense of danger is so strong, it just came tumbling out." He gently gripped my arm. "Take care, is all."

I didn't know Mike Bentine that well, I'd only met him the previous September when he'd first started in *Starlight Roof*, and I was filling in backstage. And I looked at him, this skinny young bloke just starting to go places as a comedian, and I was touched he wanted to help me, a stage-hand he'd once had a few laughs with, because he'd sensed I was heading into some sort of trouble. "Thanks, Mike," I said. "I've got a touch of the sixth sense, myself, and I've learned it pays to listen. Break a leg, eh?"

"Break a chair leg, you mean," he said, laughing. "You go safe."

I thought, at first, Mike Bentine had just picked up on the NOB caper that was looming, but it was soon evident he'd sensed something else, as well.

I spent the afternoon going over the scenery logs with the fly team; familiarised myself with what needed pushing and pulling, when and where. I popped out for a quick bite to eat, did my double shift, and was paid cash in hand. Afterwards, I drifted with the crowds over towards the Circus, intending to pop into a little Greek restaurant round the back of the Regent Palace Hotel. I'd just crossed over to the traffic island at the bottom of Shaftesbury Avenue, when a big black motor car swished past, its wheels sending up a spray of water. "Thanks a lot, you stupid sod," I yelled and the motor car screeched to halt. "That's all I bloody need," I muttered. Then two large gentlemen appeared out of nowhere, gripped my elbows and steered me towards the car, and then they stood back, which was a mildly encouraging sign. The rear window wound down, and idle curiosity being at times an unfortunate part of my nature, I leaned forward to see who it might be.

It was Jack Spot. "This is business, Jethro," he growled. "Get in."

"Is this really necessary, Jack?" I said. "Only it's a bit late and I was—"

"Just be a good lad and get in; don't let's have any non-sense," he said, with just enough annoyance to make me think I'd kept him waiting.

"Right then, Jack," I said. And someone opened the rear door, and I got in. Jack nodded, and that was the last I saw of him for a bit, because someone leaned in and tied a scarf over my eyes. They didn't tie my hands, though, which was another good sign. And I tried chatting about things; football, the weather, the price of fish, how Billy Hill was doing, anything at all that came into my head, but Spottsy said, "Just shut it, lad." So I did. But it didn't stop me thinking. If Spottsy was being this cautious setting up his next job, then maybe Tommy was right, it really was the big one. I was impressed. Most jobs got grassed to Scotland Yard long before a team ever left their hideout to go commit a robbery or take down a wages lorry. It was truly pathetic how often the Old Bill was lying in wait to ambush the unwary thief. There were so many grasses and narks knocking about the place, it was enough to make you want to go straight.

The journey lasted about fifteen minutes. Then I was

helped from the motor car, guided across the pavement, up some steps, through a front door, and down a long corridor. And from the echoing sounds, I reckoned it had to be something along the lines of a hall or a meeting place. I was led along another corridor. We turned left, went a little way, then stopped, and a door opened. I smelled cigar smoke; heard the murmur of voices; and Jack saying, "Good evening, gentlemen." Then they sat me down and took off the blindfold. Light hit me like a wet fish in the face, and I blinked a few times, and slowly started seeing things properly again.

I was sitting at the end of a long, highly polished, mahogany table. There were about a dozen men; frummers, "four-by-twos," Jews; the oldest about seventy, the youngest maybe a few years older than me. Homburg hats, little round caps, beards, long curly locks, the whole business; some of them in black, as if they'd come straight from some synagogue, some in crumpled business suits as if they'd come straight from Hatton Garden. The half-empty glasses and ashtrays filled with cigar ash told me I wasn't the first to arrive. And I looked at them and they looked at me; the overhead light shining on their spectacles like pale moons reflected in so many puddles of darkness. All of them, just staring, silently inspecting me, evaluating me, like a piece of merchandise. Only I didn't feel very wide. I looked round the table, not sure whether to nod or smile. Then I came to the bloke on the end, nearest me. And he sat there, looking back at me, dispassionately, and I started coughing as if for my very life. It was Ray; black suit and tie, watch chain, waistcoat, little round *yarmulka;* Ray, slowly nodding his head up and down like the rest of them; Ray, without even the slightest glimmer of warmth or recognition in his eyes.

Someone handed me a glass of water. "Sorry," I spluttered. "Must be the cigar smoke." I don't know; it was late, I'd done two shows at the Hippodrome; but I wasn't as quick as I usually am. And I did my best to cover my surprise and just hoped no one twigged. The thing was, out there, in the real world, I wasn't supposed to know Ray Karmin from Eddie Cantor. The bloke I was known to be pally with was a loud-mouthed costermonger called Buggy Billy, not a respectable Jewish scholar and gentleman by the name of Raymond Leopold Karmin, Esq.

Someone coughed, there was a rustle of worsted, and I looked at the man sitting at the other end of the table. I expected a rabbi, but he looked like a banker; sixtyish; well-groomed, well-dressed; fiercely intelligent eyes. He looked tired, though, like he'd had a long day. I knew how he felt.

"Thank you, Mr. Jethro, for agreeing to see us at such a late hour. But we face a crisis." You could tell he was a man used to being listened to, there was no unnecessary drama to his voice; facts spoke for themselves. "We debated long and hard as to the proper course of action, but once agreed, we felt we should act immediately and called upon our good friend, Mr. Jacob Comer, for his assistance." I turned my head. He'd waved a hand at Spottsy. But then he would, Jacob Comer was Jack's real name. It was only then that I noticed Spottsy hadn't been given a seat at the table, which was interesting; it said that whatever it was, it was even out of his league.

The chairman favoured Jack with a nod. "Mr. Comer suggested that you were the best man for the job." He opened his hands and smiled. "For which assistance, of course, you would receive our full gratitude." He looked around the table and one by one each man nodded his agreement. And that was it. If I agreed to do whatever it was they wanted of me, a handshake would seal the deal and an appropriate reward would be paid at the appropriate time. *Mazel und broche.* He smiled, again. "I know that you, Mr. Jethro, are not of our faith, but we have been told by those we trust that you are of the 'finest water'; a man we can do business with."

The finest water. It was an old saying from the jewellery trade; used to describe a top colour stone, and a fine compliment. I tried hard not to look in Ray's direction. "Thank you," I said, still working out the angles.

"My name is Joseph Zaretsky," he said. "I am the head of this small group of business leaders from the Jewish community. And excuse me, please, if I do not introduce each one by name. Suffice to say, that amongst our kind we are called *Cabal*." I nodded as if that meant something to me, but it didn't. "Since the end of the War," he went on, "we have been most disturbed by the continued rise of certain extremist political groups. Sir Oswald Mosley has returned from self-imposed exile and formed the British Union Movement. And this, of course, is of grave concern to us. Yet we have recently learned such things that lead us now to believe that the New Order of Britain Party poses an even greater threat." He paused, as if crossing some imaginary line. "We must therefore find means of limiting the growth of this Party and if necessary of curtailing it."

I shivered, knowing for sure he was going to ask me to do the bloody impossible. He did. He leaned forward in that way people do when they're about to tell you a secret. "We have learned of a certain document that lays bare the inner workings of NOB, that lists the names of its members, and details those individuals who have provided significant financial support to the Party." He paused again, this time for effect. "It is our earnest wish, Mr. Jethro, that you obtain this item for us. For it is vital that we know 'who is secretly who' in this 'new' Britain, as only then can we properly protect our families, our community, and ourselves."

Jesus, was that all? I tried to remember which

Commandments he'd just asked me to break. Not that I was averse to breaking at least half of them on a regular basis; but what'd really torn it, was they wanted the very same thing Walsingham was after. And I was, as they say, in a bit of a quandary. It's never easy serving two masters. "Er, the New Order of Britain, you say? Yes, I can see why you would be very wary about those people. And I'd really like to help you, Mr. Zaretsky, honest, I would, but I can't promise—" But he didn't even let me finish.

He slammed the table with the flat of his hand. "Mr. Jethro. We appeal to you, as from our very souls. We cannot undo the terrible evil perpetrated in the concentration camps, where millions and millions, generation upon generation of our fathers, mothers, sons, daughters, brothers, and sisters were murdered." His eyes bore deep into mine. "But we must do more than say *Kaddish* for them. We must ensure that what happened in Germany is never permitted to happen again; not here in this Great Britain or anywhere else."

And I sat there, stunned, out of my depth. I mean, I'd also survived, hadn't I? I looked at the faces around the table, not really seeing any of them, and wrestled with myself. Spottsy had set me up, which told me this *Cabal* business was how I was meant to pay him back for what he'd done for me in Slough. "An eye for an eye" it's called. The bit I couldn't get my head around was Ray being a member of *Cabal*. There was nothing I wouldn't ever do for him, but still, never a word from him about it. On top of which, I had no bloody idea how I was going to handle Walsingham. I looked round at the faces; everyone perfectly still, no one breathing, not even me. You could've heard a pin drop. "Bugger," I said to myself. But there was nothing else for it. I'd just have to work it out as I went along, like I always did when I didn't have a plan. "Er, what I meant to say, Mr. Zaretsky, was it'll be my privilege to help you in any way I can."

The murmurs from around the table, and the sound of Spottsy grunting somewhere behind me, told me I'd said the right thing.

CHAPTER 16

Making God Laugh

They put the blindfold back on again, but Spottsy was in such a good mood he insisted on giving me a nip of whisky from his hip-flask, to help keep out the chill. He didn't partake himself, he believed spirits impaired his head for business, but he said he wasn't feeling the cold, anyway, as my offer to assist *Cabal* had warmed the very cockles of his heart. Then he'd chuckled to himself like a dog with hiccups for the rest of the journey.

"Go safe, now," he said, when they dropped me at the end of Church Street. I nodded, and pulled my collar up round my ears, and walked up the street. Even at three o'clock in the morning there were appearances to keep up; it wouldn't do for anyone to think Jack had somehow persuaded me to come out of retirement. It wouldn't even do for me to think that, particularly as Spottsy hadn't said one word about wanting me in on his hand-picked team. Not that I was complaining, I wanted to be left well out of it. Still, it was all a bit odd, and I could only put it down to Tommy having got hold of the wrong end of the stick.

Church Street at that time of night is about as welcoming as a cracked marble slab smelling of yesterday's fish and that didn't help my mood any. And I walked on past the door to my flat and made straight for Ray's house. Him appearing out of thin air, like that, in that synagogue, had been a real shocker and I was very put out he hadn't warned me. He, more than anyone, knew how much I hated being press-ganged into anything. And he'd never once mentioned *Cabal* to me. I'd been to the Anglo-Palestine Club, on Great Windmill Street, with him any number of times—in disguise, of course—but it'd always been for the food, never the politics. So a little chat was definitely on the cards. And as it was only a couple of hours before he had to get himself kitted-up as Buggy Billy, I knew he'd push on through till morning and not bother going to bed. So I stood in the shadows across the street from his house and waited.

Whoever it was said, you couldn't step in the same shit twice, had never walked in my shoes. Not that I'd had any say in the matter, but I'd landed myself in the very situation I'd told Walsingham could never happen. I'd become the servant of two masters; one, MI5, the other, *Cabal*. It wasn't as if I'd set out to double-cross anyone, but I sure as hell couldn't count on Walsingham seeing it that way. I shook my head. The days when I'd just had me to answer to seemed long gone. Then a big old Daimler purred up and out of the darkness and pushed my thoughts off-stage. I saw Ray get out and make straight for his front door. I waited until the tail-lights had disappeared, then slipped across the road like a fast-fading shadow. The door was on the latch. I let myself in.

"I bet you're expecting a cup of tea, you scrounging

bugger," Ray yelled from the kitchen. "You probably think you deserve one, too."

"After that performance, tonight," I said, making my way through to the kitchen, "I was thinking some single malt might be more in order."

He cocked his head and sniffed the air, but carried on making the tea. "You'll have tea and lump it," he said. "No time for the hard stuff, Buggy Billy's got to appear in the market by five-thirty, or there'll be questions asked in Parliament, let alone the Victory cafe." He turned round, a pot of tea in one hand and a bottle of milk in the other. "You did a good thing tonight, Jethro, but I wish to Moses they hadn't picked you."

"Well, you've got to admit, Ray," I said, "it was a bit fucking odd."

He nodded, then immediately started taking the wind out of my sails. "It was. It was. And I can well understand your irritation," he said. "You deserve an explanation, Jethro, you do. So, let's make this a family conference, eh? The things we need to talk about are better served up around a kitchen table. Anyway, it'll be warmer in here." I sat down. He poured the tea, then the milk; then he sat down and pushed the sugar bowl towards me. "You can put your own bloody sugar in." I nodded, and began heaping spoonfuls of sugar into my tea; I was family.

He lit a cigarette, pushed the packet and a box of matches to the centre of the table, and waited until I'd finished stirring. "I didn't set you up, Jethro. You have your life and I have mine; what you do has always been your own affair." He put his hands flat on the table. "You've always known I had other lives." I nodded. "Well, this one came into being around about the time you first appeared round my stall as a cocky young tearaway, so it was none of your damn business. And as close as the two of us are, I'd fully expected it to stay that way." I nodded again; that was reasonable. "But seeing as you've now been dragged into it, Jethro, you've got a right to know who and what you're dealing with." I looked at him and waited. He pinched the bridge of his nose, then opened up. "*Cabal* has existed in one form or another since before the turn of the century; New York, Amsterdam, Paris, London; and before the War, in Berlin, Vienna, Warsaw, Prague. It's secret, in that the only way you ever come to hear of it is when you're invited to help. There are no badges, no rules, no rank, no regalia, no secret passwords; *Cabal* is simply made up of men who, because of their positions in the community, recognise they have an obligation to do whatever best serves the larger Jewish cause."

That was all very well. I was as fascinated by history as the next man, but having the full weight of it dropped on your head from a great height felt suspiciously like blackmail. But as I was to discover, history is all but impossible to get out from under, whether it's your own or everyone else's. I played with the spoon in the sugar bowl; still very disgruntled about the whole business. "These *Cabal* people must carry a lot of weight, then, judging by the effect they had on Spottsy."

Ray nodded. "They do. *Cabal* reaches many, many levels." I raised my eyebrows. He ran his tongue over his teeth. "Let's just say, that *Cabal* can lay down with dogs and get up without catching fleas." He raised his eyebrows at me, then, and I nodded, and he poured us both another cup. "I was invited to join *Cabal* back when Mosley and his British Union of Fascists first began raising their arms in salute. That's when I first came across the young Jack Spot, or Jacob Comer as he was called then, and even though he was a right tearaway, he had the lip and the fists to back it up. So we had him and a few other Jewish lads put up barricades and put a stop to Mosley and his mob when they tried to march through the East End. Then fearing a full-scale riot, the authorities stepped in and demanded that Mosley turn round and march his black-shirted Fascists off elsewhere."

That was a turn-up for the books. I'd had my suspicions, but that was the first time Ray had ever confirmed he was one of the people behind the events in Cable Street. "So you helped Jack Spot become Jack Spot?"

"No, he was already a well-known East End face. But he was the perfect figurehead and kept attention away from *Cabal*. Even now, years later, there are still people who say the Battle of Cable Street never took place, and he was never really there. But that tells you how *Cabal* works. The best way to cover your tracks, is sow dissent behind you; people argue about that then, and never bother to look any further." He took a swig of tea, which must've gone cold, but he didn't seem to notice. "Mosley was interned in May 1940 for the duration of the War. Yet despite that, he still had enough friends pulling strings in high places to ensure he and his wife, Diana—that Guinness woman—had a nice, cushy war. The two of them were even allowed to live together in Holloway prison, while all their followers remained in isolation cells. It tells you that whatever the crime, there's still one law for the rich and powerful, and one law for the rest. That's why *Cabal* does what it can to even out the balance."

He pushed back his chair and went over to the stove and began to move pots and pans around. "In England, it's always been the Jew can do no right and the King can do no wrong. Even if a Jew is born and bred here, it's all but impossible to shake off the thousand little snubs thrown at him every day that remind him he's still a man without a home or a country." He slammed the kettle down, making both the lid and me jump. "You know how much I love this country, Jethro. But if I go out in rags I'm dismissed with contempt as 'a dirty Jew.' If I put on a nice suit and set foot in a Mayfair restaurant, the whispers soon start about 'those flashy Jews.' " He rubbed his hands across his brow and cheeks like an actor wiping off heavy stage make-up, and stared at me, his face dark. Then as if by some magician's trick, his voice began to change from the cultured tones of Ray Karmin into the harsh rasp of Buggy Billy. And soon he was shouting. "It's only because I act and sound more like a bleedin' Londoner than most Londoners, that I friggin' get away with as much as I do. The friggin' bowler hat, spotted bow-tie, velvet-collared coat; the friggin' bugs crawling up and down my bleed-in' arm; is all the lousy buggers ever see. It's still all bread and circuses out there in the markets." He coughed up some phlegm. "But at least the sods jeer you to your face, and you can give as good as you get." He scoured his throat and spat into the sink and turned on the tap. "Bloody cigarettes will be the death of me. Maybe I should just kill off Buggy Billy, all the good I've done; let the buggers out there all scratch themselves to death. The lousy sods don't deserve me or my bug powder."

"No need to take the lead off the roof," I said. "Without Buggy Billy to give us a hand; help pull us up out of the shit, how many of us dead-end kids do you think would've ended up in Borstal or worse?"

He turned round and filled the kettle with fresh water from the tap. "Yes, there is that," he said, suddenly, the very pic-ture of reasonability. "And I did help you and those other bloody layabouts to better yourselves, didn't I; just so you didn't all end up in the poor-house or in prison. My good deed, you could say. But they do say that what goes round, comes round, don't they?" He blinked like an owl, and struck a match and re-lit the gas underneath the kettle. "Another cup?"

"Yes, ta, Ray," I said. "Go down a treat." I shook my head;

it was the same as when he worked the market crowds. He could take hold of any hostility that came at him and gather it up, and steer it off and away to one side, like a matador with a red cape. I knew of old that he railed in anger at the oddest things, and sometimes terrifyingly so, and it confused the hell out of me, at first, because he seemed so very calm about it all afterwards. It took me years to realise he only ever did it for a purpose, and could turn it on or off like a light switch.

Ray did the business with the teapot and I had a cigarette. And once he'd poured the tea, I told him about Walsingham setting me up to burgle NOB headquarters and that he was after the exact same thing as *Cabal,* the NOB Party master list. "Strewth," he said. "That's dropped you in the cart, hasn't it?" He scratched his chin and glanced up at the ceiling as if looking for an answer. "And unless NOB has been doubly good at record keeping, someone's going to be very disappointed."

"Which one?" I said. "Our Mr. Walsingham or your Mr. Zaretsky?"

He gave me the bent eye. "Better twelve good friends than one bad enemy." And I gave him the bent eye right back, and reminded him that Walsingham still had us both by the short and curlies, or had he forgotten. "Course not," he said. "All I'm suggesting is you use your camera and a bit of imagination. It wouldn't take long to photograph the stuff; you could develop the film later. It's the information *Cabal* needs, not the list itself."

"Trouble is," I said, "I'm supposed to rendezvous with Bosanquet's men, afterwards, and hand over whatever it is I've found. But, okay, let's say for a moment, I did manage to give them the slip. If I had the camera all set up on a stand and had weights ready to hold the pages down, I suppose I could do it before they even knew they'd missed me."

"You'd be surprised what you can do when you set your mind to it," he said, blowing his nose. "By the way, Jethro, thanks for helping out."

"No thanks necessary, Ray," I said. "Not between you and me. Separate lives, maybe, but secrets never." I smiled.

Ray put his handkerchief back in his pocket and scratched his chin again. "Well, as we're being so open about everything; a little word to the wise. You weren't the only one *Cabal* spoke to tonight." I raised an eyebrow. "No," he said, shaking his head. "Not another creeper; the '43' ."

"The '43'?" I said, shaking my head. "What's that when it's at home? It sounds like something out of *The Thirty-Nine Steps*."

"It might as well be. The '43' are forty-three Jewish lads, all British-born, who fought in the War as paratroopers or Commandos; and they've all sworn to do whatever's necessary to keep the dream of a new Jerusalem alive. And they're not talking about Britain's new Welfare State; they've got their eyes on Palestine being the new Jewish homeland. They mean business, too. So, for God's sake, you watch your step."

"What is it they say down Petticoat Lane?" I said.

"Buggy Billy's Bug Powder is Your Best Bet for Killing Bugs," he said, straight-faced. Then he climbed the stairs to go back through the wardrobe into the other house to change into the King of Bug Powder.

And I laughed, then; I don't know about God.

CHAPTER

17

Dressing the Part

I slept late, had breakfast at lunchtime, and in between endless cups of tea, read the linens to keep my mind off things. Most newspapers agreed that a war between the Arabs and the Jews was inevitable, now the British Mandate in Palestine was in its final weeks; the general opinion being the Arabs would win hands down. One or two papers, though, weren't so sure an armed conflict could ever produce a clear winner. And I thought back to the faces of *Cabal* and shook my head. The linens had similar thoughts about the two teams headed for FA Cup Final; most said Manchester United would soundly beat Blackpool, but again one or two reckoned Stanley Matthews, Blackpool's wizard on the wing, would ensure it was a close game. Olympics fever was starting to grip the country and there were stories galore about how London was being spruced up in readiness. But even though people had high hopes Great Britain would give the rest of the world a run for its money, few expected we'd bring home any gold. We would if they gave medals for cat burglary, I said to myself.

There was a lot on the ceremony taking place in Grosvenor Square, the coming Monday, when Eleanor Roosevelt was to unveil a statue of her late husband, Franklin Delano Roosevelt, to commemorate all the U.S. President had done for Britain during the War. The statue had been fully funded in one day by donations of from sixpence to five shillings, from people all over the country. Churchill and Attlee were expected to attend, as were the King and Queen, but then we all knew we'd never have survived without "the mighty tide of aid" we'd received from America.

I left a tip under the saucer and was at the door before I noticed there was a new face working behind the counter. Blimey, I thought to myself, I really must've been off in my own little world, and I waved a "cheerio" to all the girls, making a point to smile at the new girl. I turned to port and drifted on over the Edgware Road to the far end of Church Street, then tacked to port again, past the Children's Hospital and down across Paddington Green, before setting course for the Turkish baths on the Harrow Road. And afterwards, feeling as steamed and cleaned as newly laundered clothes I secreted myself away inside the telephone booth in the entrance foyer and dialled a number given me by Bosanquet. The voice on the other end said for me to take an umbrella as it looked like rain, which meant the job was on. I suddenly felt very peckish for some reason, so I bought a cheese roll from a nearby cafe, and although it was a bit stale, I happily ate the lot as I headed for my lock-up just off North Wharf Road.

It looked like a small disused machine shop from the outside, the faded WOLVERTON'S TOOL AND DIE-CASTING on the gates and battered FOR SALE OR FOR LEASE sign on the wall giving substance to the lie. The outer office was full of rubbish and smelled of mould and cats' piss, but it was very different inside, if you knew the secret way in. And as I let myself inside, I thought of Seth, the last person I'd let visit my inner sanctum. Joanie had told me at lunchtime that she'd had a nice chatty letter from Dilys, saying how Seth was finally out of hospital, and how they were off to Yorkshire and then North Wales to stay with relatives. She'd sent her love and had thanked us both for all we'd done for them. I'd got a pat on the shoulder from Joanie, for that. I was just pleased, though, that Seth had taken my advice. But then he always did have more sense than I did.

I didn't want to chance getting nicked on a technicality. So I gave my little Austin van the full once-over; oil, water, and tyres, all topped up; front and rear-lights, okay; commercial licence disc, up to date; proper-coloured petrol in the tank. Thing was, even though red-coloured petrol, earmarked for agricultural use only, was much cheaper on the black market, there was hell to pay if the authorities ever stopped you and found out you weren't someone called Farmer Brown. The next thing I did was load film into the Leica I'd bought for an arm and a leg down Loot Alley, or Cutler Street to give it its proper name. I fit the camera into the copying stand I'd made, screwed in a shutter release cable, and switched on the two sets of brights attached either side of the work-table. I weighted down the corners of a large book, peered through the viewfinder, adjusted the focus, and stuck strips of paper tape down as positioning guides.

Then, like a dutiful assistant stage-manager, I laid out my creeping kit on a work-bench: brown leather turtles, glim, set of diamond-tipped skeleton keys, Fairbairn-Sykes knife, small petercane, "creeper's friend." And as much as I disliked the idea, I had no choice but to take along some jelly and all its attendant paraphernalia; 9-volt battery, detonator, length of wire, stick of chewing gum, and "rubber Johnny." I put everything into a black canvas satchel, then turned my attention to my props cupboard. I pulled out a black Trilby hat and a stone-coloured Burberry trench coat. Then came a white shirt with epaulets and flapped pockets, plain black tie, black woollen V-neck sweater, and black twill trousers; all standard police issue, and all purchased from a very obliging surplus store near Euston Station. I put on a pair of double-welt, heavy black leather shoes. And that was it. With the tie tied in a full-Windsor knot and the Trilby hat pulled down over my eyes, I looked every inch a fully paid-up member of NOB. It wasn't a uniform in the strictest sense; similar clothing could be found in most men's wardrobes, but as an outfit it had an unmistakably authoritarian look and feel, and was perfect for any aspiring Fascist.

I looked at myself in the full-length mirror and did a wobbly, stiff-armed salute like Charlie Chaplin in *The Great Dictator* and tried not to fall about laughing. Then I added the finishing touch: a highly polished, saddle-brown leather map-case; the strap worn diagonally across the chest like an Army officer's Sam Browne belt, a look much favoured by senior NOB officers, and again, straight out of an army-surplus store.

Day or night, a uniform renders its wearer invisible, because as long as the uniform fits its environment, everything appears as normal. And I'd decided on the old hide-in-plain-sight-in-a-uniform routine, on that particular Friday night, because the headquarters of NOB would be all but deserted. According to Walsingham, all NOB senior officers and most rank-and-file members would be attending a weekend-long rally in the grounds of a big manor house, near Bedford, a good fifty miles north of London. The rally, itself, being just one of many right-wing gatherings scheduled to take place during April. All of which would then culminate with NOB, BUM, and all the rest of them, all joining forces for a huge May Day rally and march through Dalston, in the East End of London.

And what is it they say, while the mice are away, the cat can play silly buggers? Just to be safe, though, I drove within the speed limits, gave all the proper hand signals, and was even more careful than when I drove the cab. But I still made Camden High Street in decent time. I veered right at the tube station, drove on for a mile or so, then parked near a parade of shops, across from a line of railway arches. The constant sound of goods trains shunting back and forth rendered any extraneous noise superfluous, so it gave perfect cover. I waited in the darkness, glad the rain had held off. And when the night had finally settled again, I left the dark anonymity of my little van, slung both satchels over my shoulder, and strode forth as one of Britain's new order of would-be supermen.

I didn't so much march, as walk purposefully, as if I had serious business to undertake and would brook no interference. Again, all to blend in. And I came to the OUT gate of the big Georgian-style house that was NOB HQ. I could see through the trees that lights were still on in the upper floors. It didn't deter me, though. I'd been told they were always ablaze, as a symbolic beacon to the Party faithful. I gave the padlock a tug, as if to check it was secure, but really just to confirm NOB was still using their standard-pattern padlock. Then as I walked up the street to the IN gate, I took the pick and tiny torsion bar I had pinned behind the trench coat's storm flap, and held them as if I was holding the requisite key. And with the second padlock wedged between the thumb and forefinger of my left hand, I inserted the torsion bar at the bottom of the key opening and held it in a clockwise turn with pressure from my ring- and little fingers. I inserted the pick, stroked the padlock's hidden innards and the spring-loaded shackle popped open, and I was in and through, and the gate and padlock closed again, before you could say "boo" to a goosestep. I stood for a moment and sensed the night air. Then with each step of my heavy leather shoes on the gravel sounding as loud as a drum roll, I approached the big, porticoed front door with as much nonchalance as a squaddie on his way to a court-martial.

I could see through the fanlight the hallway light was on inside. Added to the pale glow from the upper rooms, it cast a yellow pool of light over the gravel forecourt that seemed as bright as a bank of floodlights. Even so, I paused outside the front door for maybe a second or two longer than was necessary. It wasn't the sight of the big alarm box, high up on the side of the building that made me stop, I just had this funny feeling I was being watched from the shadows. And I knew, then, I'd arrived at the point that comes in every creep, the point of no return.

I opened the front door with the first key "Keys" had made me, and let myself in to the little vestibule, then closed and relocked the door. No alarm bells went pealing out into the night, which was a good sign. "Keys" had told me the alarm system's on-off switches were masquerading as a bank of light-switches in a panel on the right wall. There were sixteen brass-domed switches, in all; four across and four down; the top-left switch at a different angle to the rest. The key was in knowing that the centre four switches controlled the alarm system for the entire house; and a simple enough puzzle, but still a very tricky little barrier for the unwary thief. "Keys" had demonstrated it for me in his workshop; starting from the bottom, you clicked all four anti-clockwise in sequence, for "off."

Click. Click. Click. Click.

Again, no alarm bells went pealing out into the night. Another good sign. I put the second key into the lock of the inner door, turned it slowly, opened the door even more slowly, and there I was, inside NOB HQ. And still no bells. But something nagged at me and it took a moment to realise what it was: the light bothered me; I missed not being surrounded by a comforting cloak of darkness. I shrugged off the feeling, stepped back into the little vestibule, slid home the heavy bolts at the top and bottom of the front door; then did the same with the bolts on the inner door. Now, if anyone came knocking, they'd need more than a key to get in, and I'd have more time to slip out through a back door.

I turned and faced the interior of the house. If I was stopped or challenged by a caretaker or anyone, I'd try and bluff my way, at first. After that it was anybody's guess. But to help weight the odds in my favour and to give any challenger pause, I reached inside my pocket for a black armband displaying the Party's symbol, and slipped it on. It showed the Red Cross of St. George on a circular white field, with the initials *N.O.B.* picked out in blue on the red horizontal arm. It also had a gold-wire crown atop the red vertical arm to denote my rank as a major. For as the officer class has known for centuries, bullshit might well baffle brains, but high rank outflanks rank and file, any day of the week.

CHAPTER 18

Bread and Sardines

The place smelt like a gymnasium and looked like a cross between a local council office and a school for wayward boys. I sent all six senses flying through the building, but the air seemed to have already settled to the disturbance of my entry. I didn't intend spending any time checking out the place for real, as the caper was more a smash and grab than a creep, and thanks to "Keys" and his floor plans I had the house well mapped out in my head. So, time being of the essence, I dashed upstairs and made for the double doors leading to the main first-floor corridor, and ignoring the sign that said, PRIVATE—OFFICIAL PERSONNEL ONLY, I pushed through and made for the third door on the right, the administration office.

It looked like a regular office, with desks, chairs, lamps, typewriters, and filing cabinets. The safe stood in one corner. Over in the other, there was a tiny green-and-cream-painted kitchen cupboard, a gas ring, a small sink, and a tin-tray with tea-mugs turned upside down to dry. You could tell these people took their tea-breaks very seriously. It all looked so very normal until you saw what was on the walls. But it wasn't so much the flags; the black swastikas entwined around the Red Cross of St. George or the jagged silver lightning bisecting a red circle at the centre of a Union Jack; it was the posters. They were all very near the knuckle and showed the very worst depictions of ugly, slavering, big-nosed Jews doing the sort of things to flaxen-haired maidens that you wouldn't ever want your saintly old mum to see. It was all very nasty. Then I noticed a poster showing a picture of two men hanging from a tree. I knew the photo. Two years earlier, it'd been the front page of the *Daily Express* and a lot of the other linens, too. Along the top, it read, REMEMBER SERGEANTS MARTIN AND PAICE; at the bottom, ZIONISTS MURDER BRITISH SOLDIERS. And I felt my heart sink. It's hard, sometimes, seeing both sides.

Jewish terrorism was rampant in Palestine after the end of the War; the Haganah, the Irgun, the Stern Gang were all at it; each one of them an illegal political group fighting for the right of the Jews to exist in their "Promised Land." And as it had been trying to do since it'd been granted the Mandate soon after the First War, Great Britain was in the middle of it all trying to keep some sort of balance between the Arabs and the Jews. The worst atrocity happened in 1946, when the Irgun blew up the King David Hotel in Jerusalem, the seat of the British administration in Palestine, killing over ninety people. For which act, three Irgun members were sentenced to hang by a British court. The Irgun then threatened that unless the sentences were commuted, British soldiers would be kidnapped and hanged in reprisal. The Zionists were duly hanged, and so, too, were two British sergeants; with land-mines buried beneath their bodies to blow up any fellow soldiers that went to cut them down. There were anti-Semitic demonstrations all over England when people heard about that, and in Palestine, some British soldiers took the law into their own hands and beat or killed the first Jews they came across. I don't know how many died in the end, but it wasn't a very pretty episode, whichever way you looked at it. And here I was, on both sides of the fence. I was British. I'd served in the War. But I also might just as well have been Jewish, it'd been so much a part and parcel of me and my East End world since I was a nipper.

I blinked. I don't know how long I'd been standing there. But I knew, without even looking at my watch, it was well past high time to get a bloody move-on. I went over to the safe standing in the corner and stared at it. It was a Burmah, with horrible horizontal pins. It would be. I'd opened a similar safe in front of "Keys" in record time. But I'd done that with the safe up on a bench and not on the floor, which meant that as good as I was at the old Chinese chopsticks routine, it would take a lot longer if I tried to attempt it now. (It's the difference between being balanced on the balls of your feet, with your arms, wrists, and whole body perfectly free, as opposed to lying flat on your stomach and leaning on your elbows.) It was much too heavy to lift by myself, so I had no choice, but to blow the bloody thing. And with that decided, I slipped off the satchel holding the jelly and bent down for a closer look. I looked, and looked, and looked again. I felt like that cartoon cat, that's always chasing that bloody cartoon mouse, I couldn't bloody believe it. And for the second time in almost as many minutes my heart sunk. Only this time it felt like what happens when you go over a humpback bridge in a motor car. They'd gone and taped over the keyhole with electrician's tape, which meant that whatever was inside might be of some importance, but was hardly likely to be the sorts of things I'd come looking for.

The Blitz had changed a lot of people's minds as to the true destructive power of fire; filing cabinets couldn't withstand the intense heat, but a good few safes had come through with their contents intact, even if a little bit on the dry side. So a lot of firms used a safe simply as a fire precaution and in offices where people came and went at all hours, and needed ready access, they left it unlocked or stuck the combination on the outside for all to see. I turned the handle, not hoping for much, the caper now pretty much a washout, and pulled the safe door open. There *was* a ledger, as it happened, but it was the stuff of shillings and pence, not thousands of pounds, and looked to be the weekly subs or tea money register. There was also a desk diary that among other things recorded the name of each weekend's duty officer, and I turned to April 16 and found it still blank. Another book listed everything to be found in the stationary cupboard, so I checked. There were a couple of those new Biro ball-point pens, which I slipped into my satchel, and a pile of Party membership application forms, which I left untouched. There was a box-file full of old copies of *Action*. But there was no ledger, diary, file, or red-coloured book; or anything else for that matter that resembled a top-secret master list of who was who, and who was giving the Party bags of money.

I stood up and looked round, wondering whether any clever sod had read his Conan Doyle and had come up with the wheeze of hiding the master file in plain sight; suitably covered in dust, of course. But a quick look around proved me wrong. Though, I did turn up quite a few Hank Jansen novels among the copies of *The Protocols of the Elders of Zion, Mein Kampf, Unfinished Victory,* and *The Alternative,* so I knew I was dealing with what might pass for the intelligentsia in some book-burning circles.

I pushed back my Trilby, and looked at my watch. Time or

no, I had to check out all the other rooms along the corridor. Only one office was locked, the first on the right, as you came in through the double doors. It was also the only door with a shiny new Yale. I got to work with the little torsion bar and pick, and I knew even before I got inside it was a whole different kettle of fish; the smell of the furniture polish was the same as in the house in Berkeley Square. I did the curtains and switched on the light. It was obviously a VIP's office; there was carpet on the floors, leather on the chairs, and oil paintings on the walls. On the desk, was an impressive pen set and leather-edged blotting pad; two telephones, one black, one red; and presiding over everything, a small black enamelled bust of Adolf Hitler; the twin of the one I'd used to weight the handle of the Berkeley Square safe. I shook my head. Was there no getting away from him? And that's when I noticed that an oil painting of a woman sitting astride a horse threw a very uneven shadow against the wall. And before you could sing, *"Hitler has only got one ball . . ."* I had the frame pulled back.

The wall safe had a brushed steel fascia, a stainless-steel treble-dial combination lock, a stainless-steel handle stamped with the symbol of a growling lion, and as a finishing touch to the vision of impenetrable strength, no keyhole. It was a thing of real beauty, even if that's all it was. And however impressive it might've looked in the manufacturer's showroom and catalogue, it presented no more difficulty to me now than a sardine tin. And I reached into my satchel for my "creeper's friend."

The sad truth is most safes aren't, despite what it says in the manufacturer's pamphlet; wall safes are the very worst for the punter and the very best for the likes of me. Most wall safes get fit into walls by poorly paid workmen, whose first job is to bash a big hole at the point where the safe is going to reside.

Sometimes, they come up against a load-bearing wall made of brick, but more often than not there's nothing but plaster and lathe behind the wallpaper. And as soon as the rough edges have all been smoothed out, they fit a steel frame into the hole, pick up the safe-box and slide it into the frame. They seal the edges as best they can, finish off with an impressive-looking steel surround, and hand over a set of keys and the combination number printed on a card, and off they scarper.

Now what man has wrought, man can . . . well, you get the idea. For as any creeper worth his salt will tell you, it's impossible to seal a corner. And "the creeper's friend" was tailor-made to exploit such a weakness. It looked like one of those wooden mushrooms women used to use to help darn the holes in their husband's socks, only bigger. But for creeping purposes, the shank was a three-quarter-inch hardened-steel chisel, on to which was affixed a highly polished wooden mushroom-shaped head. (Mine, custom-made for me by John Clague and his son Neal, in Birmingham; a much-respected family business that'd been supplying all the better villains with quality tools for well over a hundred years.)

The real beauty of it was you didn't need a hammer, you just hit it hard with the palm of your hand, which meant you could work fast, and in relative silence. It only took a couple of hits to get the chisel blade behind the metal lip. Then having worked on each corner in turn, you levered the front of the safe away from the wall, like you'd pry the lid off a cocoa tin with the end of a spoon, and just slid the whole thing out and stood it on its face. The dirty little secret that would've shocked the safe's owner rigid, was that the metal at the back of the safe was always paper-thin. All that was needed was another quick bash of the chisel into one of the corners at the rear; another twist of a wrist; and you could wind down the metal sheet like you were opening a tin of sardines. God's honest truth. After which, as they say, it was loaves and fishes all round.

I stuffed my hand down inside the back of the safe, and tried not to choke from all the dust still in the air. But there was no book or ledger; nothing; which was very odd, as I'd got a very definite feeling there was something special inside, and I wasn't often wrong about that sort of thing. I felt around again, taking extra care not to snag the sleeve of my trench coat on the jagged metal edges. Then I tilted the metal box and something fell against the back of my hand. I withdrew my arm, thumbed the glim and peered inside. It was difficult to make out at first, but the ribbon-ties gave it away. It was an artist's portfolio, in royal blue, and foolscap in size, by the look of it, and much too large to pull through the gap in the back of the safe. So I spent the next five minutes smoothing out the sharp edges and making the hole bigger. I tried to think what could possibly be inside. A sheet of rare postage stamps, maybe, or perhaps an ownership-certificate of a South African gold or diamond mine. I even had a mad idea that, with the way the creep had gone, it'd turn out to be an original watercolour signed by Adolf himself. But when I undid the bows and looked inside the portfolio, there was a couple dozen or so hand-written letters; all signed by someone with the initials "EP," whoever that was, when he was at home.

I slipped the letters back inside the portfolio and slid the whole thing inside my leather map case. I had to take something back to Walsingham, or he'd be peeved, and probably end up blaming me for another failure. I checked my watch. "Bloody hell," I said, brushing the white plaster dust off the front of my mackintosh. "Here we go again, I should've been gone hours ago." I looked up and caught Hitler's little black head frowning at me from behind one of the telephones. "I thought I told you to fuck off," I said. Then my eyes alighted on the red telephone, and I don't know quite why, but I leaned over and picked it up. And I was very glad I did, otherwise more people might've died that night, and I might've been one of them. Because, on the other end of the line, I heard a crackly voice repeating, over and over again, "Attention! Attention! There is a burglary currently in progress at NOB HQ, Inckerman Road, Kentish Town."

And that told me that somewhere in the house was a gramophone set up to start playing its recorded message down an open telephone line. All it needed was for some unsuspecting soul to open or close a particular door to complete or break an electrical circuit, and Bob your uncle was on his way to the cop shop. I was sure "Keys" would be very interested in adding that little titbit to his security file on the New Order of Britain, if I ever managed to get out of the place in one piece, that was. Because that was the exact moment I heard the quiet crunch of motor-car tyres on the gravel outside. The sneaky bastards must've turned off the headlights coming down the street and gently inched open the big iron gates. But, I tell you, gravel on a driveway is always a right bugger when total silence is called for.

Thank God.

CHAPTER 19

Pillars of Salt

I was running back down the corridor before the motor car outside had rolled to a halt. I'd only heard one set of tyres on the gravel, so the way I reckoned it, that meant a driver and three or four passengers; five men at the most. It had to be the NOB heavy brigade; determined to keep me and the whole business quietly contained, which was just fine by me. And as I madly pulled things from my satchel and started gathering stuff together in the administration office, I ran through the rest of the house in my mind.

The ground floor had a large assembly room, several small offices, a room with a printing press, and the kitchen. The first floor, where I was, contained the main offices, a committee room, and the officers' mess. On the second floor was a small barracks room with camp-beds, a common room, various storage rooms, and on top of that, the attic. All of it just one huge rat-trap. And once the people outside realised there was no coming in through the front doors, they'd leave a man front and rear, and come in through the back. Then two men would search the place, with a third man backing them up. Well, that's what they'd do if they had any military training. I just prayed they weren't amateurs, who'd charge in, willy-nilly.

It was no good me going up to the roof, as there was no adjoining building to escape to. If I tried sliding down any of the drain-pipes, there'd be someone waiting at the bottom to bash me one. There was no going out the windows, for the same reason. So the first thing I had to do was even out the odds a little, which meant Plan B. And with that decided, I suddenly felt that old black-magic feeling of time slowing down and billowing out all around me like a cloak, and I moved with a purpose and a flow that made every second seem like a minute.

I picked up a metal wastepaper bin, emptied its contents out into the corridor, then stepped back into the office, stood the bin on a desk and rammed a London telephone directory down inside it. I went over to where the tea things were kept, pulled the lid off the biscuit barrel, pushed some jelly down in among the biscuits, pushed a detonator inside the jelly and attached the two ends of the wire flex onto its two prongs. I placed the biscuit barrel inside the waste-bin, then took several boxes of drawing pins and staples from the stores cupboard and emptied the whole lot into the bin. I grabbed hold of another telephone directory and wedged it between the door and the jamb so as to leave a gap, then took a high-backed chair and angled it against the door, up under the doorknob, so it was balanced on its two back legs. I picked up the tin tea-tray full of mugs from off the filing cabinet, carried it over to the chair and balanced it so it formed a triangle with the chair's seat and back, and stood a couple of empty milk bottles on top of the mugs for added effect. I set the waste-paper bin down under the chair and fed the detonator wire under the door and out into the corridor. I slid a blotting-pad over the top of the bin and piled the two remaining telephone directories on top of that. I now had all of London covered. But as they say, there's always safety in numbers.

I inched my way out into the corridor, through the gap between door and jamb, and trailing the electrical wire out along the baseboard, I made my way back towards the commandant's office. I knew a coffin's length before I got there I was going to come up short, and in the end I barely had three or four inches left to push under the door. I stuck the wire to the floor inside the room with some chewing gum, then went back out into the corridor, and using the hilt of my Fairbairn-Sykes, I reached up and broke every light bulb all the way back to just beyond the administration office. Then I went back to the double entry doors and jammed a Biro into the armature of both door-return mechanisms. I turned to look. The lights at the far end illuminated the wastepaper I'd strewn on the floor outside the office just enough to catch the eye. But where I was standing, there was full shadow. It wasn't much as theatrical lighting goes; I just had to hope the fill of light from the stairwell wouldn't reveal the telltale trail of wire when the corridor doors were opened.

I slipped back inside the commandant's office, locked the door, stepped around the upended wall safe, and pulled the plug of the desk lamp out of the wall socket, and cut and stripped the flex at both ends. I twisted one set of bare wires onto the ends of the detonator wire, peeled the chewing gum off the floor and used it to insulate the connections. I trailed the wire across the carpet, sat on the floor, and attached a bare wire to one of the battery terminals. Then I pulled my hat down, and focussed all my attention on the darkened corridor on the other side of the door.

I had two sound cues to listen for, which in the absence of red or green blinking lights was as good as any direction I ever got when working backstage at any theatre, and I tried to calm my mind, still my breathing, and prepare for the coming drama. It'd taken me no more than four or five minutes to set everything up, which was more than enough as it turned out, as it was a good couple of minutes before I heard the plastic Biros crack and splinter into pieces. "Curtain up," I whispered. All the supporting actors had to do now was follow their parts in the play.

I held my breath, ready to touch the remaining bare wire to the second battery terminal. And my hand all but twitched as I saw and heard someone slowly turn the door handle and push against the door to the commandant's office. But the fact that it was locked seemed to satisfy whoever was outside and I heard them—or imagined I did—make their way further along the corridor. I counted off the steps in my mind, my ears now on total alert for the clatter of an upended tray of crockery and the distinctive crash of empty milk bottles. Nevertheless, the racket surprised me when I finally heard it, but I think my hand had the wire to the terminal and the contact closed even before I could say, "Boom!"

I heard the thud of bodies being flung back against the corridor wall, although it was probably just the office door blowing out. And I was up and on my feet, the Yale unlocked and the door to the commandant's office opened, even before the dust had had time to settle. I peered down the corridor to the two bodies in tattered mackintoshes that were lying under a swirl of paper and what was once a door. There was a faint moaning, which I suppose was a good sign, but as I turned and opened the double entry doors I heard a voice echoing up from the floor below.

"Ashton? Lawson? I say, are you men okay?"

The man had used surnames, which said he had to be the officer of the group, otherwise, as was proper amongst equals, he'd have used first names. He called out again. "Ashton? Lawson?" And by the sound of it, he was coming up the stairs, too. Then the bloke stationed outside in the driveway started pounding on the front door, but chummy on the stairs ignored him and just kept on coming. "Ashton? Lawson? Are you there?" I shook my head; good officer material is always hard to find. "Ashton?" I dashed back into the commandant's office looking for anything heavy that I could use as a Halifax Persuader.

"Lawson?" The man was getting closer and closer.

I waited for him to call out again. And when I judged him to be near the top of the stairs, I pulled my Trilby down over my eyes, and coughing and spluttering like a good 'un, I burst through the entry doors; right arm held across my front; left arm pointing back from whence I'd come. I must have looked quite a sight and not at all what the NOB officer expected to see. I was covered in plaster dust from messing with the wall-safe earlier, but I still looked every inch a fellow officer, as he could see from the gold crown on my armband, and my leather map case. It stopped him short for a second or two; which was just as well, really, as it was only then I saw that he had a Luger pistol in his hand. But he was still taking it all in, still responding to the uniform, and still not quite sure of what was what. But I knew that wouldn't last long, so quick as a flash I produced my rabbit from out of my hat. And as I stumbled down the stairs, I held the black enamelled bust of Adolf Hitler out in front of me.

"Thank God, you're here," I shouted, hoarsely; James Mason to the life. "Ashton and Lawson still need help, but I have to save der Führer." And I know it sounds corny, but it's like a skeleton key made of tin, it only needs to work the once. And he nodded and hurried up the stairs, and I was just about level with him when he blinked and the illusion was lost. And I don't know what it was; it might've been something as simple as me having the armband on the wrong arm, or the fact I didn't salute, but he pivoted around to strike at me with his left arm and to bring his pistol to bear. But I was already going through the same motion, and I swung the metal bust up across his knee and carried on all the way up until I hit him right under the chin with enough force to knock his hat off. His lights went out and he went down like a ton of bricks. But as I fell against him his finger twitched on the trigger and the Luger fired and the bullet went under my arm, nicked the edge of the map case, and hit the wall. And as I pushed myself upright, Hitler's head rolled down the stairs and ended up at my feet. I don't know which of us was looking the worse for wear, so I gave it a hefty kick. I'd had quite enough of Herr Hitler, thank you. But the sound of the metal bust tumbling down the stairs made me realise the bloke outside had stopped banging a tattoo on the front door, which meant he and his chum would soon probably be coming in through the back.

I shot down the stairs and made straight for the front door. And I had the bolts of the inner door pulled back before I heard the shouts. But there was no stopping me now, and I was through and the door banged shut behind me as the first blast from a shotgun hit the other side. I threw back the bolts to the outer front door and pulled it open and yanked it closed and ran for the gates; hoping the buggers hadn't thought to relock them. But then something the size of a tree stood in my path. He was a big bastard, six foot four, at least, and his Trilby hat added a few inches on top of that. Sod it, but I was getting too old for this; I was supposed to be a bloody cat burglar, not a Commando on a night raid on Dieppe.

I noticed he had his shotgun held across his body and not pointed directly at me. And only then did I twig the NOB officer's uniform was still working in my favour, because as if on cue, he said, "You said I wasn't to leave my post, sir. Only I heard a—" I pretended to stumble so he didn't get a close look at my face, and seemed to get caught up in the strap of my map case. Then he began to move, questions at last forming in his mind, and he started to swing his shotgun round. But I was already leaning back and swinging the map case round on its leather strap like a hammer throw; my case travelling faster than the arc of his gun barrels. And I think he was quite surprised when a hard corner of the leather map case hit him smack on the temple, almost knocking his eye out. Though to be honest it was probably the lead weights I'd fitted along the bottom of the case that really did the trick. And he let out a gasp, and just sort of pirouetted and fell in a heap. But the momentum of the swing took me down, too, and I landed heavily on my shoulder and lay there on the gravel, stunned and seeing stars. I rolled over and pushed myself to my feet, kicked the shotgun away, and aimed a few other well-aimed kicks at the bloke's head to ensure he stayed down. Which might've led to my undoing as an officer. Because a voice shouted out, "Stop that, you bastard." And I turned around; not always a good thing to do in such circumstances; and saw another NOB guard aiming a double-barrelled shotgun at me.

"God help me," seemed an appropriate prayer, though I don't know whether I managed to get more than the first word out as I dived for the ground. The blast ripped the curtain of night to tatters. And I honestly thought I'd had my lot. It's strange, though, what your mind goes through when it thinks it sees a brilliant flash of white flame billowing out towards it. My mind was already working out what I'd say to God when I met him; wondering what death would feel like; would it be long and drawn out, or just, click, like a light being switched off. My shocked brain cells had also registered that it was only the one-barrel that had been fired and not the two; which was odd, considering someone was supposedly going for the kill. I began to feel the stings that were the herald of me being shredded into pieces of steaming flesh. Funny thing was, they didn't seem half as bad as my imagination said they should be, but they were bloody painful nevertheless. It might've been the leather map case or even the Burberry that did the trick, as trench coats had seen a fair bit of shellfire in their time. Or maybe God had heard my prayer. I had no idea what'd deflected what, but something had helped keep death at bay. And, as they say, few ever doubt in God when they're being shelled or shot at.

It hit me, then, the shotgun barrel must have been loaded with rock salt, and not lead-shot; an old gamekeepers' trick. The salt stung like buggery, but unless discharged fully into the face, when it'd probably blind you for life, it didn't kill you; as not even a keeper wanted to hang or spend the rest of his life behind bars on a murder charge. As it was, I took most of the blast on my back and shoulders, and I'm very glad to say even though moaning loudly, I was still in one piece. And I rolled over on the gravel, the small sharp stones stinging my face almost as much as the rock salt, but I was soon up on my elbows and pushing myself up onto my hands and knees. And that's when I heard the unmistakable crunch of boots striding my way. I began to scrabble away, making for the tress and bushes that rimmed the gravel driveway. But something long and hard was stabbed in between my legs and as I tripped and fell I had to twist round onto my back or one of my feet would've broken off at the ankle, right then and there.

I peered up at the dark shape looming over me. "Not your lucky night, is it, sunshine?" the NOB guard chuckled, as he gave me a couple of hefty kicks. "I don't give a tinker's cuss whether you're a fuckin' Communist or a Jew, you scum are all just a waste of fuckin' space." He stepped back, raised his gun in mock salute, and made an exaggerated play of clicking back the hammer on the loaded barrel. "So, it's high time you said your fuckin' prayers." He swung the shotgun down in an arc towards my head, but just as suddenly arched backwards, his finger twitching on the trigger sending the blast of salt straight up in the air. And as he twisted and fell to the ground, I noticed a small silver arrow sticking out of his shoulder. I knew what it was; I had a set of them back in the lock-up in Paddington; it was a steel dart shot from a modified Colt semiautomatic pistol, known to all Commandos as a Bigot.

I praised God forty-three times in the time it took for my heart to beat twice, and scrabbled hurriedly to my feet. Only for some reason this time the approaching scrunch of gravel under someone's foot didn't make me wish for a sudden cloak of invisibility or a safe distance of about a hundred miles. I peered into the darkness.

"Shalom," said a voice softly from out of the shadows as a black-clad figure lent over the still-writhing body of the guard.

"You can say that again, my friend, whoever you are," I said, my voice hoarse with relief at the sudden dispatching of the NOB guard who'd been about to give me a passport into the land of the blind.

Then a second voice, somewhere off to my right, said, "Shalom."

"Shalom," I said. "And a long life to you both." Then I got the hell out of there.

A Walk in the Park

"I thought we might have a little chat," Walsingham said, as we walked across Green Park. He spoke softly, but there was that edge to his voice that said he was carrying a very big stick, so right away I knew something bad was up and I steeled myself for the high jump.

The message had been telephoned to the Victory just before eight that morning, and with me having not appeared until gone nine, I'd really had to get my skates on. The Universal Theatre Co. was urgently looking for stage-hands, and the stage-manager wondered whether I was interested in being interviewed; the location and time, their office near Green Park tube station, at eleven o'clock. The words "stage-manager" meant "raid your props cupboard" so I wore a dark blue, double-breasted chalk-stripe, a "snap brim" hat, and carried an overcoat over my arm as the Burberry was looking a little worse for wear. I also had on horn-rim glasses and a moustache worthy of an insurance salesman. Even I didn't recognise me.

I caught sight of Bosanquet as I crossed over Piccadilly from the tube station, but he waved me off as if signalling for a taxi. Then Walsingham appeared, in bowler hat and British "Warm," a tightly furled Swaine & Adeney umbrella under his arm, and without a flicker of recognition he marched off in the direction of Green Park. I glanced along Piccadilly, clocked everyone on the pavement by their walk and their clothing, waggled my right ear, then turned and walked after him.

I entered through the gate and, as I always did, nodded at the park bench over on the right, just inside the railings. A soldier and his girl had been sitting on the original bench, flirting the night away, when the first bomb that fell in Green Park fell on them. And I know they, at least, went together, but still, what a way to go. London County Council had replaced the bench, but there was no plaque or anything, and I know a lot of people died in the War, but some you can't seem to forget because of the circumstances. A nod, in remembrance, was the very least I could do.

I caught up with Walsingham about a cricket pitch's length into the Park. But he didn't even turn his head; he just bowled a leg-break at me. "Simon will ensure there's no one following us. It's a little melodramatic, but a necessary precaution given the circumstances." I nodded, wondering whether those circumstances had anything to do with the events of the previous night. "Good morning, by the way," he said. "And thank you for coming at such short notice. But a report came in from Special Branch this morning, about an explosion that occurred last night at NOB headquarters. For the moment it's being put down to a leaky gas main. But indications are that a number of people were injured, one or two quite seriously. There'll be an official inquiry, of course, ostensibly undertaken by the National Gas Board, but I was wondering if you'd care to comment."

I kept right in step. "A carload of NOB guards arrived brandishing shotguns, due to a telephone-linked alarm system no one knew anything about. So I used some jelly to create a little diversion. And I may have banged a few heads escaping afterwards, but nothing too drastic."

Walsingham gave me a sideways glance. "Checking the gas mains will give ample opportunity for our people to install a number of listening devices; so it worked out rather well. The only negative, I can see, is NOB will now be on round-the-clock alert for any further intrusions."

Before my brain could get itself around the notion there might be a third break-in in the offing with my name written all over it, he asked me if I'd go over the exact sequence of events from the previous night. So I told him everything, up to and including me braining the guy on the stairs with the bust of Hitler, and my battle with Goliath. I didn't think it wise to mention that the bloke had been brought down by a steel bolt rather than a pebble, so I left the men of '43' out of the story, too. Walsingham asked me why I hadn't made the rendezvous with Bosanquet's team of Watchers, so I told him the honest truth; that I'd noticed a motor car following me, soon after I'd left Camden Town. "It might've been Simon's men tailing me, but it could've been members of NOB in hot pursuit. I couldn't take the chance, so I gave them the slip until I was sure I wasn't being followed any longer. Then I found a telephone box and called into the exchange."

He nodded. "The motor car wasn't one of ours, Jethro," he said. Then he dropped the issue, which was heartening, because as it happened I had made a quick detour to my lock-up down Paddington Basin before I'd telephoned in. The way I reckoned it, if someone had gone to all the trouble to lock those letters away in a safe, I should at least take the trouble to copy them, as you never knew how valuable they might turn out to be. Then without even the slightest run-up, Walsingham bowled a slow one at me. "The letters in the portfolio, did you look at them, by any chance?"

Having just hit one over the boundary, I decided to play it safe and hit the ball straight back down the wicket. "Yes, I did give them a glance, Mr. Walsingham, but most of them looked to be in German."

"The letters meant nothing at all to you, then?" he said quietly.

I shook my head. "The handwriting was pretty bad, but the one or two letters, in English, seemed harmless enough; just friendly chat, really."

He turned his head a fraction. "Nothing else?"

"Well," I said, trying to stop myself from scratching my chin, "other than that the letters were all dated from some time just before the War or during the early stages of it, and were all signed with the initials E.P., no."

Walsingham skimmed his umbrella back and forth across the path and pinned a piece of litter to the ground. "As it happens, Jethro, those letters and items like them, were what I hoped you'd find at the house in Berkeley Square. You see, it's not entirely inconceivable, that in the wrong hands, those letters could push the Realm into turmoil, even anarchy."

I stopped dead. "I don't see how a few letters could do that."

He turned, his blue eyes hard and cold. "Unfortunately, they are the very crux of the matter. Those chatty letters, as you call them, were all addressed to intermediaries between the writer and Adolf Hitler. A top Nazi economic advisor; the German ambassador to London; a top Nazi general; all rather odd pen-pals for a British EHU, wouldn't you say?"

"I still don't follow," I said. "I know from that business, last year, with the stolen government directory, that EHU stands for 'extremely high-up' and is way above the level of VIP. But it's well known a lot of the aristocracy supported the Nazis before the War. I mean, Sir Oswald Mosley got married in Goebbels's apartment in Berlin, with Hitler himself as one of the guests. What's so different about all this?"

This time it was Walsingham who stopped in his tracks, although he did it with a precision that would've made any parade-ground sergeant major proud. "As much as Mosley aspired to higher office," he said very quietly, "he never sat on the throne of England."

I followed his gaze and found myself staring at Buckingham Palace, still trying to fathom what he was getting at. A moment before, I'd been strolling in the Park on a spring day; the next, I was back on the other side of the looking-glass and London itself seemed to have tilted. I slipped my overcoat on and looked around, nonchalantly. Bosanquet was hiding in plain sight a hundred yards back, a camera and pair of binoculars over his shoulder, a guidebook in his hand. He didn't fool me for an instant, but I still thought of asking for a quick butcher's in his book, I felt a little lost.

As if reading my mind, Walsingham turned and said, "You may well feel a little lost, Jethro, but do please be patient. For reasons I hope to make clear, events now compel me to reveal to you a story involving acts bordering on treason by a man who was once King of England." And with that stunning opening speech, worthy of Shakespeare, we marched across the Mall and into St. James's Park, with me feeling, with every step, as if I was about to take part in some modern-dress production of *Richard III*.

Walsingham slowed his pace to not quite a slow march and shot me a look. "Everything I'm about to tell you, Jethro, is covered by the Official Secrets Act. Is that understood?" I nodded, aware of the increasing chill in the air. "The initials E.P. stand for 'Edward, Prince'. It's how the Duke of Windsor, formerly Edward VIII, signed his letters when he was Prince of Wales and heir to the Throne. He took to using the two initials as his signature, again, soon after his abdication." Blimey, the Duke of Windsor. I kept my eyes fixed firmly on the ground, and wondered again what it must be like to be in Walsingham's shoes. He cleared his throat and continued with his tale. "Edward's Fascist sympathies were apparent long before the War. During his year as King he argued repeatedly against the Government's policies toward Hitler, opposed any response to Germany's militarization of the Rhineland, and sided with Mussolini in his invasion of Ethiopia. And by early 1936 it became clear to MI6 that state secrets were being passed to Berlin that could have only emanated from Edward."

He let me digest that little lot while he stole a glance at Bosanquet, but I could tell from the look on his face there was worse yet to come. I nodded for him to continue. "The story for public consumption was that Edward gave up the Throne so he could marry the woman he loved, the American Wallis Simpson, and that as a double-divorcée and commoner, she was unacceptable to the British aristocracy. However, that's not strictly true, EHU's in government were very worried the two of them were meddling too much in politics, and that Edward was using his popularity and influence as King to seek ways to bring about a peace agreement with Hitler." He turned to look at me, his gaze blank and pitiless. "Why else do you think Mosley suddenly began calling the British Union of Fascists the King's Party?" I nodded. The linens had been full of it, but the whole idea had faded faster than a spiv into a dark alley, once Edward's brother, Bertie, had taken over the throne, as George VI.

Walsingham turned; eyes front. "Even after the abdication, there were further indiscretions. The couple often stayed at a château, in France, owned by a well-known Nazi sympathizer; they were married there; top Nazi officials were regular guests there. The newlyweds even accepted Hitler's personal invitation to tour Germany and met him at his mountain retreat in Berchtesgaden. The following year, the Windsors wanted to visit England, but the request was denied as the Duke's presence was deemed not to be in the public interest. The Government feared that he might yet seek to challenge the Throne and help create conditions in the country that could lead to public demonstrations or disorder. All of which was entirely possible, as the BUF at the time was almost fifty thousand strong and Mosley was focussing all his speeches on the former King. And although they all proclaimed their loyalty to the Crown, it didn't necessarily follow that they were loyal to King George VI."

He let that all sink in for a minute. It was funny how shocked I felt at the thought of the ex-King of England meeting Adolf Hitler. But here it was now, a world war and more than ten years later and there still hadn't been a single word about it in any of the linens. That in itself, said something about the power of people in the know. But the shock I felt was as nothing, compared to what Walsingham threw at me next; it sent the bloody bails flying off the wickets; and me along with them.

"Then comes the rather unsavory matter of the Duke's activities during the early part of the War. He was given the rank of Major-General; assigned to the British Military Mission in France, and as such, was privy to all Allied military plans." He paused. "Evidence has come to light since the end of the War that suggests that an intelligence leak that leads directly to the Duke of Windsor played a significant part in prompting Hitler to order his generals to change long-standing battle plans. The net result of which, it's now thought, brought about the all-too-speedy collapse of the Maginot Line, the French Army, and led to the fall of France."

I stood there, trying to get my head around what he'd said; that Edward had somehow personally betrayed France. And I tried to remember where I'd been when I'd heard of France's surrender; which convoy, which ship; but I couldn't place it, I was in such a spin. Why on earth would the ex-King do a thing like that? I know he'd gone on about another war being uncalled for and that the British aristocracy had already lost too many of its young men in the First World War, but for him to try and get his way by betrayal on such a scale beggared belief. No wonder the Royals hadn't wanted the Duke to step foot back on British soil. But Walsingham hadn't finished.

"Then, in the summer of 1940, with German troops marching on Paris, the Duke essentially abandoned his post and fled France for Madrid. And while there, he and the Duchess were wooed constantly by German secret service officers who urged them to hold themselves in readiness for the Duke's assumption of the English throne in a soon-to-be Nazi-dominated Great Britain. In the end, Churchill had to threaten the Duke of Windsor with a court-martial before he would agree to leave Spain."

I didn't need to hear anymore. I knew the Duke had ended up as the governor of the Bahamas, during the War. But it was pretty clear now, it was to keep him as far away from the front lines as possible, which was just as well; I think I'd have shot him myself had I known what he'd done. And I stood there under the trees, blinking like an owl suddenly thrust into harsh daylight. But Walsingham was unstoppable now.

"In the closing months of the War, the Royal Family initiated a secret military mission into Germany; the sole purpose of which was to locate and retrieve all files relating to the Duke and Duchess in the German Ministry of Foreign Affairs archives. A great number of those documents have since gone missing. And with the current mood in Britain being what it is as regards the Government's continuing austerity measures and its program of nationalisation, it's not unreasonable to imagine the disastrous effects the disclosure of such material could have on the public. It would not only seriously embarrass the King and Queen; the Government fears it could also lead to calls for the abolition of the monarchy itself. And if that were to happen, it would create a social and political vacuum, the consequences of which neither they, nor the leaders of His Majesty's Government in Opposition, wish to contemplate."

So that was it. They didn't want the applecart upset. Because, if it became known "the once and future King" had colluded with the Führer himself, the remaining Royals might well suffer a Humpty Dumpty. And then all the King's horses and all the King's men couldn't put the King or Queen back together again. Not ever.

I scratched my chin. Walsingham never did anything without a reason. He'd tried wrapping me in the flag before, but even in my wildest, I'd never once thought I'd be invited to peek behind the Royal Standard itself. And that's when it hit me that most of what we clap and cheer, and stand to attention and salute, and think of as the United Kingdom, is all stage-managed. All the pomp and circumstance and ceremony resemble the lights and scenery and painted flats you find in a theatre production, only on a much grander scale. But all of it designed to do much the same thing, to catch the heart, mind, and eye. And now here I was being asked to help move scenery around again, so the whole bloody lot didn't come crashing down. No wonder the Royals wanted to keep a tight lid on things.

CHAPTER 21

Canard

The idea of the Royals sending people into Germany to get their hands on what they considered was their private property didn't surprise me. As any scholar of crime in the Smoke will tell you, the Royals had been the talk of the screwing fraternity ever since the disappearance of the Duchess of Windsor's jewels from Ednam Lodge, over in Sunningdale, back when the abdication crisis was at its height. And even though a lot of tongues at the time had wagged my way, as I was one of two or three up-coming faces thought worthy of the caper, I had nothing at all to do with it; those were Germans other than mine at work that night. And not to give too much away, but if you ever wanted to know the truth about the haul; word was, it included a ruby the size of a duck's egg; I'd suggest you pop round the Palace to ask if they'd got any ideas as to the jewellery's whereabouts. Titled tealeafs have been getting away with it for years; nicking whole countries sometimes; so reacquiring a suite of jewellery that once belonged to Queen Victoria, was as nothing.

We came to the lake, my favourite bit of St. James's Park, and were about halfway across the old iron suspension bridge when Walsingham stopped dead again. They'd drained the lake a year or so earlier in search of an unexploded bomb that was thought to be too close to Buckingham Palace for comfort, but that now seemed a mere bagatelle compared to what Walsingham had just dropped on me. He looked out towards the little island where the ducks gathered under the willow trees. "In all conscience, Jethro, I couldn't ask you to go into danger again, without you knowing what's fully at stake." The willows stirred. So did I. I nodded for him to continue. "Letters sent by the Duke of Windsor to his Nazi friends first began coming to light last year. The Palace insisted they were all forgeries, until we proved the letters contained information that could have only originated from the Duke. They then admitted that a number of files on the Windsors had gone missing from private Royal archives, but were adamant that the Secret Services take no further action." The unspoken question hung in the air. He glanced at me. "The audacity of the robbery at the Palace fitted Von Bentink like a glove and had all the hallmarks of being a Soviet operation, and there was no way I could ignore that. So, as Von Bentink was based at the Bulgarian Embassy, I put the building under surveillance. And then you burgled the place and came to my attention."

"Back in the halcyon days when I was nothing but a humble cat burglar and jewel thief?" I said, perhaps a little too wistfully.

"I wanted Von Bentink caught red-handed and put on ice for a while, to see what the Soviets would do. But as he came to a sticky end in that incident with you, last Christmas, that rather put an end to that."

"The bastard had me trussed up like a turkey and was torturing me to death," I said. "He deserved to die."

"Perhaps he did," Walsingham said. He turned and looked in the direction of Buckingham Palace. "But, on New Year's Day, while you were still recuperating in hospital, a young under-butler on the Palace staff was found floating in the Thames, near Waterloo Bridge. A tobacco tin found among his personal effects contained one of the missing Windsor letters and a Communist Party of Great Britain membership card. The timing may well have been coincidental, but it was all a touch too neat, for my taste."

I scratched my chin. "So, what are you saying? That the under-butler wasn't really a Red, and that he didn't really steal into the Palace archives?"

"No," he said, tapping his umbrella on the pathway. "That's what one's supposed to think." He paused, and it was all I could do not to lean forward. "The PM recently introduced legislation to establish new, more stringent procedures for vetting people seeking clearance to classified material; which means that Communists, as well as Fascists, are now excluded from work considered 'vital to the Security of the State.' The real intent though is to weed out secret sympathisers and fellow travellers of either ideology." He paused again. "Those cases that are deemed especially sensitive are passed to my department for a more stringent vetting. In one such security sweep, one of my teams happened upon a cache of missing Windsor documents in the London flat of a very senior civil servant. The items were all brought in, photographed, and returned. We put a tap on the man's telephone, a team of Watchers on his tail, and started inspecting his mail. His file says, he flirted briefly with Communism at Cambridge, but quickly became disillusioned with it; since then, he'd never been party to anything more extreme than the Rotary Club. But as the only people up until that point who'd been found to be in possession of missing Windsor material had all had Communist affiliations, we assumed he did, too."

"Blimey," I said, eyeing one of the ducks out on the lake. "Those Reds are getting everywhere. What happened then?"

"Nothing, for a time. Over the course of the next few weeks, our VIP-CS never once deviated from his usual routine. Then, in short order, there occurred a series of seemingly random meetings between him and others that led us, in due course, to the house on Berkeley Square."

"Was that how you knew I'd find all those red leather-covered books in the safe?" I said, helpfully. He shook his head.

"I didn't know they existed, Jethro. I was simply trying to determine the source of the missing Windsor letters."

"Well, if you don't mind me asking, whose house did you have me burgle? Who is it lives on Berkeley Square?"

"Lord Belfold, the City banker," he said. "Or, as he prefers to be called, since his recent elevation to the peerage, Lord Ernest St John Belfold, First Baron Belfold of Bray."

"It's nice to know I'm still stealing from England's richest and finest," I said, with all the irony I could muster. "But why trust me with all this, Mr. Walsingham?"

"For the same reason I needed you to burgle Belfold's house. Other than you and Simon, there's no more than a handful of people in all of England I can trust at present. Whitehall and Westminster are riddled with secret sympathisers; Communist; Fascist; pro-Zionist; pro-Arab. It would be folly for me to think MI5 hasn't been penetrated. That's why I moved the department out of Regent Street, and now have it in limbo."

"I did wonder," I said, feeling in a bit of a limbo myself.

He humoured me with a slight raise of an eyebrow. "One has to be so very careful, Jethro. Take, for instance, the break-in in Berkeley Square. No official police report was ever filed at West End Central or Scotland Yard. Yet, within days, there was a flood of enquiries from MPs and civil servants of every stripe into the Home Office Deputy Secretary responsible for MI5. With everybody suddenly extremely interested in high-value burglaries in London or the Government monitoring of political groups. And much too much activity, for it not to have been a concerted effort."

Someone had to be very important to be pulling that many strings. He'd even got Walsingham on edge, and that was a first. I looked to see if I could see Simon Bosanquet, tourist and spy at large, and saw him circling the far side of the lake. I thought his throwing crumbs to the ducks was overdoing it a bit. But wasn't that what Walsingham was doing with me? I looked over the trees towards the domes and spires of Whitehall; if I hadn't known it was London, it could've been a city in some far-off country; it'd certainly begun to feel like one. "Then, what's the connection between those red books and the Windsor letters?" I asked.

"The NOB elite refer to the books and the letters as being 'the Keys to the Kingdom.' There are other Keys, too, apparently."

The red book I'd peeped at had been enough to make my eyes water, but I couldn't let on. "So what makes those books I took from Belfold's house so important? What's inside them, exactly?"

"Pornography, of the very worst sort," he said, matter-of-factly.

"Charming," I said. "So, is that what I risked life and limb for?"

He shook his head. "I had no idea the photographs or the books existed until you dropped them into our lap, Jethro. Truly."

"But I don't see how any amount of dirty photos could be the keys to any kingdom," I said, "unless, perhaps, it was Darby Messima's Soho."

"The levers of power assume many forms, Jethro. And the photographs show many of the country's VIPs in rather less than a perfect light. Peers of the Realm, MPs, government officials, City businessmen, even one or two judges, so I gather. A rather rum bunch to have revived the Hell Fire Club, wouldn't you say?"

I nodded. Every schoolboy had heard tales of the notorious Hell Fire Club, where Sir Francis Dashwood and his cronies had all dressed up as monks and got up to all manner of mischief out at his country estate: orgies, witchcraft, torture, murder; they'd done the lot. But that'd all happened two hundred years before. "But why all the photographs?"

"Blackmail," he said, in a tone of voice that said he wasn't guessing. "You see, we weren't the only ones to have had the civil servant under observation. All three Red Books show graphic black-and-white studies of him with various women and, in one or two instances, other men. Suffice to say there are no snaps of his lovely wife. So, I had a little chat with him about it all. And as I suspected, the photographs were how NOB persuaded him to spy for them in Whitehall. In many ways, though, I think he was very relieved to have been found out. He seemed only too eager to tell me all about the Keys to the Kingdom and the part the Windsor letters play in the scheme of things; he even confirmed Belfold as being the source of them. All in all, he was so very helpful, I thought it best to leave him in place and run him as a double agent; as our man on the inside."

"Like you did with Twenty Committee, during the War?" He nodded. "So what has our man on the inside got to say about events?"

"Not much, I'm afraid, he was found dead in his Chelsea flat this morning, with a bullet hole in his right temple and a suicide note in his typewriter saying he couldn't face being revealed as a Communist spy."

I shot him a look. "You're joking," I said.

Walsingham stabbed repeatedly at the pathway with his umbrella. "The troubling thing is, he was left-handed; something I happened to notice when he was signing his statement; and although not exactly proof of foul play, it does rather suggest he was murdered." He shot me a look. "And, in all probability, in response to last night's events at NOB HQ."

"Now, you really are joking," I said.

"I wish to God I were, Jethro," he said, quietly.

"So, are you saying he wasn't really a secret card-carrying Red?"

He shook his head. "Again, that's what we're supposed to think."

"I don't follow," I said. And I didn't.

"I rather suspect that NOB and other extremist right-wing groups are stage-managing events so it appears there's a Communist-inspired plot to topple the Monarchy. And that the Duke of Windsor's letters to the Nazis are but the means to them achieving that end."

"But that doesn't make sense. Why would NOB use the

Duke's own letters to discredit him; him being such a staunch supporter of Fascism?"

"You must always remember to look at the larger picture, Jethro. Their single aim is to discredit Socialism, reverse any attempts at nationalisation, and steer the country very firmly to the right. They want to force a crisis that will lead to a vote of no confidence in the Labour Government. And widespread publication of the Duke's letters would substantially serve to dissipate public confidence in order and institutions, in general, and the Monarchy, in particular. They'd then use the spectre of a growing Communist threat as their rallying cry and cite the new vetting initiatives as precedent to demand that the trade unions purge themselves of all Marxist and Communist influence. They know, full well, it would lead to more dock strikes; bring factories to a halt; put men out of work; perhaps even cause a general strike. But they'll do whatever they have to, to manufacture an economic crisis, even if it means manipulating the stock market so as to cause a major fall in prices and a run on sterling. Anything and everything that would give rise to a nation-wide cry for NOB and the other extremist right-wing groups to come together as a new King's Party. And if they were then not swept up into power, they'd take over control of the Conservative Party, at the very least."

"So, it's really a big double-bluff? NOB drops poisoned titbits into whatever Communist shell-like ears they can find. It all goes round and round until the Communist Party can piece it all together; then when they go public with it, they get blamed for trying to bring down the Monarchy."

"That's it, exactly," he said, stabbing at the ground.

"So is that where all the dirty photographs come in; NOB uses them to blackmail key people and guarantee support for their King's Party?"

He nodded. "NOB, in effect, is planning to stage a political coup."

I stared at him, my mouth opening and closing like a drowning fish. "A coup?" I said. "But this is Great Britain, not some third-rate country where bananas come from. I don't see how they could get away with it."

He smoothed his moustache. "They could. And with the country in its present state, Jethro, all too easily, I fear."

I shuddered. Ray had told me once that wherever power resided in the United Kingdom, it was definitely not in the House of Commons, it was somewhere in the triangle made up by the City, Whitehall, and the House of Lords. I'd told him that by my reckoning that put it very near Cleopatra's Needle on the Embankment. Ray didn't even laugh; he just said I'd missed the point, entirely, as per bloody usual.

Walsingham waved his umbrella at the rest of London. "The fate of the country rests with whoever garners the support of the country's elite, or who at the very least can guarantee their non-intervention. Whoever holds the key decision-makers, effectively holds the Keys to the Kingdom."

The world had done more than tilt; it'd turned upside down. I grabbed at names. "Do you think the Duke of Windsor or Sir Oswald Mosley are behind all this?"

"No. Even given his wretched past, I don't think the Duke would still be such a bloody fool as to be involved. But Mosley still hungers for power, and would appear on any platform that might validate his visions."

"Well, what about Belfold? Why don't you just lock him and all his friends up? I mean, given everything you've said, they're all traitors."

"If only I could, Jethro. You call them traitors, but they no doubt see themselves as patriots and would use all their considerable influence, as well as the full panoply of the Law, to defend their position. The fact of the matter is, MI5 doesn't have any powers of arrest, and even though Special Branch does, they can't go and arrest half of the country. But I do have some inkling of how I might yet bring Belfold and his friends to book."

I swallowed. "Yes, but if he's so powerful and well connected, I don't see what part I can possibly play in all this. I'm just a humble London cat burglar and scene shifter, or have you forgotten?"

"No, Jethro, I haven't forgotten. Nor have I forgotten my earlier attempts to coerce you. But, as I said, there's no one else I can trust. And as you've so ably demonstrated in the past, you're at your very best when fighting to protect family or friend, or a cause you truly believe in."

I nodded. Well, it was true. They're the only things ever worth fighting for. He favoured me with a smile. At least, I think it was a smile.

"If you do come and help me defend the Realm, Jethro, and the mission proves successful, I give you my word, I will destroy the file I have on you, and leave you free to go about your business."

Surprisingly, he didn't add, if I was still alive afterwards, which was an encouraging sign. The funny thing was, I believed he'd follow through on his promise. So I told him, straight out, he had a deal. Then, as if the two of them had planned it down to the minute, Simon Bosanquet appeared at the Birdcage Walk end of the bridge, and came up to us in that tentative way tourists do when enquiring something of the natives. He waved his guidebook at the Park, and said he hadn't seen anybody following us. Then Walsingham got into the act and turned to me as if he was asking me something. But what he said was, "Simon is going to use his society connections to get you invited for the weekend, to a country house where the NOB elite and others will soon be gathering. And while you're there, if you can possibly find time to tear yourself away from all the usual goings-on, I want you to rob the place blind for me."

I blinked and looked out over the lake and saw something floating in the water. I hoped it wasn't a dead duck or another dead body, as that would've really been a bad sign. But it turned out to be just another piece of discarded litter. I didn't point it out to Walsingham, though; he had enough worries to be going on with. Then so did I, because it started to spit and then to rain, and before long it was bucketing it down. And by my reckoning there was only the one umbrella between the three of us.

CHAPTER
22

A Cut Above, A Cut Below

It wasn't only the Royals that didn't want the applecart upset; Walsingham didn't want the boat rocked, either. The ship of state had to be seen to be sailing on, calm and serene and unperturbed. After all, this was Great Britain. And as with the practice of stopping for afternoon tea, even if there was a war on, there were rules masquerading as niceties that needed to be observed. So there would be no mass arrest of the country's wayward elite; no Army standing at the doors of Parliament; no Police Commissioner, reading the Riot Act in Trafalgar Square; everything had to appear as normal. But I knew just how much toil, tears, and sweat went into producing even the most ordinary of drawing-room sets before it could pass for real on the stage.

Based on all he'd learned from his "man on the inside,"

before the poor sod went and got himself topped, Walsingham was now pretty certain that most or all of the Keys to the Kingdom would be found in a certain manor-house in Bedfordshire. The place was called Vashfield Hall and was the home of a certain upper-crust family who'd long been known for their dabblings in things political. By which, Walsingham explained, he meant hundreds of years of behind-the-scenes string-pulling; not simply their involvement in the political ferment that'd bubbled up between the two World Wars. Lord Belfold had been a guest at the Hall the night I'd burgled his place in Berkeley Square. And the NOB rank and file had gathered in its grounds the weekend I'd burgled their headquarters.

As with any top-class creep, it was the date of an upcoming posh do that'd determined the actual timing of the caper. In this case, a special May Day's banquet being held in honour of none other than Sir Oswald Mosley. All of the extreme right-wing elite was expected to be in attendance and if Bosanquet could pull enough societal strings, I would, too. But instead of me just swanning around in a dinner jacket, my job was to locate whatever Keys to the Kingdom were on the premises; red books, blue photos, documents relating to the Windsors; and spirit them away. After which, so that the burglary didn't appear to be politically motivated, I was supposed to lift any jewellery that'd caught my eye.

Don't laugh, but the crux of the plan called for me to pass myself off as someone of breeding and education, with wealth and connections enough to make me of interest to NOB. But, as Walsingham had pointed out with his usual aplomb, I might well be able to get away with it for an hour or so, but to have any real chance of pulling off such a deception for an entire weekend, I should perhaps consider polishing up my "gentlemanly demeanour." And, I mean, coming from him—Eton, Balliol, the Guards, and Whites—who was I to argue? Even I'd read enough Buchan and Sapper to appreciate that you needed the cloak of being a gentleman to step into the ungentlemanly world of dirty tricks.

It was Simon Bosanquet who came up with the idea I should play a Canadian, the scion of a wealthy family of Scottish ancestry with vast timber and mine holdings. "Your success in your guise as a Canadian businessman gave us the idea," he said. "It'll be that much easier for you to stay in character." So, while Walsingham called on what resources were still available to him to build a suitable background cover story for me, Simon was charged with looking after the cut of my jib, my clothes, and my shoes. And on the following Monday morning, he took me first to Savile Row and then on to Jermyn Street, where in short order he introduced me to his tailor, his bootmakers, his shirt-maker, and the people from whom he purchased his hats. I was, he explained, a distant cousin, which was enough it seemed to open all doors and clear all appointment books. I didn't have the heart to tell him I already had a good few of the necessary items in the moth-proofed props cupboards back at the lock-up, but I did get a good brush up on the finer points of an upper-class gentleman's wardrobe. Other than the hats and the shirts, though, it was more a question of time, than a matter of taste. There were some things, it seems, that couldn't be rushed, even with the requisite number of clothing coupons and a wad of Government cash. That's when I finally told him I had one or two resources of my own, and all he needed do was give me a list of what I should have packed for the weekend, and I'd see to it myself. He raised an eyebrow, but handed me a buff envelope stuffed with used fivers, and a half a dozen books of clothing coupons.

"The money's from the department's Irregular Activities

fund," he said. "Given what's at stake, Colonel Walsingham thinks no expense should be spared; everything has to be one hundred per cent pukka. None of the serial numbers can be traced back to any bank or account."

I nodded. What else could I do? If the Government were paying to put on a first-class production, I'd be a brassbound fool not to play along and get myself some nice threads out of it. I asked Simon if I could borrow the same two elegantly-battered leather suitcases he'd lent me on the Embassy caper; the ones covered with luggage labels from the world's finest hotels and ocean liners. I knew most of them from my time with Cunard-White Star Line and thought they'd add a nice touch. "No problem," he said. I could have them just as soon as another one of Walsingham's "gifted irregulars" had finished fitting them with false bottoms.

"Don't tell me," I said. "Big enough for a couple of red books about the size of a ledger?" He smiled a conspiratorial smile. I shook my head. "It could be risky. Once things go missing, the very first thing our hosts will do is search everyone's luggage, so you're going to need a Plan B." I suggested that his motor car get the same treatment as his suitcases. I told him I'd fitted secret compartments in all my motors, and I'd do the same for him if he came up with a suitably-equipped garage workshop, about twelve-square feet of eighth-inch steel plate, and an oxyacetylene bottle and torch. Again, I didn't let on that I had all the necessary in my lock-up, down Paddington Basin. We might be starting to dress alike, but I didn't know him anywhere near well enough to start letting him in on everything.

He then insisted on taking me to a little, out-of-the-way place on Sackville Street. And we each had a pork-pie, some cheddar cheese, a stick of celery, and a glass of sherry. Then we shook hands, and I took my leave and walked off into Soho. If I was going to be putting my best foot forward to help defend the Realm, I already had all the proper boots and shoes, but Savile Row or no Savile Row, I needed the best tailor money could buy.

Solly was Morrie Templeton's brother, the genius who made my turtles. Gloves, shoes, anything in leather, Morrie was an artist, and in a pinch even the head of the workshop at Lobb's—cobblers to royalty and American film-stars—would call him in. But Sol was in a league of his own. His was the secret hand behind many of the best names on Savile Row, and even the most fastidious cutters who worked there would hold up tailor's shears in admiration and respect if ever he stopped by. And if there ever was a master tailor's master tailor in London, it was Sol. Ray had introduced us when I first started setting up capers where my clothes needed to speak silent volumes. For as any gentleman or rogue will tell you, there's nothing better for opening the right doors than the right clothes. Sol had come up trumps for me then; I hoped he would again.

The brothers had adjoining workshops in Broadwick Street; the Berwick Street end. Up two flights of stairs from the street, there were three small rooms that acted as joint reception, office, and fitting room, with the warren of workshops tucked away at the back and on the next floor. There was always a strong hint of steam and singed canvas in the air, but the smell of lavender polish and fresh flowers from the market always made it very pleasant. For me, the best part of any visit was when Sol took me into his inner sanctum for a glass of sherry. Two entire walls were covered in shelves holding bolts of cloth. The crown jewels, Sol called them. And the rumour was; just as the King had done with his treasures during the War; Sol had had everything carefully packed away and stored up North somewhere. Sol waved me to a chair. "Always pleasure to see friend of Mr. Karmin." He raised his glass in salute. "So, for what can I be of assistance, a nice suit perhaps?" I nodded and gave him a list of what I needed and by when. He rocked his head from side to side in slow equivocation. "What am I, a craftsman or a cook? You want to make a meal, try Goody's."

I laughed. The oldest kosher restaurant in England was just down the street, and I knew he had a favourite table there. "Better a good friend than just a friend," I said, smiling and pulled out the envelope and counted out twenty white five-pound notes and more than the required number of clothing coupons. "A little on top for your trouble." Thirty guineas was the going rate for a suit on Savile Row, but that wasn't anything like what Sol and his staff were paid for their work. He beamed. "For you, express is pleasure." Then he pulled a tape measure from his waistcoat pocket, and called for his assistant and got to work, checking to see if I'd lost or gained any inches, anywhere. Then my measurements were written into a black book about the size of a desk ledger. Funny thing, I couldn't help but see its similarity to the Red Books; so much riding on a colour, so many intimate details hidden between its covers.

I slipped into Moroni's for a midday *Evening Standard,* stopped in next door to Patisserie Valerie for a cup of coffee, then strolled in the direction of Shaftesbury Avenue. I know they say a change is as good as a rest, but I'd found I'd really missed the theatres. All the pettiness and vicious back-stage back-stabbing seemed like so much childish banter, given what I'd been hearing went on behind the curtains down Whitehall and the Palace. And I started down towards the Circus, and stopped outside the Lyric.

It being a Monday, everything but the box office was

closed. So I stared at the photographs of the current production they had up outside. Another drawing-room drama, starring . . . My mouth went dry, as my legs turned to water. There she was: the porcelain-skinned, dark-haired English beauty that could've been Vivien Leigh's sister; smiling at the world, so very sweetly, with a mouth that could've roasted horse chestnuts. But some pictures can be so deceiving, for I knew it for what it really was, the cruellest mouth in London theatreland. The previous year I'd done a stint backstage at His Majesty's, another Terence Rattigan play, and had fallen in love with the leading actress's portrayal of the title character. I'd been told she was a bit of a flirt, but the lady she was playing was so sweet, so tender, yet so alluring, she was spellbinding. And when several times during rehearsals she'd stopped and fluttered her eyes at me and said how charming I was, I'd fallen like a ton of bricks. But it was all just an act; just more playing of the part she was playing. And when a little later I'd approached her, flowers in hand, at a cast party that one of the young actors had invited me to, she'd cut me dead. "Go away you pathetic person, I never fraternise with the hired help." Then she'd laughed her tinkly laugh, and thrown her glass of wine over both me and the flowers.

Well, quick as a flash, I started picking and eating the petals from off the stems and saying to anyone who'd listen that I thought the bouquet was rather good. I'd seen Charlie Chaplin do much the same in any number of his films, and if ever a way of picking yourself back up off the floor was worth stealing, that was. Anyway, my remark set my young actor friend off laughing like a hyena with hiccups and the incident was soon forgotten. It must've stuck with me, though. And a lot of it, I suppose, could be put down to the posh-looking Yank the actress had made a big point of draping herself over for the rest of the evening. A real charmer and debonair ladies' man that flashed his perfect white teeth at the drop of a hat or a handkerchief and laughed loudly at anything said by anyone remotely important. He was some sort of diplomat, apparently, the flash bastard; I could've happily smashed his face in, he was so very smug about everything. Then you know how it is; it's like a word you've never heard before, that once you become aware of it, you seem to hear everywhere. Well, after that first night, I couldn't turn round in the West End or Soho without him being there; across the street; coming out of a theatre, restaurant or hotel bar; going into some posh shopping arcade or store. And each time, if not with her, then with some smashing piece of upper-crust crumpet on his arm. Maybe he was two-timing the actress, I don't know, but if he was, he was having a whale of a time doing it. And not that I was jealous or anything; but there are limits. "What the bloody hell's he got, that I haven't?" I remember saying to myself. "Damn Yanks; over-sexed, over-paid, and still over here."

I sneered at all the photographs of "the actress" that lined the walls of the box office, then tore my eyes away. But who was I kidding? For, as well you know, beauty provoketh thieves even more than gold. I lit a cigarette, took a long drag, then threw the bloody thing into the gutter; it tasted sour and me along with it. And hands stuffed deep in my pockets, I walked down to Piccadilly Circus tube station and took the first Bakerloo Line train back home to Edgware Road.

CHAPTER

23

Smoke and Mirrors

It never rains but it pours, and it was fair chucking it down when I got out at Edgware Road. And I trudged up the street and through the puddles, and by the time I got to Church Street I felt like I could murder a cup of tea. It wasn't far off closing time when I pushed open the door and set the brass bell ringing at the Victory cafe. But the girl behind the counter, the new one that'd taken over Vi's old job, looked up and smiled the biggest smile I'd seen all day, and that did wonders to break the cloud hanging over me.

She was a big girl, in every way, but pleasant looking, with blonde hair, rosy red cheeks, and dimples. I could see why Joanie had hired her. Vi had left a big hole to fill and this girl couldn't have been more different. But where Vi had had a mouth like a fishwife, this one just giggled. I wondered how long it'd be before one of the "Jack-the-lads" in the market reduced her to tears. I made a mental note to put the word round that I'd thump the living daylights out of the first one that did her wrong.

"Cup of tea please, love. I'm Jethro, by the way."

"I know," she said, "I saw you last Saturday morning. There's four messages. Mrs. Mac, the cleaning lady, was in and your shirts and vests have all been ironed. Your friend Seth called; said he's fine. The gentleman you play chess with called and said he's going to be at the V and A, instead. And Mr. and Mrs. Aitch are off down the pictures. And here's your tea."

"Thank you," I said, a bit taken aback. "What's your name, then?"

"Mary," she said. "I'm Pauline's cousin on her dad's side; my dad is her dad's brother. Pauline put in a good word for me, with Mrs. Aitch."

Pauline had been at the Victory since the day it'd opened, and she didn't put up with nonsense from anyone, which I could now see ran in the family. I knew then, it'd be the blokes in the market that'd have to watch out, not little Mary. I'd still put the word round, though; some men can't ever resist a challenge where women are concerned. Pathetic, really.

The Victoria & Albert pub wasn't that far from Church Street, but as it was part of Marylebone railway station, you never got too many locals going in. People used it more for a quick one, before the train ride home. We used the larger of the two bars, as Ray said, with all its dark panelling, fancy wallpaper, huge gold plate-glass mirrors, and marble fireplaces, the V&A felt more like the reading room of a gentlemen's club than a station bar and buffet. So we always dressed accordingly, as if we were spending time before catching the 7:20 or 8:10 back home to the lady wife. I had on the same hat and dark blue, chalk stripe I'd worn to meet Walsingham; Ray arrived in a Homburg hat, nice grey suit, and a raincoat. He didn't look at all like Buggy Billy, which was just as well; they'd have thrown him out otherwise.

"Fancy bumping into you, Mr. Karmin," I said. "Do let me get them in." And I returned with a Bells and a half-pint of India pale ale.

He looked at the double measure, then stared at the IPA. "I see the Government's still watering it down." He took a sip of whisky, followed it with the chaser and gave me the bent eye. "Okay, sunshine, what happened? Did you get your hands on that master list, or what?"

I shook my head and took him from the break-in on the Friday night, to my meeting on the Saturday morning with Walsingham in St. James's Park. I told him about the Duke of Windsor's many betrayals; how the Government and the Royals had covered it all up; and how the Duke's missing letters could blow the lid off everything. I touched upon the secret vetting of civil servants and what'd led Walsingham to Lord Belford and the house on Berkeley Square. And how the Communists seemed to be mixed up with the deaths of an under-butler from the Palace and a senior civil servant. He stopped me, to get another round in, which was a sure sign he was thinking. Then armed with another beer and a chaser, I told him about the Keys to the Kingdom and how NOB was going to try and engineer a crisis in the country, then use the dirty photos to blackmail VIPs into supporting their coup. I downed what was left of my whisky. "I tell you, Ray, it bloody amazes me how amazed I can still be. I feel like a bloody schoolboy. I mean, it all starts with orgies and blackmail, then quickly ends up in treachery and murder. And for the life of me, I can't understand why the

Duke of Windsor did what he did. It beggars belief."

Ray rubbed his chin. "People don't only suffer austerity on the outside, you know, Jethro," he said, quietly. "Why do you think it is people love going to the pictures or go boggle-eyed over film stars? Or why it is they love reading racy novels or detectives stories? People are desperate to have their imaginations tickled and their emotions enflamed, and for most, that's all there is to it. But some will go to any lengths to achieve satisfaction. And never more so, now we've all survived the War. You tempt people who have the means, with whatever they think is expressly forbidden them, like those orgies, for instance, and they'll not only go potty, they'll quickly go blind to any consequences."

"No wonder they say ignorance is bliss," I mumbled into my glass.

"Not in this case, it isn't, Jethro, because the whole business with the Duke of Windsor points to it being something else, entirely; something that makes his catalogue of betrayals seem almost inevitable." His voice dropped, I leaned in towards him. "And if I'm right, Jethro, then you're talking about the people who really run this country. And if you're about to go up against them, then God help you."

I looked at him, daft. "Are you talking about that triangle of power you once told me about; the City, Whitehall, and the House of Lords; the one I said must be located somewhere near Cleopatra's Needle?"

"The very same," he said. "Ever since those twenty-five barons made King John sign the Magna Carta, back in 1215, power has always been in the hands of those same, few, titled families that have owned the vast majority of the land. It's little changed, today, from when it was a feudal system."

Here we go again, I said to myself, more history. I waggled

my empty whisky glass, got in two more Bells and two more half-pints of IPA. "Okay, Ray," I said, "but I still don't see how all this nonsense with NOB and Fascism can stem from a bunch of barons having held on to all the land since the days of Robin Hood and his Merry Men," I said, shaking my head.

"I know you don't," he said, glancing at me as he trickled water into his whisky. "The last thing to ever know it's a gold-fish in water, is a goldfish in water." He held up his glass, in salute. "You're subject to it all, me old cock. You can't see it, for looking. Cheers."

"Charming," I said, swirling the whisky around in my glass. "But you just can't put all our history down to the luck of the blanket, surely?"

"I can and I do, Jethro. Just take a look at the society that's evolved in England. It's been fixed so the people that have always had continue to hold onto it for themselves and their descendants. Nothing's ever allowed to threaten or to take away the aristocracy's continuing possession of the land itself; it's the very substance of their lives. That's the foundation stone of what you think of as democracy, and, incidentally, why the upper classes hate the very idea of Communism with such a passion and why so many of them were only too eager to embrace the ideals of Fascism. With Edward VIII on the throne, they believed they'd come through it all, with all or most of their property secure and intact. It's never really been anything to do with ideology or politics; it's whatever will guarantee the con-tinuance and survival of the families at the core of British socie-ty. It's conservatism and pragmatism, rather than Fascism or Communism, or any other kind of 'ism' that they look to give support to, nothing else."

I lit a cigarette and took a long, slow drag, and blew the smoke out in a long, blue stream. I watched the smoke rise up into the air and saw it reflected in one of the huge mirrors on the wall. I coughed, and reached for the chaser. "Roll on the revolution," I muttered into my beer; draining it.

Ray sighed, wistfully. "Look, I love England. I chose Great Britain, the United Kingdom or whatever you want to call it, as my home. I'm one of thousands of people that came here to escape persecution, in search of a better life. And as long as I don't set out to challenge the accepted order of things and keep the peace, no one ever bothers me, I'm free to go about my business. That's freedom enough for most people, given the alternatives. Just because I know the truth of it, doesn't mean I go around worrying about it. God's Holy Trousers, Jethro, there's a thousand and one things I could start a revolution over, if I had a mind to. But I don't. For me, knowing it, is enough. I look behind the curtain and I see things that others don't; that's why I study history and study the Mysteries. There are people out there that know things, but they don't tell you. But I can, and I do. My quest in life is to stick my nose in until I find the truth of something, then quietly slide it back out again." He paused. "I told you about *Cabal,* Jethro, because *Cabal* asked for your help. But what if I was to tell you there exists a secret council that steers the destiny of these islands; a council elected exclusively from the descendants of those same twenty-five barons of Magna Carta; the Duke of this, the Earl of that, the Marquis of such and such. Its members hidden behind the very flags and banners, insignia and coats of arms that everyone else salutes, and hidden behind all the laws of the land, too, seeing as most of them are based on laws of possession. Because, if it's them you're going up against, then even I fear for you. They've been masters of this 'promised land' of theirs for over seven hundred years. They've had a lot of practice defending it and dying for it, too, if they must." He cleared his throat. "And killing for it, if necessary."

"A secret council that's got the whole country by the short and curlies?" I said. "And no one knows anything about it? I should cocoa."

"But that's it, only a very few people ever do come to know about it. The secret council is clothed in the very fabric of English history, and so is rendered invisible. But it's always been there, in the background, and even those nominally in charge of the country feel the strings on them, and wonder just who it is that's doing all the pulling."

I honestly didn't dare ask him how he'd come to know all this stuff. And I sat there, staring off into space. "What is it they say, about possession being nine-tenths of the law?" I said, my voice trailing off.

"Yes, well it's nine-tenths of your history, Jethro, that's for sure."

"Check-fucking-mate-and-match, right from the very start," I said, feeling angry and upset, but with what or whom, I couldn't really say.

"Here, I didn't come here to get into all this," he said. "Life's far too short, as it is. Drink up. Let me buy you dinner at that little French restaurant, round the back of Selfridges. Only, I've got a feeling you're going to need a good nosh to get you through what's ahead."

"Very kind of you," I said, draining my whisky. Then, as we were putting our hats and coats on, he turned and said, "A word to the wise, sunshine, given Mr. W's plan that you pass yourself off as some sort of gentleman. Just remember that the English aristocracy, having no reality of their own, use 'style' and all its accompanying tiny details to destroy everyone else's. So, always act as if you don't need a bloody thing from them, not even their approval; they'll respect you all the more, then."

"Yes, Professor Higgins," I said.

He gave me the bent eye. "Alright, George Bernard Shaw, but you're the one playing Pygmalion, not me. And another thing, while we're at it, I got a call to ready myself for a meeting of *Cabal,* later this evening, which is why the bespoke whistle and flute." He brushed a handful of fingertips across a lapel. "But even more than that, me old china, I was told you'd be definitely putting in an appearance."

That was news to me, of course, but then wasn't everything?

The taxi dropped Ray off at his house and me near the lock-up. I changed into a tweed jacket and flannels, and began walking home, fully expecting to run into Spottsy's big black motor car somewhere along the way. They were waiting for me up by the Edgware Road. Then it was much the same as before; the same black blindfold; same smoke-filled room, same secret East End synagogue; the same Mr. Joseph Zaretsky and *Cabal.*

I told them I hadn't found anything remotely resembling a master list of extremist right-wing groups, which was true, and I was very sorry I hadn't been able to do more. And Mr. Zaretsky nodded. Then he totally floored me. He said *Cabal* had learned that not only was there a carbon copy of the master list, but there were also carbon copies of all the documents reputed to contain information of such importance they were said to be the keys to NOB's power and influence. And that as these special keys or their copies were bound to come to light, sooner or later, would I be so good as to continue to try and secure one of them for *Cabal.*

I just sat there with a stupefied grin on my face. And all I could think about was how in hell he'd come to know so much about the Red Books or indeed that they were referred to as the Keys to the Kingdom. And I wondered if Walsingham even knew about there being duplicate copies of everything. So, I nodded and said I'd do my best. What else could I do? Then, still lost in thought, I reached for a cigarette, thumbed the Zippo, and took a long, slow drag. And after a bit, Spottsy had me driven home again. This time he offered me a swig of single malt. My reward for having given the right answer again. I don't remember much else. I'm sure I must've dozed off at least a dozen times behind that bloody blindfold of theirs.

CHAPTER

24

Hard Acts to Follow

If you think about it, life's just one long parade of faces flashing by in front of you, and depending on what you're met with, do you have a good day or a bad day. That Thursday was both good and bad, and seemed to go on forever. But in a week full of long days, I hardly noticed at the time.

Things went non-stop after that second meeting with *Cabal*. I spent the next couple of days fitting a hidden compartment into Bosanquet's motor car; something called a Bristol 400; a beautiful, handmade job with a big, throaty six-cylinder engine. He told me it was based on a German BMW model, from before the War, but the engine and the designs had been appropriated by a British company as part of war reparations, and they were assembling them out at Bristol Airfield. It was a lovely-looking motor car, long-nosed and sleek, and it gave the impression that if ever pushed to its top speed it would take off and fly. All it needed was a couple of canons mounted along the bonnet, and you'd be well away. Anyway, when I'd finished the job, Simon Bosanquet was well pleased, and was like a kid with a new toy when I gave him the barrel key to the hidden compartment nestled between the boot and the rear seats.

Thursday found me back in the West End, on my way to Sol's for my first fitting. I was well dressed, but nothing too flash; I wasn't in character yet, even though the moustache I'd started growing was coming on nicely. I took a bus down to Marble Arch, hopped another one to go along Oxford Street, then changed my mind and got off at the top of Bond Street. It was a pleasant morning, there was no sign of rain, there were pretty girls out and about, and as I had time, I fancied a walk. So I made my way down towards Burlington Arcade and along the way admired a few paintings in a few art gallery windows and priced the larger stones on display at Asprey's and other fine jewellers' shops. I crossed the street and ambled through the Arcade, making sure not to run or whistle, so as not to catch the eye or ear of the uniformed beadles on duty. Then I headed down Piccadilly in the direction of Sackville Street, so I could go up the Row to Regent Street, then cross over into Soho.

I turned into Savile Row and froze. The "actress's" posh Yank boyfriend was just paying off a cab, before venturing into one of the Row's many tailoring establishments. I looked away as if I'd got a piece of soot in my eye, and waited for him to be gone. The flash bastard looked as if he'd stepped out of one of those gin advertisements you always see in *Life* magazine. It was amazing how very English some Yanks always looked; always so very poised and polished. He fair made me want to spit, but I held off. And I'd just about reached the end of the Row, having stared, unseeing, at the endless parade of tailors' dummies in all the window displays, when a police Railton slid past and stopped dead in a squeal of tyres. Obviously my suit, that day, wasn't up to snuff. I stood stock-still. I had nothing to hide, nothing incriminating on me, and no earthly idea why I was about to get my collar felt. The other thing was there was a large man breathing down my neck that looked just like a plainclothes detective. And he must've been following me on foot, for some distance, because he had his hat and coat on. Then he surprised me a second time, because he stepped around me, opened the rear door of the Railton, took off his hat and swept it in front of him in mute invitation for me to get in. Very funny, I thought, but I got in the drag, anyway.

And there, almost taking up the entire back seat, was Detective Chief Inspector Robert Browno of Scotland Yard's Flying Squad. I smelled, rather than saw, why he hadn't got out to collar me himself; he was in the middle of eating a huge sausage sandwich. Browno made a grunting noise and the detective sergeant slid into the front and the police driver slipped into first gear and accelerated out into traffic. I just stared in fascination at the thing Browno was eating: the tomato sauce and fried onions made it look like so much pulped flesh; it put me off meat for weeks. And I sat there, as still as a mouse in a trap; trying to ignore the sticky, wet sounds he made as he champed down on what could so very easily have been the remains of whoever he'd just interrogated.

There were very few men guaranteed to put the shits up London's criminal fraternity. Messima was one; Jack Spot and Billy Hill, two others; there were a couple of coppers down the Yard, like Bob Fabian and John du Rose. All hard men, at the top of their trades, and with reputations that went before them into every pub, club, spieler, or cop shop in the Smoke, and the one thing you noticed about them all was that not one of them ever had to raise his voice. But Browno made the lot of them, even Billy Hill, seem like wind-blown foghorns. The awful sound he made grinding his teeth was enough to impress most people. So I stayed stumm. A still tongue helped keep your head on your shoulders where he was concerned.

"I thought it was you, toe-rag; poncing up and down, like King Dick. We've been eyeing you, ever since Bond Street. Setting one up are you, scumbag? Well, don't you even think about it, you flash git, or I'll have your guts for breakfast, dinner, and tea."

It was awful, his voice was no louder than the sound of a razor being honed on a strap and I had to lean in to hear him. And as he licked his fingers clean, I just stared at him, mesmerised. After about a hundred years or so, sounds came out of my throat that might've been words. "I was just taking a stroll, before going round a few stage doors to see about picking some work up, Mr. Browno. That's all."

"Don't come it with me, smart arse. I may have been away up North these last few months, but I'm not fucking daft. Or blind. And I very definitely didn't like seeing you eyeing all those jewellery shops. Gave me fucking heartburn, it did. So, you just count yourself bloody lucky the Yard says there's still a fucking red card on you, and you're to be left alone. But I know you're up to something and I don't mean you shifting scenery around in some poxy theatre, neither. Your arse needs locking up for twenty years. So be warned you. Now just fuck off out of it."

He grunted again and the driver pulled into the kerb. There was a screech of tyres behind us, and a taxi angrily hooted its horn, but no one in the Railton paid it any mind. The detective sergeant got out, opened my door and let me out, and without a word, slid into the seat I'd just vacated. Then the Railton roared off into the traffic. The whole episode couldn't have taken more than a couple of minutes. And I looked around me, feeling dizzy from lack of food, probably. Then I laughed. Partly out of relief, but mostly because they'd dropped me not twenty yards from Sol's workshop. And it looked as if it was about coming on to rain.

I didn't mention it to Sol. He didn't like coppers in plain clothes; they reminded him too much of secret policemen back in Russia. And he quietly got on with the business of seeing whether I'd changed enough in a week to put his cutting pattern out of true. But even for a first fitting, everything looked and fitted beautifully, and if it wasn't for all the tailors' thread, canvas and horsehair, I'd have taken every piece, there and then; it all felt so natural on. "Magic, as always, Sol, you're a bloody wonder."

"Is good you appreciate good work; this means, is not waste of time and good cloth. You want a second glass of sherry, maybe?"

I left Sol's to find Soho smelling as clean as ever it can after a shower, and I nipped down to Patisserie Valerie's for a cup of coffee and a slice of cake. I'd been in enough, recently, to earn a flicker of recognition from the waitress, and I'd just ordered when two faces walked in and sat near the window. I'd last seen them that first night in The George, in Slough; Tweedle-dum and Tweedle-dee; Darby Messima's top bagmen, which meant they carried money, threats, or retribution; whatever was called for. The word around Soho was they'd use a cosh or a razor at the drop of a hat, and choppers or shooters if they had to. I wondered if perhaps they'd been following me, but they didn't seem to pay me any mind, and as they didn't ask to borrow the sugar or to lick their boots or anything, I quietly got on with perusing my *Evening Standard,* midday edition.

It said on the front page that due to huge public demand, Danny Kaye was returning to the London Palladium. And I thought back to when I'd seen him perform there, on his first visit to England, some two months before. I'd just begun to feel more like my old self again, after all my time in hospital, and I thought it'd make a swell night out for my girlfriend Natalie and me. Danny Kaye had been sensational and had had everyone eating out of his hand with his new-style act. He was a brilliant singer, dancer, mimic, and comedian, and his crazy antics could have you clutching your sides one minute and crying your eyes out the next, amazing to watch he was. He made all the other acts; the dancing horses, the whirlwind roller-skaters, the old-time comic; look very tired and old-fashioned. At one point, he sat down by the footlights at the edge of the stage, asked for a cigarette, and just chatted away to the audience and made the Palladium seem as intimate as a supper club. And we'd all just sat there spell-bound. Nobody had ever seen anything like it.

I had another reason to remember that Saturday night at the Palladium. A nasty thick fog had settled over London, and once I'd got Natalie back to her flat, she'd insisted I stay with her rather than get lost or catch my death or anything. I'd have been a right mug to argue with that. So, I stayed right through to the Monday morning, then popped back into Soho for a late breakfast. And it was right after that, that Bosanquet had come up to me on Old Compton Street, and asked if I'd mind, awfully, taking a little ride. And I'd finished the morning sitting in an office high above Regent Street, on the other side of a table from Walsingham.

It's funny, isn't it, how your life goes in circles, and some days you see it so very clearly and other days you don't. And I finished up my coffee, slipped a tanner tip under the saucer, and stepped out into Old Compton Street, ready to take on the world. And I'd just stopped to look in the windows at Danny's, the outfitters, across the street, when I heard a taxi screech to a stop outside Wheelers. I turned and gave it a quick butcher's, and the passenger door opened and a peel of tinkly laughter emerged, along with a pair of high heels and never-ending legs. I was just about to really give it the eye, when I heard a man's voice ask the cabbie, "What's on the meter, my good man?" And my blood went as cold as yesterday's coffee, and I pulled down the brim of my hat and stared, fixedly, at the shop window. It was the actress that'd snubbed me, and her pain-in-the-arse Yank boyfriend, again; both of them, no doubt, in for a quick glass of wine and a plate of oysters before her matinee performance at the Lyric Theatre around the corner. Seeing the two of them, like that, narked me no end; and I thought, Blow this for a lark; and I marched off down Shaftesbury Avenue to Piccadilly Circus, and took the Bakerloo Line back home to Edgware Road. Some days, though, I tell you, it's as if I'm forever stuck, going round and round on the Circle Line.

God is in the Boodles

I told Joanie and Bubs as much of the truth as I dared, then quietly put the word round Church Street that I was disappearing up North for a few weeks, to help out an old china I'd known on the boats. Ray had me write out a stack of postcards with messages like "Wish you were here" and "Weather awful; food awful; reminds me of home," which he'd have posted for me, from places like Scarborough and Harrogate. "It's always best to give people something to chew on," he said, "they'll swallow anything, then. But just you go careful. And Walsingham or no Walsingham, make sure you don't get dropped in the cart." And I'd nodded and told him to keep his chess-board set up. Then I took my leave and made my way over to the lock-up. I changed into the appropriate clothes and slipped across to Paddington Station. I retrieved the two suitcases I'd left earlier at the Left-Luggage Office, took a taxi to Victoria Station and waited for the boat train to come in. Then I joined the crowd and took a cab into the West End.

I took a room at the Mayfair Hotel, under the name of Jeffrey Hannay, paid a month in advance, using a Canadian bank account set up for me by Walsingham. I was profuse with my thanks for the hotel having held all the cables and telexes that'd come in for me from Canada, and then even more profuse with tips for the staff. And by the following morning I was well on my way to being one of the Mayfair's favourite guests. After breakfast, I walked round to Trumpers, on Curzon Street, for a trim and a shave, then went back to the hotel. I decided on the dark-blue suit Sol had made for me and even if I say so myself I looked a million dollars. And with my handmade shoes polished to perfection and sporting the tie Walsingham had chosen for me, I had the Mayfair doorman hail a cab to take me to Boodles. The cabbie gave me a funny look; it was barely a two-block walk from the hotel. So I told him to go along Piccadilly, down Haymarket, and back round, via Pall Mall and St. James's Street, and he needn't bother taking the short cut down Duke Street, past Fortnum's. And he nodded, tipped his cap, and without any more ado, off we sped. I wasn't being flash; going the long way round gave me time to get into character.

I recognised the doorman, though he'd have a hard time placing me as the old cabbie he'd once threatened with bodily mischief. He opened the cab door with a "Good morning, sir," and I got out and paid the fare; feeling the doorman's eyes measuring me, as well as the size of the tip I gave the taxi-driver. I turned and glanced at the cream-coloured columns and bow-fronted window; it certainly was a nice-looking building, once you stopped to look at it. "Lunching with Colonel Walsingham," I said, airily. "Certainly, sir," he said. "Welcome to Boodles, sir. The Hall Porter will attend to you." Then he pulled open the front door to one of the most exclusive gentlemen's clubs, in all of St. James's. The Hall Porter greeted me, told me I was expected, and straightaway escorted me to the bar.

I looked about me; it was all very impressive, a world away from the hustle and bustle of the rest of London. And then there was Walsingham, looking as immaculate as ever, as if he'd stepped out of a Pont cartoon, and ever the professional, he slipped smoothly into the business at hand. "Ah, Jeffrey," he said, "so good of you to come. London must be a trifle warmer than Toronto, this time of year." He turned to the porter and said, "Thank you, Davy," and then addressed me, "A drink, for you?" And with that, I was launched, or should I say, lunched in London clubland.

The rule is, one never talks business. So I didn't have to go on and on about timber or mining or anything, but a word or two dropped here and there, would have me pegged by anyone who mattered, by the time we got to coffee and brandy. "The food, of course, is quite dreadful," Walsingham said jovially, "even worse than Brook's across the street, but rationing or no, I think Chef might manage something palatable. And the club does serve a very decent claret, so all is not lost."

But I wasn't there for the food or the wine; I was there to cast an eye over the manners and mannerisms of my supposed betters, and to be seen by one or two of the right sort of people. By which, Walsingham meant certain club members who leaned a little too far to the right and whose paths I might later cross. The other issue, of course, was whether or not I'd be exposed as an arrant fraud. And I asked Walsingham whether it'd give the game away, me being seen in his company. "No," he said, quietly. "People think I'm War Office, not Home Office, and so there's no reason for anyone to connect me with MI5. And, as for Simon, even though it's well known he's Scotland Yard, people assume, because of his title, that he's simply being groomed for senior administrative office."

"You mean our Mr. Bosanquet's got a title?" I said, surprised.

He nodded. "Hereditary baronetcy."

"Well, he's never tried lording it, or once mentioned it," I said.

"Nor would he," he said. "He only assumes the mantle of Sir Simon Bosanquet, Bart., when it affords him a degree of anonymity; mostly on those social occasions when people tend to look no further than his title."

"Blimey, a right Scarlet Pimpernel," I said, shaking my head.

"One reason I recruited him, Jeffrey. But do watch the accent; it was a little wobbly, just then." He cleared his throat and as if by magic drinks appeared on a silver tray. He nodded and waited for the waiter to depart. "And as to establishing your bona fides, I'm sure the cut of your suit and the stripe of your tie will have already been noted." He raised his glass.

I fingered the silk material. "But why the Highland Light Infantry?"

"It fits your cover. Given the casualties suffered in the War, a regimental tie gives far more room for manoeuvre than would a school or club tie." He glanced over my shoulder. "I've asked a couple of friends to join us; I'm sure you'll enjoy them. Take a little from each, and you'll have exactly the right touch of insouciance your new identity calls for."

"Who's coming," I said, "Cary Grant and Errol Flynn?"

"Hello, Bill," said a voice I instantly recognised, "I hope I'm not late. I do so hate to keep a good malt waiting." And I looked up, and you could've knocked me down with a feather.

"David, I'd like you to meet Jeffrey . . ."

"Hannay," I said, standing up and offering my hand, "Jeffrey Hannay. A pleasure to meet you, Mr. Niven. I'm a great fan of yours. *Prisoner of Zenda, Charge of the Light Brigade, Dawn Patrol, Raffles,* and, of course, *A Matter of Life and Death.*" It was funny, rattling off all his pictures like that; it was almost the story of my own life; but I could tell he was pleased I hadn't come on aloof or as if I was above that sort of thing. He sat down.

"How very kind, thank you. Some of the older members still can't resign themselves to having a film actor in the club; they think it upsets the natural order of things. Please, call me, David. Any friend of Bill's is a friend in disguise." He chuckled and touched his tie, a patterned affair that spoke of New York or Hollywood. "Canadian, are you? Only, I can't help but notice you're wearing the colours of my old regiment."

Walsingham steepled his fingers. "I suggested he wear it, David. Mr. Hannay, here, is about to play the phantom for me, and I thought the tie would be a useful touch."

Niven raised his eyebrows. "Something on, is it, Bill?"

Walsingham blinked, slowly. "A little subterfuge, a little playacting, but all in a worthy cause, David, I can assure you."

"Quite," Niven said, pulling at his earlobe. Then he turned and grinned at me. "Well, Mr. Jeffrey Hannay, being a Scot who's invariably taken for an Englishman, I'd say a Canadian Scot is entirely appropriate for the Highland Light Infantry. So, have at it, and with my blessings." The waiter appeared with his glass of single malt and Niven took it, and sniffed at it, approvingly. Then he looked abashed and adjusted his tie. "Gosh, Bill, it quite stirs the blood again, doesn't it? How exactly can I help?"

"You already are, David, just by being your usual charming self. I'm hoping some of the polish will rub off on Jeffrey here."

"Flattery from you Bill, that's a sure sign of impending

danger." He turned to me. "I've just popped over on the *Queen Mary* to reshoot some scenes for *Bonnie Prince Charlie,* for Korda. I look a right bloody Charlie in it, too; the blonde wig they have me wear is simply frightful. So if you take anything at all from me, Jeffrey Hannay, I'd suggest you steer well away from wearing a wig or the kilt; that'd immediately mark you out as a fraud." We all chuckled, but he'd come uncomfortably close to the truth, and I wondered if I had any chance at all of pulling off the deception. He pulled at his earlobe again. "Although, if I remember correctly, Bill, wasn't the Scarlet Pimpernel a member here, and all his gang, too?" Walsingham nodded. And Niven turned his head as if struck by a thought. "Oddly enough, Sam Goldwyn wants me to play the Pimpernel in a remake, when I get back." He made a show of looking around the room, then turned back to me. "On second thoughts, Jeffrey, maybe a periwig is called for, after all. I'll best leave it to you. Though, personally, I have to say, I can't stand bloody costume dramas myself."

I nodded. I knew exactly what he meant. But we all chuckled again, a merry band of conspirators, and I became as a sponge, and tried to soak up as much of David Niven's easygoing charm as I could, even while all the other eyes in the bar worked hard at ignoring us. Walsingham had given me a little set piece, to ask the steward; the sort of posturing you might expect of someone from the New World. I was to inquire about the quality of the meat and insist they not fob us off with horsemeat or anything. And then add, *sotto voce,* that if I had to pay black market prices to secure better cuts for the table, I'd see him and the chef were properly rewarded, afterwards. Of course, it wasn't done to talk of such matters, and not at all my place to discuss the bill, that was between the club and Walsingham. And the steward looked suitably askance at me, then at

Walsingham, who just happened to be locked in conversation with David Niven, so he nodded politely, even if a trifle stiffly, and took his leave. Walsingham knew it'd soon get round that I was what passed for a gentleman in Canada; someone rich enough to demand the best; and hang the rules. Tiny things, I know, but as Walsingham had explained, "Big oaks from little acorns grow." And I'd replied, "I hope so, I might need to hide myself up in its branches, before this is all over." And my little act with the steward all played out, I felt someone approaching, even as I saw Walsingham look over my shoulder.

"Hello, Ian, you know David, of course. May I introduce you to . . ."

He smiled at David Niven, but he'd already taken in my tie, the cut of my suit, shirt, and hair, as well as my gold Rolex, gold cigarette case and lighter, gold signet ring and cuff links. "Hannay, Jeffrey Hannay," I said, holding out my hand. "How do you do?"

"Fleming, Ian Fleming," he said, his voice as firm as his handshake.

"Drink, Ian?"

"Yes, thank you, Bill. But I only ever drink one thing before lunch, and that's a very large and very cold vodka martini; shaken not stirred."

We adjourned to the dining-room on the first floor. And so began a joyous lunch, with old stories recounted and banter thrown from all sides. I think I just about managed to hold my own, but in all my life I've heard no funnier raconteur than David Niven and no one better able to deliver a clever or cutting aside than Ian Fleming. And all the while, Walsingham quietly steered the proceedings like the masterful ringmaster he was; and me, I felt as comfortable as if I'd been down the Duke of York, raising the elbow with a bunch of old mates. And before

I knew it, it was time for coffee and liqueurs.

David Niven declined both; saying how delightful lunch had been, but, unfortunately, he had a meeting to go to in Soho Square. He glanced at me, a bashful look on his face, and pulled at his earlobe again and made me promise on pain of death never to go and see *Bonnie Prince Charlie*. And I said that wild horses wouldn't drag me there, and we shook hands. "Good luck, Jeffrey Hannay," he said. "Up the Highland Light Infantry." Then he said his goodbyes to the other two, and departed.

"A good man," said Walsingham, staring after him. "Don't let his easy-going manner fool you for a minute, he had an extremely interesting war." And he and Fleming exchanged glances and for the very briefest of seconds I felt like a true outsider, but it passed just as quickly, and as Walsingham turned to the wine steward, Fleming excused himself. And I sat back and took a moment to reflect on the man who was Ian Fleming.

He was older than I was, and handsome in a bland sort of way, in that he could stand out in a crowd just as easily as he could disappear into it. He had that effortless sort of assurance that spoke of a private income and a public school education. But he also sported a blue-spotted bow-tie, an ebonite cigarette holder, a gunmetal cigarette case and a black oxidised lighter that said he didn't give a fig about fitting into anybody else's idea of what was proper. As lunch had progressed, it'd become pretty obvious he was someone who followed his own tastes and amusements; and in that, I suppose, we were very similar. Most of the time he'd had a faint hint of a smile on his face that could've easily been read as supercilious had it not also looked so knowing. And I could see how his sardonic grin and wicked humour could easily be taken for arrogance and cynicism. It didn't bother me, though, I just took it as his way of testing people and gave as good as I got; which seemed to go over well. Another thing, he always seemed to be veiled in smoke, like a destroyer on convoy duty, and I put him at thirty or forty cigarettes a day, and not cheap ones, either, but Turkish and handmade. And I suppose that summed him up, really; he was as restless as blue smoke caught for a moment in a spotlight, before it drifted and disappeared from view. One thing he couldn't conceal, though, was his hunger for excitement, and I could see why Walsingham liked him; it could've been him, himself, ten or fifteen years earlier.

"I hope you found lunch helpful, Jeffrey," Walsingham said.

"More than helpful," I said. "And not just for picking up manners and mannerisms, or funny stories. It showed me that a lot of spying is simply acting the part. Having the right attitude; having confidence, even when confronted by someone who thinks they know better. Then it seems you can break almost any rule, as long as you show you know you're breaking it, but don't give a damn; then it seems you can get away with almost anything, probably even murder. It's just like the East End."

Walsingham gave me a look that was pure Ray Karmin. Then Ian Fleming plopped down in his chair, again, and the moment broke. "A wonderful lunch; delightful company, thank you, Bill," he said.

"My pleasure, Ian. Only, I was wondering if you'd mind helping my young Canadian friend, here, in the art of backgammon and other assorted skills. You see, he's about to go play at Red Indians, for me, and anything at all you can pass on, I'm sure, would add immeasurably to his success."

Fleming narrowed his eyes at Walsingham, then at me. "So the game's afoot, is it, Bill? I've often wondered how I could repay my debt to you." His face split into a devilish grin. "It'll be my pleasure, gentlemen. I'll take immediate leave of absence, and say I'm on special assignment." It was as if somebody had just let loose a dog of war. "It'll be a damn sight more exciting than bloody publishing; that's for sure. When do we start?"

CHAPTER

26

Train Hard, Fight Easy

Ian Fleming was no mug; I had ten years on him, if not more. And so it wasn't him that had me on the judo mat, it was a gristle-hard, ex-Marine sergeant, now employed as a PE instructor at a posh sporting club, out Richmond way. "Mr. Carter will take you through a few basic moves, Mr. Hannay," Fleming said, "and we'll see how we go from there." It was back to surnames, so right away I knew they meant business, and I wondered again why Walsingham had thought it necessary for me to be put through the ringer. The only answer I could come up with was he wanted to make sure I had my head on straight. I only hoped Mr. Carter had been instructed not to cripple me.

But I was determined to go through with it. After all, why not? I'd as much steal a skill, as an idea. And in that, it was no different from creeping or the theatre, rehearsal was the work, performance the enjoyment. Mr. Carter put it more bluntly. "Train hard, fight easy," he said, pulling me up off the floor for the umpteenth time. "Still a bit too much faffing about, in your attack, Mr. Hannay, sir, for my liking. So do please try and remember to keep it simple. Shins, groin, stomach, throat; that's always the ticket. If your attacker is bigger than you are; then fight defensively to tire the bastard out, before you move to incapacitate or move in for the kill. If he's a counter-puncher; then your only focus is to give the bastard back what he gives you, until such time as, again, you can move to incapacitate or kill."

The War would never end for some; for me it was enough to put someone down long enough to give me time to get away, but I didn't think it the right time to be arguing the niceties. We started with hands, fists, and feet, then moved on to weapons. "Now just try and stick me with your knife, if you would, please, Mr. Hannay, sir." So I tried and he took it away from me like I was a kid with an ice-cream cornet. "The cross block, Mr. Hannay. Use a two-handed cross block. Have both thumbs open and overlapping. Catch your attacker's arm as close to the hand as possible. Good. Keep hold of his forearm, twist your body away, and bring his arm down quickly to throw him off balance. Then hit the bastard in the face with your elbow. Good. That's it. Better yet, once you come in with the cross block, just knee the bastard hard in the testicles."

When it came to knife throwing and hitting a target with the point or the hilt, even Mr. Carter was impressed with what I could do. But he didn't give me time to gloat; he marched us straight into the indoor shooting gallery. He locked the door behind us, unlocked the gun safe, and handed Fleming and me a revolver each, as well as some earplugs. "About time you knocked off some of the rust, Mr. Fleming, sir. And you, Mr. Hannay, sir, let's see what you can do with a Colt .38 revolver." I raised my arm, sighted, and got three out of six on the paper target. "That's bloody awful, Mr. Hannay, sir," Mr. Carter said, wheeling the target back. "This isn't a fair ground, you know; the only prize here, is you not ending up dead before your time. Now try again, sir, and forget all the nonsense they teach officers in the Army, just do it by instinct." He handed me six more bullets and I reloaded. "Right, on your toes, bring the gun up to waist level, and as you step forward, point. Keep the elbow in; the left arm out for balance, if need be; now grip tight, and fire two." He had me do it again twice; and I got four on the target, and two cutting the edge of the paper. "The bastard's probably down, if not dead, but I need you to have tighter grouping, Mr. Hannay, sir. And now, you, Mr. Fleming, if you please."

He handed Ian Fleming six rounds, watched him break open the gun and load the empty chambers with a practised hand, then he nodded and stepped back. "Rapid fire, if you please, sir." Fleming went into a crouch and brought the gun up and fired off two rounds, three times, in quick succession. He did much better than I did, he got all six bang on the target; the first three in the outer ring, but with the last three shots all nicely grouped, left of centre of the middle ring. Mr. Carter, however, was not satisfied. "You've been polishing too many chairs with your arse for my liking, sir. That's terrible, that is. You used to be able to at least give me a run for my money back at Camp X." Then he loaded his Colt .38 and fired off three "double-taps" in about as many seconds.

From where we were standing the target looked like it hadn't been touched, but you knew by the almost matter-of-fact way Mr. Carter wound the target back that he'd shredded the centre ring. "All it comes down to is practice, gentlemen; that, and not having your weapon jam on you. Which is why I always recommend a revolver over an automatic pistol; but if you have no choice, then go with the Browning 9mm Hi-power, like this one here." And with that, we set about shredding more paper targets.

Ian Fleming's enthusiasm proved inexhaustible, and a few days quickly blurred into an entire week. He was every bit as much of a stickler for details as Walsingham; each tiny detail, he told me, was an important thread woven into the pattern of a cover story; and he had no argument from me on that. But it did make me wonder what kind of war he'd had. And my evenings turned out to be as jam-packed as my days, as each night, after taking dinner at a different restaurant, he attempted to polish up my gamesmanship. I'd thought that learning the finer points of backgammon would be a walk in the park. But he revealed it to be as bloody a field of combat as any you could imagine; the unskilled and unwary as hapless on their side of the board as if lost in some dark alley in Soho. "Attack, always attack," he said. "Apart from it being the best defence, it's always the best way of upsetting your opponent's game. Rattle them hard; redouble, regroup; then bear off with a will." He reached for his gunmetal cigarette case. "That's enough for tonight."

I toyed with the doubling cube and happened to glance at the date in the little window on my Rolex watch as it began to slide into tomorrow. "Today was St. George's Day," I said. "Funny, isn't it, him being the patron saint of England, and him not having a drop of English blood in him."

Fleming looked at me, oddly. "Have another glass of Tattinger. Then let's toast to St. George and the success of your coming mission."

"Thanks for all you've done, Ian," I said, smiling. "Truly. But if we toast anyone, tonight, let's make it to old Bill Shakespeare; April twenty-third is his birthday, too, you know."

He narrowed his eyes. "You know, Jeffrey Hannay, you're a damn funny sort, for a Canadian."

"Funny you should say that, Ian," I said. "That's exactly what Colonel Walsingham always says about me."

"You're a damn funny sort, Jethro," Walsingham said. "And, yes, as it happens, we are trying to find a beautiful woman for you."

I was sitting in a big leather armchair, sipping a large glass of sherry, in the big front room of the nice little house Simon Bosanquet had in a nice little tree-lined square off the King's Road, Chelsea; the Sloane Square end. Walsingham was already there, when I'd arrived by taxi; the two of them busy going over Ian Fleming's assessment of me. They both seemed pleased I'd passed all my tests, but they didn't show me the report. And I'd sat there, quietly sipping away, as the two of them had discussed some Wren officer who, it turned out, was on duty out in Hong Kong, and one of the secretaries over at the Registry, who apparently had just got married. Then the two of them had gone back and forth, dropping women's names like Ping-Pong balls at a bad table-tennis game, with me left sitting there, all but forgotten. It was only when I finally twigged it was all because Bosanquet had got me invited to a cocktail party at some posh publisher's, and that they thought a posh bit of skirt on my arm would make Jeffrey Hannay appear all the more convincing, that I spoke up. "Er, excuse me, you two, but I think I know someone that fits the bill perfectly." Two sets of eyes swivelled towards me and blinked in unison. "Her name's Natalie," I said, "and she's very classy and very smart."

Walsingham gave me a blank look. "Is she trustworthy?"

"I'd trust her with my life," I said. "She and me are very close. I'd just tell her I was setting up a caper, and as long as no law was broken while she was with me, she'd be game."

"It's highly irregular," said Walsingham, giving nothing away.

"Then just think of her as being a 'gifted irregular,' like me?" I said.

"Does she live in London?" Bosanquet asked, narrowing his eyes.

"Yes," I said, "she works as a mannequin for most of the better West End dress houses; she also models furs and expensive dresses for Harrods."

But Bosanquet still looked troubled. "Could she alter her appearance sufficiently, so that she wouldn't be recognised by anyone afterwards? Only, as she's a civilian I'd hate for her to be put in jeopardy."

"That's good of you to think of it," I said, not missing for a second they had no such concern about me. "But believe you me, I'd be the very last person to put Natalie in harm's way. And if as you say it's all only a cocktail party, she'll be fine. She can paint her face as good as any actress, her accent can cut glass, and she speaks French, fluently." And they looked at one other, then back at me, and then they both nodded, and for better or worse, Natalie got cast for a walk-on part in the caper.

A quick word about Natalie. Like all mannequins at the very top of the game, her job was to imitate upper-class women and do it with more style than any of them could ever muster. So with her nose and chin stuck firmly in the air, she affected a haughty disdain and modelled the aristocracy in photographs in fashion magazines, the showrooms along Great Titchfield Street, and on the catwalk at Harrods. She looked every inch the real thing, too. She was tall and willowy, and raven-haired. She had flashing blue eyes and a complexion that made peaches and cream look like condensed milk. Her long, long legs covered in nylon stockings were enough to make a vicar seriously question his calling. And like most men, I'd wanted her from the very first moment I'd set eyes on her. But she'd seemed so cold and aloof, so reserved and unattainable, that I'd thought I didn't have a snowball in hell's chance. So, I bided my time, waited outside Harrods, for several nights in a row, and when at last I saw her, I raised my hat and presented her with a bunch of red roses. I told her how very beautiful I thought she was, and asked her if she'd care to join me for cocktails. And she'd looked at me from under her lovely, long eyelashes and to my delight agreed to meet me on the Friday evening.

The thing that made her so special was that unlike the clothes she modelled, she could never be bought or owned. She was very much her own woman and her constant allure was that, one day, she might confer her blessings upon you, but in her own time and in her own way. And in time she blessed me, but in that time I also came to realise I could never give her what she really wanted in life, which was a title of some sort, and all the security that she thought came with it. It didn't have to be an English title, she wasn't that much of a snob; all that mattered was, that once conferred it could never be taken away from her. So, until such time as I lost her forever to some Lord this or Count that, I did my best to treat her like a lady, and in private, I called her "princess."

On our second date, at the Savoy, she'd put down her champagne, and looked at me, her eyes flashing. "It's high time I told you the truth," she said. And, maybe there's a point when you realise you want to get closer to someone and you start by taking down your own walls. Anyway, we both dropped our masks at one and the same time.

"No, let me go first," I said. "I come from Hackney, originally."

"I'm from the East End, too," she said, her upper-class accent utterly flawless. "From Bermondsey, actually." And I can still remember her laughter, which like her voice, was like the tinkling of little silvery bells.

The cocktail party at a big house in Russell Square, not far from the British Museum, turned out to be a posh do to mark the publication of a thick new book by some thin-on-top historian, who was the latest darling of the upper classes and landed gentry. The only thing I could tell from all the piles of his books on display, though, was that he'd stolen all his titles from Shakespeare. But I suppose I couldn't hold that against him.

We'd addressed Simon Bosanquet's concerns about Natalie being recognised; she wore a pale face and a shoulder-length red wig; another Willy Clarkson creation from Gainsborough Film Studios, once worn by no less a beauty than Margaret Lockwood. As worn by Natalie, with a long, bare-shouldered, black cocktail dress and stunning jewel necklace, supplied by yours truly, it was more *Gilda* than *The Wicked Lady,* and she was about as unnoticeable as a manor-house burning down on a dark night. But as Bosanquet had said, the whole purpose of the mission was to get noticed.

For my part, I had to drop hints at how well the Hannay family had done since leaving the old country, while vehemently expressing my concerns about Britain going to the dogs. "Something must be done about it, and soon, or else there'll be nothing left, *but* a fabled history, irrelevant to the modern world," I ranted. It wasn't that I had to offer to write a cheque, there and then, to help keep the Kingdom afloat, I just had to appear an over-opinionated, rich, young Canadian looking to be royally plucked. Simon Bosanquet was there, too, his title now very much to the fore, to introduce us around and to help keep anyone too inquisitive at bay. As he'd suggested, though, I had genned up on all things Canadian. I didn't think anyone would ask me how far Winnipeg was from Montreal, but I'd looked it up anyway; third city of Canada, capital of Manitoba, a distance of one thousand, four hundred and twenty-six miles; and all the rest of it. But I was buggered if I was going to say; "Am I right, sir?" at the end of it. I mean I was only prepared to go so far as Jeffrey Hannay.

But the conversation couldn't have been more deadly dull, and it was all I could do to stop yawning in people's faces. Natalie proved to be a brilliant partner in crime, though, and her tinkly laughter more than added to my fund of witticisms, courtesy of Messrs. Niven and Fleming. And, to be honest, I thought I was doing rather well, Canadian accent and all. But then, of all people, "the actress" swept into the room with her stuck-up boyfriend in tow. There was another bloke in her wake, too; only, unlike her regular pet Yank, this one was in uniform. It's funny, what causes you to take a second look, sometimes, and in the end I just put it down to the new bloke having a shock of red hair. Then I saw "the actress" see red as she realised she'd been upstaged, and she looked deadly-daggers at Natalie. Then, stripe me, but when she saw that didn't work, she started flashing admiring glances at me; not that she knew it was really me, mind you; me, who she'd once so cruelly reject-ed. Women can be so very contrary.

The room hushed as the historian stood on a polished wooden box and began to thank his publishers and his well-heeled well-wishers. And I stood there, Natalie's French perfume clouding my thoughts. Then, despite myself, I found myself being drawn into the silky-voiced web being spun by the balding, bespectacled, grey-suited Oxford don. It was as honey-tongued a piece of jingoism as ever I'd heard and it wasn't long before he even had me humming along to the strains of "Jerusalem." Everything he said echoed with the myth and legend of a bygone Britain, and the divinity of *"this Sceptred Isle."* Even the horrors of the two World Wars he saw as being but marks of England's necessary sacrifice for the sins of the World and further proof of the burden the country had been fated to bear, because of its sacred destiny. A destiny that needed to be preserved and defended by those that the Land itself had chosen as being worthy of the task. Then he looked around the room, and in the silence you could sense everyone feeling just how very worthy they all were.

To my ears, though, it all seemed like a nice bedtime story for grown-ups; with all the good things multiplied and all the dark horrors made as nothing. It didn't so much make a mockery of past sacrifices, as recast them as payment for some new and as yet unspecified end. The room filled with waves of applause, and I blinked awake. It was time for Natalie and me to be off.

The way Simon Bosanquet reckoned it, there'd be no better time to get myself noticed and remembered. "Act as though you're dismissive of it all," he'd told me, sounding very much like Ray. "They'll be all the more intrigued by you, then." So that's what I did. I gave a loud snort, and just loud enough to be overheard, I said, "As ever, those that can, do; those that can't, teach." Then I took Natalie by the arm and left. And from the looks on people's faces, it had the desired effect. But that's life, isn't it? Men, women, actors, politicians, even vicars and intellectuals, no one likes seeing people dismiss them and their cherished ideals, do they?

In *The Thirty-Nine Steps,* it says the secret to playing a part is to think yourself into it and that you could never keep it up unless you really managed to convince yourself you *were* the part. And I'd done that. I *was* Jeffrey Hannay. But even I'd had enough of it all, by that time, and the country going to the dogs or no, I'd promised to buy Natalie dinner at the Café Royal for her being so wonderful. The day before, I'd even popped in and greased the headwaiter's palm with a fiver, so we'd be guaranteed a good table. Some things you never leave to chance.

CHAPTER 27

Alarums and Merry Meetings

The funny thing about pretending to be someone else is how often you cross the paths of the real you. It's always very alarming. Take that night, after the book party. I was standing there, paying off the taxi-driver, Natalie already halfway across the pavement, when I happened to glance up at a double-decker bus going up Regent Street. And staring at me out of a window on the lower deck was a bloke I knew from the fly floor at the Palladium. I realised then he was looking straight past me, at Natalie; so okay. But as I turned round, I caught sight of someone turning round to get a second look at me. It was Michael Bentine on his way down to the Hippodrome. It was coming on dark, but I couldn't chance it. So I hunched my shoulders, pulled in my stomach, and called out, "Hold on, honey. I don't wanna miss your entrance," and strode after Natalie in what I hoped was the manner of a man who thought he owned half of Canada. And out of the corner of my eye, I saw Mike shake his head, and walk on down towards

Piccadilly Circus. And, a close call averted, I ventured into the glittering interior of the Café Royal.

A pound note changed hands and the headwaiter, all but purring, escorted us to our table. Waiters appeared as if out of nowhere to tuck in our chairs, menus were placed before us, and a wine steward appeared with a bottle of bubbly. I looked over at Natalie and she at me, and I pushed away all thoughts of things happening in threes. "You look very lovely, tonight, princess," I said. "Red hair suits you; it brings out the fire in you." She gave me a look that all but melted the ice in the ice bucket, then smiled and reached for her handbag, which I knew was a signal she was about to excuse herself and visit the Ladies Powder Room. I stood and watched her move between tables as if on castors, marvelled at her again, and sat down. And anyone looking at me might've thought I had the world on a string, and in some respects I did, but I was still on edge.

All it takes is those first tickles on the back of your neck. I tapped my fingers up and down on the table. "You'll drive yourself mad, anymore of this," I said to myself. Then I thought of Natalie in that very long, very tight black dress, and I thought, I've just got time for a quick pee; get there, get back, before she does. So I nipped into the gentlemen's toilets; did the business; and I'd just picked up a hand towel, when the outer door banged shut. I didn't look up. I just continued drying my hands and began twisting a knot into the end of the towel, in case there was a knife. Then I heard footsteps stepping towards the urinals. There was a moment of echoing silence, followed by the sound of someone peeing, and then a long sigh.

"Napoleon probably lost the Battle of Waterloo because he couldn't pee; he all but poisoned himself; it killed him, in the end."

"Hello, Mr. Messima," I said, looking up into the mirror.

"Hello, Jeffro," he said, buttoning up his fly. "Long time no see." The Emperor of Soho took up station at the wash basin farthest from me, and slowly undid the sleeve buttons of his jacket. Like Napoleon, he never travelled alone, so I knew there had to be at least two of his goons standing guard outside to keep other patrons at bay. I also knew they'd charge in and cosh me senseless at the very first sound. So, as Messima reached for the soap, I kept on wiping my hands, and slowly undid the knot in the towel. He turned on the taps, then looked at me in the mirror. "Didn't recognise you, at first. You're looking very natty and polished, I must say."

"Thank you," I said, neatly folding the towel in half.

"Must be what, four, five months, at least?" he said. "My, but how time flies. I did hear, though, you'd been away. Have a good time, did you? Of course, you did, I mean look at you; and look at that Natalie of yours. What a lovely-looking girl, and so very classy with red hair; very Rita Hayworth." He let that soak in, while he soaped and washed his hands. There was no blood in the water that I could see, so that was a good sign. "So you're obviously keeping alright then, Jeffro? Only, I've been meaning to have you in for a little chat, seeing as your name still crops up from time to time." His forehead crinkled into a frown. "Come to think of it, now, it did just before last Christmas when some very high-class jewellery went missing from an embassy over Belgravia way." He rinsed the soap off his hands and slowly flicked the excess water into the basin, like someone miming a conjurer. "Funny, that, knowing how you'd sworn to me you'd given up the game for good." He reached for a fresh towel, but left the tap running. "But be that as it may, you should know that when a certain foreign gentleman came offering top money for the names of London's top creepers, I did put you in the frame along with Eddie Chapman and Don Machin." He wiped his hands very fastidiously. "Nothing personal, though, Jeffro, merely business." He scrunched up the towel and dropped it in the used-towel basket. "Then a funny thing. Those nasty sods in Special Branch gave me a right-earful about not mixing with foreigners. I tell you, the things they do hear. But then you couldn't have had anything to do with that, could you? I mean, you being away and all. And, of course, you knowing that if you ever tried to stitch me up, I'd have both your thumbs cut off just for starters." He waggled his thumbs for emphasis, then leaned over and turned off the tap. "So tell me, for old time's sake, are you back to creeping? And be straight, Jeffro, or I'll have those two outside drop you in the piss until you start gargling up shit."

Well, I was no longer a creeper, in the classic sense, was I? So I told the truth, always the best way. "No, Mr. Messima. Creeping, as I knew it, has gone right out the window. I'm a different person now, honest. I just help move bits of scenery around these days. But as I did manage to put a little bit aside, before I retired from the game, I can still afford the odd night out with a girlfriend. But that's it, really."

He nodded like a priest hearing confession; a sure sign I'd said enough. But as Ray always said, "Give people something to chew on, and they won't end up biting you in the arse."

"Fair enough," Messima said. Then he stared at me, hard. "Still getting your suits run up by old Solly Templeton? A very nice job he does, too. I should go and see him myself, next time. I tell you those snobby gits down the Row are happy enough to take my money, but I'm sure they fob me off with less than their best." He did up the buttons on his cuffs and brushed his lapels with his fingertips. "I'm glad we took the time to have this little chat. You mind how you go."

And in the blink of an eye he was gone. But that was

always the way with Messima. You never knew where or when he'd come at you next. Or whether you'd survive it, when he did. And I stood there, with the sound of the urinals flushing in the background, and splashed cold water on my face. I ventured slowly out into the corridor, caught sight of myself in one of the huge gilded mirrors, and immediately got that itchy feeling again.

I tried to put on a good face for Natalie; enjoy the food, let the bubbly buoy me up; but she knew me too well and could tell I was on edge, and in the end, I told her about my run-in with Messima. But she just shook her head. "You act a part with Messima, you do the same with Jack Spot and Billy Hill, and they do the same with you; it's a never-ending game of cat and mouse, and always will be. But this job you're involved in, now; it's different, somehow." The sharp-eyed girl from Bermondsey looked out at me from behind her beauty mask. "I don't want to know what it is you're involved in, darling, or why, I just want you to be very, very careful."

"You're wise beyond your years," I said.

"All women are," she said, reaching for her handbag. This time it was a signal for us to leave. I stood up to pull her chair out; shaking my head at a waiter that'd been hovering to do the same thing. She looked up at me and said, "You know I'd do anything for you."

"Anything?" I said, suddenly Bogart to her Bacall.

She smiled and set some more ice melting. "Anything, but marry you, Jethro, darling, you know that," she said sweetly. "But if it's any consolation, I do believe I'd contemplate murder for you, if I had to."

"Let's hope you never have to then, princess," I said.

I had the doorman hail a taxi and tried not to look up and down Regent Street too many times. The neon lights around

Piccadilly Circus were still off thanks to Government austerity measures, but the way my nerves were jangling, I could've lit up half of London by myself. It's always that way, though, when I feel someone's eyes on me; in daylight or darkest shadow, it's always the same itchy feeling.

We didn't speak in the taxi, but Natalie squeezed my hand from time to time and did her best to keep me earthed. Then the cabbie turned off the Strand, down towards The Savoy, down the only street in all of London where motor cars travel on the right-hand side instead of the left. Only that night, it made me feel as if I was forever trapped in the world on the other side of the looking-glass and that there was nothing at all I could do about it.

I paid off the cabbie and we headed for the American Bar to have a nightcap. Natalie removed her cloak and draped it elegantly over a leather chair and then, still holding her handbag, she reached over and gently touched my arm and whispered in my ear. I looked at her, and she looked at me, and I nodded, and she went back out through the door. I watched her go, as did every man in the place. Then I turned round, beckoned a waiter over and ordered a double brandy and soda. I sipped my drink and smoked a cigarette, and made a constant play of looking at my wrist-watch, like a man impatient for time's winged chariot to get cracking. And after ten minutes, exactly, I gathered up Natalie's cloak and sauntered over to the door, leaving the brandy unfinished. The faces that watched me go were full of envy at my coming good fortune, and I couldn't blame them for thinking it. But I didn't head for the lifts or the stairs. Instead, I walked along the corridor and gently knocked on the door to the Ladies Powder Room. The old lady that opened the door looked like Jessie Matthews's much older sister, but she was really one of Natalie's legion of aunties.

"Hello, Dolly," I said—Jethro now, not Hannay—"Here's Natalie's cloak, and a bit for your troubles. Thanks, love." She pushed the fold of fivers back at me, but I gently closed her hand around them. "No, go on, have a treat on me on your next night off." She smiled with her eyes, and without saying a word, disappeared back inside the Powder Room; her domain. Miss Dolly Doyle, one of London's late joys, a lady who'd once graced all the best music-hall stages with her singing and dancing. And looking at her, even at her age, you could tell good looks ran in the family. Smarts did, too. For Natalie had gone by then; her face cleaned, her dress changed, the Willy Clarkson wig hidden in a box; and she in a head scarf, old coat, and flat shoes; gone out the hotel employee's rear entrance.

I went back along the corridor and slipped into one of the phone booths. I dialled a number and waited, dropped pennies in the slot, said half-a-dozen words, then made my way back to the foyer. I walked head-down, so as not to catch any inquisitive eyes, and pushed through the revolving door, and had the top-hatted doorman call me a cab to take me to the Ritz. It was the one thing Walsingham and Simon Bosanquet had been adamant about; if I got any sense, at all, I was being followed, Natalie and I had to split up immediately and go our separate ways.

But that's the funny thing about itches; if they don't go away, once you've scratched them, it usually means something much more serious.

CHAPTER 28

The Third Act

I stared out the window of the taxi, and let London slip by in a whirl of wheeling shadows and splintered thoughts. The first time you feel a tickle on the back of your neck, you note it; the second time, you're already waiting for the third; and by then, you know someone's got their eyes on you. And all you can do is wait for whatever's going to happen, to happen.

I paid the cabbie and waved off the Ritz doorman. "Thank you, no. Just taking a stroll before bedtime." He tipped his hat, said, "Good evening, sir," and went back to searching the horizon for approaching taxis. I walked towards Green Park, hearing Walsingham's footsteps echoing alongside me, all too aware I'd come full circle and was still nowhere near the Final Act. I looked up and down Piccadilly and waggled my ear; to remind myself to really concentrate on what I was seeing. (I'd picked up the habit from Ray, and the funny thing was the more you did it, the more it worked.) There were a couple of taxis; a double-decker bus on its way to Hyde Park Corner; a few motor cars, a van or two; a dozen or so vehicles parked along the pavement; half as many, again, in Stratton Street; but nothing ominous. And once I was certain I'd clocked the lot, I crossed over.

The Mayfair was at the far end of Stratton Street, and the only sign of life between me and my hotel was a cab waiting outside the Coq d'Or, over to my left. There was a brief explosion of laughter as a couple exited the restaurant, then the taxi drove off into the night, the growl of its engine almost supernaturally loud. The echo died away, and I walked on into the now deserted street, still feeling very itchy. I'd just crossed Mayfair Place, about halfway to the hotel, when a shadowy figure stepped out of nowhere and stuck a gun in my back. "Hands all the way up and go careful, now, I'd hate to have to put another button-hole in that fancy jacket of yours." It was a bloody Yank. Not, at all, what I'd been expecting. I slowly put my hands up in the air. "Just keep them up, nice and easy, now," the shadow said, pushing his gun hard into my back.

And quite unprofessional of him, really. I can't say now I even thought about it, I just responded as per Mr. Carter's instructions and spun left, bringing my left arm over and down and up, trapping the bloke's gun-arm in mine. And the heel of my right hand was swinging round to push his soddin' jaw up into his head, when I heard Simon Bosanquet say, "That won't be necessary, Jeffrey. Stand back." But it was too late, all I could do was swing wide, and my attacker and me ended up looking like a couple of drunks dancing in the street. "I have a gun trained on you, Mr. Russell," Simon said. "So, if you'd be so good as to drop your weapon."

"The hell, I will," my dancing partner growled. So I pulled my head back and butted him hard in the face. He let go then, and his pistol fell onto the pavement, and so did his hat.

Bosanquet kept his revolver trained on the man and kicked the fallen pistol into the gutter. "Now, now, James. Play nice."

"Play nice?" he spluttered, indignantly. "This lousy son of a bitch almost broke my nose. Train your gun on him; he's the bad apple."

I knew who it was then; it was the red hair that nailed it for me.

"Couldn't be more wrong, Russell, old man," Simon said, as casually as if he was chatting with someone in a pub, rather than confronting them at gunpoint. "James Russell, let me introduce you to Jeffrey Hannay, a cousin of mine, from Canada, currently assisting His Majesty's Secret Service on matters pertaining to the defence of the Realm."

"Like hell, he is," the American said, shaking his head. "He's no damn spook. But he's up to something, I know he is." He glared at me and stepped back, and bent down to pick up his hat. And Bosanquet, gun very much in hand, matched his every move, and stooped down and retrieved the fallen Colt automatic from the gutter. Then as I stood there, looking like a lemon, he presented it, handle first, to the mad American.

"Are you bonkers," I yelled. "This Yank bastard just tried to kill me."

"If he wanted to kill you, Jeffrey, you'd be dead," he said smoothly. "So I'd wager that the intrepid Mr. Russell, here, simply wanted to have a little chat with you." He looked around. "My club's nearby, let's all go have a drink, shall we?"

And so we did. Bosanquet, the hopping-mad American, and me.

I'd played my part, though, and by Walsingham's reckoning a single foray into enemy territory was more than enough to begin with. If I was seen to be too eager or too accessible, I might be taken as a sacrificial piece, and that, he said, would never do. So now it was up to him and Bosanquet to make whatever moves were necessary to get me further up the chess-board.

And, just as Walsingham had planned, over the next few days the other side sent out their bishops and knights to make discreet inquiries about J. Hannay, Esq. at the Mayfair Hotel and in Boodles. Walsingham told me later that one or two members had even approached him directly, which he'd considered very bad form, but given the situation he'd overlooked it. "Hannay? Hardly know him," he'd told them. "Only invited him to lunch as a favour, really. He's more a friend of David Niven's. The story is, Hannay's father met the young Niven back in the Thirties, sometime, when he was working for a New York firm, importing liquor in from Canada." It was a fanciful enough tale, but it seemed to go down well enough. And with David Niven safely back in Hollywood, it wasn't as if anyone could just accidentally bump into him, to check the facts. It was a similar story with Simon Bosanquet. Someone at his club, who'd also been at the publishing house party, casually asked about, "That Canadian chap, with the stunner on his arm; Hannay, or something; timber and minerals, wasn't it? A cousin of yours, I hear?" And he'd responded much like Walsingham. "A distant cousin; brought letters of introduction; met for the first time a month or so ago; frightfully nice chap, though. Generous, too, but then there's a lot of new money in Canada." And there it was, their built-in deniability should there ever be any awkward questions later. I tell you, with all the thinking ahead they did, I reckon either of them could've given Ray a run for his money, if they ever sat down for a serious game of chess.

Much later, I was told that inquiries had even been made at the Board of Trade and the Canadian Trade Commission. Walsingham had once let slip that he had one or two high-ranking civil servants in his pocket, but I still wonder how he got the fix in at Canada House.

And so there I was, back in Simon Bosanquet's living room, with me sitting on a well-worn toffee-coloured leather chesterfield, sherry glass in hand, quietly waiting to be told what the next move was, and Walsingham standing silent at the window looking down into the square. "Your run-in with Russell notwithstanding," he said, over his shoulder, "your Mr. Hannay appears to have gone over rather well."

"Yes," I said. "I can't say the Yank and me really hit if off."

He turned and gave me one of his looks and then resumed his staring out of the window. "Nevertheless, he is an ally, Jethro."

"Well, I'm not sure he knows that. He wasn't at all friendly, when Simon took us to the In and Out Club," I said.

He gave me another look. "He's OSS. North Africa and the Middle East during the War; then Berlin and Vienna; now, here, in London. So I think you disarming him, like that, must've rather ruffled his feathers."

I wondered why Walsingham was giving me the ten-cent tour, so I threw in my own sixpence worth. "OSS? What, is that like SOE, and the Twenty Group, and all that malarky Eddie Chapman was involved in?"

He let the net curtain fall back into place and turned to face me. "It's all still covered by OSA, of course, but yes, the U.S. Office of Strategic Service was modelled on our Special Operations Executive. Your new chum Ian Fleming had quite a lot to do with setting it up, as it happens."

"I bet he could tell some stories, then," I said.

"Not out of school, he can't. But if anyone were to ever find a way around the Official Secrets Act, it would, like as not, be Ian."

"Yes, I could see him taking to cloak-and-dagger like a duck to water," I said. And, as we were being so chummy, I asked again about the Yanks, in general, and Mr. James Russell, in particular.

Walsingham poured two very pale, very dry sherries. He took one, and then sat down. "The Americans were rather taken by surprise by the Labour Party's victory at the last election, and they're determined not to be wrong-footed at the next. So now they monitor all British political groups as a matter of course."

"So what's Russell's role in all this, then?" I asked.

"I gather, Mr. Russell's mission is to keep a close eye on the activities of Britain's more extremist political groups."

"What's that got to do with me as me or me as Jeffrey Hannay? The only group I'm a member of is the National Association of Theatrical and Kinematographic Employees. So why stick a gun in my back?"

"The Americans tend to take rather a dim view of anyone that gets too deeply involved in another country's politics, unless, of course, it's at their express request. And it appears one of their own people is giving them some cause for concern. Russell told Simon that he mistook you for someone that's been shadowing the person he has under surveillance."

"Well that's daft, that is. Unless Mr. Russell frequents Church Street market or has been moonlighting back-stage at theatres round the West End, there's no way in hell our paths could cross. And the only time I've been near Grosvenor Square, recently, was to go see Roosevelt's statue."

"No, it does seem rather improbable. Simon thinks so, too.

Russell must be mistaken. It was, after all, only your second outing as Hannay. One thought, though, given Russell's current focus, it's very likely it was he that followed you the night you broke into NOB House. But, again, even I can't see how he could connect that episode with you as Jeffrey Hannay. But whatever his reason, he was intrigued enough by your little display at the publishing party to want to talk to you. Anyway, I've since made it very clear to our dear Cousins at the U.S. Embassy that while I quite understand their need to gather intelligence on U.K. politics, it might be better for all concerned if we try not to trip over one another in pursuit of our respective goals. So, do please remember, Jethro, that if and when your paths do cross again, Mr. Russell should be regarded as friend, not foe."

"I only hope, someone's put our Mr. Russell in the picture, then," I said. "There's no telling what could happen, if he tried coming it again."

"All I ask, Jethro, is that you play your part." I nodded in agreement. "One other thing," he said, sipping his sherry. "I've taken the liberty of arranging for your lady friend to go to Paris. I thought it best she be out of London for a little while. She's travelling as a diplomatic courier, but she'll be staying with people perhaps a little more suited to her particular line of work."

I stared at him, suddenly caught again between two worlds; was he holding Natalie hostage? He'd once done that with Ray, to keep me on a tether, but a lot of water had run under the bridge in St. James's Park, since then. No, it was the smart move, safer all around. "Thank you," I said.

"It was Simon's idea," he said. "His father put money into a French couture house, before the War, and it's doing rather well now, so I hear. She should enjoy her stay."

It was Walsingham, playing chess again; protecting his pieces.

Then the Special Branch representative of *Burke's Peerage* sashayed back into the room. He went over to the sideboard, stood for a moment, then turned around, a glass of sherry in one hand and a cream-coloured envelope in the other. And I suppose you could say that's when the third and final act of the caper really began. He took a sip of his Tio Pepe, savoured it, and then as if it was nothing too important, he handed me the envelope. But before I could even open it, he grinned at Walsingham, then at me. "I gather, Hannay, old chap," he said, raising his glass, "that you've been invited for a weekend in the country."

CHAPTER 29

Knight to King Four

A long, winding drive has always been a well-planned way for a house to impress itself and its setting upon its guests; like the opening scene in a play, it sets the stage for everything else that follows.

It wasn't Blenheim Palace, but it had nice, classical lines, and even though the two wings and the stable block had been added onto the house at later dates, you could tell that generations of Vashfields had done their utmost to keep everything in proper proportion and character. Unlike their politics, however, where the family not only had a long history of going to extremes, but even more tellingly, perhaps, had an equally long history of surviving them. Simon Bosanquet gave me the potted version of the Vashfield dynasty on the drive up to the Hall, but it was only when he'd mentioned that they'd always fancied themselves as "kingmakers" that I got the message. "What, like Warwick the Kingmaker in Shakespeare's history plays; *Henry IV* or something?" I said.

"No. Much more, *Richard III,* and by hook or by crook," he said, not smiling. "The ends always justifying the means; sacrificing family member or friend, if need be, to achieve their ends or atone for their sins."

"They sound like a right charming bunch," I said, but he didn't hear me, he was staring off, already midway through a quote from something.

"How oft the sight of means to do ill deeds, make deeds ill done."

"Is that from *Richard III*?" I asked.

"No," he said, "*King John.* I looked it up."

I turned to him. "Ray Karmin is always saying to me, 'Read your Shakespeare; it's all in there. It's all happened before, and will again.'"

"He's a smart man," Simon said, not taking his eyes off the road.

"You can say that, again," I said, staring out the car window, at the unending hedgerows flashing by. "For a start, he's not here in the motor car with the two of us nutcases, is he?"

Simon had timed the drive up from London, that Friday, so we'd arrive at Vashfield Hall well before the light faded. I'd studied plans of the house during a session down in "Keys's" dungeon workrooms, but I wanted to see it in the flesh before I stepped foot inside the place. There was a team of uniformed footmen, brawny lads all, to attend to our bags on arrival. And I got out of the motor car and yawned and said I needed to stretch my legs and as per Simon's instructions, I requested that they leave my suitcases in my room and that they needn't bother to store them once they'd been unpacked. Then before anyone had time to suggest otherwise, I wandered off around the grounds. The ground was wet, April having thrown its last shower an hour or so before, the cloud grey and overcast.

Otherwise, it was a picture of genteel tranquillity, and if not Constable, then a watercolour by Turner. It could've been anytime in the last two hundred years, but for the posh motor cars and limousines all lined up along the drive and on round into an area off the stable yard. And every single drag supposedly there on business important to state or commerce. It looked more like the line-up for the British 1000 Miles Race, at Brooklands. Though when I walked back up to the house, the chauffeurs seemed to be having the hardest time with Bosanquet's Bristol; where was it in the pecking order; above or below a Daimler; the equal of an Alvis, or a Bentley? Life could be such a bugger if no one knew your proper place.

By the time I was shown to my room my bags had all been unpacked and everything neatly placed in drawers or hung up in the wardrobes. It was as good as Cabin Class service aboard the *Queen Mary*. And as good a way to find out all about me, from the name of my shirt-maker, to what book I'd brought along to read myself to sleep with. Bosanquet, as cunning as ever, knowing the historian from the publishing party was also going to be a guest, had loaded me up with copies of the professor's best-known works: *Thy Inward Greatness, This Other Eden, The Triumphant Sea,* and the very latest, *Naught Shall Make Us Rue.* I'd skipped through them all, appreciating very little, but had carefully left in place the slips of paper Bosanquet had used to flag the most purple passages; especially liking his little touch of using neatly-torn pieces of a cablegram from All Canada Timber Consortium. For my part, I'd also brought along a book called *Birds of the British Isles* and a pair of binoculars, not my Afrikakorps field glasses, but a smaller pair I'd bought for a song down Portobello Road. For his cover, Bosanquet, special agent and jobbing spy, had two well-thumbed volumes of Agatha Christie; the source, I'm sure, of all his better ideas.

I dressed for dinner, gave myself a quick once-over in the wardrobe mirror; marvelled again at Solly Templeton's artistry with cutting shears; did a quick impersonation of Sir Thomas Beecham conducting the Royal Philharmonic; then went down to the drawing-room for preprandial drinks. The room was only a little bigger than the bar at the Metropolitan music hall, reputedly the biggest in all of London, but it was much better appointed; there wasn't a single cigarette-end or speck of saw-dust on the floor. But just like the Met, you could see the stage from anywhere in the room, by which I mean the open expanse of richly hued Oriental carpet where I was to make my next moves in the great game.

I was introduced to everyone as a distant cousin of Bosanquet's, newly arrived from Canada. As Jethro, the cat burglar, my normal procedure would've been to observe from the fringes, price all the jewellery, and put markers on the pieces I fancied; and I did all that, without thinking. But I was there to mingle and to reprise the role I'd played at the publishing party, that of the overly wealthy, overly opinionated Mr. Jeffrey Hannay. But as they say, it's always the honey that catches the bee. And like flies round a money pot, various guests came up to engage me in conversation; the opening gambit always some variation of, "Very cold, Canada; and very large, so I hear." So I didn't have to work too hard to establish myself as one of Canada's brightest sons, but then out of the blue two gimlet-eyed gentlemen suddenly confronted me with detailed questions regarding the state of the Canadian mining industry and timber business. I professed total ignorance of the first; "Not my side of the family, I'm afraid," I blithely explained, before parroting-off figures on timber exports that Bosanquet had rustled up from the Board of Trade. It seemed to satisfy them, though. But I've often found, in life as in disguise, that an admitted-to ignorance adds its own credibility to any situation.

I'm sure I wasn't supposed to feel like I was being vetted, but that's what was going on. But, again, thanks to Messrs. Niven and Fleming I was never at a loss for a witty comment or a cutting aside. And, dotted as my conversation was, with all the necessary political opinions Bosanquet had crammed into my head, I managed to skewer Communism, Socialism, Clement Attlee's Labour Government, the National Health Service, the Black Market, the Jews, and just about anything else the locals considered not right with the world. Including, for good measure, my ongoing dismay as regards the abdication, as well as the loss of India and Empire. But as the Bard once said, better a witty fool than a foolish wit. And by the end of it, the only thing they didn't know about Jeffrey Hannay and his world, was whether he beat his dogs, his horses, or his women.

Then, just as I was running out of puff, if not powder, who should sail into the room, all eyes flashing and guns blazing, but "the actress," "Madame heart-breaker" herself, done-up to the nines and then some. She looked absolutely stunning. Then the thought hit me. She'd seen me as Hannay at the publishing party, but what if now, up close, she recognised me, as me? And worse, as always, she was accompanied by the all-too-self-satisfied Mr. Trent Tyler; America's turgid answer to "gentleman" Jack Buchanan. And if that wasn't enough to take the wind out of my sails, there again with the two of them, was Bosanquet's OSS friend, James Russell, resplendent in the dress uniform of a U.S. Navy Commander. And that was a bit unexpected. I tried to catch Bosanquet's eye, but ever the Scarlet Pimpernel, he was on the other side of the room doing his Sir Percy Blakeney impersonation. He was very good at playing a duffer who'd only got the position as Scotland Yard assistant deputy assistant liaison to the Home Office because an old school chum's pater had interceded on his behalf. It was obvious, no one there had the remotest idea of who he really was or of his link to Walsingham; to them, he was simply Simon. "It's all very nice, but I don't even have a bally policeman's whistle," I heard him telling one elderly lady, who was still complaining about a burglary she'd suffered some twenty years before. "You'd think they'd at least give a chap his own set of handcuffs," he said. I wanted to lean in and tell the old bat to emigrate to Canada; the Mounties always got their man, there. But I didn't.

I took another gin and tonic from off a proffered silver tray, then all but had the glass knocked out of my hand by someone bumping into me. I swung round, to find James Russell apologising profusely in that way Americans do when they want to impress you with their manners. He dropped his voice, "I'm here as a last-minute guest; you and I have never met," he said in a very clipped, almost British accent. Then with a sharp, little explosion of laughter, as if he'd just matched me witticism for witticism, he walked off. I nodded, and chuckled as if I'd found him unimaginably charming. Fat chance of that ever happening, I thought.

I turned to see "the actress" parading about, batting her eyelashes and basking in the worship of her legion of admirers; a very smug Trent Tyler strutting by her side like a peacock. "Sod this for a game of soldiers," I said to myself, and went stoppo with a schooner of fino sherry in one hand and a gin and tonic in the other. It's a ruse I've used many times, at all sorts of society gatherings; it works a treat, too. As a waiter, you're searching for the couple that ordered the drinks; as a guest, you're in search of the person that asked you to "hold their glass for a moment." If anyone comes across you with your hands full, it's that they respond to then, not you being where you oughtn't to be.

I slipped out into the corridor and arched my eyebrows into a look of innocent surprise, which is the only proper face to have when you're nosing around a strange house full of strange people. I rounded the first corner and found myself in a long oak-panelled corridor that, if memory served me, led to the library and the billiards-room, and beyond that, the family wing. I did my "I must say, that's a very interesting-looking painting or vase or suit of armour" walk, which meant stopping and staring at something every so often, but again only ever to stay in character. And I stopped to look at yet another portrait of yet another Vashfield ancestor, but there was something about this one that struck me a little differently. It was modern painting, but done in such a way as to capture the look and feel of the past. The gentleman in question was in white tie and tails; tall, dashing and very debonair; but he was also wearing a dark blue sash and a Garter Star, that I knew I'd seen before; and the last time, on the writing desk in Ray's front room. And that wasn't all, you could plainly see the bloke's ring finger of his left hand was all but missing. The artist had highlighted a ring on the tiny stub of finger. I leaned in to get a closer look at the crest engraved on its centre stone, and heard muted voices. I turned my head and saw a part of the wood panelling start to open inwards.

I stepped quickly to one side and stood in the shadow of a suit of armour and waited to go into my "I'm awfully sorry, but I seem to have lost my way" act. But the bloke who appeared as if from out of the wall, didn't even bother to turn round to pull the oak-panel door closed behind him, he just walked off down the corridor towards the family wing. And as I stood there, my mouth still agape, the secret door slowly and silently closed on its hidden hinges. I blinked. Striped-trousers, a fitted black jacket, stiff white collar; the man who could walk through walls was a government civil servant, a banker or a butler. I plumped on him being the butler. I heard people murmuring again. So I took a quick butcher's around me to get a fix on the hidden panel, then nipped back to the cocktail party, sharpish. Old manor-houses were famous for their priest-holes, secret passages, and back-corridors, and I wondered where the one I'd just stumbled upon gave access to; it was odds-on it led to the library; but where else? But wherever it led to, it was right up my street.

Supper was a simple affair requiring only three forks and three knives, plus spoons of various sizes; the full canteen of silver, no doubt, still being polished for the following evening's banquet. As it was Friday, fish was the main course, but as they also served oxtail soup and duck in aspic, it was probably more tradition than religious observance. It wasn't whale meat or snoek they served up, either, and it was very telling that the topic of food rationing never came up once in any of the conversations I heard. So it was obvious the Vashfields had a good pipeline into the black market.

On one side of me was a horsy-faced woman who, having once determined I didn't ride to hunt and that I was a Canadian, to boot, didn't talk to me again for the entire meal. But that sat fine by me, as there was a very pretty young girl on my right, who appeared to be as much of a stranger to the place as I was. She told me her name was Jennifer Manning. And that she'd finished finishing school and was thinking of finishing with her job as a secretary to a director at a big advertising agency in London, and was at Vashfield Hall because she really wanted to pursue her dream of becoming an actress. Especially now, that she'd also arranged for an audition at the Webber Douglas Academy of Dramatic Art, in London, that coming July, hopefully then to start in the September term. And I nodded, as if it all made perfect sense. And she laughed and said, No, no, no, someone she'd met at an agency function had invited her for the weekend so she could meet a certain famous actress and, perhaps, try out for a part in a special theatrical production. "How very lucky for you," I said, the penny nowhere near to dropping. "You're the first really nice person I've talked to all night," she said, gaily. "Everyone else seems to be avoiding me for some reason." "Oh, really," says I, "where's this kind gentleman that invited you, then?" A loud laugh erupted from the far end of the table. "That's him," she said, brightly, "darling Trent." I looked at her, in all her delicious beauty; her peaches-and-cream complexion and her lovely long—what I'd once heard a GI describe as—strawberry-blonde hair. But it wasn't for me to tell her what I thought of Mr. Trent bloody Tyler and she blushed at my unrelenting gaze. "Are you, by any chance, here for the theatrical masque on Sunday night, Mr. Hannay?" she asked.

"No. I'm afraid I wasn't invited," I said. "Anyway, I'm off back to town, Sunday afternoon. But I'm sure you'll be tremendous in whatever part you're asked to play."

And she smiled a sad little smile and told me that her father was dead set against her being an actress. But that if only given half the chance to show what she was capable of, she was sure he would relent, and that until then she was adopting her mother's maiden name as her stage name. And seeing the passion in her eyes, I said that I didn't doubt it. "You're so very kind, Mr. Hannay," she said. "Do tell me all about Canada."

So I said, "Call me Jeffrey." And I told her I loved the theatre, too, and instead we chatted about what was on in the West End. She didn't seem to notice the occasional glances she got from people up and down the table, but I did. And for the very first time since arriving at Vashfield Hall I didn't feel like the spotlight was only on me.

But I missed the significance of it all. And looking back on it, I can only think I had too many other things on my plate. For a start, as soon as everybody was abed, I had to suss the place out in preparation for the following night's creep and become as familiar as I could with the dark, shadowy ins and outs of Vashfield Hall. And all I could really focus on, in my mind's eye, was the picture of a certain section of the oak panelling in the corridor outside the library.

Seeing Red

The gossip columns all said Lord Vashfield had married well, by which they meant the sizeable fortune his American wife, close friend to Nancy Cunard and Lady Astor, had brought into the family. It certainly explained the number of servants. Life below stairs had mostly gone the way of the dodo since the War, but they could afford troops of chambermaids and footmen. One odd thing, though, other than the senior staff and the chef, who was a Frog, most of the men seemed more suited for the Services, than a life in service; they seemed clumsy, awkward even; without polish. And I wondered why Vashfield put up with them; he seemed such a stickler about everything else; shows you how blind I can be sometimes.

Breakfast was taken in the breakfast room, where all the dishes were laid out on long refectory tables and kept warm by hot plates, and once I'd determined everyone was supposed to serve themselves, I did, too, with unabashed relish. It was almost as good as Saturday morning at the Victory cafe, but not quite, there was no black pudding or fried bread; funny how you can still miss certain things, even in the midst of plenty. Afterwards, everyone was left to their own devices until dinnertime; for those so inclined, there was riding, shooting, lawn tennis; for those who enjoyed more leisurely pursuits, there was walking, reading, or gossip. I had my book of British birds and binoculars on open display, as playing the earnest amateur bird-watcher was the only way for me to be left alone to walk the grounds, unescorted. Even so, I had the distinct feeling I was being watched the entire time, so I acted the part, and stopped every now and then to peer at distant trees and hedgerows. There was a lot of shooting going on at the far end of the estate, and the only oasis of quiet appeared to be the beautiful glass conservatory, right out of Kew Gardens, that'd been added on to the end of the family wing during Edwardian times. I was just about to go and have a closer look, when a couple of other houseguests appeared out of nowhere to insist that I come and try my hand at shooting. I got the sense I was being vetted again, so I stuck a smile on my face and joined the people milling around the shooting ground, and stood and waited my turn.

I'd first seen one of the catapult machines that threw little clay discs up into the air, set up on an after-deck of the *Queen Mary* when I'd watched no less personages than Douglas Fairbanks, Jr. and Charlie Chaplin try their luck. Fairbanks, as you'd expect, turned out to be a pretty good shot, but Chaplin much less so, and even though he'd tried to make light of it all, you could tell he was right put out about it. But, I suppose, even a genius can't be good at everything.

Vashfield's set-up, however, was of a different order

entirely. He called it his little trap shoot, but the huge area of ground he'd given over to it gave the lie to that. One of his Lordship's helpers looked me up and down and picked out a gun from a dozen or so double-barrel shotguns all neatly arrayed in a special wooden carrying case about the size of a small steamer trunk. He broke it open to show it was unloaded and snapped it closed. I nodded, took hold of the gun, got a feel of its weight and balance, then turned away towards the open field and shouldered it. I pushed the stock hard into my cheek and moving in an arc from left to right, I sighted along the barrel. "Bang, bang," I said. I turned back, nodded, broke open the gun, and held it across my arm. My helper handed me two cartridges from out of his shoulder bag and I took them and held them down between my fingers like two fat cigars. Then I watched and listened and learned.

A round of trap consists of twenty-five shots; five each from each of five different posts or stations. The target clays or "birds" are then catapulted up into the air at different angles, from a concealed trap house, sixteen or so yards in front of where the trap shooter is standing. In the early days, I was told, it'd simply been a matter of hiding pigeons under top hats and releasing them, one by one, to be shot at. But England being England, it was soon turned into a sport with rules, so that people could bore you to death with details of how much better than you they were at doing it.

In the end, I approached it much the same way I'd throw a knife. I took a deep breath, relaxed, and kept both eyes open. I shouted, "Pull," tracked the "bird" with my eyes, swung the gun quickly past it, and "bang," it was in smithereens before I realised I'd squeezed the trigger. I didn't do too badly; but I wasn't the best shot there; not by a mile. That was a toss-up between Simon Bosanquet, of all people, and Lord Vashfield, stubby finger and all, and I willingly joined in the chorus and nods of approval at their shooting skills. Someone handed me hot coffee from a thermos flask. "Jolly good, aren't they? I can't say as there's much between them, myself," he said. But with him being shorter than me, and with his tweed cap pulled down over his eyes, I couldn't see who it was. "Yes, jolly good," I said, nodding my thanks. He glanced up at me. "Hannay, isn't it? You didn't do too badly, yourself, considering it was your first time." "Thanks," I said, sipping at the hot coffee; but his voice and manner of speaking made me pause; I had the oddest feeling I'd met him somewhere before, and not just at breakfast. "The American chap seems to be doing rather well, too, doesn't he?" he said, sounding as if he was biting off each word and chewing it. It was the sound of a shotgun blast that brought it all back again. It was the officer chappy I'd brained on the staircase at NOB HQ. He still had a mark down the left side of his face, but he didn't seem to recognise me. I nodded and looked over at James Russell doing his impersonation of Buffalo Bill. "Yes, a real Buffalo Bill Cody," I said, handing him back the cup. "I wonder where he left his horse."

Thankfully, Simon Bosanquet appeared at my elbow, and saved me from having to make any more small talk. "Good show, Jeffrey," he said, slapping me on the shoulder. "I know the 'birds' aren't anywhere near the size of caribou or elk, but you did well." It took me a moment to realise he must be talking about what people shot at for fun, in Canada. I just stared at him. "Fancy a quick walk up to the house?" he asked, loud enough to be overheard. "There's a telegram for me, apparently."

But of course there was; that was another little piece of his plan coming into play. The telegram from Scotland Yard would request his presence there, at 9:00 A.M. sharp, Sunday morning, and give good reason for his crack-of-dawn departure. It also meant the Red Books and whatever else I managed to get my hands on that night would be well on the way down to London before the Vashfields and their guests awoke to find their morning routine had been shot to pieces.

When we were out of earshot of the shooting party, I turned and said, "What the bloody hell is that Yank, Russell, doing here, Simon? Navy commander now, is it? The flash bugger; someone should've told him Portsmouth Dockyard is on the south coast, not fifty miles north of London in the middle of the English countryside. What's his game? He's being so bloody chummy with everyone, it's scary."

He gave me a narrow-eyed look, like a card player forced to reveal his next card. "Russell *has* to play the part to the hilt, Jethro. Everyone believes he was once an aide to Joseph Kennedy, when Kennedy was U.S. Ambassador here. Given that Kennedy backed the Nazis to win the War, it gives Russell impeccable credentials."

"And all very impressive, I'm sure," I said. "Just as long as you're also sure the slimy bugger's not out to double-cross us."

A certain testiness crept into his voice, which was a bit unusual for him. "Damn it, Jethro, how in hell am I to convince you Russell's mission here in no way conflicts with ours? The Americans have given us their word, and if it's good enough for me it should be good enough for you."

I shot right back. "Look, Simon, that might be how it works in your world, but it doesn't hold water in mine. It's actions that speak the loudest where I come from. And anyone that's ever drawn a gun or a knife on me is marked double dodgy until proven otherwise. So despite what you or the Yanks may say, I still don't trust that Russell character any further than I could throw him."

Simon stopped in his tracks, shook his head, clearly exasperated, and turned to face me. I noticed though he still had the presence of mind to make it appear, to anyone looking on, as if he and I were sharing a joke, but the tone of his voice said he was deadly serious. "Look, Jethro, just stay focussed on your mission, and not on Russell. Even I'm here, having to act the part of a fool to the hilt, so that I can provide you with support and cover. But believe you me, I'd change my act in an instant if anyone or anything endangered the mission or us. Now, is that absolutely clear?"

It was a reasonable enough response. And sudden flareups happen even between the best of friends. The pressure for him to act the fop "Sir Percy Blakeney" and me the Canadian "hooray" Hannay must've been getting to both of us. "All right, Simon, hold your horses, no need to bridle," I said. "It's just that when you get an itch on a job, you have to scratch at it to see what it means or suffer any consequences. For instance, what's Vashfield up to, on the far side of the trap shooting ground, over near the woods?"

He looked over towards the woods, then back at me. "Interesting you should ask, Jethro," he said, all irritation now gone from his voice. "He's all but finished putting in a large 'sporting clays' course that more closely mimics the actual field conditions and flight of live game: grouse, pheasants, hares, rabbits; almost anything; all manner of clay targets can be tripped and thrown from every conceivable angle, across all kinds of terrain. He's had whole platoons of the ground staff working on it for months, apparently. I overheard Vashfield telling Russell that similar shooting grounds were going in, all over England."

What is it they say about a tree falling in the woods making no sound if there's no one there to hear it fall? Well, for me it was like being hit on the head by a well-planed piece of two-by-four. "God's Holy Trousers, Simon. It's a wonder how much I can't see the wood for looking at it, sometimes." I stared at him, eyebrows raised. "Don't you see?"

He gave me another narrow-eyed look. "What now?" he said.

"Try this on for size," I said. "I reckon all this 'sporting-clays' malarky is ideal for training up a private army right under everyone's noses. For a start, it'd explain why there are so many beefy servants and helpers around the place, all the time. I couldn't understand why he had so many blokes around, before. But if as you now say, Vashfield and his mob are putting in these special shooting ranges up and down the country; well, think about it. They'll have groups of fully trained men strategically positioned all over England, all armed and ready, and waiting to do whatever it is they call on them to do."

He shot me a very odd look, nodded his head towards the house, and we walked on in silence for a bit, then he nodded again for me to continue. And by then the trees were falling around me like mad. "And another thing, Simon, they're not daft having you here. Even if they do think you're pretty low on the Scotland Yard totem pole, inviting you here is still the very last thing anyone would do if they had secrets to hide; it's really very clever of them. That young Jennifer Manning, me, and all the other people here for the first time; even the Yank, Trent Tyler, for all I know; we provide them with all the cover they need to hide in plain sight. But your presence, here, allows them to claim reasonable doubt, should there ever be any charges of conspiracy. They're playing you as cleverly as you're playing them. That's why they've fallen over themselves to be so accommodating to you; letting me come here is only part of it; they want to ensure they keep you sweet. You're an important part of their alibi."

He stopped again in mid-stride and turned to me and gave me another slap on the shoulder. "Bloody good show, Jethro. Colonel Walsingham said you'd work it out if you didn't get too caught up in your own role as Hannay. It's like a great game of chess, isn't it? They move, we counter-move; they make another move, and so on."

A game of chess? I should cocoa. At least on the chessboard, you could always recognise each piece for what it was; you knew how it moved. The white pieces were always white, the black, always black; the red, always red, if that's how they were coloured to start with. But on this side of the looking-glass black could be white; or a pawn be taken for a knight. And black hats or blackshirts, as Walsingham had said, people saw themselves as patriots. Traitor or hero, double agent or spy, it all depended on how you looked at it. I gave him a narrow-eyed look, then. "Well, I can only hope, Simon, the end-game doesn't also turn out to be a game to the death."

"Never say die," he said, turning to face Vashfield Hall again.

Yes. My old dad had said that, apparently, the day he died, and people always said how I took after him. "Onwards and upwards," I said. And Simon nodded and continued on round to the front of the house and I veered off around to the rear for one last look before the light faded. I stayed in character, even if only to satisfy the two estate-workers that'd had us in their sights since we'd left the shooting grounds. So I stopped every now and then, my binoculars glued to my eyes, and moved back and forth, and round and round, as if to capture the flight of some elusive tiny bird, and soon I'd seen all I needed to see. I didn't plan on climbing up or down any drain-pipes, later, but if a quick exit through a window was called for, I wanted to have all possible lines of escape well-mapped-out.

I went on round, past the west wing and the conservatory, and was passing through the stable yard when a commotion broke out in one of the stable blocks. I heard a horse whinnying like mad, and I ran over to see if anyone needed help; not that I know the first thing about horses; I prefer motorbikes, but Jeffrey Hannay, from the wilds of Canada, was another story. So I dashed in through the open stable doors and I came face-to-face with the front end of a big black stallion standing on its hind legs and the rear of a horsewoman holding a carriage whip. It looked like something out of a circus act. But the woman wasn't whipping the horse; it was more like she was waving her arms like a conductor. Then she stepped back and the horse gently dropped its forelegs down onto the ground and the woman went over and patted it on its muzzle and blew in its nostrils, and she cradled its massive head in her arms and stroked its forelock and its ears. The horse whinnied again, and maybe I did, too, and the woman turned around, and of course it was "the actress," herself, doing another special one-woman performance.

Her riding breeches were on so tight, for one giddy moment I thought she wasn't wearing anything, save for a black velvet jacket, crisp white shirt, and black leather riding-boots. Then she moved, and I heard the rasp of material against material; not quite silk on silk, but still the same promised whisper of earthly delights yearning to be released from bondage.

"Do you know who I am?" said the haughty lady, on her high horse.

"I have no idea," I said, feigning ignorance, with just the right touch of indifference. "The bored, but dutiful wife of one of the other guests?"

She threw her delicious neck back in a gale of tinkly laughter, just as I'd seen her do a thousand times on the stage. And she did it so very well; just long enough for any admirer to admire the swell of her breasts, her beautiful swan-like neck, and her partly opened, oh, so inviting lips. But as I said, she'd had a lot of practice, even down to the little start of realisation that you were staring at her, followed by the lowered chin, breathy voice, and the slow, demure batting of her long and so very luscious eyelashes.

"I'll just call you Rosalind," I said; the very first words out of my mouth. Well, what with all the dressing up in disguise and not being who you really were, it only seemed appropriate. And I know it sounds funny, what with everything else going on, but I couldn't bring myself to call her by her real name; that was linked to me and my past; not Jeffrey Hannay. "And you can call me Orlando or Touchstone; or as you like," I said.

"I like it well," she said, quickly getting into the act. "And you, really, don't know who I am?" she said, still flirting with the whole idea, her voice at once both cajoling and cruel.

"No, who are you, really?" I said.

"I am . . . I am all the women of Shakespeare, Sheridan, and Shaw," she said, doing her coquettish throwing-her-head-back routine again. I wanted to add that she'd been a good few of Terence Rattigan's dishy dames, as well, but no fool I, I stopped myself just in time, and we exchanged those looks that men and women do that suggest desires as yet unfulfilled, very soon might well be. And we might've made hay, right then and there, on the stable floor, if it wasn't for the big bloke in a footman's uniform that came into the stable yard and started calling out her name. And the horse whinnied again and the moment was lost forever.

CHAPTER

31

New Worlds, Old Empires

It was formal, with full regalia expected: all medals, orders, insignia, sashes; and tiaras, too, where appropriate. It was as grand a display of privilege and position as might be seen at a State banquet. And for much the same purpose; to affirm to all that there were those present that not only had the right to rule, but also the duty to do so. It was a cross between *The Prisoner of Zenda* and a Nuremberg rally.

The guest of honour, Sir Oswald Mosley—Tom to his friends—and his coterie had swept in from a big May Day rally and parade in the East End, and had immediately gone upstairs to change. His wife, Diana, Lady Mosley, had been the first to reappear; flanked by two muscle-bound Mosley supporters who thought themselves very dashing; but all eyes had gone straight to Lady Diana. She was a legendary beauty, and if looks could kill, "the actress" would've done murder right then and there. What she had in dark sultry brunette, Diana Mosley had in icy blonde, but in social terms there was no real contest. Lady Diana had had the benefit of title and fortune before she'd left her husband to marry Sir Oswald Mosley. Even beauty has its own aristocracy. Not that I'd had much time to give her the once-over. As even before I'd taken my first sip of champagne, I was cut away from the rest of the flock by two retainers; their whispers as efficient at steering me out of the room as a couple of border collies snapping at my heels. "Lord Vashfield wonders whether you'd spare him a few moments in the library, sir?" said the one; "Please follow me, sir," said the other; neither of them waiting on a reply. So, of course, I threw my shoulders back and followed. It all seemed informal enough, but on entering the library I could see from the way the men were positioned in the smoke, that they could've set up enfilading fire at the drop of a handmade cigarette. "Come in, dear boy. Shan't keep you long. Just wanted to say hello, introduce myself and a few people." He looked like George Sanders; same manner, everything; and as he gestured to his other guests, I tried my utmost not to stare at the stub of a finger on his left hand. "Lord Whorley, Lord Ogilvy-Jordan-Stewart, Lord Hammondon, Lord Belfold, Sir Oswald Mosley."

I nodded at each of them, in turn, but stopped short at bowing. Then I just stared at the two men whose shadows had seemed to darken my every step for months; no one moving; no one saying a word.

"You did well, if that was your first time at traps."

I turned to Lord Vashfield, grateful for the diversion. "I think it was more a question of beginner's luck, your lordship," I said.

"A glass of sherry?" he said, turning to an exquisite lead-crystal decanter to pour me a schooner the size of a tea-clipper.

"Family originally from Scotland, I hear," one of the other men said. I think it was Lord Ogilvy-something-something.

If he couldn't tell, my accent was very definitely slipping. "Glencoe, my lord," I said, with a pronounced burr, quietly thankful I hadn't slipped and said, Glenlivet, by mistake. "Three brothers, all emigrated to Canada around 1876; one of them my great-grandfather. All the boys in the family are sent back to school, in Scotland, lest we forget; went to Fettes, same as my father." Bosanquet had sweated cobs over the details; just enough of the past to give basis for a believable history; just enough, to carry the story forward to the present, and no more.

"Understand, your family's in timber?" said a voice that verged on patronising. I turned; somehow not surprised to see it was Lord Belfold that'd spoken. He looked like Claude Rains, gone completely bald.

"And mining, as well," I offered, helpfully. But he didn't care; none of them did; they were there to assess the character of my politics, the cut of my jib, and whether my family name could add weight to their cause.

"Couldn't find a listing for your company, anywhere," he drawled.

"Entirely family-owned," I drawled back. I smiled and put down my glass, took out a gold cigarette case and slowly tapped a handmade cigarette up and down on the outside of it. "Might I have a light?" I said, lightly, a man amongst kind, if not entirely amongst equals.

"Knew Lord Tweedsmuir, did you?" asked Lord Whorley.

"No, my lord, but many of the family did. Canada has had no better Governor-General. A good man and, of course, such a splendid author," I said, thankful yet again for Bosanquet's head for details. He'd known the Hannay surname would come up at some point; how could it not? "The family think it a hoot they may have been the source for the hero in *The Thirty-Nine Steps* and those other books Buchan wrote. Though one or two were rather put out when Hitchcock made the Hannay in his film a mining engineer from Canada, and not South Africa, as in the novel. My Uncle Dickie is still trying to live it down." I allowed myself a chuckle. "Though, he tends not to, whenever ladies are present."

"Was just going to say, I met Buchan when he was called to the Bar," Whorley said, now quite indifferent to the Hannay pedigree.

Vashfield cleared his throat. "Heard you'd been expressing some interesting opinions, Hannay. And was wondering whether you'd care to share some of them." He gestured with his left hand, leaving a trail of cigarette smoke in the air. "We're just a few friends who share a common concern for the weak-ened state of the country and the all-too-rapid decline of Britain's cultural and commercial influence abroad. Friends, who share the belief that to succeed society needs to adopt the longer view, as much in regard to past glories, as in how best to deal with present uncertainties."

I opened my mouth and jumped in with both feet. "If, my lord, you mean, do I believe the only proper way to harness the future is by holding onto the best of the past, as only then can we be assured of a prosperous and stable present? And that those few men capable of creating such a brave new world have a moral duty to do so, and by whatever means are neces-sary. Then I do." I didn't really know what I was blathering on about; I'd lifted it lock, stock, and barrel from *Naught Shall Make Us Rue.*

"But I'd understood Professor Tybarn's work wasn't at all to your taste," Lord Belfold said, with a feigned air of puzzlement.

"Only that it doesn't go far enough, sir," I said. "In my book, history is for making; not for gathering dust in universities and libraries." And that got me nods of approval all round, even from Belfold. Mosley leaned over to light my cigarette, which made my flesh creep, but I forced a smile. And they all stood there, in the glow of the fire, radiating effortless authority and nonchalant power, a club so exclusive it didn't exist unless they acknowledged it as having substance. And I held onto my cigarette as if to a rope and waited to see whether I'd managed to bag another string of birds. Though, it was less a question of whether I'd be blackballed from the club or not; it was more, whether I'd be taken out into the woods and shot.

"Well, Tom," Vashfield said, "let's hope there are others out there, like young Hannay, here. Because if, as you were saying earlier, today's rally in London points to a growing wave of popular support, then it does indeed suggest the political tide may well be turning in our favour."

There must've been a hundred people attending the banquet. "Very grand; very pre-War," I overheard one bejewelled lady utter. It was, too. I looked around me and it's true what they say, the rich are different. They didn't look so battered and knocked about; there wasn't a gaunt or haunted face in sight. And all dressed up as they were, in black-tie and elegant new gowns, it was obvious they lived in a different world to everyone else; not for them, the unrelenting drabness of deprivation and rationing.

Drinks were served in the drawing-room and dining-room, as well as the antechamber, and I wondered where they were going to seat us all. So I drifted through into the dining-room and saw that the glass-panelled doors at the far end had been opened, and everything set up in the space beyond, in what the house plans had identified as a large gallery. But at some time or another, it'd been turned into a ballroom, with tall French doors on two sides, opening onto narrow corridors. The wood panelling was painted cream and the walls pale green. Details were picked out in gold. And there were floor-to-ceiling columns in a green so deep as to be almost black, that on closer inspection revealed themselves as heavy velvet hangings tied back with tasselled, gold-silk ropes. It could've been a film set; it looked so grand; and had someone proclaiming himself to be the Emperor Napoleon Bonaparte marched in at that point, I for one wouldn't have been at all surprised.

I felt someone slip their arm through mine and I knew the evening was back on course when Miss J. Manning asked me if I'd be kind enough to escort her into dinner. "An honour," I said. And with a quick shuffle of the place cards, so snooty Cmdr. J. Russell, USN, sat next to the snotty horse-lady, the Hon. Lady something-or-other and I sat next to Jennifer and, as they say, I was off to the races. She was giddy with pieces from Shakespeare she was learning for future auditions. So I played along and delighted in her joy, and spoke what few verses of the Bard's I could remember, and for much of dinner we were off in our own little world.

Then in a voice loud enough for a Church Street coster on a slow Saturday, the toastmaster called everyone to silence for Mosley's speech. "My lords, ladies, and gentleman, please pray you silence for Sir Oswald Mosley." There was a brief murmur as Mosley rose to his feet, then an expectant hush. He was a pariah to much of English society, having once been its golden boy and would-be saviour, but you could tell by his manner he felt that he and his ideas were still more than worthy of an audience; the self-assurance was quite undimmed. The face was fuller, the hair not as slick or as black as it had once been, but it was unmistakably Mosley: the dark, piercing, button-like eyes; the flared nostrils and military moustache overshadowing a too thin-lipped smile; the arrogant tilt of the chin. In the early days he'd been dubbed "the Sheikh," but once he'd abandoned the politics of Parliament for those of the street, his followers called him "the Fox." There was no preamble. No it's nice to see you all again. He just looked down his nose, cleared his throat, and launched into his speech, and spoke for twenty minutes or more without notes.

"Our present-day Government is guilty of a great betrayal, and one day it will stand before the bar of history and be utterly condemned. There is a lack of meaning and commitment in modern Britain, but I tell you it is not true that all the great causes we fought so valiantly for, in the Thirties, have been lost to history. There are great and brave causes left, and though the building of Europe is but one of them, it is arguably the greatest one before us. And what glory then." He resembled nothing so much as an over-aged Romeo playing Hamlet. He adopted the stance and postures of a younger man and tried to call up all the passionate intensity of youth, but the heavy jowls and thickened neck and waist robbed him of any real drama. Even the abrupt tosses of his head and pointed jabs of his outstretched arm seemed strangely ponderous and out of place.

"The decline of British power; the loss of Empire because of an unnecessary war against Germany; the fact that Britain's then leadership hesitated to work towards unity with Europe, which alone could have made Britain independent of the powers of America and the Soviet Union. This is history we cannot change. But the dream of our once-promised future is not lost; it is still within our grasp, if only we choose to act now." He thrust out his chin, held his fist across his chest. "Do you not hear the steady drumbeat of progress? How can you not? For it is within us all, the heart that built an Empire the like of which the world had never seen. And I tell you it is time you heed that stout British heart again. For in the New Europe, there would not only be a common government for a people that have shared over two thousand years of history, but also a common market with the New Britain at its heart. A New Britain from whence we would look out upon a New Empire that is Africa."

He hooked his arm out, like a boxer, as if to pull the crowd in closer. "Yes, Africa will become Europe's new Empire. Yes, Africa. That vast land will provide Europe with all the minerals and raw materials it requires and, with proper husbandry, much of its food. It has the space to absorb all of Europe's unemployed. And soon Europeans would have the highest standards of living in the world. And Europe's success under an enlightened system of benevolent, but properly informed leadership would be seen by all, and could not therefore be denied. Then, my friends, Communism would collapse. For how could it not?"

His vision revealed; the spittle flying, now; he jabbed the air with his fist, as if to knock some sense into those who could not grasp what he could so plainly see. "And as if harbinger to this success, this May Day has been made glorious by the growing wave of support I have witnessed on the streets of London, and here again tonight; support that comes from Britain's brightest sons, its Dominions' brightest sons. And I tell you that this glorious tide will continue to rise up until it lifts Britain's beleaguered ship of State back onto the course it was always destined to follow."

The foxy old bastard pointed straight at me during the bit about the Dominions' brightest sons. So I lost the flow, then. But he went on and on about "Europe a Nation, Africa the Empire." Punching home the point, again and again, that it was imperative Great Britain move towards a union with Europe. It would, he promised, be a brave new world, and the British Union Movement could most assuredly lead us all there, to our true destiny and rightful future. All we need do was listen to our stout British hearts. "And may God save the King," he said. Then he sat down.

I don't know if talk of a new Europe was quite what people had been expecting; there was only a polite smattering of applause afterwards. But Belfold rose to his feet to thank Mosley for a most challenging and edifying speech, then went on to praise Lord and Lady Vashfield for their noble patriotism. And even I noticed that whereas Belfold's response to Mosley was very cut-and-dry, his praise for the Vashfields almost knew no bounds. I thought at first it might be simply because Mosley had trumpeted his Union Movement, and not the united forces of the New Right. But then I noticed the two men seemed to be avoiding even looking at one another, which was interesting as it suggested that perhaps something was out of joint between Mosley's British Union Movement and Belfold's New Order of Britain. Of course, it could've just been me imagining things, and I thought to ask Simon Bosanquet whether he'd noticed anything amiss. But then the toastmaster called out for all present to charge their glasses, so that he might lead their lords and ladies, and honourable guests, in a toast to the King. And I found myself standing, glass in hand, lost in thought, and not really there, at all. It shows you how daft I can be sometimes, because I completely missed the look in Miss Jennifer Manning's eyes. And given what transpired later, she wasn't the only person in the room giving me a second look, apparently.

I tell you, it never rains but it pours.

CHAPTER

32

Miscue

The rule is dukes go first, then marquises before earls, viscounts before barons, and pearls before swine. So, of course, I found myself in the baggage train again, bringing up the rear. But when I spied their lordships all quietly slipping off in the direction of the library . . . etiquette, be damned, I excused myself from Miss Jennifer Manning and made a beeline for Sir Simon Bosanquet, Baronet, swaying a little, as I went.

I caught up with him in the billiards-room, already racking up balls for a game. "It's vital I disappear for half an hour or so, Simon. So make up an excuse for me; say I'm feeling dizzy or something, and need to get some fresh air." He cottoned on quickly, and his face a sudden mask of polite concern, he patted my arm and wished me well. Then with my own face suitably blank, I turned and made for the door. But as I'd learned from Ray, if ever you want people not to notice you're missing, give them a reason to forget you, and anyone who can't seem to hold their drink gets pushed out of people's minds faster than a lame joke.

I didn't overplay it, though, I just acted as if I was trying to appear my usual sober self, and made my way a little too slowly down the corridor, stopping every now and then to hold onto the wall panelling. I'd done much the same when I'd searched high and low for the hidden doorway in the dead of night. But the way I saw it, if the butler could locate it, night in, night out, I should be able to without too much trouble. It took me nigh on twenty nerve-wracked minutes, but in the end I found the key to it; you pushed a certain wood panel inwards, while pressing down the lower bevelled edge of the adjacent panel. Sounds complicated, I know, but once you'd got the hang of it, you could do it in your sleep.

The risk was that the passage might not be empty, but faint heart never a fair lady or full pocket yields. And so with a last look up and down the corridor, I did the business with the wood panelling; counted, one, two, and on three, pirouetted inside. The first time in, I'd discovered two large wooden discs the size and thickness of boot-polish tins, high up on the wall; push the top one in, the secret door opened; push in the bottom one, and it closed. So I shut myself in and stood in the silence and let my eyes adjust to the darkness. I was alone. I gave Lady Luck a nod of thanks, then shook off Hannay and became Jethro.

The passageway was just wide enough to admit a man wearing a cavalier's hat and sword. And with my hands touching against both walls, I inched my way through the darkness, feeling for the first of two small recesses that stood either side of the chimney-breast. Cut high into the wall of each alcove, were a number of teeny, tiny, diamond-shaped holes tailor-made for spying. And the very first thing I'd done when Vashfield had had me in the library was to try and locate those same secret spy holes, from the other side. It was obvious, though, once you knew where to look; they were discreetly hidden behind patterns of latticework in the ornate, carved wooden panels that surrounded both mantelpiece and fireplace. I pressed an ear to the wall and from the commotion going on inside the library, it was clear I'd come in at the tail end of a heated argument and that tempers were still roiling, despite Lord Vashfield's attempts to cool things down. "Gentlemen, gentlemen, please, we must agree to disagree. For us to fall out amongst ourselves, now, would be the utmost folly."

"The utmost folly, Lord Vashfield, would be for us to continue with Belfold's scurrilous plan, despite his silky assurances to the contrary. As if recent events at NOB HQ weren't warning enough, there was the incident at his house in Berkeley Square that resulted in the loss of several of the Keys. And as we have it on good authority someone in MI5 is setting up an operation against us, it's imperative we display the utmost caution. Especially now, when so much is so clearly within our grasp. We must destroy any and all evidence that could possibly be used against us."

"What, destroy the Keys, ourselves? Are you mad, Mosley?"

"We have no more need of them, Belfold. Don't you realise what's happening out there? Are you that blind? The people are speaking."

"But only to you, Mosley, is that it?" snorted Belfold.

Vashfield stepped in, again. "Gentlemen, please. Our unity is our strength. But you have made some telling points, Tom, I grant you. Deeds planned and deeds done in secret are one thing; but evidence that gives them proof, is quite another." He gave a little chuckle, as if to try and lighten the situation. "After all, was it not but a single letter of her assent to insurrection that lost Queen Mary of Scots her head? The Keys have already achieved much for us, in opening the way forward, perhaps now is the right time for their destruction; for the security of all we hold dear."

Belfold spoke up then, now all honey-tongued reasonableness. "The theft of those Keys was unfortunate, Tom, I grant you, but is of no real significance; the photographs have all been reprinted. The master file was never in jeopardy; as you can see it's safe, there, on the table in front of you. Even the loss of a few Windsor letters is inconsequential; there are more than enough Nazi documents on the Duke's activities seeded throughout the Kingdom for even those dullards in the Communist Party of Great Britain to be able to piece it all together, ten times over. A legerdemain, I need hardly remind you, only made possible by us having the necessary means for blackmail. How else do you think it was that we acquired a copy of the CPGB's very own master list?"

"As usual, Belfold, you miss the point," Mosley shot back. "If MI5 ever got their hands on the Keys, it would condemn us all. And I, for one, do not intend to spend another night at His Majesty's pleasure. Prison is absolute hell, as you'll no doubt soon discover. As for me, my duty's clear."

There was the sound of a scuffle. Then Vashfield said, his voice incredulous, "You'd actually point a gun at me, Tom?"

"To save the future, yes," Mosley said, in a steely voice. "Now get back, all of you." It was like something out of John Buchan. Blimey. I'd thought he'd just made it all up. I heard the sounds of paper being ripped and torn, and my imagination ran riot. Then I smelled smoke. I pressed my face into the wall, desperately trying to see what Mosley was doing.

"What the hell are you doing, Mosley? Have you lost your senses?"

"No, if anything, I've come to them. I detest you and your grubby little books of blackmail, Belfold. Whatever early successes they might have brought us, I see now that they can only lead to disaster. You cannot win by alienating so many important people; you have to win hearts, as well as minds, if you are to build anything that will last. If only you had the patience to wait for that support to grow, it would deliver us Parliament, the country, an empire, everything. If only you had the eyes to see that there are hundreds, thousands of people out there, people like that young Hannay, with a real hunger for change and for proper leadership."

"Again, just as long as it's you that leads them, is that it, Mosley?" drawled Belfold. "You're ruining everything, you damn, conceited fool."

"Not fool enough to want to stay in the same room or circles as you, Belfold. You, who it now appears, will stop at nothing, even murder, to see that your evil schemes succeed. You are despicable, an utter disgrace to the cause. I'll have no more of you."

"Tom, Tom, I beg you to reconsider." Vashfield again. Then I heard more pages being torn and ripped. "Tom, please. If you destroy the master file, you'll do very great damage to the cause."

"It's too late, Vashfield. I must do my duty and follow my destiny."

"Oh, tosh, Mosley," Belfold snarled. "You didn't succeed with your blasted Blackshirts. What makes you think you can win people over now with your empty rhetoric about a united Europe? You fool, the Marshall Plan means the Americans will have a stranglehold there, for years."

"All the more reason for the great British people to act now," Mosley shouted. I heard the sound of a poker being scraped back and forth against the fire-grate. "There, that's done for you." He threw down the poker and stormed out of the library. "Damn you, Belfold, damn you to hell."

It went deathly quiet. Then Vashfield said, in a low voice, "Gentlemen, I wonder if you'd be so kind as to offer Sir Oswald Mosley every assistance as he prepares to depart. Please ensure that he doesn't unduly upset any of the other guests, especially any of the new people attending tomorrow evening's masquerade. Lord Belfold and I will join you, shortly."

There were mumbled responses as the three lords dutifully filed out of the room, and I stood in the passageway, in a spin; and not just from the smell of burning paper, but because it seemed as if the whole bloody caper had just gone up in smoke. Then I heard Vashfield say, "Well, Baron, what's your opinion, now, of our *'yesterday's man'*?"

"It couldn't have gone better, Number Two. Your idea of appealing to his vanity was admirable. The London rally, this evening's banquet, the episode here in the library will have boosted his ego, immeasurably. He'll let nothing stand in his way, now that he believes he's destroyed the master file. You stage-managed everything brilliantly. We are in your debt."

"It was my pleasure to serve, Number One," Vashfield said. "Mosley was like a hungry dog that sees nothing but the bones placed down in front of him."

"It is indeed fortunate that Mosley is so predictable, Number Two. But now we must ensure that the other shoe drops with sufficient force. Therefore, cease all NOB activities and leave the playing field clear for Mosley and BUM. Call on our friends in Fleet Street and ensure that Mosley gets onto all the front pages. Then arrange for demonstrations of support whenever and wherever he speaks. Have banners calling for the establishment of a new King's Party and for the abolition of all

Communist groups. Flood London with pamphlets that draw from *The Protocols of Zion* and that warn against the secret treachery of the Jews. It's imperative we do everything we can to draw the Communists out and force them into using the Windsor letters to try and discredit the Monarchy. And when they do, we'll fan the flames of disquiet until it appears it is the Communists, themselves, who threaten the balance of power. Then we'll unleash an anti-Communist backlash the likes of which has never been seen."

"Number One, it is you who are brilliant," whispered Vashfield.

"Thank you, Number Two, but there are also times when even we must heed a fool. Therefore, as to Mosley's concerns regarding MI5, please ensure that all necessary arrangements are made for the remaining Keys."

"Perhaps, Number One, we should call upon our American friend?"

"Yes, Number Two, now would be the perfect time to use him."

Number One? Number Two? Belfold, telling Vashfield what to do? Call upon our American friend? The world was turning upside down. And if I'd heard it correctly, Mr. James Russell had very cleverly put himself right in the frame; and us out of the game. And I slipped out of my hiding place, and headed in the direction of the billiards-room, wondering whether Bosanquet and me had been completely snookered or not.

CHAPTER

33

A Horse, A Horse

I don't know about any "back-lash" business, what I couldn't get over was the master file going up in smoke, just hours before I was set to do the creep, and I wondered whether Simon Bosanquet would call off the whole caper. I found him all by himself in the billiards-room, cueing up a shot. He looked up from the green baize table. "Word of Mosley's departure spread like wildfire," he said, cannoning a red ball into a corner pocket. "So everyone's gone off for a night-cap and a final gossip before bed."

I told him about the events in the library, and he all but mis-cued at the bit about Mosley burning one of the all-important Red Books. He was as puzzled as I was about the "Number One, Number Two" business and the setting up of Mosley to be the spark in the tinderbox. But he dismissed outright any thoughts I had about Russell being involved. "Colonel Walsingham's oppo-site number at the U.S. Embassy assured us that Russell's involvement was strictly an internal security matter."

"They're pulling the wool, more like," I said, still not convinced.

"Either way, we have no choice, but to carry on," he said. "And given tonight's events, I think it wise we show our faces in the drawing room, and go have a nightcap; we may hear something more."

But we didn't. What conversation there was, was muted, and most of the other guests had already called it a night by the time we arrived. And so I sipped a brandy and watched the die-hards get more and more tipsy, before they, too, drifted off to bed. It'd been bad enough the night before, more a French farce than anything, what with all the creaking of the floorboards and the opening and closing of bedroom doors that went on for a full half-hour after everyone had supposedly retired for the night. I'd had to give it another full hour before I'd ventured out in search of the secret passageway, and I didn't see how tonight would be any different.

It seems it was custom, for those guests that elected to play, to switch bedrooms. And I only mention it, because I went the long way round to my room and just happened to find myself on the corridor that went past Miss Jennifer Manning's bedroom, and an envelope slid out from under her door and stopped right in front of me. And inquisitiveness often being an unfortunate part of my nature, I picked it up and read it.

> *Thou know'st the mask of night is on my face,*
> *Else would a maiden blush bepaint my cheek*
> *For that which thou hast heard me speak to-night.*

There was no signature, just a *Wherefore art thou?* at the bottom. And my first mistake was in not immediately walking away, because then I heard the key turn in the lock and saw her door opening. My second mistake was in thinking I had the time; my third, that even before I knew it myself, I was standing inside Jenny's bedroom and she was leaning back against the now-closed door, her pale hand to her brow. *"What man art thou that thus bescreen'd in night, so stumblest on my counsel?"*

I had to think. "Er, *there lies more peril in thine eyes than twenty of their swords,"* I said softly, pleased I could remember a little of what comes before a favourite line. *"I have night's cloak to hide me from their sight."* Then I looked around and realised that Jenny was perhaps more eager for the Bard, than for bed. For on the floor, amidst a sea of writing paper, was her diary, a copy of Shakespeare's *Sonnets,* a big, illustrated book of his plays, and a heavily underlined paperback text of *Romeo and Juliet.* And suddenly, it was all too clear how truly innocent it all was; she simply wanted to pick up from where we'd left off, earlier. I'd encouraged her and this was my reward, a private performance. But that's the funny thing about encouraging someone: if the person then embarks upon the course you've helped set for them, the consequence is that you become partly responsible for the outcome. That's how it is with me, anyway. And so there I was, suddenly feeling very protective towards her, like an older brother, and we just sort of sat there, cross-legged on the floor, with her reciting lines and me listening and quietly applauding. And time flowed gently by, then I said I had to go, and gave her a hug and told her she should get a good night's sleep as she had an important audition on the morrow. "Break a leg," I said. "Knock 'em dead." And she stood up on tiptoes and kissed me on the cheek, then she blinked, and I was gone. It was the oddest start to a caper I've ever had; but I tell you, it beat lying on the tiles in a cold, wet, miserable London fog into a cocked hat.

Out in the darkened corridor, I cupped my hand over the luminous hands of my watch; it was not yet a quarter of one.

More than time enough to prepare and be out on the creep by two, and be done by four, five at the very latest, and be back before cockcrow. And I moved as drifting smoke back towards my room. The burned and blackened piece of matchstick I'd left wedged between door and frame was still in place, and I unlocked the door and pushed it open to find my room bathed in red light. And what is it they say, "each time a door closes, another door opens?"

She'd thrown red scarves over the lampshades and lay on her stomach leafing through my book of British birds, naked but for the tiny golden leather slippers on her feet. There was no need for any come-hither smile or beckoning crooked finger, for even in repose, she was like Salome dancing her veiled promises of unearthly delights. The line that ran from each delicately turned ankle, up across the curve and flow of her calves and thighs, would've made Rubens or Rembrandt beg for a stick of charcoal. Her legs were a wonder worthy of a lengthy poem, but she topped them with the most splendiferous arse I'd ever seen on a woman. It was breathtaking in form; like on one of these Greek statues you see down the British Museum; the curves so beautifully proportioned you're afraid to touch them in case your hand might blemish their glory. And feeling myself harden, I crossed the room as silently as ever I'd done when creeping after diamonds, and leaned over and drew my hand slowly from behind her knees, all the way up to her bum. You could've rolled glass marbles down either side of it all day long and not one of them would have wobbled out of true. I leaned forward and kissed both cheeks, and she sighed and moved languidly, and pushed her hips into the bed, and slowly turned over onto her back.

"Where have you been, you naughty boy? I've been waiting ages."

"Er, I went outside to have a smoke and clear my head," I said. "I couldn't sleep. I couldn't, er, get you out of my mind. I was bewitched and I hoped I might find your room and . . . and yet here you were, all the time." It was just a stream of blather, really; the first words that came into my head, but it seemed to mollify her. And she moved her body in that way that women do that says you're welcome. And I stood there and looked at her in the red-shadowed lamplight and marvelled. For she'd shaved herself, or her maid had. It was how dirty pictures looked after the photo-retoucher had had his way. But to see it there, in all its stark nakedness, just as she'd been as a young girl, was strangely breathtaking. It teased as much with the promise that you were not only the first man who'd ever seen her naked; you were also the first man she'd ever gone with.

I got down on my knees by the side of the bed and began to worship at the altar of life. I kissed her belly and then slowly slid my lips down until my tongue found the first gentle fold of skin. And she moved and her legs opened a little and I couldn't help myself, I growled; the musky scent of her was as intoxicating as the smokiest Highland malt. Then she moved her legs again, closing the path, and pulled my head away. And as I looked up, she brushed the fingertips of both hands up over her skin, tracing a line from her belly all the way to her neck. And I followed as if led by a silver cord and sat astride her and covered her like a cloak and began to kiss and explore her face and body with my lips and fingertips. But just as I was getting into my stride, a groan of pleasure starting to rise in my throat, she wriggled from under me and pushed me gently but firmly onto my back.

She went up on her knees and slid a leg over me and sat back on my stomach; my prick caught between the cheeks of her behind, like a bicycle wheel caught in the bars of a fence. Then she inched her way back and back and I thought, Here we go. But she continued to shuffle, back and back, on her knees until she was sitting astride my knees and my cock was standing to attention and saluting her repeatedly like a confused private on parade. And she leaned forward and took me in hand and caressed the family jewels as if she were stroking a diamond necklace from Tiffany's. I could get used to this, I thought. I groaned as she pulled the skin down and began to lick the helmet with her tongue, then she wet her lips and opened her mouth into an O and took me inside; the long dark curtain of her hair drawing a veil over the all-too magical proceedings. "Oh, oooh," I went, but she suddenly slipped from her lips and tongue, to her teeth, and bit me hard and nipped me in the bud. The shock, quite painful, but not entirely unpleasurable; which was a bit odd, in itself.

"No, not yet, my beauty. Not just yet," she said, her voice low, like she was gentling a horse. Then as I started to relax, she slapped my thighs hard, and shook her body as if to awaken sensation elsewhere. And I swallowed and gazed hypnotised at her breasts, and she slid forward and using both her hands she guided me into her as expertly as any stallion put to the tup. Then she sat up and began to squeeze me with her thighs. And I thought it was high time I got back into the act. I mean; fair's fair; but this was supposed to be my game; giving pleasure, so as to take it. And I started to push myself up onto my elbows.

"No, lay back," she said, in a domineering voice. "Let me."

At first I wasn't sure how far she was intending to go. But I thought, Just go with it. And so I lay back and went along for the ride, and at first she rode around the paddock getting the feel of the beast between her legs; sensing its possibilities; and I only say that, because even I'd begun to suspect that's all I was to her. She went from a walk to a trot; up and down, up and down;

that glorious arse of hers slapping against my thighs; her body perfectly erect; her neck, high and proud. Then she took us into a canter and squeezed her thighs and began to gather me up, and we went into a full gallop; up and down, up and down, up and down. Her breath a rasping sound that came from the back of her throat; mine, a deep grunting coming from God knows where. On and on she rode to the first jump, and up and over we went, and undaunted she headed straight for the second, the double-barred gate; and she gathered us up, and we went up and over again. Then it was man and rider going hell-for-leather for the water jump and she screeched with delight at a perfect round with no faults, no dismounts, and no refusals.

I went limp from all the effort, but she stayed in the saddle, a fine sheen of perspiration glistening all over her body. She leaned forward, her hair touching my chest, and I waited for the kiss, but she just took my lower lip between her teeth and bit me until she drew blood. "Now you've been properly blooded," she said in a mocking voice, suddenly devoid of all allure. And I didn't much fancy anything else after that and I shoved her away. "Bitch," I said. And she snorted loudly and shuffled backwards and I rudely fell out and without so much as another glance, she slipped off the bed in one easy, fluid motion and stepped into her leather slippers and silk dressing gown. She turned, the legendary coquette taking her curtain call, but she didn't wait for any applause, she just shook her mane of hair and made a neighing sound. "Good horsey," she said. Then she walked over to the wardrobe, opened the door, stepped inside, and was gone.

I replayed that last bit over again in my mind. So it was the secret-door-in-the-wardrobe routine, was it. At least that explained why the matchstick had still been jammed in the doorjamb. I felt the cold wetness on my belly and slid off the bed and went over to the wash-basin and used the hand-towel to dry myself. I turned and looked at the crumpled sheets. It'd been very pleasurable in lots of ways, but there was no feeling of warm elation spreading through me; nothing; I just felt sort of empty. Not that every time's a winner, but I always have to love the woman I'm with; even if only a little bit. Then all of a sudden it dawned on me, and it was such a new sensation I wasn't sure how I felt about it. I'd been used, pure and simple. It really hadn't mattered to her who I was, I'd just been a new horse that'd caught her eye when we'd all been paraded round the show ring, champagne glass in hand. Or maybe she'd even been put up to it; to draw Hannay further in; and that was a sorrowful thought. I snorted myself then and turned and looked at my face in the oval mirror on the wall. "Not one of your better nights, my old cock," I said. And the man in the mirror nodded his head in agreement. But I couldn't stand around like a horse feeling off its food, I had work to do. And I poured cold water into the bowl and splashed it all over my face. Then I began to assemble my proper screwing clothes and ready myself for the creep.

CHAPTER 34

Holes in the Night

I had a black, brushed cotton shoe bag with holes cut in appropriate places to use as a balaclava. Hanging in plain sight in the wardrobe, was a short black, zip-up golfer's jacket on one hanger and a pair of black twill trousers on another. My black roll-neck sweater and black-leather turtles were in a chest of drawers with my other clothes. In a games bag, I had a pair of black plimsolls, a jockstrap, a rugby shirt I'd had dyed black, and a small black canvas satchel filled with assorted socks. My twirls were nestled in amongst the scissors, tweezers, nail-file, and safety-razor inside my toilet kit; and coiled inside the false bottom of one of the suitcases was a length of black silk rope and a collapsible grappling hook. The cherry, though, was a walking stick that unscrewed into two; the top part of which became a very useful petercane. And Bob's yer uncle; I was ready to do the business.

I unlatched the window; half-turned the key in the door; then stepped into the wardrobe. I slid open the rear panel that

Madame had so obligingly failed to lock earlier, and gave the wardrobe door on her side a gentle push. She was lying on her back, snoring away. I stepped through into sleeping beauty's boudoir, unlatched her bedroom window, then opened her bedroom door a hair and pushed tiny squares of felt into the holes in the striker plate, so the latch and bolt couldn't engage. Then I slipped out into the corridor, closed the door behind me, and flattened myself against the wall to let my eyes adjust.

Small decorative wall sconces, each end of the corridor, gave just enough light for guests not to bump into furniture when hopping between bedrooms. But it was still far too bright for my liking, and I shape-shifted from shadow to shadow, making for the main staircase. About halfway there, I heard the scuff of shoes on carpet, so I edged myself back beside a long, narrow table and crouched down into a tight ball.

A figure appeared from around a corner, as nonchalantly as if he was taking a stroll in the park. It was Trent Tyler, in smoking jacket and open-collared shirt. He looked straight at me, but as I was a misshapen shadow amongst other shadows, he paid me no mind. He went into his room, left the door ajar, and the light from inside spilled out into the corridor. I stayed stock-still, heard small sounds of small things being moved, then the light-switch suddenly clicked and the door opened to a deeper darkness and Tyler re-emerged and went back along this corridor. I followed and peered round the corner in time to see a shadow moving in his wake. It was Russell. I watched them both disappear. Quick as a flash, I was inside Tyler's room. I turned the key in the lock, flashed the glim, pulled a rug up over the foot of the door and switched on the light. I scooped up his wrist-watch—a very nice gold Breguet—his gold cufflinks and gold signet ring, then I rifled through his calfskin wallet and trousered all his money.

I scanned the room and my eye was immediately drawn to a smart, black-leather valise the size of a large Gladstone bag standing on a chair by the window. It sported a bright-red Cunard luggage label, of the kind that was only issued to First-Class passengers on the *Queen Mary*. There was a second valise on the floor, next to the chair, that was identical, even down to the Cunard label. So, like me, it seemed he preferred to keep his bags close to hand. I examined both leather name tags, but there were no names written in, just an impressive-looking gold seal showing a bald-headed eagle clutching ears of wheat and a bunch of arrows. I looked inside the first valise. It was empty. So I picked up the other one, and the bottom fell out of it onto the floor. The secret compartment was entirely lined in red leather and had a rectangular space cut out of it that was about twelve-by-nine, and two inches in depth; the exact same size as one of the Red Books.

I picked up the first valise again and pushed the catches every which way, slid my fingertips around the bottom of the case and all along the seams, but no result. Lost in thought, I tapped my fingers up and down on the *Queen Mary*'s three famous red funnels, as depicted on the luggage label, and accidentally hit against a decorative stud on the side of the bag's metal locking bar. I pressed it and it moved, but nothing else happened. Then for some reason, I remembered having to do two things at once when opening the door to the secret passage-way. So, as I pressed in the stud, I slid one of the catches on the top of the case. There was a click and the false bottom fell out, same red-leather lining, everything. I put it all back together again and put it back on the chair. Then I searched every drawer in the room, looked under the bed, on top of the wardrobe, inside the wardrobe, everywhere, but came up with nothing.

I clicked off the light, moved the rug back into place with

my foot, and stood in the darkness, listening. I blinked and it was as if I was seeing a negative, pale shadows on black, and suddenly it was all as clear as day. Trent Tyler wasn't the fool I'd always taken him for; he and James Russell had to be a two-man team pulling their own caper; the very mirror of Simon and me. That had to be it. One man inside; the other giving cover; the two of them maybe even switching roles now and then. And all of it done in plain sight. It would certainly explain Russell's appearance at the publishing party and his presence at Vashfield Hall. That was why he'd tried to see me off. He thought I was a freelance agent and he hadn't wanted me to spoil his pitch. Even then, he'd only backed off when he'd found out I was working for Walsingham. But by the looks of it, it still hadn't stopped the Yanks from going ahead with their plans to nick the Red Books for themselves. "An internal matter?" I should cocoa. What is it they say about honour amongst thieves? I stared into the darkness, as if seeing the two black-leather valises in a new light. Of course, they were empty; it was how the tricky sods planned to get the books out, once they'd got their hands on them. The two of them were doing the old *smuggler's safe* trick, the same as us. So much for us being on the same side. I let myself out of Tyler's room and made for the main staircase, and once I sensed it was clear, I scurried like a black spider down to the ground floor. And moving from deep shadow to deep shadow, I slipped across the hall and into the corridor that led down to the library.

Looking for one or two books amongst hundreds and hundreds of dusty tomes, with just a pencil-torch would've been worse than looking for a needle in a haystack. But when Vashfield had summoned me to the library, I'd taken careful note of which shelves had runs of books with red-leather spines. It wasn't exactly scientific, I know, but it was a start. I flashed the glim and would you believe it, the very first thing I saw was a Red Book on one of the side-tables, near the fireplace. I had it open in a trice, but there was nothing but a thick curl of torn pages inside. It was the one Mosley had burned. So I did some gentle poking with a fire iron, and right at the back of the grate, in amongst the ashes, I found half a dozen or so partial sheets of scorched paper with blackened edges. I lifted them out and shook off the ash. The typewritten letters and numbers looked a little smudged, but I cradled the precious pages as if they were scrolls from some ancient monastery, and looked around and found a copy of *Horse and Hounds* and slid them inside the magazine and slid the whole lot inside my satchel. Then I quartered the room, scanning all the books out on the tables, as well as those on the shelves, but again came up with nothing. I shook my head, thumbed the glim and made for the door.

I padded silently along the corridor, past the billiards-room, down towards the family wing. And I thought things were looking up when I saw there was an alarm system outside Lord Vashfield's study, but it wasn't even armed. It was a cosy little room, almost the size of my entire flat, and by the looks of it, it was where Vashfield usually finished up his evenings. A round mahogany table near the door was littered with all the usual paraphernalia of wealthy men; the little accoutrements that flash quiet signals to others of kind: the gold watch, the heavy gold ring with the family crest, the gold lighter, gold cigarette case, the gold cuff links. But it was a groin; a ring, set with a red gemstone; that caught my eye. It was jasper, probably, and engraved so that like a gold signet ring it'd reproduce its design in relief when pressed into wax. It was the same ring as in the oil painting, the one showing an octopus or a spider. I popped it in my satchel, then rummaged through bookshelves and cupboards and desk drawers, but found nothing of any consequence. Out of sheer habit, I looked behind a painting over the fireplace and found a wall safe. "About bloody time, too," I said to myself. And I turned the handle and the bloody thing opened, so of course, it was empty. What was going on? The place was cleaner than a novice's Sunday-best wimple. I shook my head. Maybe this was what Belfold had meant when he'd given orders to Vashfield to make all the necessary arrangements. Or worse, maybe Messrs. Tyler and Russell had already half-inched everything. It was very frustrating. And there was nothing else for it, but go to Plan B: go for the diamond jewellery, tiaras, and rings and stuff; set the place in a roar; then just sit back and see what happened. I slipped out of the study and made for the Vashfields' bedroom.

And by the time I'd done all the bedrooms on my list, I'd missed two rendezvous times, and even then I only barely made the third. It was one of the very few times I ever heard Simon Bosanquet swear. But that was understandable, as I completely surprised him when I stepped out of the shadows, not three feet from where he was standing. I lifted my balaclava and gave him a wan smile. "Where the hell have you been, Jethro?" he whispered, hoarsely. "I've been worried stiff." He must've been, too, because he called me by my real name, and never even realised it.

He had a dressing gown on over his dress shirt and an unlit cigarette in hand, supposedly in search of a match; an old ruse, but no less effective for that. I handed him the satchel, full of some very tasty trinkets, and shook my head. "No Windsor letters and no Red Books," I said. "I did manage to retrieve half a dozen or so partial pages from the fireplace. But one thing's for sure, the Yanks are definitely up to something, and Russell and Trent Tyler are in it together." He shook his head. "I know what you said, Simon," I said. "But I've seen them at it. So you just watch your step taking all this stuff back to the Bristol, and if you run into them, don't trust either of them a bloody inch. Got your barrel key?" He nodded and was about to say something, when we heard a noise. And I threw him a quick salute and stepped back into the darkness, and the last I saw of him, he was disappearing through the French doors that led out onto the back terrace.

I turned and set sail for my last two ports of call. I mean, I couldn't very well leave Lord Belfold and "the actress" out, now could I? So I made for the main staircase and had just about reached the bottom step, when a footman came out of a doorway on the other side of the main hall. It was odds on he'd see me if I stayed where I was, so I dissolved back into the dark at the foot of the staircase and prayed he hadn't been called upstairs. Then something very odd happened. Commander James Russell, USN, stepped from out of nowhere and headed straight for the footman. "Gee, it's so good to finally find someone," he whispered loudly, his accent suddenly much broader than ever I'd heard before. "This little old place of yours is so big, a guy can't fail to get a little lost. Reminds me of your wonderful Hampton Court maze. And excuse me, but could I possibly get a glass of milk? Only, I'm having a dickens of a job getting off to sleep." I don't know who was more taken aback by it all, the footman or me, but when the two of them went off in the direction of the butler's pantry, James Russell still breezily whispering away, I scurried back up the stairs as if lifted by a prevailing wind. But, as they say, any port or friend in a storm.

Then the gods of Petticoat Lane laughed again. Belfold turned out to be the only other person in the entire house to have a half-turned key in his bedroom door, so I had no choice then, but to go in through his window. I nipped back into sleeping beauty's bedroom, removed the tiny squares of felt from out of the striker-plate, and went out through her window. I inched along a narrow ledge until I came to a main stack-pipe, climbed up to the roof, and then used a rope to let myself down to Belfold's window. I balanced on the ledge, did the catch, then curled into his room like smoke caught in a draft. Then another funny thing: his bed hadn't even been slept in. I scratched my chin. Then I heard noises coming from the wardrobe. The door was partially open; so I leaned in as far as I dared, and heard a male voice whispering in the next room, and a second male voice whispering in reply, and they weren't whispering about whippets or racing pigeons, either. And so very, very gingerly, I inched back out of the wardrobe. I quickly searched Belfold's bedroom. But again, there were no Windsor letters, no Red Books, no safe, nothing. So I swept the room of all its gentlemanly trinkets. Snatching up another very nice gold Breguet with Roman numerals in the process, as well as a large gold-and-jasper signet ring identical to the one I'd taken from Vashfield's room; the one with the octopus or spider or whatever it was, engraved into the red stone. They're both probably members of some terribly exclusive club, I said to myself. I gave a shrug and without a sound was gone out of the window.

Red Herring

The noise built and built; first a click and a clack, a humming and a bang; then something akin to a clap of thunder, as when a tube train hurtles out of a tunnel of darkness into the light. Then endless screeching, metal upon metal, as if a host of angry spirits were calling me ever closer to the edge. And I all but jumped out of my pyjamas when someone began knocking furiously on my bedroom door, a little after six. But I'd had a long night, and the world that exists somewhere between sleep and wakefulness can be a very odd place. "Come in," I shouted. "It's not locked." I switched on the bedside lamp, to see Lord Vashfield's head butler framed in the doorway. "Whatever is the matter?" I said, rubbing my eyes.

"I'm sorry to disturb you, Mr. Hannay," he said, "but, were you by any chance robbed during the night?"

"Robbed of what?" I said, all innocent. "No, I don't think so. I'm sure I'd have heard something. I'll take a look." I got out of bed and began moving this and that, then stopped dead.

"Good Lord, I seem to be missing a few things ... my gold watch, my cigarette case, gold lighter." I snatched up my leather wallet and opened it to show that it was devoid of five-pound notes. I looked up, now rather indignant. "I say, what's going on?"

"It appears the house was visited by a gang of jewel thieves, during the night, sir," he said, very calmly.

"Burgled?" I cried, with just the right hint of disbelief.

"I'm afraid so, sir," he said. "Would you mind if a member of my staff takes a look at the window to see if it's been forced in any way?"

"Of course not," I said. And he turned and nodded, and a beefy-looking servant walked in carrying a torch. "I'm afraid I slept with the window open," I said. "It's the cold night air, it reminds me of home." Steady boy, I said to myself, no need to overdo it. I put on my dressing gown and stood, yawning, seemingly fascinated by chummy examining the window frame for evidence of entry. Out of the corner of my eye I saw the head butler take a quick peek inside the wardrobe. All the clothes hangers were still pushed to one side and the secret panel was still unlocked. But he must've already known that, given the noise I'd dreamed earlier was probably him trying to awaken sleeping beauty next door. Anyway, if it helped confirm his suspicions about who'd slept with whom, the night before, it couldn't harm. Though, how he managed to keep a straight face about it all beats me. It's all down to the proper training, I suppose.

I washed, shaved, splashed on lots of Geo. F. Trumper's Extract of Lime Cologne and After-shave to shock myself awake, then went down to breakfast and was shocked to see Simon Bosanquet talking to one of the footmen in the hallway. He was supposed to be halfway to London. "Ah, Jeffrey," he said, looking up, "running a bit late, due to this beastly burglary business. Had to telephone in a report to the Chief Superintendent, county police. I think he was rather relieved, though, that I had to get back to the Yard; they don't like us nosing around, unless we're invited in. Must dash. Oh, yes, I asked Commander Russell to give you a lift back to town."

I looked at him as if he'd lost his marbles. "You did what, Simon?"

He gave me a look that said, "Don't argue with me on this," then he smiled and said, "Says he'll drop you back at your hotel, in time for tea."

"How very sporting of him," I said, feeling increasingly like a character in a bad drawing-room farce. I raised a very inquisitive eyebrow.

He turned and dismissed the footman, then stepped forward to shake my hand. "Trust Russell, as you would me," he whispered.

"You've got to be kidding," I whispered back. "We've come up empty-handed, and all because of him, probably."

He gave me a steadfast look. "Not every operation is an unqualified success in our game, Jeffrey, and even a draw can count as a win. As I said, never say die." Then with a too-cheery "Cheerio," he turned and strode down the hall and out through the open door to his waiting motor car.

"Have a safe journey, old man," I called after him, suddenly very tired of it all. And I went on into the breakfast room, feeling as if I'd just walked off-stage and into the wings. Failure never sits well with me. But as I stood at the buffet table I noticed I was attracting more than a few odd looks. I looked down to see if my fly was open. It wasn't. So I shrugged, lifted the lid on the serving dish, and then twigged it. I was food for gossip this morning. Word must've spread that "the actress" had given me her stamp of approval. Funny that, seeing as she'd also provided me with the perfect alibi. It's an ill wind, though, that blows nobody any good.

I forked some kippers onto a plate, and was carrying the plate over to a table, when I chanced to look out of the window into the forecourt. The head butler was talking to Simon and pointing back towards the house. "Here we go," I said to myself, and got ready to drop the food and go to his aid. Then I saw two footmen carrying various items of luggage out to the Bristol. The boot was opened; the bags and suitcases stowed inside; then everyone did that awkward military two-step that happens when any ceremony, however trivial, gets interrupted or added to. Then the dashing figure of Trent Tyler strode out to the car; looking even more puffed up than usual. He shook hands with Simon, turned and said something to the head butler, who nodded and pointed to the boot. The footmen stepped forward, held the car doors open, and Simon and Trent Tyler got in, and moments later, the Bristol sped off with a roar, its wheels kicking up little clouds of gravel. It looked just like a fighter plane taking off. I stood and watched it fly down the drive until it was gone from sight. "That's it, then," I said to myself, "all over and done with, bar the shouting."

It's said that any landing you can walk away from is a good landing. It holds true for capers, too, but the very worst of times is at the arse end of a failure. And despite all the planning and scheming, all I'd really managed to come up with were a few burnt pages from one of the Red Books; for once, the jewellery I'd nicked didn't count. I stared out the window at England's green and pleasant land, lost in a world that seemed to me to be about as real as the ones you see in a Fred Astaire or a Marx Brothers film. A staged world filled with people I'd happily steal from, but at all other times would strive to avoid. And suddenly I couldn't wait to take off the mask of Mr. Jeffrey bloody

Hannay. I felt like I was locked in a gilded cage and I couldn't wait to get out and get back to the Smoke. I could see things more clearly there. Royal letters? Red Books? Secret lists? I might just as well have been chasing ghosts. I shivered, and started rubbing the back of my neck, then sensed rather than saw someone move to stand next to me. It was Commander James Russell of the I don't give a toss.

"Mr. Tyler is leaving early, so as not to involve the U.S. Embassy." He paused, then added, "Though, it's unlikely the local constabulary would ever have troubled him, given that he's covered by diplomatic immunity. Living proof, that even bad apples sometimes get covered in candy."

"Coated in toffee, you mean; they call them toffee apples, here," I said with enough of an edge to say I was in no mood for pleasantries. "So why didn't you go with him?" I said, not turning my head.

"I'm staying to show the flag, so the Brits can see it's not the American way to cut and run. Then I'm going to be interviewed by a wonderful British 'Bobby.' And then, as masquerades and amateur dramatics are not at all my cup of tea, not that I would want to be invited, I'm going to drive you back to London. But, as for now, I'm going to try and do my best to enjoy an English breakfast."

If that was his idea of humour, I preferred him being standoffish, at least I knew where I was then; and as if by a common consent we sat at separate tables. And just as well, really, as I all but dropped my fork. It'd been staring me in the face, only I hadn't been able to see it for looking. If I hadn't disliked Russell so much, and discounted Tyler so very readily, I might've seen it earlier. It's funny, isn't it, what the mind continues to sift through even when you've gone on to think of other things. It was Russell mentioning "diplomatic immunity" that had all the shoes finally banging home with an almighty thud. It was the luggage. And I'd almost missed it.

I tried to picture all the pieces I'd seen being carried out to Simon's Bristol, cursing myself I hadn't thought to waggle my ear. Then like a camera lens coming into focus, I saw Tyler's three matching tan-leather suitcases, his tan briefcase, tan shoes, tan gloves, then the two valises I'd seen in his room, not of tan saddle leather, mind you, but black. And not much, in itself, I know, but the mismatch just didn't fit with Tyler or with his fussy fastidiousness. And suddenly I just knew that he hadn't brought the black valises from London with him, and that they weren't his or from the Embassy. Vashfield or Belfold must've given him the Red Books to secrete away in the bottom of the bags that very morning; though where they'd had them hidden, God only knew; in another secret priest hole, probably. But what could be better than to have them driven away by a Scotland Yard police officer; and a baronet, no less? Who'd ever search bags with diplomatic tags, bound for the U.S. Embassy? No one, that's who.

It was as if someone had thrown a switch up in the limes; I felt lit-up again and alert to everything around me. What had been noise before were now vital snippets of conversation. I was like a playwright hearing the chatter of a first-night audience as they streamed back in from the bars for the Final Act. At first, I thought the whole place would still be aflutter over the burglary, but it wasn't. Mosley and his speech weren't really mentioned at all. And even the prospect of being questioned by the police was being treated as nothing more than a minor inconvenience. It was very odd.

Lord Vashfield stopped in to say we should all amuse ourselves while we waited for the police to arrive, and that he hoped it all wasn't too much of a bore. Then off he went to shoot traps with Belfold and the rest of his cronies. Russell, I noticed, went along, too. So some people went riding, others simply decamped to the drawing-room for a game of backgammon or bridge. Me? I went and got my binoculars and bird book from my room. It'd been searched again, of course. Though, it's marvellous what a faint dusting of talcum powder or a hair stuck across a door or drawer opening can tell you. My suitcases had fingermarks all over them, but it was clear, neither one had been forced to give up its hidden secrets.

Talking of which, I went back downstairs and asked if I might call London, and was shown to a little alcove, just off the main hallway, at the head of the corridor leading to the butler's pantry. It was probably the telephone Simon had used earlier, but it was far too public for my liking. On top of which, I had to go through the local exchange, so after asking the operator for the number, I knew I had to watch my p's and q's. And I went through all the usual rigmarole about it being a wrong number, until the woman on MI5's secret switchboard at last agreed to take the call. Then I pretended it was Simon's housekeeper, and called her May; knowing full well that was really the name of Walsingham's Scottish housekeeper.

"Hello, May," I said. "It's me, Jeffrey Hannay. I forgot to tell Simon before he left, that I think I know where Uncle Bill's keys are. I'm pretty sure he dropped them at the Commander's house. Tell him to rustle up some help and go get them. Yes, that's the message. Tell Simon I'll pop round for drinks as soon as I get back. Thank you, May. T.T.F.N." It was right off the top of my head and I know that "Ta-ta for now" was a bit of a stretch for "Trent Tyler," but it was all I could think of at the time. At the very least, I hoped the message alerted them to the fact the game was still afoot. And that done, I strode out through the front door, binoculars and bird book in hand, and scrunched my way across the gravel forecourt. I saw a line of police cars coming up the drive. The long arm of the law. I wondered if I should go and tell them that the butler did it.

I carried on around the grounds and noticed the stables and the yard with all the motor cars were hives of activity. It was the same in the gardens and over towards the shooting grounds and woods. It looked to me like everyone was searching for evidence of trespass, before the police trod over everything. And I'd just got as far as the main house, when Jennifer Manning came out onto the terrace, looking radiant. "Good morning, Mr. Hannay," she said. "May I accompany you on your walk?"

"Good morning, Miss Manning," I said. "That would be my pleasure. You're looking quite radiant, I must say."

"People said the same at breakfast," she said, smiling. "I just told them how very excited I was about my debut this evening. And they all said they were looking forward to my performance with great interest."

"You'll be wonderful, Jenny, really, you will," I said.

"I was hoping to spend a few moments with Miss Felicity Larsen," she said, unknowingly cutting me to the quick by putting voice to the actress's name. "But apparently, she's so distraught over the loss of all her favourite pieces of jewellery, she won't even think of coming down."

I smiled. "She's probably madly learning her lines for tonight," I said, "so she's not totally eclipsed by you and your performance."

"Oh, Jeffrey, you are such a dear," she said, touching my arm.

Then as fate and the local constabulary would have it, one of the footmen called me up to the house for my interview. Jennifer walked with me, arm in arm, and that was almost the last time I saw her, so radiant, so pretty, so full of the joys of spring. "I leave for London, immediately after this," I said. "Then, I'm afraid, I must home to Canada. It was wonderful meeting you, Jenny. I won't forget you and I'll be sure to keep a look out for your name in lights. The very best of luck, tonight. Break a leg."

"Parting is such sweet sorrow," she said softly. "Goodbye, Jeffrey." Then with a little wave of her hand she was gone.

I watched her go, knowing full well that one day she'd meet a Romeo worthy of her. And I turned and went back inside the house, and made my way along the hall to the waiting room that'd been given over to the police to do their interviews in. I gave my address to the Detective Inspector as "the Mayfair Hotel, London, W.1." and told him my Canadian passport was in the hotel safe, and that I'd be happy to present it at Savile Row police station, on the morrow. I handed him an All Canada Timber Consortium business card; a very posh affair on good quality card that Walsingham had had printed up for me. And that went over very well. In fact, the DI personally apologised for any inconvenience caused me. "I'm afraid there's been a spate of these country-house robberies of late, sir. The London gangs seem to be getting bolder by the minute. I do hope it hasn't caused you to form an adverse opinion of our country, sir."

"Not at all," I said, thinking, "If only you knew the half of it, mate."

What did have me seeing red, though, was the shooting party were so tardy in returning to the house, James Russell ended up being almost the last person to be interviewed. And for most of the afternoon, I was coerced into playing backgammon with all sorts of ghastly people. I ended up winning a fiver, but even so, it was almost five o'clock before Russell's black Ford V8 Pilot was brought around to the forecourt. I can't be more precise, my watch had supposedly been stolen, and it would've given rise to some very tricky questions had it suddenly appeared back on my wrist. As it was, it was inside one of my suitcases in the boot of the Ford, along with the rest of my gear, Belfold's knick-knacks, and the actress's favourite jewellery. Anyway, once Russell finally did appear, we quickly got things stowed and then sped off down the driveway into the fast fading light.

But the farther away we got from Vashfield Hall, the more it was as if another pair of blinkers fell away from my eyes. And all the little voices suddenly let loose in my head were yelling at me that I'd been as blind as a bat and as dumb as an ox. And so I tried to fit all the leftover pieces together. Amateur theatricals. Jenny Manning. A masquerade. Men and women in opera masks. It all seemed innocent enough on the surface: a little diversion at the end of a long weekend, a final flourish to all the round-the-clock socialising; but it nagged at me all the same.

Sometimes, though, the missing bit of a puzzle is in not having sufficient distance from it; you have all the puzzle pieces, only you can't see the picture of the wood, for all the oddly shaped trees. Then out of the blue, it's as if the last tumbler in a lock gets pushed up into line and a door swings opens and you see everything from a new perspective. And the truth was, what with the constant strain of being Hannay and always having to watch the accent as much as what I said, I'd only had eyes and ears for my own problems. For a start, everything was riding on me pulling off the creep without being tumbled. There were all the ups and downs at finding the secret passageway, but not the Red Books. Then there was that little riding episode with you-know-who. And then the euphoria at knowing for certain where the Red Books were hidden and being dead chuffed that I'd succeeded again in pulling Walsingham's chestnuts from out of the fire. So, it stands to reason I didn't have my head on straight.

But once that'd all been put behind me, so to speak, what remained stood out as plain as day, and I knew for sure then that I had to get back to Vashfield Hall and be bloody quick about it. Mind you, all this came together in less than a tenth of the time it's taken for me to tell you; but that's how fast the world turns, sometimes.

CHAPTER

36

New Frontiers

"It's Sunday," I said, spying a church steeple in the distance. "What county are we in?" I thought for a moment. "No, we're okay. It isn't dry." I stared out the window at the growing darkness. "And by the look of it, it's already gone opening time." Russell gave me an odd look. "Fancy a drink?" I said. "There'll be a pub coming up in a minute." He nodded, but didn't take his eyes off the road, and within minutes we came to the outskirts of a village and the beckoning glow of a pub sign. We pulled up outside. "Looks friendly, enough," I said, as I pushed open the red-painted door. The regulars in the public bar all pretended not to notice they'd been invaded by foreigners and I pretended not to notice they'd noticed, and when I saw the saloon bar was empty I took us in there. The barman came through from the public bar, his eyes narrowing as he placed our clothes as being a cut above. All the same he treated us with the same courtesy he would anyone else. "Good evening, gentlemen," he said. "What can I get for you?"

I turned to Russell. "Whisky; Johnny Walker," he said in a quiet, American voice. "Make that two doubles, please, and have one yourself, landlord," I said in passable Canadian. I handed over one of the fivers I'd taken from Tyler's wallet. The landlord dispensed our drinks, put them on the bar, along with a soda siphon, then turned back to the upturned whisky bottle in the bank of optics and poured himself a double measure. "Thank you, gentlemen," he said. "And welcome. I'll look in from time to time."

We took a table near the fire. "To our neighbours in the north," Russell said, raising his glass. It took me a moment or two to realise he was toasting Canada. "To our neighbours in the south," I replied, throwing in "and to our British cousins," for good measure. He nodded. "Yes, up the Brits," he said, with no hint of insult. He drank his whisky neat. "You were here during the War, were you?" he asked.

I paused, mid-sup. The trouble with legends, as Walsingham called them, was you never knew where you stopped and myth began. "The Dominion of Canada did its fair share and more," I said affably, "we were in it from day one, you know. But as you ask, yes, I was here and there."

But he persisted. "With your family background you could have easily got out of it; got a cushy posting, somewhere."

I looked him square in the eye. "As could you, I suppose?"

"Fair enough," he said, smiling. "Just making conversation."

I'd been wary of him ever since he'd stuck his gun in my back. And despite him having been given repeated "thumbs-up" by Simon Bosanquet, I still had serious doubts. Save for the episode by the stairs, and at breakfast, he'd remained cold and aloof at Vashfield Hall, and there was no way of knowing whether he'd been playacting then, or was now. And even though he'd thawed a bit in the motor car, I thought it best we keep our distance. The thing was, though, I needed his help or, more accurately, I needed his motor car. And if he wasn't going to play ball, as they say in America, then I was going to have to resort to Plan B, which meant I'd have to incapacitate him with a bottle, a brick, a bat, or with my bare hands. "What about you? Come over with Ike, did you?" I said.

His grey eyes hooded over, for a moment, almost as if he'd been reading my thoughts, then they opened, and so did he. "I was a major in the Army Air Corps," he said. "And like yourself, once we came in, I was in from day one, and was here as much as I was there."

"A flyer?" I said looking at him over the rim of my glass.

"In a manner of speaking," he said, sipping at his Johnny Walker. "So, your family is in mining, as well as timber?"

I took a sip of whisky, too, and tried to remember some of the things Bosanquet had drummed into me. "Yes, with Canada being so rich in minerals and timber, there was room enough for all branches of the family," I said. "Timber, bauxite, copper, zinc; all vital to the war effort."

"My father was a mining engineer," he said, staring into the fire. "So was I, before all this started."

"Really?" I said. "There's far too much explosive around for my liking. At least, when they cut down a tree someone has the courtesy to shout, 'Timber!' Take after your father, do you?"

He looked up at me, I think, a bit surprised to find himself talking about his dad with a relative stranger; but you've always got to be wary if you're truly proud of your family; other people can never see them as you do. "Yes," he said quietly. "He was my hero; utterly fearless above- or belowground; always a man of his word, whether dealing with friend or foe. He was shot dead by bandits while heading up a mining project, in Peru."

"Shot by bandits? And in Peru, too? Blimey," I said, my Canadian slipping dangerously into Cockney. "Er, let me get them in again."

"No," he said, deliberately, getting to his feet. "It's my shout."

Funny, I'd had him marked as being another Trent Tyler: a Yankee snob, acting the Brit. I'd come across boatloads of them when I'd worked on the *Queen Mary,* and they'd got right up my nose. I mean, when I'd asked if I could call him Jim, that first night, with Simon Bosanquet, at the In and Out Club, "No," he'd said, getting all shirty about it, "It's James, if it's all the same to you." I blinked; looked at him standing at the bar; he had the swash of Errol Flynn, but the buckle of Spencer Tracy; the look of action matched with a quiet confidence. Five-foot-eleven; thirteen stone; slight, but muscled. Mining engineer, U.S. Army Air Corps Major, OSS agent, acting Commander USN; he was no simple stranger in a strange land, that was for sure. But just where did he start and end, and who was he really? And was James Russell even his real name? And then, of course, how could anyone with red hair be so reserved and controlled?

When he came back with the drinks I asked him what his father's name was. "Branch," he said, not hesitating. I held up my glass. "Then, here's to Branch and to Harold, my own father," I said. "God bless them."

Bugger, I remember thinking, it was going to be all the harder hitting him with a bottle, now. It's so much easier when you see the man you've got to cosh on the head as the enemy and nothing more. But needs must when the devil drives. I downed the rest of my whisky. "I think I need to get a bit of fresh air," I said, "stretch my legs, before we drive on."

I was first out into the darkness, and I ducked down and away to find the empty beer bottle I'd seen lying on the ground when we'd arrived. It's an old trick if there's going to be punch-up at a pub; get outside fast and first, get your eyes used to the dark, then turn and hit the bloke, framed by light, as he's coming out of the pub doorway. Trouble was, they probably knew the same trick in the bars out in Nebraska, or wherever it was he came from, as he was right behind me, all but treading on my shadow. And gun in hand, he said, "Now, Jeffrey, play nice." And he meant it, too.

"Nothing personal," I said, "but I need your motor car and I couldn't be sure you'd let me have it." He looked at me, his grey eyes flat and dangerous. "Look," I said, "I've got a feeling something bad is going on at Vashfield Hall, a theatrical masquerade or something, only it doesn't add up, and there's an innocent girl caught up in it all, so I've got to go back."

He nodded and his gun swiftly disappeared back into his pocket. "My one reason for staying on, was to see if anyone let slip anything more about Trent Tyler. We suspect he's engaged in political activity not in keeping with or conducive to his diplomatic status here, but we have no idea to what extent or to what purpose. And the only thing everyone seemed to agree on, was that despite the many new faces attending this evening's event, friend Tyler was going to be badly missed. So, masquerade or no masquerade, for once, Mr. Hannay, you and I have got the same itch. And what I'm saying to you is, I'm coming with you."

"But I thought you and he were buddies; on the same team," I said.

"Nothing could be further from the truth," he said, flatly. "It's simply a case of keeping your friends close; your enemies closer still."

"But why didn't you just arrest him?" I said.

"That you never do; not until you see the whole game," he said.

Blimey, I thought, there's no stopping him when he gets going. "Great," I said. "Just one question, though, have you got any thick woollen socks in your suitcase?"

Back in the Ford V8 Pilot, hurtling through the night towards Vashfield Hall, my directions got us lost a few times, but we found our way in the end. At one point, Russell turned to me and said, "I'd kind of got the impression, earlier, you knew the area real well. How did you know the pub was going to be there?"

"Because there always is one just over the next rise," I said. "If a village is big enough to have a church, there's bound to be three or four pubs along the high street; same, all over the country."

He looked at me for what I thought was a little too long for someone driving on strange roads at night. Then he nodded and turned to face the road ahead, the glow from the dashboard outlining his profile. No, not Errol Flynn, I said to myself, more John Barrymore.

"One thing," I said. "In my book, 'James' isn't at all a name you can shout out in a fight. Do you mind if I call you 'Red,' instead?"

He chuckled. " 'Red' was my father's nickname. It's also mine."

"Right, 'Red' Russell," I said. "I'm glad we've got that sorted out. Let's go and lasso ourselves some bandits, shall we?"

CHAPTER

37

A Darkness in the Night

Vashfield Hall looked like a theatre set that'd gone dead. Even the tiny sliver of moon had all but disappeared from view. Here and there, there was a suspicion of a glow, as if a single candle had been left unattended in some upper room, but it was nothing more than a trick of the light. The entire house was just a greater darkness in the night. And but for the fact there were enough posh motor cars to fill Jack Barclay's showrooms ten times over, all lined up in the courtyard round beyond the stable block, any sane person might deduce that the house was still closed up for the winter.

"Red" drove the Ford off the road and onto some hard ground, and came to a stop behind some bushes so the motor car was hidden from view. He opened the boot—the trunk, he called it—and produced a big hand torch. I did the business with my two suitcases and took out the gear I needed; golfing-jacket, turtleneck, two shoe-bags to use as balaclavas, a pair of thick woollen socks to slip on over my shoes for when we got down to the serious business of breaking and entering. I told "Red" I'd read in a novel it's what professional burglars did to deaden the sound of their footsteps. He gave me another one of his looks and reached into his own suitcase, and pulled out a pair of dark-grey argyle socks. They matched his automatic pistol perfectly. He put on a dark-brown leather flying-jacket and held up a pair of black plimsolls. I shook my head and stuffed my tie in my pocket. "No, keep your heavy shoes on, they're better in a fight," I said. "Set watches." We both fiddled with our wrist-watches. "Set," I said. "Turtles?" He gave me a funny look. "Got your turtles?" I asked again, then realised my slip-up. "Name of a glove manufacturer back in Manitoba. I meant, gloves." He nodded. "Good," I said, slipping a shoe-bag balacla-va on over my head. "Use this," I said, handing him one and without a word, he put it on and both our faces disappeared into the night; and us with them.

I had my Fairbairn-Sykes, a length of silk rope wrapped around my waist, my twirls, pencil-light, and the petercane end of the walking stick. "Red" had his torch and his pistol. At first, we kept close to the trees and walked in single file. Then we made our separate ways across the open field until we got to the landscaped outer-grounds and the manicured lawns that swept up to the Hall. I stopped next to a line of rhododendron bushes and lay full-length on the grass and just stared at the house; my chin resting on my hands, my elbows spread out on the ground like a pair of dividers. It usually takes a few minutes, but when you're bringing your night vision into play, there's a big differ-ence between moving and when you just wait patiently for the night to surrender up its secrets. It's also a good way to calm down if you've walked a distance or had a long climb. "Red" joined me and assumed the pose. "Six men, patrolling in twos," I whispered. "Light-coloured mackintoshes, Trilby hats, Sam Browne belts."

"Where?" "Red" whispered.

I held up two fingers and pointed towards the stable area. Then I held up four fingers and waved them in the direction of the east wing. He nodded. "Follow me," I said. And he did.

It took ten minutes of slow-slow, quick-quick, slow moving between bushes and ornamental hedges to get ourselves situated, then another five minutes to wait for the first set of guards to pass by on their circuit of the house. One of them carried a shotgun. I counted off a full minute, then followed them round to the other side of the east wing. At the corner of the building, just off the path, was what looked to be a cast-iron telephone junction box, just like you see in the street; shorter than a pillarbox, but square, and with slab sides. The humming noise it emitted told me it must be a high-voltage transformer of some kind. We took refuge behind it and I chanced a look and saw the two guards disappear off round the corner where the east wing abutted the main house. "Red" tapped my arm and pointed towards a set of French doors. But I shook my head, and pointed to the far end of the building; I wanted to come in at the opposite end from where the stage was. I took off like greased lightning over the grass, with "Red" hard on my heels. When we reached the flagstones, I flagged us to a stop and went straight into my silent-step routine; one foot down, one foot up; like Charlie Chaplin on roller skates, only in slow motion. "Red" copied me exactly and before you could say, "How's-yer-father," we were across the terrace and up the stone steps, crouched down by a set of tall French doors that opened into the vestibule outside the banquet hall.

I cupped my hands round my eyes and peered in through the glass door. It was pitch-black. I did the business with the twirls and reached in and touched the blackness, which turned out to be a long velvet curtain hung across the entrance. I flashed the knife, peeked through the slit, then turned and nodded, and "Red" joined me in the tiny space between curtain and door. I pointed to my shoes, pulled the woollen socks from out my pocket and slipped them on. "Red" did the same. I felt for the edge of the curtain, held it aside, and we slipped out into the vestibule. I call it that, but it was really little more than a narrow passageway between the dining-room and hall, that allowed for both sets of entrance doors to be pushed back to form a short connecting corridor, as had been done for the Mosley banquet. Now, both sets of double doors were closed and curtained off.

I stopped and cupped a hand to my ear. There was a strange noise coming from inside the hall that sounded like a one-note foghorn repeating itself over and over. I inched open the door to the corridor that ran down the left-hand side of the hall, took a quick peek, then pulled back and shook my head. I pointed to "Red," then back at the French doors, and made a two-handed, downward gesture that said, "Wait over there." He nodded and disappeared back behind the curtain. I shape-shifted over to the far side of the vestibule, crouching down as I passed the main doors into the hall, then I inched open the door to the far corridor and peeked in, and just as quickly pulled my head back out again. It was the same down both corridors, standing room only, with about a dozen or so people, all peering intently at whatever was going on inside the hall. I turned and slipped back across the vestibule, only this time I took a quick peek in through the main doors. And bingo, I had our way in.

I skated over to where "Red" was hiding and got his pistol stuck in my nose for my pains. But he just twitched his mouth in apology and then sticking like glue, he shadowed me back over to the entrance doors. I took another peek inside, opened one of the doors a hair and slipped through, beckoning "Red" to follow. I gently pulled the door closed behind us and we stood there in the dark and tried to still our breathing. It was very clear then, that the foghorn sound came from dozens and dozens of people singing the same word in unison, over and over again. We couldn't see anything, though, as there was a heavy curtain hanging down three or four feet in front of our faces. Just like the ones you see at exits in theatres and cinemas to prevent any out-side light from distracting the actors up on stage or to prevent ghost light from falling across the screen. I stepped forward, flashed the Fairbairn-Sykes, and cut two slits in the curtain, and "Red" looked through one hole and I looked through the other.

It was a simple enough stage set as semi-professional pro-ductions go. All the walls were draped from floor to ceiling in dark velvet curtains, so the eye was drawn immediately to a huge blood-red banner hanging at the far end of the hall. At the centre of the banner was a large white circle, containing a black swastika entwined around a Red Cross of St. George. In each corner of the hall, huge "brutes" threw up columns of white light that seemed to support the very roof itself, and that bathed the entire room in an eerie diffused light that was almost devoid of shadows. It was like something dreamed up by Himmler or Goebbels. And you could bet a tanner to a sixpence, that who-ever had done the lighting, had worked at one of the film stu-dios, at one time or another. At least, I knew now why they needed the high-voltage transformer outside.

The platform where they'd had the head banquet-table the night before had been raised and extended outwards at the mid-dle to form an apron about twenty feet square. And the only prop, on the otherwise empty stage, was a large round table on top of which was what looked to be a large wooden box, five or six feet wide, painted black and draped in black velvet. As for all the people in the hall, everyone appeared to be wearing hooded black cassocks and at first glance it could've been taken for a gathering of monks learning Gregorian chants. But the more I listened, the more I became aware of the constant drumbeat beneath the noise. It didn't sound too saintly, though.

I looked over at "Red" Russell, but it seemed he was as transfixed as I was by what he was seeing. I bet this is a first for the OSS, I said to myself. Then a blast of trumpets pulled me back to the scene on the other side of the curtain. And peering through the tiny slit, I felt just as I'd done as a lad, when ever so slowly turning the handle, I'd had my eyes glued to the flickering images inside the "What the butler saw" machines down the penny arcades.

In Camera

Three figures in blood-red hooded cloaks appeared, as if out of nowhere, and walked slowly downstage. And from the sway of their hips you could tell they were all women. The two on the outside stopped and the one in the middle stepped forward like a bride abandoning her bridesmaids. As she reached the table she produced a long silver dagger from out of the sleeves of her red cloak and pointed it at the velvet-draped box. The chanting started up again and she walked anti-clockwise around the table, her dagger always pointing to the box. The circle completed, the trumpets blared and a spotlight picked out a fourth hooded figure cloaked in red, standing centre-stage right, only it was a bloke this time. He said something to dagger woman and she slow-stepped back across the stage and knelt at his feet as if in penance and held the dagger above her head, and the hooded man took it and held it aloft and the crowd immediately stopped chanting. I tell you, it was as good as anything you could see down the Palladium:

leggy girls, colourful costumes, movements in perfect time with the drums. I couldn't see how they could top it. But they did.

A deep voice boomed and echoed around the hall. *"I am Paracelsus, Saint Germain, and Cagliostro,"* it proclaimed. *"I am Albertus Magnus. I am Mesmer. I am all. I am He. I am Patriarch and Prince. I am Grand Master, and Commander of the Temple. I am Magister, Ippciccimus, and Great Beast. I am that I am. Dost thou swear fealty to me?"*

The audience all roared that they would.

"Then swear thou thy allegiance," the hooded one commanded.

"Magister, Magister," they cried over and over again, until they were called to silence. *"So mote it be,"* he said. *"Then let our sacred ceremony begin."* The drums started up again and the hooded man touched the top of the kneeling woman's head with the tip of the dagger, as if "knighting" her or something. He pointed to each breast, touched her on both shoulders, then he kissed the dagger and threw back his hood. A mask of a goat covered most of his face. Then the trumpets sounded again and the woman in red stood up and turned round and threw back her hood to reveal she was wearing the mask of a cat.

Blimey, I thought, It's Harlequin and Pierrot; what next, Puss in Boots? But, no. Cat-woman slow-stepped to the very edge of the stage and stood there, her arms out in the shape of a cross, then to the beat of the drum, she crossed her arms back over her chest, uncrossed them again, and stepped out of her robe. And there she stood, naked but for her mask, a black, silk cord around her waist, and her black high-heeled shoes. The audience surged forward, but I knew who it was, I didn't need to see her face, I knew the lines of her body as well as if they were a favourite poem. But to my eyes, now, it'd resembled nothing so much as the kind of show you'd see down the

Windmill Theatre, only without the comics. Or a flashier version of the cabarets that got put on occasionally in some of the very, very private clubs that dotted the outer fringes of Mayfair.

And once everyone had got an eyeful, Cat-woman, high priestess of desire, turned and slowly walked back upstage towards the round table. And as she did so, her two hand-maidens slow-stepped their way downstage and reached down underneath the table and pulled a lever or something, and the round table and its odd-shaped box began to tilt forward. "What now?" I said to myself. "Sawing a woman in half?" But as the whole thing continued to tilt, the two assistants pulled away the black-velvet covering, and my words all but cut my throat to pieces. The box was a five-sided, silk-lined coffin and inside it there was a naked woman lying spread-eagled; her hands and feet bound with red rope. And as the audience moved left and right, like waves on a black sea, so as to get a better look, I did, too.

I couldn't see clearly, at first, as Cat-woman was standing in the way. But then as her handmaidens sang, *"Blessed be thy lips that shall utter the secret names,"* she leaned forward and kissed the girl in the coffin full on the lips and then bent down to kiss her breasts. *"Blessed be thy breasts formed in beauty and strength"* the handmaidens sang. Then Cat-woman bent down even lower and my heart just about stopped dead in my chest. I recognised the strawberry-blonde hair. Jenny Manning was staked out, stark naked, like a broken butterfly pinned to a board, and by the look of her, she'd been well drugged. My absolute worst fears, realised. And that was it, they'd crossed the line. So that was the part Trent fucking Tyler had invited Jenny to play, was it? He was going to need a box of his own, when I got my hands on him, the slimy ponce. And as for Miss Felicity Larsen; she whose name I'd been unable to utter for months; I'd drop the iron on her the very first chance I got. I prodded "Red" in the shoulder to get his attention and told him what I wanted him to do. I gave him the petercane and took his glim, but I could tell from the look on his face he knew I was very close to losing it. "Watch the gimbals, Jeffrey," he whispered. "Stay balanced, or we've lost before we've even begun."

I almost told him where he could stick his bloody gimbals, but I didn't, because I knew he was right; I had to stay on an even keel or we were all sunk. But that's the trouble when anyone does damage to family or friend, I tend to run a bit hot before I get cold-blooded. I nodded. "Okay, I'll watch the gimbals 'Red,'" I said through clenched teeth. "Just as long as you get a bloody move on and go do what I asked." And he twitched his mouth and disappeared without another word.

On the clock now, I peered through the slit in the curtain again and it took everything in me to stand there and not rush out and go berserk. Felicity Larsen was pointing out into the audience and the black sea parted, and gave way to a very tall hooded figure, dressed all in black. The man marched up on stage and knelt down on one knee before cat-faced Larsen, and she just stood there, her arms held out wide, loving every minute of it. The trumpets sounded again and the man in black got up, and then held his arms out like a pair of wings, cloaking her from sight. Then he lowered his arms and turned around to face the audience, and Madame Larsen quietly walked off in the direction of the man in the goat mask. But as was no doubt the intention, all heads now stayed fixed on the man in black, and he threw back his hood to reveal the mask of a fox. At least I think it was a fox, it might've been a dog. And he stood there, hands on hips, his cloak held out and away from his body, so everyone could admire the black-leather Sam Browne belt across his well-muscled bare torso, his skin-tight black riding breeches, and his highly polished black riding boots. Then, I had to look, again, because it appeared that he had an uncooked turkey leg pinned to the front of his trousers.

Then the voice of the man in the goat mask boomed out, *"The Horned One now stands before you."* And he was right, because I realised then, that the turkey leg was really a cock standing up, getting ready to crow. Then, behind him, I saw Jenny begin to struggle against her bindings. But all I could do was stand there behind the curtain, my hands opening and closing in impotent rage; praying that time itself would dissolve, so I could be let loose on their world.

"Will you pass now through the veil and the gates of dark and of light?" cried the voice behind the goat-mask. And the bloke in black answered, "Yes," and held his cloak out like a pair of wings, only this time he unclasped it and let it drop to the floor. And then so did everyone else. *"I am the light and thou the dark,"* the women all sang. *"I am the dark and thou the light,"* the men all chorused back. And as the women twirled around to face the men, I saw that they, too, were naked but for opera masks, black silk cords around their waists, and black high-heeled shoes. And as the men turned, they mirrored the man in black, and wore highly polished black riding boots and black riding breeches with the fly cut out of the front so that every man's cock and balls were fully framed, but free. *"Nothing must now come between us,"* the men and women all chorused, and then they all began to partner-off. It was a masked ball for the debauched and depraved. It was the pornographic photos I'd seen in the Red Book come to life. And maybe it was because my senses were so heightened and I was so on edge, but that's when I heard the clicking of camera shutter releases and the whirring of motion-picture camera motors.

I stared at my watch, willing time to move ever faster. And

I dropped the cloak of Hannay and became Jethro, the avenger. And I pulled the Fairbairn-Sykes from its sheath and gripped hold of the heavy torch and counted off the final seconds. And as I held the knife to the curtain I dared one more look through the slit and saw the man in black with the enormous prick turn towards Jenny, now writhing madly in her coffin. And that was the exact moment everything went black, and the women stopped moaning with pleasure and started screaming their heads off.

CHAPTER
39

Over My Shoulder Goes One Care

"Red" was turning out to be as reliable as a brand name. He'd jemmied the lock on the transformer box and thrown the main power switch, bang on the dot. In an instant, I slashed a hole in the curtain and was through and running; the torch beam stabbing out, in front of me. I straight-armed and shouldered people aside, like a prop-forward intent on making a try. "Out of the way; out the fucking way," I yelled at wild and frightened eyes. Then I jumped for the stage. I kneed Mr. Big in the balls, elbowed him under the chin, knocking him into the middle of next week. I pushed Felicity Larsen to the floor and she went sprawling across one of her handmaidens. I swung the knife hilt up across Goat-man's face, knocking his mask askew, and for the very briefest of seconds, in the torchlight, I saw the startled face of Lord Ernest St. John Belfold, First Baron of "who gives a stuff." So he was the secret master of ceremonies was he, the creepy little swine. I wondered whether his playmate, Vashfield, had been in the hall with him, along with the others from the library. Fuck, but I was angry.

I spun round and sliced through the silk ropes binding Jenny's wrists and ankles, slid the knife back in its sheath, and hoisted her up onto my shoulder in a fireman's lift, scooping up the discarded red robe from off the stage as I did so. Then with a quick flash of the glim I exited upstage right and went down the back stairs to where I hoped "Red" was waiting by the rear entrance doors, pistol in hand, ready to dissuade anybody from following. And that's when torch beams began to stab and probe the dark interior of the hall, as the NOB guards rushed in to investigate. "Red" loomed up in the beam from the glim, shaking his head and directing me towards the side corridor. "Go that way, I'll follow," was all he said. Then he fired three shots up into the ceiling, and of course that set the women screaming all the harder.

I pulled open the doors to the corridor, and took a moment to shift Jenny's weight on my shoulder, and but for that I'd have probably tripped over the bodies and tripods and stuff that littered the floor. They'd had cameramen positioned along the corridor, all shooting through removable glass panes in the French doors and flapped-holes in the wall hangings. But it seemed "Red" had been busy in the time it'd taken me to free Jenny. And he came barrelling past me, then, a bloodied petercane in his hands, and I followed and tried to light his way forward like a spot-operator up in the limes. A NOB guard jumped out and struck at "Red" with a truncheon. But he blocked it with his arm, and twisted and hooked the wooden baton from out of the bloke's grip and jabbed him in the face with the petercane, and the guy was down and writhing on the floor as I stumbled past. Then with me wildly swinging the torch and "Red" swinging the petercane or the butt of his gun at anything that moved, we fought through to the end of the corridor and out into the vestibule to find it empty.

I slipped Jenny from off my shoulders and leaned her against the wall and did my best to cover her with the red cloak. She was still out of it, and I was just readying her so as to lift her back up on my shoulder, when a bloke in a mackintosh came bursting out of the corridor. He had a truncheon in his hand and his arm back ready to strike, and he came straight at me. And suddenly, I was on the mat with Mr. Carter, again, seeing it all in slow motion. "The first rule when it comes to defence against weapons," he'd told me, "is to avoid them at all costs." Then he'd added, "However, it is prudent to learn how to deal with them." So I tried to balance myself, and stepped forward and in, and threw my left arm up and out in a blocking motion, and the truncheon missed my head and went down past my shoulder. And I brought my left arm over and around his weapon arm, and trapped it in mine, just as I'd done when "Red" had stuck his gun in my back. I pushed outwards with the left, drove the heel of my right hand up into the bloke's chin, and followed up with a knee to the balls. Then "Red" finished the bloke off, with the petercane.

I turned to see Jenny sliding slowly down the wall. "Hang on, love," I said. And as I reached for her, I saw "Red" clutching his wrist. I was just about to say something, when the noise from inside got louder and torch beams flashed across the glass panes of the main doors to the hall. "I think it's time we left," "Red" said, pulling back the curtain over the French doors that led outside. And in a blink of an eye, we were through and out and running across the terrace towards the rear of the main house.

"Why are we going this way?" I shouted. A shotgun blast and an angry chorus of shouts and barking dogs sounded from behind us. "Okay, then, whose bloody idea was all this?" I gasped. "Red" glanced back over his shoulder, fired off two double taps over the heads of our pursuers, and gave me a look. "In through those French doors, on the left," I yelled. And he launched himself at the doors and jemmied them open with a speed and a skill that impressed even me. And in a flash, I was in and through, carrying Jenny over the smashed glass and broken wood, and into the antechamber that separated drawing-room from dining-room. "Down along that corridor towards the library, quick."

The light was better in that part of the house, but the sounds of pursuit now echoed all around us. And, of course, that was the exact moment Jenny Manning came to, and started to struggle and scream. I gave her a quick smack on the bum. "If you don't shut it, dear Juliet, your Romeo won't even live through Act Three." And I know it might sound a bit lame, but I had to say something that'd tell her it was me that had her over his shoulder. "Jeffrey?" she cried. "None other, Jenny, love, now shut it, we're in a bit of a tricky situation, here."

I still had the torch in one hand. "Here, 'Red,' cop hold of this and hold her up, will you?" He looked at me as if I'd really lost it, this time, but as economical as ever with words, he simply glanced up and down the corridor, slipped his gun into his pocket and nodded. I faced the wall, pushed and pressed the appropriate places in the two wood panels and the door to the secret passage sprung open. The look on his face was priceless. "Just another of England's many little secrets," I said. And in we went.

I hit the button on the wall that closed the door, and moments later we heard men running past, outside in the corridor. I turned to Jenny. "Can you walk, love?" The torchlight made our faces look so sinister, I don't think she really believed it was me at first. "Jeffrey?" she said. "Yes, it's me," I said. "I never miss a first night, if I can help it. Can you walk?" She nodded, still trying to make sense of it all. "Good girl. Give nice Mr. Russell, here, your other hand and follow me." Then like blinded soldiers in a trench, we stumbled along the narrow corridor. "This comes out near the other end of the family wing," I whispered. "We can't stay in here, though, it'd give them too much time to get organised." Then I heard a little whimper and turned round. Jennifer Manning was limping, badly.

"She's got cramp in her legs," "Red" said.

"I think I've sprained my ankle," she said, close to tears.

"Not your fault, Jenny, love," I said. "Throw your arms round my neck and I'll carry you. 'Red,' give her a hand up onto my back, will you?"

"A little difficult. I think the wrist has gone," was all he said.

I looked at him, my mind suddenly whirring like mad. "I was planning on taking one of the motor cars from the yard. But I needed you to fend off any guards while I wired the bloody thing."

"I can still shoot with my other hand," he said flatly.

"What? Fight them off from all sides; and all of them with shotguns; and all while holding on to Jenny? It'd be Custer's last stand, all over again. No, it's time for Plan B." He stared at me. "Could you carry her, fireman's fashion back down to the Pilot?" He nodded. "And drive, one-handed?" He nodded again. "Right then," I said. "Let's get out of here." I had Jenny throw her arms round my neck, and we shuffled down the narrow passage until we came to a dead end. "Hang on while I take a look," I said. I felt for the button on the wall, pushed it, there was a click, and the door opened inwards. I inched forward and looked left and right. The corridor was empty. But I'd expected it to be. It was bare of furnishings and I'd pegged it as a servant's back-corridor the night I'd first gone exploring. I waved the others forward, did the business with the door, and I'd just bent down again, so Jenny could put her arms around my neck, when a NOB guard in a mackintosh stepped out of the shadows. He had a shotgun in his hands. "Jesus," I said, as "Red" reached for his gun. But the guard just shook his head and held up a finger to his lips. "Shalom," he said, and beckoned us to follow. And that was good enough for me. I turned to "Red" and said, "He's kosher," and we followed our new friend along the back corridor until it crossed another one. He pointed for us to go left. "The orangery is at the far end," he said. Then he nodded and disappeared back the way we'd come. I gave Lady Luck another big nod of thanks.

"What the hell was that all about?" said "Red," stuffing his gun into his belt and reaching into a pocket for another ammunition clip.

"I've come across blokes like him before," I said. "Members of a Jewish brigade called the '43'. They must've infiltrated NOB, somehow."

"Just as well it was them, then, as my gun was empty," he said.

We both digested that little titbit as we made our way to the orangery: a hot-house conservatory, full of exotic flowers and palms, rattan armchairs, couches, and silk cushions so people could while away their days in quiet contemplation. To me, though, it was a dark jungle full of ambush. I couldn't use the glim; what with all the windows, it would've been like lighting a beacon fire. And it's funny what sticks in your mind: but for me, the smell of all the tropical plants just made the danger all around us seem all the more dreamlike and deadly.

I peered through the glass doors at the end of the orangery, out into the darkness, then I turned to "Red." "If we stick together, 'Red,' they'll get all three of us, for sure. So, I'm going to try and lead them a bit of a dance, while the two of you get away." He stared at me, unblinking. "Just tell Simon," I said. "I think Trent Tyler's got hold of one or two of the Red Books, maybe even the NOB master file. Tell him Tyler's two black-leather valises are smuggler's safes, and for him to slide the left-hand catch, as he presses in the tiny round stud just above the picture of the *Queen Mary*'s funnels; he'll understand."

There were no mock-heroics, no speeches insisting he be the one to stay behind; the way posh actors always do in films. There were no questions, either, just a look and a nod. I handed him the glim and he handed me his pistol and the ammunition clip. "That's all of it," he said.

"I better make all seven count, then," I said, releasing the old clip and inserting the new one. I snapped back the slide to load a round into the firing chamber, and flicked on the safety. Then I quietly opened the doors and peered out into the darkness. "All clear," I said. "See you in Piccadilly."

He twitched his mouth in what might've been a smile, then vanished into the night with Jenny Manning slung over his shoulder. And the last I saw of him, he'd just crossed over the pathway and was cutting diagonally across the grounds.

CHAPTER 40

Bringer of War

"Who dares not stir by day must walk by night." My one quote from *King John*. I had the Fairbairn-Sykes in its sheath and "Red's" pistol in my hand, but I knew the Colt .45 was more for creating a diversion, than for killing. Even at that stage of the game I didn't really want to top anyone, at least, not intentionally. I just had to give "Red" enough time to carry Jenny down to the Ford Pilot and get away to safety. I did the reckoning. A fireman's lift over that distance, Jenny unable to walk over much of it; they'd need a good half-hour, maybe more. It was going to have to be a long Third Act.

"God, help me," I said to myself, and remembered Ray once telling me, "Pray, as if everything depended on God; but act, as if everything depended on you." So be it. It was up to me to keep everyone away from the main road by making sure they had their hands full elsewhere. And I headed for the stables, not in search of a horse, but a stick about the length of a whip. I searched around by the light of my pencil-torch, found what I needed, and made for the yard where all the motor cars were parked. I spotted a big Riley RMA, pulled open the driver's door, leaned across the seat, stuck my hand up under the dashboard by the steering-column, got hold of the wires, and pulled. I separated out the two I wanted, cut away the covering and twisted them together. The car horn that blared out into the night made me jump, I don't know about anyone else, and with my own nerves like stripped wires, I started counting off the seconds. I slid out of the Riley and dashed along the lines of motor cars until I spied a brand-new Jaguar Mark V saloon. "That'll do nicely," I said to myself. I stuck the pencil-torch between my teeth and unscrewed the petrol cap. I pulled out the tie I had in my pocket, hoped David Niven and the Highland Light Infantry would forgive me, and poked the narrow end down inside the petrol tank. I pulled it out, pushed the wide end in, let the narrow end fall to the ground, flicked my lighter into flame and set it alight. I snatched the pencil-torch from my mouth, pulled my shoe-bag balaclava back down over my face, and disappeared into the night faster than thought.

My Molotov cocktail on wheels erupted with a sound and fury that made even me turn and stare in awe. There must've been a full tank of petrol in that Jaguar. I watched the flames spread like wildfire, but I knew it was the reflections in all the windscreens. Then I heard the sharp crack of glass shattering in the heat and saw, in the glow of the fire, a black column of smoke billowing and twisting angrily up into the night sky. And behind it all, the mournful wail of the motor horn and the growing tumult of shouts and cries as if to herald the Second Coming.

I headed for the ha-ha. Not that I'd known what that was before coming to Vashfield Hall, but they do say travel broadens the mind. And a ha-ha is an unseen sunken ditch that prevents cattle from grazing the plush expanse of lawn that extends out from the terrace at the rear of all the better country houses. A red-nosed Major had pointed it out to me the previous day—not that you could see anything from where I was standing—and I'm very glad he did, because the ha-ha made a perfect pathway in the dark of night. Hee-hee. I ran along the bottom of the ditch; the main house veiled from view as if by magician's trick; and gauged distances in my head. I skidded to a halt, scrambled up the ha-ha and peered over the edge. The barking of the dogs seemed much too close, but it was just the sound echoing along the side of the hall. Lights were ablaze in the main house and family wing, but the east wing looked as dark and as forbidding as a prison. It was the last place anyone would think to look for me.

I'd noticed the casement windows high up on both sides of the banquet hall when I'd first walked around the place. But as they were all covered over by the floor-to-ceiling velvet hangings inside, I'd forgotten about them. I ran across the lawn and onto the paved terrace, pulling the remains of the woollen socks from off my shoes as I went. It was a two-storey climb up onto the roof of the passageway, and as I couldn't count on the tiles being strong enough to hold me, I lay full-length and wriggled across them on my belly. Then with my feet pressed hard against the outer wall, I set about doing the first window. I jammed the blade of the Fairbairn-Sykes into the wooden frame, forced the latch, then levered out the retaining brackets so the window fell in against the inside windowsill. It was darker than night on the other side; as black as black-green velvet could ever be; and I took the knife and cut into it as you would flesh and peered through the gap, down into the ballroom.

The big floods were all still off, but there were a few lights at the back of the stage and a pale wash of light was coming in through the main doors. There was a harsh, scratchy sound repeating over and over in the background, but other than that, the place was dead. I widened the hole and stuck my head through. It was a thirty-foot drop down to the floor, and the black-painted Tannoy loudspeaker box was an arm's-length away to my right. I cut deeper into the velvet curtain and pushed my whole body through, and keeping a firm hold on the outside window frame, I balanced on the ledge and reached over and unhooked the speaker box and almost dropped the bloody thing, it was that heavy. But I managed to change my grip and pulled it towards me and stood it on the window ledge, facing outwards. Then hugging the wall very closely, I stepped gingerly along the tile roof and went in through another window and did the business with a second Tannoy speaker box. I did a third speaker, a bit further along. Then I sat on the ledge, facing inwards, and looked down at the hall's polished wooden floor. It was too high to jump and there was nowhere to secure a silk rope, so I had no option but to do a Fairbanks.

I pulled out the Fairbairn-Sykes, made a deeper gash in the velvet, then turned and slipped my whole body through the opening. I held onto the ledge, lowered myself down and hung there for a moment. Then I reached over as far as I could and slashed the velvet again. I re-sheathed the knife, flexed the fingers of my free hand; prayed Morrie Templeton's stitching would hold; took a deep breath, let go, and grabbed for both edges of the torn curtain. The whole bloody thing would now come away from its retaining rings or it'd rip all the way down to the floor; either way, I was counting on it being enough to break the fall.

The velvet ripped as if on cue, and I rolled as I hit the ground and came up into a crouch. I still had my balaclava on over my head, so I was but a dark shape against a dark background in case anyone rushed in to see what the commotion was all about. But the only sounds were of the dogs barking off in the distance. I looked at my wrist-watch. It was just ten minutes since "Red" had carried Jenny off into the night. I took a deep breath and knife in hand, crept across the floor towards the stage.

The person responsible for sound effects is usually found prompt-side, same side as the stage-manager, and even amateur productions in village halls try and follow tradition. This lot had set up opposite-prompt-side. It was only a record player on a table, but the stack of records they had wouldn't have been out of place at the BBC. The label on the record going round and round on the turntable said: *Empire Film Studios. Sound FX Library. Military trumpets and timpani: rising crescendo. Do Not Remove* "Give me Glenn Miller, any day," I said, as I lifted the needle-arm from the record's inner groove. I quickly sorted through what else they had, and it didn't take too long to find something better suited for a Sunday night in hell. *Gustav Holst: The Planets. (Selections from.)* I pulled the record from its cardboard sleeve and exchanged it for the one on the turntable. "Mars, the Bringer of War," was one of Ray's most favourite pieces of music, though he'd all but turned me off it for good, by playing it most Monday nights so as to put me in mind of my coming defeat at chess. I turned the volume knob to MAX., put the needle to the edge of the record, and turned and took it on my toes. And as "Mars" erupted into the night with the sound and fury of coming war, I'd already disappeared through the nearest exit, and by the time the brass section reached its first thunderous plateau, I was running like mad towards the woods.

There's a lull that comes just after the cymbals and timpani and everyone have all been crashing away together for a full minute or so, and that was the point I turned and fired twice into the air. It stopped the dogs barking for a bit, but they soon started up again, even louder than before.

I came to a fork in the path, chanced a quick flash of the glim, and had a quick look over my shoulder, then wished I hadn't, because I wasn't sure at first what I was seeing. Lights were moving at speed, down both sides of the house, ten or so feet off the ground, and they were coming fast in my direction. I blinked and pulled up my balaclava and took a deep, cooling gulp of night air. Then I knew exactly what it was. Riders on horses; with lamps on their saddles; and carrying God-knows-what in their hands: shotguns, sabres, lances, pig-sticking spears. It could be anything, with this lot. Then all the points of light seemed to gather together and stop and mill round and around, and my blood ran cold. They were going to let loose the dogs.

But I had no choice but to draw them after me; they could still very easily run across "Red" and Jenny's trail. So, I turned and fired twice more into the air just before the distant trumpets, drums, and cymbals all crashed together for the very last time. Then I turned and ran for my life. I was Jethro the fox, Jethro the stag, Jethro the hunted one. Of course, I should've known they'd use their bloody horses, but I'd been too caught up in conjuring chaos up out of thin air. I still had three rounds in the Colt, more than enough for mischief, but the stark truth was they outnumbered me fifty-to-one and had shotguns, and I dug my heels in and ran and ran and ran. My only focus, now, the dark wood ahead and the stream that ran through it, so I could throw the dogs off the scent; my only hope, that I didn't trip and break a leg or brain myself running into a tree.

One of John Buchan's "Thirty-Nine Steps" was that if you ever found yourself in a patch of land, hemmed in on all-sides, and there was only one possible chance of escape, you had to stay in the patch and let your enemies search it, and not find you. Only, I wasn't hemmed in yet, was I? I still had the whole woods to lose myself in. And I flashed the pencil-torch, on and off, as I ran, to keep myself on the path, and tried to remember what Simon had said about the layout of Vashfield's new shooting grounds. There had to be an easy way through it all, but it was the only part of the estate I hadn't had a chance to walk over, so I was running blind.

Then Belfold's voice assailed the night, amplified by a megaphone: "I want them taken alive. Use salt, not shot. That's an order." And I thought, "Good. They still think they're chasing all three of us." Then from out of nowhere two large dark shapes the size of brick shit-houses on stilts appeared in front of me, and two powerful torch beams stabbed me with light, blinding me completely. And I spun round and ran, willy-nilly, back the way I'd come, and ran straight into a wall covered with what felt like shaved coconut matting. Then a black shiny boot kicked me in the face and the butt of a shotgun smashed down on the top of my head. And as the scratch of a gramophone needle stuck in a groove sounded over and over again, far off in the distance, I fell into a dark muddy pool that smelled of warm horse piss.

CHAPTER

41

Not Exactly Up to Scratch

A sharp smell went right up my nose and out through my ears, and my head flopped about like a dead fish, and I coughed and spluttered and my eyelids fluttered open. I blinked and blinked, but couldn't see a bloody thing, then I realised I'd been blindfolded. "Here we go, again," I said to no one in particular. I tried to move my hands, but couldn't. I'd been bound hand and foot to a chair, and a broken one, at that. Or at least, it was broken at the bottom, as most of the bit you sit on was missing. I started shivering. I could feel the cold on my arms and legs, on my chest, my back, and my backside, then it registered, I was stark, bloody bollock-naked and strapped to a fucking chair. It wasn't a good sign. And suddenly it was as if my whole life was a broken record, a needle stuck in a scratch, endlessly repeating itself.

I heard the sound of a cat meowing, but didn't know if it was real or not. Then it meowed again, and I don't know why, but stuck in a darkness I couldn't alter, it made my blood run cold. Then someone tore off the blindfold and I blinked through the blaze of light, and yelled out, "What's your game? What are you playing at?" But all I heard were footsteps disappearing off and a door opening and closing somewhere behind me. "Oi, cloth-ears, I'm talking to you," I yelled. "What's your game, then?" But there was only silence. I yelled some more, then stopped, bewildered as to why I should find myself amidst a forest of candelabras. It was very eerie; whichever way I looked, a hundred candle flames became a thousand points of flickering light, disappearing off into infinity. And in the middle of it all was something pink and blotchy. Me, all pinched and shrivelled like a squashed sausage; me, as naked as the day I was pulled howling into the world. I looked down at myself. I was one mass of bruises, and the only good thing I could see was that I hadn't been trussed up with electrical flex. It said that whoever they were, they weren't planning on electrocuting me, anytime soon, which was a huge relief; I'd already had enough of that nonsense to last several lifetimes.

But now I knew exactly where I was. I was back in that room of mirrors in Baron Belfold's house, in Berkeley Square. Only, this time, I was fixed to a chair in the middle of the circle painted on the floor. "Jesus," I croaked. "I'm a bloody sacrifice in a black magic ritual." I nearly lost my bottle then. By which I mean, I almost peed myself. But I held it in, just. I stared, unseeing, at the candles, then forced myself to focus. My reflection seemed to go on and on forever. And I think I must've sighed, or something, because I heard a swishing sound, like an echo, and I looked over to starboard and for a few moments I really did think I was seeing things. Two white shapes danced up and down against the backdrop of the long black-velvet curtains. It looked like a little white bird was fluttering madly, back and forth, trying to keep out of the reach of the claws of a large white cat. Then I saw it wasn't a bird at all, it was a bunch of feathers fastened onto the end of a line. Then something began tickling my bum and my balls, and it shocked me as much as if someone had swiped me with a newly honed chiv. I jerked my head down and saw a black line scribbling itself repeatedly across the floor. It was a coachman's whip; made for tickling the ears of a lead horse in a coach and four; a good five- six-feet long before the line began, and as supple as a fly-rod in the right hands. But why would anyone stick feathers on the end of it?

I heard meowing again and looked up and saw the cat padding purposefully across the floor towards me. It was a big white fluffy smudge of a cat, with a diamond-studded collar that seemed to catch the flickering light from the candles and set its head and neck ablaze. Then suddenly it seemed there were hundreds of the flaming things, a whole army of cats, one big blur of white coming straight at me, and for some reason I couldn't fathom, I broke out into beads of sweat as all the cats disappeared under my chair. I felt something tickling me. Then something scratched me. And for the briefest of moments it felt like nothing at all; then suddenly, it was as if I'd been lashed by a cat-o'-nine-tails and I was one big open wound, wet with blood and sweat. And I yelled and screamed blue, bloody murder. The cat swiped at the feathers over and over, and tore at my arse and my balls and my poor, poor willy. It was worse than being done over with razors by a frenzied mob. And I heaved and yelled and swore and screamed, but the chair was fixed to the floor and I was fixed to the chair, and well on the way to being fixed forever. And I couldn't help it, my guts turned to water and I peed all over the floor.

I heard a snort and a swish of the whip and the feathers flew away and so did the cats, the smoke from the candles rippling in their wake. And I blinked and blinked and heard a bell ring and the door open and I shouted for help. But a hand appeared from out of nowhere and clamped a wet rag over my nose and my mouth and I screamed silently as the chloroform clouded my senses. Then everything went black.

And in the blackness, the same old dreadful dream rode at anchor, awaiting me. The eternal fires above, the ice-cold waters forever swirling below; the darkness lit only by the snowflake flares and the orange glow of things burning; and flesh and steel and tanker oil all one flame, lighting a pathway to Hell. And as always happened I could feel the bitter, acrid smoke squeezing the last living air from out of my scorch-scarred lungs. Then the sickly-sweet smell went up my nose again but I didn't care, I just gulped in great lungfuls of air, glad not to be down among the dead. But Belfold cut into my reverie. "Rather un-sporting of you to pee on my pedigree Persian cat, old man; really very unbecoming of you; terribly vulgar. I'd have thought that you, at least, Mr. Hannay, with your fine upbringing would've been able to hold on just a little longer."

I yanked my head round. Belfold was sitting in a black armchair all dressed in black and all but invisible against the black-velvet curtains. All I could see was his bald head and his pale hands stroking the cat on his lap. But all I had eyes for was the nasty red wheal across his face, where I'd hit him with the hilt of my knife. I blinked and looked into two sets of eyes staring at me as if I was nothing more than a pile of cat's meat. And Belfold continued gently stroking the cat and the cat continued to purr contentedly and everything looked so calm and un-troubling that I began to shiver uncontrollably. Then the feathers fluttered up into the air, the cat moved its head, its fluffy white body slid down onto the floor, and I burst out in sweat again. I yelled out, "What the fuck's your game, Belfold?"

I don't remember much after that. All I know is, there's

pain and there's pain. A woman's nails raking your face, a tear-away's razor cutting your cheek open to the bone; you know you can come back from it; marked maybe, and perhaps for life, but you know you'll eventually heal. But when someone starts in on the family jewels, well, you can very quickly end up being the last of your line, and I suppose it's the thought of that that really scares a man the most. I don't know what they did to me after those first few times of cutting my arse to ribbons and me blacking out; one of Belfold servants might've covered me with Germoline or jabbed me with morphine, I don't know. All I recall was the darkness being ripped apart by the sickly-sweet smell going up my nose, and me being sick down myself.

I shook my head, feeling the first stirrings of despair, then froze. There were men in uniforms standing all around me, like judge, jury, and executioner. And I began to shiver again. Then I twigged it. It was all done by mirrors; nothing more than a magician's stage trick; though the real trick was that the figures weren't people, at all, they were all life-size oil paintings. Full-length portraits of Hitler, Alexander the Great, Julius Caesar, George Washington, and Napoleon. There were some I couldn't place; one of a man from the time of the French Revolution; and of a man in the red robes of a cardinal; and even one of a man in what I took to be Elizabethan dress. There must've been a dozen, or so, paintings in all. I stared at the last one, knowing I'd seen it before. The figure wore an ostrich-plumed hat, a long dark-blue velvet robe, a heavy gold chain, and a blood-red sash. He had a large eight-pointed diamond star over his left breast and stood with one leg forward to reveal the blue garter buckled around his leg. It hit me, then, the figure was dressed in the robes of the Order of the Garter, and the funny thing was, I knew I knew the bloke in the picture. I stared and stared, and all but gasped out loud. It was Belfold. I looked at the other paintings, and saw that they were all of Belfold; even the one of Hitler. Belfold, in Hitler's brown jacket and black trousers, swastika arm band, and iron cross; the same stance, same haircut; the light source in the painting cleverly casting a shadow under his nose so as to resemble the Führer's bottle-brush moustache; it was him to the life. Then Belfold's voice, bored, languid, and larded with culture, cut into my fevered musings. And, as if on cue, the awful pain burst through into my senses again and I was one writhing mass of tatters and shreds.

"You stand before your accusers, Mr. Hannay, as a fraud and impostor. So you can begin by telling us who you really are."

"Fuck off," I croaked, through a reddening veil of pain.

"I think that only confirms our suspicions," he said smoothly.

I flinched even before I heard the sound of the whip. Then I flinched for real, as the leather lash cut deep into my shins and the fluttering white feathers mocked my pathetic attempt at bravado.

"Let's try again, shall we? For a start, you're no gentleman, and you're certainly no scion of a wealthy family, Canadian or otherwise. You're a damn Cockney." He cracked the whip again and I could do nothing but flinch and shiver. "But, as they say, 'Blood will always out.' Or at least yours will before I've finished with you, my tiresome friend, of that you can be assured." He whipped me again. "This is not some adventure story by Buchan in which the villain is finally routed and the hero wins the girl. Such things do not happen in real life." He started cutting into me thick and fast with his questions then. "So, who are you working for? MI5? Special Branch? The Communist Party? Who sent you, and how much do they know? Where are the red-leather-covered books of photographs? It was you that stole them, wasn't it, and the Garter insignia, too? You, that broke into NOB House, and that robbed and desecrated Vashfield Manor? You scurrilous swine, who do you work for?" And to help concentrate my mind, he began to whip me again, even harder.

Well, I mean, where to begin? How do you talk your way out of all that? So in between me gasping for breath I tried some more bravado. "You can't get away with it, Baron. They're on to you and have been all along. They probably even followed you here. And knowing them, they've no doubt already nobbled 'Number Two,' and 'Three,' and 'Four,' and all the rest of your mob and are racing up the stairs as we speak. So, you're well and truly buggered, Belfold, whatever you do to me." Of course, I knew there was no way in hell of that happening. And Belfold knew it, and he whipped me across the face, so that I got the message that my insolence would not be tolerated. He stopped after a bit and put the whip down and flicked a lighter, and even through the blood in my nose I could smell the Turkish tobacco and three-star brandy.

Belfold leaned back in his chair, drew on his cigarette, and blew two perfect streams of smoke out into the room. It didn't seem to bother the cat any, but my eyes just couldn't seem to stop from watering. His indifference cut me as much as anything else he'd done, because it said the swine was in no hurry and was going to relish every moment of my torture, and I broke out into beads of sweat again at the thought of him and his fucking cat. I tell you, an unfettered imagination can be a right bloody nuisance, sometimes. And that's when I imagined I heard noises off. So I thought what else have I got to lose, certainly not my dignity, and I started yelling my head off, and I kept on shouting even though Belfold whipped at me, again and again. Then I heard the door burst open, and so did he, and he stopped in mid-whip like a conductor down the Albert Hall that's come to the end of a particularly taxing movement. It must've been his manservant, because he turned and said, irritably, "I told you, Mathers, under no circumstance was I to be disturbed."

But Mathers didn't answer. Then there was the sound of a heavy thump, like a body or something falling to the floor. Then it got really weird, because above the sound of me howling—I might've only been whimpering, I can't recall—I heard the sound of teeth grinding. And I thought, it can't be. I really must've been pushed way off my trolley to start imagining that, but some sounds are like deep scars, and once heard, you never forget them. Then this unmistakable voice growled, "Put the whip down, if you please, sir, or I'll be forced to shoot."

I tried to turn my head round, but the effort was too much and my head slumped down on my chest. And I think I must've lost it for a bit, and probably out of disbelief, because even in my wildest dreams there was no way on God's green Earth that I'd ever be rescued from anything by DCI Robert Browno of Scotland Yard's Flying Squad. But Belfold's breeding didn't betray him; he didn't even stand up. "How dare you burst in here, like this? Who the hell are you? And what's your business?"

"Detective Chief Inspector Robert Browno, sir, of Scotland Yard's Flying Squad. And if you're Lord Ernest St John Belfold, First Baron Belfold of Bray, then you're my business."

Belfold slowly got to his feet, still the king in his own castle. "I am, indeed, he, officer. Have you a warrant to enter these premises?"

"Indeed, I do, sir. And not only that, but I also have a warrant for your arrest. So please put the whip down, your Lordship." He waggled the gun in his hand. "Or, as I believe I said, I may be forced to shoot you, sir."

"Let me warn you, officer, I know the Commissioner personally."

"So do I, sir. So, I say again, please put the whip down on the floor."

When Browno didn't back down, Belfold became like silk. "But surely, this can be of no concern to Scotland Yard, Chief Inspector. We were simply playing a game, my friend and I. I'm sure in your line of work you've heard or come across such practices. It may shock the innocent, but there are those that acquire a taste for it. It's essentially quite harmless."

"I see, sir. One man's meat is another man's cup of tea, is that it, sir?" I heard Browno come over to where I was sitting and felt a gloved hand under my chin. I peered up into Browno's face. He looked down at me for a moment, then at the floor beneath my chair, and I heard him say, "Jesus Christ," then I heard this awful grinding noise as he gently lowered my head back onto my chest. "I can assure you that your little goings-on, here, have nothing do with why I'm here to arrest you, your Lordship.

"Then, on what charges, pray?" Belfold's voice was now full of disdain. If being caught red-handed over my naked and bloody body was not an issue; then whatever the charges, he knew all the right people; and as usual, everything could be brushed under the carpet.

"The warrant for your arrest, sir, is in regard to the theft of certain items of regalia pertaining to the Order of the Garter, as were once awarded to Lord Charles Henry Hugo Vashfield, by the late King George V."

"But, surely," Belfold protested loudly, "there's been some mistake; the pieces were loaned to me by Lord Vashfield him—" He raised a hand, as if to point out the painting of himself in the robes of a Garter Knight, then stopped, realisation slowly dawning. "Oh, I see. I'm the one to be given up, is that it, officer? The one marked for sacrifice?"

"I'm sure I don't know what you mean, sir. Now, drop the whip."

I heard the whip clatter to the floor. Browno grunted, appreciatively, and went over and kicked the whip away. Then switching his gun from his right hand to his left, and without any warning at all, he lunged forward and jabbed Belfold in the Adam's apple, and suddenly Belfold was coughing and spluttering like a man surprised to find a bunch of chicken bones stuck in his throat. And as his whole body sagged, Browno turned and dipped and punched him hard; first, in the kidneys, then high on the thigh, dead-legging him. Browno stepped back and Belfold dropped to the floor, making very uncouth sounds. "I'm awfully sorry, sir, did you trip? Please let me help you up." And he sounded full of concern as he stepped in, again, and gave Belfold a hefty kick to the side of the head. He leaned down, grinding his teeth like mad, and pulled back an eyelid. "Or, perhaps you'd prefer to just lie there, sir, until proper assistance comes."

That's when I heard Walsingham's voice outside in the corridor and I knew, then, I really was saved. Browno called out to him, "In here, sir. Your poor sod's in a terrible way by the look of him and Lord Belfold is unconscious. He must've slipped on all the blood on the floor and hit his head. If you ask me, it's a bloody wonder he didn't kill himself, sir."

Walsingham came over to my chair and I heard another whispered, "Jesus Christ." But by then I was so choked up about my unheralded resurrection—I mean, rescue—that I happily fell headlong into the valley of darkness that some call sleep. Though, it's true, to everyone else in the room, it probably looked as if I'd just fainted clean away.

CHAPTER 42

End-Games

I lost another week of my life, with no memory of it other than an endless procession of dreams where I drowned in blood and the sea was always aflame and the burning bodies of seamen were clawed clean of flesh by white cats as big as tigers. It was nightmare enough to scar the soul and even now I'd give both my thumbs to forget. But each day I swam nearer the surface, then one bright morning I came to, floating on my back, and after a while I knew I was lying on a bed. I tried to move, but couldn't, my arms and legs were strapped down, and for one terrible moment I thought I was back in the room of mirrors and the torture was about to begin again, and I cried out for release. Then I heard a rustle beside my pillow and a vision in starched white rose up into sight and I dreamed she smiled down at me and touched my forehead with a cool cloth that smelled of lavender and I smiled back and sank down again into exhausted sleep.

The next time I looked up I saw someone had drawn

mountains and valleys on the temperature chart above my bed and I came over all dizzy. I tried to swallow, but my throat felt like the bottom of a parrot's cage, a rough sea of sandpaper, split seeds, and dried shit. And I said, "Please, dear God, give me some water." Then I heard the rustling sound again and another vision of loveliness arose into view and held a cup of water to my lips and I prayed that she was really real, and as she gentled my head back down onto the pillow, I whispered, "Thank you, nurse."

"Welcome back," she said softly.

"How many of the convoy made it home?" I asked, steeling myself.

"All your ships came in," she said as she put her hand on my pulse.

"That's wonderful," I said, "really wonderful."

She smiled. "I'll go get the doctor, he wanted to be told the moment you regained consciousness," she said. Then she left me.

My head felt woozy, but apart from my wrists and ankles I couldn't feel much of anything, other than the bristles on my face; it was as if I'd been wrapped in cotton wool from head to toe. I inched my head up off my pillow, but all I could see was a tent of white that looked disturbingly like a coffin. "Blimey," I croaked, "a burial at sea is expected soon, is it?"

"No, Mr. Hannay, a full and complete recovery is expected. If you'll just be patient, and play your part."

I almost lost it then; the man playing the doctor was the spit and image of Robert Donat: voice, Scots' burr, easy smile, pencil moustache, everything. He didn't see the joke, of course, but I did and I told him I'd play whatever part he wanted, just as long as all my important parts ended up in good working order.

"Your injuries were serious and you lost a considerable amount of blood, Mr. Hannay, but your life is in no danger. And none of your, shall we say, usual functions will be in any way permanently impaired."

It's remarkable how quickly your brain un-fogs when a doctor starts talking to you about matters of your life and death. I stared up at him, relief flooding through the length and breadth of me. "How long?" I said.

"As long as it takes," he said. "But another week or two should see a marked improvement. Until then I intend to keep you restrained so as to prevent you from scratching yourself to pieces. We'll do what we can to dull the pain. And I've put you on a course of penicillin."

My eyebrows raised at that. "Penicillin? Blimey, it must be serious."

"Your body was very badly abused, Mr. Hannay. It's imperative we do all we can to keep infection at bay. Torn and lacerated tissue needs time to knit and to mend properly. But with luck there'll be no permanent scarring to your genitals, your rear, or your face."

I'd missed being scarred for life by a whisker, that was bloody lucky, it's so much harder to hide in plain sight with nasty big scars all over your cheeks. "Er, if it's not too much to ask, Doc, where am I, exactly?"

He smiled. "St. Mary's Hospital, Paddington," he said, waving an arm in the direction of the soot-stained window, as he scribbled a signature on my chart. "We're quite well known for slash and stab wounds, here."

I heard the sound of a distant train whistle and almost lost it again, knowing how close I was to Church Street and home. And I pushed my head back into the pillow and went spark out. It's amazing though, the things you can catch up on when you're asleep. For a start, I didn't reckon I was in St. Mary's by chance. Even though it was where Alexander Fleming had first discovered penicillin, I couldn't see them just popping down to his laboratory to ask if he had half-a-cup to spare. No. Knowing how rare penicillin was even then, almost three years after V-E Day, Walsingham must've pulled some serious strings to ensure I had every chance of making a full recovery. It hadn't been that long since the black markets of Europe had valued the antibiotic wonder drug as being worth its weight in diamonds. Knowing I'd been stuffed full of the incredible stuff told me I was of value as a future witness or something. Not that I believed any of it would ever come out in open court. Not when you considered the people involved. The very idea of the aristocracy rigging the political process so as to pervert Parliamentary Democracy itself, was enough to bring hordes of unruly mobs out onto the streets. So like as not, there'd be a secret tribunal, in camera, behind very tightly closed doors, but none of what'd happened would ever be allowed to reach public ears, let alone the front pages.

That also probably explained why Walsingham had an armed guard outside my hospital room. Even this late in the game, he must've known he wasn't the only one capable of pulling a few strings. So it was gratifying to know he wasn't taking any more unnecessary chances with me, or my skin. But it did give me a lot to ponder as I tried to piece it all together during the weeks of recovery that followed. I mean, I had to work out for myself why it was that I was allowed to live and Mr. Hannay wasn't.

But enough talk of bedpans and needles; how did I come to be rescued? As usual Simon Bosanquet filled in all the details later, after I was let out of hospital, but as much of what he told me fits here, I'll tell you now. The moment Simon got back to London, Walsingham had examined the few scorched pages I'd rescued from the fireplace in the library, but had pronounced them insufficient to his needs. Then they'd got my telephone message from Vashfield Hall; about Uncle Bill's keys being dropped at the Commander's house and that they should rustle up some help to go get them. And they'd put two and two together and come up with only half of it, and had concluded that Commander J. Russell was now in possession of the Red Books and was taking them to Grosvenor Square. So Walsingham had immediately got on to his contact at the U.S. Embassy. But no one yet thought to add Trent Tyler to the equation. There was some concern when I didn't report in again. And they'd thought the worst when the resident OSS station chief telephoned back, a little after eleven, with the news that "Red" had called in from a village telephone box to say he was on his way back to London and needed medical help for himself and his passenger.

And so by the time "Red" finally arrived at No. 1 Grosvenor Square, around midnight, both Walsingham and Bosanquet were waiting in the station chief's office at the rear of the building. Walsingham, apparently, deeply shocked that it wasn't me with "Red," but Jennifer Manning, the daughter of a close friend and very influential Member of Parliament. "Good grief, Simon," he said, barely able to contain himself, "I'm the girl's godfather, for heaven's sake." So they whisked Jenny off to a private hospital. And then while "Red" had his wrist strapped up by a Marine corpsman he'd told them of the night's events: the explosion and gunshots he'd heard while making good his escape; and my suspicions regarding Trent Tyler being the secret courier for the Red Books.

"What is so important about these Red Books?" "Red" asked.

"Therein lies the tale," Walsingham replied, and he

quickly mapped out how the Red Books—"the Keys to the Kingdom"—could be used to subvert the United Kingdom's entire political process. And that's when the balloon went up, and the Yanks don't exactly hang about once they decide to get going. The funny thing was, though, they thought Trent Tyler had been selling secrets, not acquiring them. But that was of little consequence; unofficial espionage activities involving allies was bad diplomacy; and so one of the Federal judges that served at the embassy was hauled out of bed to sign the necessary papers. Then "Red" led a group of very determined men to pay a nocturnal call on one Trent Tyler, senior cipher analyst and all-round ladies' man, and he was hauled off for questioning. Then with Walsingham and Bosanquet on hand as unofficial observers, "Red" searched Tyler's flat, where they duly found, in the bedroom of all places, the two black valises, open and half-full of clothes. Simon picked one up, tipped the contents out onto the bed, snapped the bag shut, and ran his fingers over the *Queen Mary* luggage label. He identified the decorative stud on the side of the bag's metal locking bar and pressed the stud in as he slid the nearest catch sideways. Then he lifted the upper part of the valise away to reveal a Red Book nestled in the red-leather-lined "smuggler's safe" inside the base. How Walsingham contained himself I'll never know. Simon said he simply nodded and said, "And the other one, Simon, if you please." And not only did Tyler have two Red Books, he had *the* two Red Books, the two original Keys. The fabled master file, that laid bare who was who and what was what; and a second master file, that detailed the how, the when, and the where. And that was when the OSS station chief called the ambassador out of bed.

The U.S. Ambassador was quick to grasp the awkward political dimensions of the situation. He acknowledged Walsingham's request that the Red Books and Trent Tyler be released into British custody so that His Majesty's Secret Service could proceed with dispatch with "the Defence of the Realm," but he insisted that Tyler first be questioned by the embassy's own security people. Walsingham, who probably ate diplomats for breakfast, immediately agreed, but requested the ambassador grant him half an hour so he could produce additional evidence that would greatly assist them in their interrogation. And so, while the ambassador retired to complete his morning ablutions, Walsingham disappeared off into the cold London night, and on his return everyone reconvened in a room deep inside the embassy. Then with Walsingham and Bosanquet looking on, via a two-way mirror, "Red" interviewed Trent Tyler in the presence of the ambassador and a couple of armed Marines.

At first, Tyler denied everything. It'd been his first and only time as a guest at Vashfield Hall. He'd met Belfold, but the once. His connections weren't political, merely social. Then "Red" showed Tyler a whole stack of surveillance photographs of him entering Belfold's house in Berkeley Square, and going in through the gates at NOB headquarters, and paying umpteen visits to Vashfield Hall. Then he undid the brass lock of the red leather-covered book of photographs that Walsingham had so thoughtfully retrieved from God-knows-where, and let him view at his leisure various images of himself indulging in all sorts of tricks with all sorts of people. And then whatever remaining resistance there might've been in Trent Tyler or the ambassador simply dissolved.

Tyler laid the blame entirely at the pretty feet of Miss Felicity Larsen. He was intoxicated with her, he said. It was she who'd introduced him into the group's inner circle; after which he'd simply been swept up and so had done whatever had been asked of him; and all, simply to please her. He explained that he'd been given the Red Books to hold secure, as they would be guaranteed the same immunity that he enjoyed as an American diplomat. "An interesting if somewhat naïve assumption," Walsingham said, on his side of the looking-glass. "Not that I believe a single word of the rest of it." And neither, it seemed, did the U.S. Ambassador, because right there and then he revoked Trent Tyler's diplomatic immunity and gave permission for him to be handed over to British authorities. Simon said, it looked like a waxwork tableau down Madame Tussaud's; no one in the room seemed capable of moving. Then Trent Tyler all but got down on his knees and made a tearful appeal to the ambassador, begging him to reconsider, but the embassy's most senior diplomat simply turned away. And then the two U.S. Marines escorted Tyler from the room.

Then events get a little sketchy. It seems Trent Tyler pulled the oldest trick in the book, and asked if he could first pay a visit to the lavatory. And then, somehow, he eluded his escort and ran along empty corridors and up five or six flights of stairs to the tiny row of offices set into the embassy roof. And I can see how it must've happened: the Marines giving chase, but not yet drawing their weapons; believing there was no possible way of escape. But, of course, Mr. Tyler always did have such a theatrical nature. And after he'd thrown open one of the small windows and got out and balanced himself upon the narrow cornice, maybe he did take a brief moment to gaze out across the rooftops of London, his adopted home. But the plain fact of the matter is: he jumped, and impaled himself on the iron railings below; the whole thing as much a surprise to him, I'm sure, as it was to the two Marines. And even now, I can't decide whether that was courage or cowardice. It's a hell of a way for anyone to go, though, especially as what he'd done was nowhere near to being a hanging offence. I mean, it wasn't as if we were at war, or anything.

CHAPTER

43

Clearing the Board

The finding of the two, key Red Books set all the other wheels in motion. There was real evidence now of conspiracy, of tampering with the official political process, and of wide-scale blackmail, and with that all in hand, Bosanquet set about obtaining the necessary search- and arrest-warrants. And come the dawn, Special Branch and Flying Squad detectives raided Vashfield Hall, NOB headquarters in North London, and the offices of BUM in the East End, and files, photographs, negatives, and film were seized and numerous people taken into custody. But, of course, there was no sign of me anywhere.

Monday lunchtime, Scotland Yard got an anonymous tip that a Canadian businessman named Jeffrey Hannay had been abducted and taken to a house in Berkeley Square. The name threw up a red card with *Contact Immediate. A.C.* scribbled on it. The Assistant Commissioner then immediately got on to his old school chum Walsingham. And I'm not casting aspersions or anything, but why Berkeley Square was the very last place anyone thought to search, was beyond me. But I suppose anyone can overlook the bloody obvious, even a brilliant spymaster like Walsingham or a smart copper like Bosanquet. Simon claimed later that Belfold's London residence was the next on the list for warrants to be issued. It was just that nobody imagined Belfold would be stupid enough to return there; so it'd been relegated to the "mopping up" part of the operation. And even though I still can't say for sure who made that all-important call in to the Yard, suffice to say, every Easter-time, I light seven candles and give "thanks" forty-three times that I wasn't passed over. But as Ray once said, "Better twelve good friends than one enemy."

A quick word about DCI Robert Browno. I'd always suspected he was Walsingham's pet pit-bull terrier, although only God and Walsingham knew what it was he had on the Detective Chief Inspector that made him so compliant. But who better to knock down doors than bullheaded Browno; the Commandos being otherwise engaged. Anyway, that lunchtime telephone call had the boys from Scotland Yard swinging into action just in time to catch the evening post. The Railtons were left parked in Hill Street. Then a young copper in a postman's uniform cycled around the corner to Belfold's house with a special delivery package. And once the lad had got his foot firmly stuck in the door, Browno led half a rugby team's worth of muscle to bear on the situation. They barged into the house, up the stairs, and the day was saved, and me along with it. I learned later, that when Walsingham heard that someone answering Hannay's description was in a bad way, upstairs, he broke the fourth wall and came on up himself. Though he did insist that Simon Bosanquet remain out of sight in the back of the unmarked police car, to prevent Belfold or anyone else from seeing "the Scarlet Pimpernel" in his true guise.

So what had the NOBs hoped to accomplish, and who was Belfold, really, and what of Vashfield and all the rest of them? Simon told me the inner council, most of whom I'd met in the library at Vashfield Hall, called themselves The Links; each man part of a chain of people that'd all sworn to bind and hobble the lawful Labour Government until it could no longer function. He said he had no idea what all the "Number One, Number Two" business was all about. So I said it sounded a lot like the Merchant Navy. I reminded him I'd gone in as Fourth Officer and ended up—because of the War—as a Number One, a First Officer. So it could be the same with The Links; men departed or died during the course of their duties and others took their place. "Number One is dead, long live Number One." He gave me a rather funny look when I said that. But he let it go, and so did I.

In the full light of day, I think what startled everybody was the extent of the operation and the number of VIPs caught up in The Links' web of deceit and betrayal. Nothing was out of bounds, it seems; no friendship, club, or old school tie was held sacred; their ends justified any and all means; they ruthlessly exploited any weakness or vanity. It turned out, though, there was no real black magic to any of it. All the hocus-pocus and Nazi symbolism was Belfold's personal contribution to the goings-on, all of it simply thrown in for added effect, or so he claimed. And whether he'd portrayed himself as Cardinal Richelieu, Napoleon Bonaparte, Hitler, or a black magician, it was all just a nasty little play within a play. A bit of theatre to get everyone in the mood and feeling naughty, and get them going at it like rabbits. As for poor Jenny Manning, she was just a tasty little titbit served up to titillate jaded appetites before the main meal.

I asked Ray why The Links had kept on taking photographs of VIP's in compromising situations. I'd have thought they'd have had more than enough for purposes of any blackmail. "It's always the same," he said. "Those in power never stop doing whatever it is that's been the means of them acquiring that power, especially if they also see it as being the means to the continuance of their power. And in politics, the power of blackmail is in never having to use it; that's why they always continue to amass it. It's the same with military power; once the cloak of legitimacy has been achieved, the power is all in the display of it, rather than being forced to use it. Gunboat diplomacy, it was once called. And once the whole process is begun, those in power daren't let up or else it's taken for weakness. It happened with Hitler, Mussolini, Franco; it's the same with Stalin. Whether it's behind-the-scenes blackmail or a visit from the secret police, they can never have too much dirt, if they're determined to fight dirty."

Over the weeks that followed Walsingham interviewed most everyone brought to light by the Red Books. And I'm sure he quietly assured each of them that everything was now in safe and secure hands. Maybe, he even promised that the offending negatives and film would be destroyed "for the good of King and Country"; although I bet he never gave any definite date as to when that might be. But it seems people were only too eager to put the past behind them, and they swore up hill and down dale that they'd stick to the straight and narrow in future. And, as Walsingham had no doubt intended all along, public and private support for NOB and all the other more extreme right-wing groups evaporated like morning dew on a sunny day. I have to admit, though, over the years since, whenever some incident involved the sudden resignation of some senior civil servant or government minister, or some big noise in the City,

Ray and I did both wonder whether it was Walsingham that'd pulled the strings. But it was never more than idle speculation on our part.

Walsingham also had a little chat with Sir Oswald Mosley, apparently, which resulted in Mosley publicly severing all ties with the New Order of Britain Party. The two also came to a gentleman's agreement, of sorts. Mosley—and BUM—would be allowed to continue to pursue his vision of taking Britain into a unified European Common Market, and MI5 would, of course, pursue all means of infiltrating the group. "They simply agreed to play the game," was how Simon put it. Though, he did add that anyone with half a brain was unlikely to take Mosley's ideas too seriously. "In fifty or a hundred years time, perhaps, but not now."

As for the rest of it, it's a bit cloudy. I'm fairly certain Walsingham must've interviewed Lord Belfold, though it was the one subject Simon was always a little vague about; and maybe on purpose. All I know is that while I was busy recovering, an obituary appeared in *The Times* of London stating that Lord Ernest St John Belfold, First Baron Belfold of Bray, eminent banker and philanthropist, had died of a single gunshot wound at his house in Mayfair. It went on to say that only days before the unfortunate incident Belfold had placed his house and holdings in trust to provide a continuing income for the many charities he'd supported during his distinguished career. It didn't sound too much like the man that'd been so keen on torturing the living daylights out of me. And maybe I've read too many mystery stories, but the only way I can add it up is that Belfold was given a simple choice: public disgrace and dishonour; his title, stripped; his fortune, forfeited; a lengthy prison term; or Plan B. Who knows what really moves or motivates such men, but apparently he chose to follow the example of the American, Trent Tyler, and do the proper thing, as was the time-honoured preserve of any gentleman who'd strayed too far from Society's norms. A fountain pen and a few sheets of headed notepaper ready on the desk. Then left alone in a room with an old service revolver, a round of ammunition, and a stiff upper lip. Though in his case, perhaps, there was an armed marksman ready to shoot him, should he reappear at the door with pistol in hand. And for what it's worth, I do admit to occasionally having odd thoughts about Simon Bosanquet, where I imagine him coming out of Belfold's room *after* the sound of a shot is heard. And I don't know why I should think that about him, but I do.

Of course, Lord Vashfield denied everything and maintained he'd been completely unaware of what'd really been going on in the east wing of Vashfield Hall. He claimed he'd simply loaned out his banquet hall to an old friend who'd formed his own amateur group of theatrical players. Even the sight of all the paraphernalia for filming the group's activities had been of little or no concern to him; after all, he was but a simple country squire with a passion for hunting, shooting, and fishing. And in the end his name remained quite unsullied, even when questions were raised, in both Houses, regarding the rumoured illegal activities of a whole covey of extremist political groups. And looking back on it, I suppose it's not that different to how the whole question of the Duke of Windsor's rumoured dealings with the Nazis was handled. The issue was simply ignored; no official comment was ever forthcoming; it was all quietly left to wither on the vine.

Leaving two applecarts, primed and ready for repainting.

They gradually took me off the morphine, the doctors began to visit me less frequently, and slowly I got better. But I did still happen to notice that there were two sets of medical charts; one for Mr J. Hannay, the other for a Mr X. One went up, the other went down, and poor Hannay seemed to be having a very bad time of it. And when septicaemia set in, even I feared for his life. And he went one way out the door and down the hallway, and I was pushed on a gurney down the other end, up onto another floor. And a few days later Simon Bosanquet handed me a strip of newsprint. "It's the obituary for Jeffrey Hannay from the *Toronto Globe and Mail.* The second, shorter clipping is from *The Times.*" It was nowhere near as grand as the obituary for Lord Ernest St John Belfold, First Baron Belfold of Bray. There was no picture; merely a few lines to say that Jeffrey Hannay had once passed this way and had played the game of life straight through to the end. But then a pawn never merits the same attention as a knight, does it?

To give "Red" Russell his due, when he read of Hannay's passing, he did telephone Simon to offer condolences. He'd got the impression I was on the mend and was shocked to read I'd succumbed to wounds suffered from an encounter with a rabid dog, which to be honest sounded a lot better than me dying from being attacked by a white Persian pussycat. Then, for appearance's sake, Walsingham and Bosanquet, and "Red" and Jenny Manning, all attended a small private memorial service for Jeffrey Hannay at the little chapel in South Audley Street, just down the road from the U.S. Embassy. The Mayfair Hotel sent flowers, too, I was told.

I felt oddly saddened, though, by the death of the other me. And in a mad effort to cheer me up Simon told me he'd recently lunched with Ian Fleming, at Scott's. Ian had asked after me, too, or rather after the man who was Hannay. And when Simon had told him of all the gory details of the horrible torture I'd suffered, and that for reasons of expediency I was to officially expire from said horrible wounds, Fleming had raised a glass in my honour and then launched straight into a discussion of people's tolerance to pain; a matter that'd concerned him greatly, during the War, when he'd sent British agents into Nazi-occupied Europe. He said it even touched on an idea he had about one day writing a novel about a new breed of post-war British spy. "You know, Simon," he said. "It would've been so much worse had the villain used something like a carpet beater on Hannay's testicles. That would've battered and crushed his balls as flat as two fried eggs; ten times as nasty, and much more bloody. Even so, the psychology of robbing a man of his manhood and using a damned pussycat to do it, suggests the villain possessed a remarkably twisted mind."

"That's it," I shouted, when I heard that. "I've had enough of playing bloody Red Indians in Defence of the Realm, I want out of here, now."

"But that's why I'm here," Simon said, my little outburst rolling off him like water off a duck's back. "You're being released, this morning, and I thought you could use these." He pointed to two elegantly battered suitcases standing by the door. "As Jeffrey Hannay's nearest relative, Russell gave them to me. But as for me, Jethro, I'd like you to have them; you more than earned them. Though, you may find them a trifle heavier than when you last packed them." He gave me a nod and a wink worthy of Donald Wolfit, and even I had to laugh. "Then I thought a spot of lunch would be in order," he said, handing me my dressing gown.

I looked at him, then at the suitcases; just possibly, my unofficial reward for all I'd gone through. "If you're saying what I think you're saying," I said through narrowed eyes, "then lunch is definitely on me. So let's go to Wheelers, I want to rewrite some history."

Wheels within wheels. False bottoms and smuggler's safes filled with jewellery. *Laces for a lady, letters for a spy.* I felt more like my old self than I had in months.

CHAPTER 44

England Made Me

The first thing I noticed back on my side of the looking-glass was there were few if any of the usual faces on the manor. From King's Cross to Ladbroke Grove and White City; all round Paddington, the Edgware Road, and Lisson Grove; it was as if all the major villains had gone off on their holidays. Or maybe word had got round that the Yard were working extra hard to clear their books of serious crimes; as happened, occasionally. Nothing too unusual, of course, but it pointed to something being in the wind.

Ray was pleased to see I was still in one piece. And Joanie was glad to have me back after my stay *'oop North,* as she called it. But that lasted exactly less than a week and I was soon being accused of getting under everyone's feet, as per usual. And, ever mindful to remain hidden in plain sight, I started making noises that I was looking around for a bit of theatre work. So, when a call came in from Universal Theatre Co.

looking to see if I could fill in for a day, again, she hardly turned a hair, although I did.

As before, I met Walsingham outside the Ritz. I thought, at first, he'd just strolled round the corner from Boodles, but the package in his hands suggested he'd come from Hatchards, the booksellers, further down Piccadilly. We headed for Green Park, again, and I realised it must be one of his favourite walks. I gave a little nod over to my right as I entered through the gate, then eyes forward, got into step.

"We're heading for Queen Anne's Gate," he said, by way of explanation. "There's something there I want you to see. Simon should have it all set up by the time we arrive." Then, without breaking stride, he turned to me, a look of genuine concern on his face "How are you feeling, Jethro? Well on the way to a full and complete recovery, I hope?"

"Yes, everything seems to be working, I'm glad to say."

"Good, good. No other concerns then?"

I thought for a moment and said, "Well, now you mention it, Mr. Walsingham, there is something I've been wondering about." He nodded for me to continue. "With respect, it strikes me that with you being who you are—Eton, Oxford, the Guards, and all that—and Simon Bosanquet being much the same, that it would've been so very easy for you to have let sleeping dogs lie. It was your lot, after all, that was behind everything."

He turned to look at me a second time. "By, *my lot*," he said, "I take it, you mean the upper classes?" I nodded. He was quiet for a moment, then with eyes still facing front, he said, "While I do admit to having benefited from a privileged background, Jethro, I do very strongly believe in the idea of democracy; the alternatives to which, frankly, appal me." He gestured across the park towards Buckingham Palace with his tightly furled umbrella. "It took five hundred years after the Magna Carta for us to achieve anything like true democracy in this country, and in many ways it's been a very unruly and untidy process, but I believe we should do our utmost to stay the course." He turned to me again. "And for better or worse, so very many of 'my lot,' as you call us, fought and died in two World Wars to defend the very idea of it. And if called upon, I assure you, they would do so again, unhesitatingly. But it's this country and what it stands for, that I believe in, Jethro, not a particular class of people."

I thought about that for a moment; he was neither defending or apologising for his class, what he'd been fighting against was a group of people who'd attempted to seize the reins of power, illegally. It mattered not that they were of his own kind, what'd spurred him to action was that they hadn't played by the accepted rules of the game.

I had to push it, though. "But if 'your lot' fought so hard and gave up so much, doesn't it follow that all those people who supported NOB and BUM would just turn round and say they earned the freedom to shout down everything they were opposed to?"

"No," he said, flatly, "that's anarchy. Freedom starts with accepting limitations, accepting compromises, and then accepting responsibility for what follows. Freedom only gives you the opportunity to assert your interests if you also acknowledge there is an obligation to hear and accommodate the interests of others."

"For the common good? For the good of all?" I said. He nodded. "Sounds just like Communism, if you ask me," I said.

"You forgot the most important element," he said. "Debate, the very fulcrum of Parliamentary Democracy; two Parties separated by a sword's length; two sides to every argument; more, if you consider the differences between front- and back-benches. Even the rise and fall of whichever Party is in power is always a reminder that 'nothing ever too much' is the very essence of symmetry and balance. It's certainly better for all parties than a dictator or a single Party standing atop the heap, killing off or obliterating all who oppose them or who one day might."

"Freedom to do whatever you like within the Law? Is that it?"

He turned, and smiled. "As Winston once said, Jethro, 'Democracy may well be the very worst form of government, except for all the other forms that have been tried, from time to time, all over the world.'"

I smiled back. "He also said, 'Democracy was no harlot to be picked up on the street by a man with a Tommy gun.'"

"Then let's just agree to agree, shall we?" he said, nodding.

"I did, the first time you invited me to take a walk in the park with you," I said. And with that we crossed The Mall into St. James's Park.

It appeared Walsingham had lately gone up in the world. He'd taken over part of a nice, four-storey Georgian house—not including attic and basement—in Queen Anne's Gate. They were still moving filing cabinets and furniture in when we got there. He paused just outside the front door and turned, and said, "Thank you, by the way, for what you did for Jennifer Manning." Then he went in ahead and we made our way past all the boxes in the hallway and through to a big room at the rear of the house. There were several desks already piled high with files and papers. Simon Bosanquet looked up with undisguised pleasure. "Ah, cousin Hannay," he said, "back from the dead, again; and so soon." He chuckled at his own wit, then turned to Walsingham. "It's in here, sir," he said. And led the way into an adjoining room, empty, but for a mahogany writing desk, three bent-wood chairs, none of which matched, and a squat grey metal machine standing against the far wall that looked like a safe with a mouthful of teeth. Walsingham moved a couple of cardboard file boxes on the table, put down his package and his umbrella, and turned and nodded, and Simon went over and closed the door and locked it.

"As you can see, Jethro, we're moving into new offices, and so there are one or two items I no longer have room for." I looked around the almost empty room, then back at him. He leaned against the table and turned to Simon, who opened one of the file boxes and produced a buff-coloured file with a red card stapled to the front of it.

I stared at it as if it was going to explode. "Me?" I said.

"You," Simon said, pulling out a second file, and then a third. And that was before he started in on a second box.

"Blimey, I didn't realise there was so much of me. So what is it you want me to do for you now?" I said, my spirits sinking fast.

"Nothing but watch," he said. "It's a variation on a confetti-making machine; it's perfect for destroying both print- ed and typewritten matter."

And as Simon Bosanquet pulled page after page from the files and stacked them neatly on the table, Walsingham looked at me and said, "Directly or indirectly, Jethro, I've twice been responsible for you having been tortured and almost killed. And I'm somewhat wary of pushing your luck a third time." I bit my tongue. "I also gave you my word that, if successful, I'd destroy what files we had on you and not involve you in any future plans as regards the Defence of the Realm." I bit down even harder, and prayed I wouldn't draw blood. "Then there's the vexing question of the missing jewellery and other items taken from

Vashfield Hall." I tasted something warm and salty, and swallowed it down. "And even though I understand Bedfordshire County Constabulary are still investigating the incident, I am disinclined to involve this department any further in a matter that is so patently outside its brief. Especially now that Simon appears to have so very uncharacteristically mislaid said items."

I watched Simon Bosanquet innocently feeding page after page from my file into the mouth of the confetti machine. It sounded like a printing press gone badly wrong, but I didn't really hear it; Walsingham's words were still ringing in my ears. He was actually standing by his word; I was going to be allowed to go back through the looking-glass; back into the normal world. I stood there as tiny bits of paper flew out the other side of the machine into a collection bin; watching, mesmerised, as little pieces danced in the air like newly hatched moths. In the back of my mind I suppose I knew there had to be other copies of my files, somewhere, but I appreciated the gesture, nevertheless. Then, to top it all, Walsingham reached into his briefcase and pulled out my Fairbairn-Sykes; I mean, his old Fairbairn-Sykes, the three-quarter–sized Commando knife he'd given me that time I broke into his house. He handed it to me, hilt first. "Yours, I think. Belfold had it on the desk in his study; no doubt, intended as a letter opener. I'm sure you can put it to better use."

I eased the knife out of its leather sheath; its edges had been newly honed. I stared at it. The blade was me; pointed and double-edged; and only deadly in a fight for my life, my family, or anyone I called friend. I put me away. "Thank you," I said. He handed me the small parcel from Hatchards. I looked at it, daft, not knowing what to do with it, then my fingers did the thinking for me and undid the knots and the wrapping paper. It was a red leather-bound copy of John Buchan's *The Thirty-Nine Steps*. I opened it to the title page. Walsingham had written, *To the real Hannay* and signed it with a simple *W.* I didn't know what to say, so I nodded and bit down very hard again on my by now very sore tongue.

What I'd come to realise about Walsingham was that he was a dyed-in-the-wool pragmatist who practised the patient assembling of what parts he had to hand and the manufacturing by whatever means necessary of those he didn't. Bosanquet and Browno were his two most useful tools, but otherwise he turned to "gifted irregulars" like me. It was all very English, in a way, like constructing "a ship in a bottle" out of matchsticks or building a model locomotive out of bits of scrap metal. But by hook or by crook, fair means or foul, he'd have things work to his pattern or he'd break them to pieces and start again. And it's that, I suppose, that made him such a formidable enemy. He was true to his lights and even though I hadn't always agreed with him or his methods and had really cursed him at times, I'd learned to respect him. He loved Great Britain and all it represented with a passion, as did Ray Karmin and Simon Bosanquet, and as I'd come increasingly to realise, I did, too; not the jingoistic tub-thumping, pomp-and-circumstance, class-riddled England; but something much deeper. And maybe that history professor was right, it was to do with the land and its history and its people; only it should be *all* of its people, not just the privileged few. After all, almost everyone's ancestors had come from elsewhere, hadn't they, even the aristocracy's. And I'd never ever thought about it in those terms before. I'd never even asked myself what it meant to be an Englishman. I'd only ever thought of myself as a Londoner, a Cockney. But I suppose, no man is an island, and nor is any city, neither.

CHAPTER

45

Thief Row

Of course, that should've been the end of the story; the villains routed; the arch-villain bearded in his den; the applecart still standing; the ship of State, nicely afloat; but it wasn't. But life never is as tidy as they make out in novels and films, is it? And if life teaches you anything, it's that there are always umpteen unseen consequences to anything you do; and good or bad, makes no difference. And more's the pity, because in many ways what happened next was the beginning of a lot of bad things that went on for years afterwards, though no one involved had the slightest inkling at the time. It was all set to be the really big one; something that'd never been attempted before and that'd have people talking for years to come: the Great Airport Robbery. Not that I was looking to be any part of it, mind you, but I had no choice, it was payback for what Jack Spot had done for me—and Seth—in Slough. Payback being another word for having to face the consequence of your actions; your history, ready and waiting to take a bite out of your arse at the very earliest opportunity.

I didn't see or hear the big black motor car slide up beside me, but then I had my collar up, I was wearing a hat, and was about to step inside a telephone box. All I had in mind was Natalie's voice, but all I heard was, "Get in, lad." And I knew then, I was on the spot, again, so to speak.

"Been away on your holidays again, have you, Jethro? Seems to be the season for it, for some reason." He chuckled, his grin somewhere between an inquisitive cocker spaniel and a hungry wolf. "And not one postcard to say, you wished I was there. It's enough to make a person think you've forgotten who your real friends are."

I was relieved it was only Spottsy and Tommy Nutkins in the motor. "Never happen, Jack. Family and friends are the key-stones to life."

"Very poetic, Jethro," he said, tapping a finger against his chin. "I must remember that." He nodded at Tommy's eyes in the driving mirror and the big black motor car slid smoothly out into the traffic. "So," he said, holding out a silver hip-flask, "Did you ever come across any of those very special red leather-covered books, on your travels?"

"Er, no, Jack," I said, quickly lacing up my tap-dancing shoes. "Truth is, I didn't have a bloody clue where to look. And with no one with any inside gen, there was no chance, as much as I wanted to help."

I had to be straight. I didn't want to end up on the same hook as before. But to my relief, Spottsy just pushed out his lower lip and slowly nodded his head, in agreement. "True, very true," he said.

"Why, has that Mr. Zaretsky been asking after me?" I asked.

"No, as it happens, he hasn't, he hasn't mentioned you at all. But everyone's got more important things on their minds, at the moment."

I nodded. "All helping with the birth of Israel?" I said, helpfully.

He turned and looked at me, blankly. "Yes," he said. Then he turned away and just stared out the window, but I don't think he was seeing the traffic on High Holburn. After a mile or so, his head still turned away, he said, quietly, "I'm setting up a really big one and I'm putting a crack team together. So, I need to call on the very best."

I'd been expecting it for nigh on three months, ever since Tommy had first given me the whisper, but it was still a bit of a shock to have it finally out in the open. But I'd rehearsed my lines and all I had to do was not bump into any furniture. "I'm in," I said, simply.

There was no need to thank him again for what he'd done for me in Slough; he'd just called in the favour. The rules were simple. From that moment on, for the duration of the caper, Spottsy was my Guv'nor. Or, in his absence, Tommy was. Even so, there was still another scene yet to play, and I told Spottsy I'd only go through with it all on one condition. The only people who were ever to know it was me he'd tapped as his key-man, were him and Tommy Nutkins, and that I'd only ever appear in disguise during rehearsals and on the caper itself, or it was no go. I wasn't casting aspersions against anyone on his team, I said. It's just that, however good they were, with the new Criminal Act in force, anybody could be pressured into being a nark. "I don't want to end up inside, Jack, just because somebody's grassed me up to save their own skin."

Spottsy's chuckle set my hairs on end. "Don't you worry, Jethro, everyone on the team is going to play by my rules. If anyone ends up inside, their family will get well looked after, whatever the result. But if anyone grasses us up before, during, or after the caper, then God help him, because he's a dead man walking. So, you believe you me, nothing's going to go wrong. I've been planning it for months. I've hand-picked everyone myself. And every tiny detail has been thought about long and hard."

When it came to relieving people of their money Spottsy was nothing if not fastidious. And since the War he'd done very well from his gambling club in St. Bartolph's Lane and his share of on-course betting at half a dozen different racetracks. But there'd also been whispers about Spottsy and Sammy the Greek, another North London villain of repute, doing a number of very lucrative lorry hijacks together. I knew Spottsy was always moving pieces about on the board so as to mess up Messima's future plans, but I did wonder why he was now so hell-bent on setting up a big one, especially with Billy Hill still inside. But as I sat there, in the back of the motor, and he told me what he had in mind, even I understood the lure. It was the perfect target of opportunity for a forward-thinking villain who had plans for taking over all of London, north of the River. The new airport out at Heath Row was still under construction. And even though a huge terminal building had recently been completed, Customs operations were still being carried on in a ramshackle collection of Nissen huts and old warehouses on the northern perimeter, near the Bath Road. And it just so happened that Sammy the Greek had got it from a friend of his that worked at the airport, that valuable cargoes of never less than £250,000 worth of goods, including diamonds, were kept overnight in the main Customs shed almost every day of the week. But the real kicker was that every now and then, they also took delivery of a million quid in gold bullion. And that of course was the very reason Spottsy had had the airport Customs sheds under observation, just watching and waiting, every single day for over three months. He'd even had bulky parcels sent over from Ireland, then had two of his blokes with kosher lorry-driving licences go in and collect them, which had enabled them to get a real close look at both the inside and outside of the Customs area.

Then Spottsy made every man Jack of us go on the official airport visitors' tour to familiarise ourselves with the area. After which, he had us move toy motor cars and lead soldiers around on a big sheet of plywood that had a plan of the airport and all the surrounding service roads painted on it. It even had little cardboard models of the Customs sheds; it was that detailed. Then he had us go over the plan again and again until everyone knew their entrances and their exits and what parts they played, off by heart. And then he had us do it for real at an abandoned aerodrome way out on the Estuary. And at the end of it all, it was just a question of waiting until word came through that a shipment of gold bullion was expected. Sammy the Greek's inside man would then kick off the whole caper by ensuring that the coffee urn, delivered each night and morning to the main Customs office to help keep the security guards awake, was well and truly spiked with enough sleeping pills to drop a herd of elephants.

Anyway, when it came to it, I sported a pencil moustache and a thick Irish accent, which although at times veered dangerously between Belfast and Dublin, was accepted by all, and without comment. Probably because Ireland and gelignite go together, like fish and chips. I did however take the extra precaution of always wearing a nylon stocking over my face, which must've also gone over well, because by the end of rehearsals everybody on the team was wearing one.

Natalie played hell with me at first for asking to borrow a couple of her old stockings, given how hard they were to come by. Although, it might well have been because she thought I was intending to give them to another woman or something. But when I told her I needed them to help keep me out of trouble on a caper, she simply nodded, and gave me two stockings with ladders in them; a black one and a tan one; and asked no further questions. So I wore the tan one during rehearsals and the black one on the job itself, and when it all went down, knowing it was one of Natalie's fully-fashioned stockings I had on over my face, somehow made it that much more bearable. And looking back on it, now, I'd say it was the only pleasant part of the whole bloody caper.

But beyond those few stipulations I'd made to Spottsy, that time in the back of his motor car, none of it was ever my call. I was just a pawn in the game, again. And in that, there was really no difference, whether it was Spottsy or Walsingham making the moves or pulling the strings. And anything I ever did for either of them, you could put down to me working to protect my family, a friend, or myself. But then as my old mum had taught me, if ever you couldn't get out of something, you stuck your arm into the pickle jar all the way right up to the elbow, and grasped hold of the pickle. You did what you had to do, hoped you'd still be in one piece at the end of it all, then you moved on.

Blue Moon, Robber's Moon

At precisely thirty minutes to midnight one Saturday night, late in July, a police car turned onto the perimeter road of Heath Row airport and sped off, westwards. "Dead on time," said Tommy, looking through a pair of night glasses. "We're on." We were all waiting in a lay-by, a quarter mile back. I was with Tommy in a big black Wolseley, like the ones used by airport security officials and police traffic patrols. The heavy brigade and light brigade were behind us, in two Austin Freeway vans. We set off in convoy. Everyone wore buff-coloured overalls; leather turtles; and had a stocking ready in a pocket. Tommy had a big hand-torch for signalling with. All four heavies had a length of lead pipe for coshing senseless anyone that deserved it. I carried a set of twirls, a pencil-torch, and a satchel with various bits of kit. I also had my cat's eyes, sixth sense, and whatever of my nine lives I still had. We turned off the perimeter road down towards the Customs enclosure. "I don't like it, Tommy," I said staring out at the two dim puddles of light that stopped the Customs sheds from completely disappearing into the darkness. "It feels iffy, if you ask me."

"Well, I'm not asking you, Jethro, I'm telling you, the job's on. The gold bullion is in there tonight and it'll be gone tomorrow. So shut it." He looked at his watch. "You're on the clock, go." I got out of the Wolseley and went over and did the padlock on the security fence gate. I pushed the gate open so the Wolseley and the two vans could drive in, closed it again, and substituted a padlock of my own so it'd look kosher when the next police patrol passed by. Then as the vans backed up to the loading doors to get out of sight, I nipped down the side of the main Customs shed to the single-storey administration building; counting off seconds in my head.

There was a light on over the entrance and lights on inside the office, but I just had to trust to Spottsy's planning and I went at the upper Yale dead bolt at full speed. I inserted both twirls, stroked the tumblers and got them all up into line, gave the torsion bar a firm twist, and retracted the dead bolt. Then I started in on the second Yale lock and I'd just got the torsion bar turned and the bolt rolled back, when Tommy appeared from around the corner with the heavy mob. I gave the door a push and stepped aside. The two biggest heavies went in first, then Tommy, followed by the third heavy carrying a stepladder and the fourth heavy, a bag of tools. After a quick look left and right and a squint up at the night sky to see if I could see a robber's moon, I pulled on my black stocking mask and followed.

It looked like the end scene in *Hamlet,* only without the swords. The bottle of barbiturates Sammy the Greek's inside man had had poured into the coffee urn had certainly done the job as well as any poisoned cup. All three uniformed Customs officers were sprawled on the floor, out for the count. Then I looked up and despite all the training, I felt real dread at seeing the wall of steel bars that ran from one side of the administration office to the other; it was my horror of a prison guardroom, sprung to life.

We all looked at Tommy. He nodded. And while two of the heavies pushed all the furniture to one side, the other two set about tying up the unconscious Customs officers and dragging them into a corner; each guard getting an extra cosh on the head before being relieved of his keys. We'd been told the steel door into the high security area was alarmed. Trouble was, the arming switch could've been hidden anywhere in the office, even in the toilets for all we knew, and as there was no time to go searching for it, it was my job to loop the alarm. So I looked for the two copper contact plates that I knew had to be located somewhere between the steel-barred door and its surrounding frame. And, luckily, they were situated; one in the door, the other in the jamb; just above the door's upper hinge, and not along the top, which would've meant us going up into the ceiling. I waved away the heavies with the stepladder and hammer and chisel, and pointed to one of the desks, and the other two heavies had it up against the steel bars in seconds. I jumped up and ran my fingers from the contact plates across to the adjacent horizontal crossbar that kept the vertical steel bars rigidly in place all the way to the wall. I stuck my hand in between the uprights and felt for the metal conduit pipe that'd been spot-welded along the top of the crossbar. I reached back and one of the heavies slapped a hacksaw into my hand. I sawed through the conduit, halfway, held the saw out, and it was whipped away and I was handed a jemmy. I pushed the head of the jemmy in as far as I could under the conduit pipe, and levered upwards until the gap in it opened wide enough for me to reach in with a pair of bent-nosed pliers and pull out the two alarm wires. I stripped them bare, snapped alligator clips onto both of them, then snipped each wire just beyond where I'd attached the clips, and turned my head and nodded.

Tommy looked at his watch and gave a nod. One of the heavies opened the outside door a crack and flashed a signal out into the night. Then I was handed three sets of keys, in turn. I had to find which keys fitted the top, bottom, and middle locks on the inner security door. The top two locks, no trouble. However, no key on any of the key-rings would open the third, which was odd. So I used my twirls and picked the bloody thing. Somewhere in the back of my mind, though, I suppose I must've been pondering whether it was entirely natural for any-one who was supposed to be dead to the world, to give out with a grunt when they got given a bang on the head. But as my part had to be done in three minutes, max, I stayed focussed. And with it done, I pushed open the security door, stuck a wedge under it, and stood back. Tommy was the first one through into the high security area, quickly followed by the members of the heavy brigade. Then I went back over and stood by the outside door and kept my ears cocked.

There was a knock on the door and I opened it and the light brigade wheeled their trolleys in like a team of porters at the Savoy. The first two trolleys were loaded with heavy canvas bags, lengths of rope, and work-lamps. The third trolley had a dustbin full of bolt-cutters, pickaxes, and sledgehammers strapped to it. The fourth one was loaded with an old ammuni-tion box containing gelignite, detonators, wire-flex, and a nine-volt battery. Spottsy had planned for every eventuality. I sig-nalled for them to hold their horses and went and peered into the dim light of the Customs shed and waited for Tommy's next signal. Two flashes, on-off, on-off. Then the glim flashed on again, and stayed on, to show where Tommy and the team were waiting. I nodded to the trolley-men and in they went, their steps as jaunty as a formation dancing team. My job, then, was to wait for Tommy's next signal. Two flashes either meant, "come and do some more business with your twirls," or "the jelly needs serving up." Four flashes meant, "go unlock the loading doors and keep your eyes peeled."

I followed the progress of the light brigade as they disappeared off towards Tommy's glim and tried to picture in my mind the plan of the warehouse. If Spottsy's information was correct, a million pounds' worth of gold ingots were stored some thirty yards down on the left-hand side. A million quid; it was enough to take your breath away. And I know, now, I must've imagined the sound of grinding teeth. Because when all was said and done, DCI Browno wasn't ever listed as being on the team of Flying Squad detectives and uniformed police officers that suddenly emerged from out of the shadows, howling and shouting like a horde of Fuzzy-Wuzzys lusting for blood. But something in me must have heard something, and responded faster than thought, because while everyone else in the place seemed to be charging in the direction of Tommy's now-extinguished torch beam, I'd already vanished back inside the administration office.

I left the security door wedged open, as it could still be a way out for someone on the team. But I swung my satchel up, and smashed the two bare light bulbs hanging from the ceiling, and slipped inside the toilets to the left of the front door. And before you could say, "Houdini will now disappear," I'd whisked off the stocking mask and slid out of my overalls, got the peaked cap out of my satchel and onto my head, and stuffed everything I could down inside one of the water tanks. And I was just about to make my exit when I heard a van screech to a halt outside. Then the outer door to the Customs office crashed open with an almighty bang, followed by what, from the sound of boots on concrete, must've been a whole rugby team of uniformed police officers. Then there was another almighty bang. And I took three deep breaths, opened the toilet door a crack, and peeked out. The security door had been slammed shut, and if the noises were anything to go by, everybody inside the Customs shed was busy thumping the living daylights out of anything else that moved. And whatever my feelings were about the situation, there was nothing more I could do, but exit stage left and be bloody quick about it.

There was a police van outside, its engine still running, and I was tempted to hop in and drive off. But then I noticed the outer gate in the perimeter fence was still locked with my padlock, which said the second lot of coppers must've been waiting for us round the far side of the Customs shed. And that was proof, right then and there, that we'd been stitched up right from the start. I looked up and saw a bunch of headlights approaching fast, and even in the dark I could make out the boxy shapes of a fleet of Black Marias against the streetlights strung along the Bath Road two or three hundred yards away. Then two headlights split off and accelerated ahead of the convoy, and that meant only one thing: there were two police motorcycle outriders in attendance. Soddin' hell. That was all I needed.

I marched towards the gate, gave a quick nod up to heaven to thank Harry Houdini, the only true begetter of the ruse, then took a deep breath and waited until the two outriders and the leading prison-van were almost upon me. Then in the full glare of their headlights, the silver buttons on my blue serge uniform gleaming like cat's eyes, I snapped open the padlock, and pulled back the gate allowing them to enter, adjusting my police driver's peaked cap as I did so. The black vans swept by and skidded to a halt outside the main Customs shed. The drivers got out, someone yelled, "Good job," and one of the motorcycle riders got off his bike and started walking towards me. And at that exact moment there was another almighty bang and the Customs shed loading doors burst open and about half a dozen bodies came flying out, which not unnaturally attracted everyone's attention. It was like a scene out of the Keystone Kops, only with real truncheons, and with no quarter given or received. Tommy and at least two other members of the team all ran off in different directions, each of them chased by a scrum of coppers. Then as I spent a moment seemingly fiddling with the lock on the gate, I noticed a lone figure slip out of the shadows and roll underneath one of the police vans. He didn't appear again on the other side, which said whoever it was, was going to try and do a "hanger" and hold onto the underside of the van, in the hope of dropping off at the first set of traffic lights, out on the Bath Road. I wished him luck. Then I slipped outside the perimeter fence and started moving in a fast crouch in the direction of the new main terminal building, a mile or so away. As the old creeping saying says, "The best place to hide, is where no one would ever expect to find you."

CHAPTER

47

Retreating North

The Gods of Petticoat Lane started laughing before I'd gone ten yards. Once off the concrete aprons, roadways, or runways, Heath Row was just hundreds of acres of grassland full of pot-holes and puddles and the rough and muddy ground made the going very hard, very quickly, and I was forced back towards the firmer ground near the wire fence. But as the whole area was also dotted with discarded building materials I had to go extra careful or I could've tripped or slipped and sprained an ankle or something. I'd just about reached the southernmost corner of the perimeter fence, when some bastard somewhere started switching on all the lights along the sides of the Customs sheds. And I hit the ground, hard, just about the same time as someone hit the wire fence a dozen or so yards from where I was lying. As luck had it, I was lost in the shadows cast by a stack of oil drums and as long as I lay still I couldn't be seen. But I could see that the bloke climbing for his very life was Tommy Nutkins. He was surprisingly agile for such a big bugger, and he went up one of the ten-foot-high steel fence supports like a rat up a drain-pipe. I could hear him puffing and groaning like a goods train on a steep slope, and I whispered, "That's it, Tommy, up, up and over." Then I saw the barbed wire coiled along the top of the security fence, and realised he was in trouble. I pushed myself up off the ground to go and help, but saw out the corner of my eye a bunch of coppers running along the side of the Customs shed, which meant they'd have Tommy in their sights in fifteen, twenty seconds, tops.

I heard a ripping sound and a dull thump as Tommy dropped heavily to the ground. He lay there for a moment, winded and dazed, but Tommy being bloody Tommy, he didn't stay down for the count, but staggered to his feet and started to stumble off, wheezing like a clapped-out accordion. The trouble was, the rough ground would soon have him bogged down, and with the noise he was making he'd be spotted immediately, which would land us both in it. I had no time to whistle or shout out a warning, as in the state Tommy was in he'd probably just turn and turn, too exhausted to know what was what or which way was which. So I reached down and grabbed a brick, and running in a crouch, I threw it at him and hit him smack on the back of the head. And he went down like a wooden skittle at the very moment all the coppers came barrelling round the corner of the Customs shed.

I lay full-length in the mud and prayed Tommy wouldn't groan or make a move. The galloping coppers were too charged up not to want to carry on chasing their missing quarry. And so after a few cursory glances through the wire fence, when a couple of fly buggers crouched down to look for any dark silhouettes moving against the night sky, they dashed off around the other side of the main Customs shed, like hounds after a fox. I waited a minute, then crawled over to Tommy and rolled him over and over, and down into a shallow ditch. I pulled the stocking mask off, so he could breathe more freely. Then I pulled a couple of wooden planks and a torn piece of tarpaulin over the hole; lay down in the mud, tried to silence the military tattoo drumming in my head, then tried to see through my ears. It seemed a very, very long way from the world of Vashfield Hall.

The sounds of pursuit ebbed and flowed, and finally faded. Then I heard the doors of the police cars and Black Marias all banging shut like the gates of doom. I swallowed hard, and wiped the mud from off my wristwatch; it was just gone two o'clock. I gave it another half-hour, then spent about a million years trying to get Tommy out of the hole and up onto my back, fireman's fashion. Then I staggered off, in the direction of the Bath Road.

My practice when on any caper, was always to leave a means of transport close by. So I had the old Austin van parked in a side road on the other side of the Bath Road, next to a line of houses. And I waited until there was no sign of any headlights coming from either direction, then looking like a giant hedgehog having a bad day I scurried across the road. I had to double Tommy up to get him in the back of the van, then I climbed in beside him and closed the doors. It was only when I heard him groaning that I realised he must be badly hurt. I scrambled into the driver's seat, spit on an old handkerchief and cleaned as much mud as I could from off my face, then drove towards Slough, the Farnham Road, and Seth and Dilys's house.

I threw small stones up at the bedroom window. No light came on, but suddenly Seth was at the front door with a pick-axe handle in his hand. He had his boots on, but was still in his pyjamas. I put my finger to my lips and nodded back over my shoulder. He nodded, slipped a coat on, then came and helped get Tommy out of the van, and only when we got inside, did he turn the light on and call up to Dilys, who appeared in her dressing gown. "Hello, Jethro," she said. "I'll put the kettle on. You look like you could do with a cup of tea." I looked at Tommy; he looked as if he could do with a week in bed with a nurse and three weeks at the seaside.

Even without all the caked mud and dried blood, it was pretty clear Tommy had a broken arm, broken ribs, and a badly sprained ankle. And I know Seth and Dilys knew something was up when I declined Seth's offer to go call for an ambulance. They were bloody sure of it, when they saw the blue-serge uniform on under Tommy's torn overalls. Mine wasn't the life they'd chosen, but they kept their thoughts to themselves; a friend was in need, that was all that mattered. There were no more questions, just a job to be done. So Seth put an oil-stove in the bathroom and we stood Tommy in the bath and cleaned him up as best we could. And while I cleared up the mess and then took a quick bath, Seth got to work bandaging and putting a wooden splint on Tommy's arm. Then he rustled up some clean clothes for me, and the two of us drove round to Dilys's sister's place.

We tapped the knocker till John appeared and, again, he just got stuck in, with no questions asked. And after we'd apologised to Betty for disturbing them so very early in the morning, the three of us drove through the trading estate to the biscuit factory where John worked. The night shift was still in full swing when we got there. But after a chat with one of the foremen, and a favour asked and a fiver given, John arranged for Tommy to be taken as a passenger in an overnight lorry slated to carry a load of biscuits up to a warehouse in Manchester. Tommy had family and friends up there, and the makings of a cast-iron alibi that he hadn't been anywhere near London at the time of the attempted robbery.

That done, we drove back to Seth's to go pick up Tommy and found him bundled up in blankets, warming by the fire, busy reviving himself with a large glass of Johnny Walker and a pot of Dilys's tea. So we all had a cup laced with whisky to warm us up, along with a plate of ham sandwiches Dilys had made. While we'd been away, Dilys, bless her, had also cleaned Tommy's shoes and brushed and sponged his clothes clean. Add a large pair of overalls that John had borrowed from a mate back at the factory, and a muffler and flat cap lent to him by Seth, and Big Tom began to look halfway decent. Then, just as we were about to leave, Dilys handed Tommy an Oxo tin full of sandwiches for the journey home, and Seth gave him what was left of the half bottle of whisky to help keep him warm. "Thank you, you two lovely people, for all your help. I won't forget it," Tommy said, kissing Dilys on the cheek and shaking Seth's hand.

"Go safe," Seth said.

I took my leave, then, thanked him and Dilys for all they'd done, and promised I'd be in touch soon. "And you go safe, and all," Seth said.

"I bloody well need to," I said. Then I bundled Tommy into the van, waved goodbye, and with John sitting in the back, drove back to the biscuit factory, where the lorry driver was waiting for us, smoking a cigarette.

"Right then," he said. "Let's be off. The A1 North can be a right bugger if you leave it too late."

"Thanks, John," Tommy said, shaking John's hand. "I owe you."

"No," said John. "You came to help Mr. Jethro, help our Seth. So, I thank you." Then he grinned sheepishly, shook my hand, and walked off into the factory to clock on for his shift.

"Good people," Tommy said. "Unlike whichever bastard has set himself up for an early grave, by grassing us up."

"Yes," I said. "The thing is, though, even with my suspicious nature, I can't see it being anyone on the team; there was too much on the table."

"Then you mark my words, Jethro, it's someone even closer," he said, tersely. I nodded, helped him up into the cab, and slammed the door. He looked down at me. "That's another one I owe you."

"No, Tommy," I said. "As young John said, there's nothing owed. You'd have done the same, if I was in your shoes."

"Possibly," he said, smiling a tired smile. "Possibly not. It'd depend on how hard I had to hit you to get you to do as you're told." He rubbed the bump on the back of his head where I'd crowned him with the brick. He looked at me, and raised his broken arm in salute.

I raised an arm, in reply. He nodded. I nodded. Then the driver let out the clutch, and the lorry's tail-lights disappeared off into the dwindling night. And then I drove slowly back into London via Beaconsfield, all the while thinking of an earlier time, when Tommy and I had come in, like conquerors, from the North.

CHAPTER 48

Red Sky at Night

The world continued turning. Summer drew to a close. And that September, Seth, Dilys, Natalie, and me got all poshed up, and went up West to the Hippodrome to see Michael Bentine in *Starlight* on the last night of its run. Seth laughed his head off, which was good to see. "Never seen anything like it," he said. The exact same reaction I'd had when I'd first seen Mike's act the year before, when all the other acts on the bill had been stars from off the radio, and a few Americans nobody had ever heard of; not what you'd call a great show. Then this scraggy-looking kid had come on and held the crowd mesmerised; just Mike holding a broken chair-back. The chair-back, first one thing, then another, in a constant blur, all the while him chattering away like a nutcase; a cartoon character come to life; it was brilliant. And though I'd had enough of broken chairs to last me several lifetimes, given what I'd suffered at the hands of Belfold, five minutes of seeing Mike's mad antics again and even that awful memory faded away and I was allowed to laugh myself out of a very dark corner.

I got a call from the Globe to fill-in for some dress rehearsals, due to one of the blokes on the fly-team being out with a badly sprained wrist. So I went down Shaftesbury Avenue and was up on the fly floor, working away, when I nearly went arse over tit down onto the stage. It was her, Felicity Larsen, as large as life and free as a bird, preparing for yet another role. It was the very last place I'd expected to see her, but I suppose if fancy applecarts could be left standing upright, then someone's favourite sleeping dog could be left to lie. And given what I'd come to learn about how such things worked, it was likely some EHU, somewhere, had decided that were such a well-loved star of the stage and screen to be accused of foul deeds, the resulting ill wind of publicity would little serve the public good. But then beauty of a certain sort rewrites most rules. Undue influence, I think it's called.

Anyway, for the rest of the afternoon all I could hear was that voice, so cajoling and cruel, echoing up at me from below, and glutton for punishment that I am, I just happened to be hanging about outside when she left the theatre. Then as she waited on the pavement for the taxi-driver to open the door for her, I had to rub my eyes to make sure I wasn't seeing things. She had hold of a large black-leather valise identical to the ones Trent Tyler had been given. And, of course, that meant another creep, *tout de suite*. Only then, I discovered she kept the valise with her at all times, and had her maid hold it during the periods she was on stage.

I abandoned any thoughts of creeping in through her bedroom window when I saw she kept all the lights in her pent-house flat on, all night, every night. Much too tricky; one good look at me under those circumstances and she might've thought Hannay had come back from the dead. So I went to Plan B and waited for the play's official first night when all the actors and actresses, and everyone front of house and backstage, are at their most nerve-wracked. It cost me a tenner to have another bloke on the fly team suffer a badly sprained wrist, the morning of the opening. Then there I was, lunchtime, in the pub around the corner from the theatre, when the head gaffer walks in. " 'allo, Jeffro," says he. "I was about to bell you. Could you help us out, again, like now?" "For you, anything," says I. And for the rest of the day I was busy relearning the play's ropes.

I had a quick butcher's in the prompt book during a tea-break, and saw I could do the business right after the first inter-mission and complete the caper some twenty minutes into the Third Act. Like so many of Terence Rattigan's plays, it was a drawing-room drama, and Madame was on stage throughout most of it. But the cherry on top was that one of the sets called for a large bookcase, and that fit my plans perfectly. I knew from the previous year, that being the star she was, Felicity Larsen always demanded a fresh pot of coffee be delivered to her dress-ing room at intermission, even if barely a few sips ever passed her oh-so cruel lips. I also knew from backstage gossip, that it was always her maid that polished the lot off, afterwards. I just hoped I hadn't overdone the barbiturates I'd emptied into the coffee-pot, earlier. And that the plan worked, this time.

Come Act Three, I excused myself from the fly floor, say-ing I had to dash to the toilets. I pulled a book from off the prop bookcase and made for the "No. 1 Star" dressing room. And with Madame's maid snoring away, like a good 'un, it was but a matter of moments to open the smuggler's safe in the valise and switch the prop book for the Red Book. I poured the rest of the coffee down the toilet, and exited, carrying an armful of linens to cover my prize. I slipped the Red Book into the prop book-case and hurried back to the fly floor, mumbling apologies about having eaten a bad bit of horsemeat, and without any more ado got on with my scene shifting. Then that night, once the theatre had gone dark, I retrieved the Red Book, dashed over to my lock-up in Paddington Basin, where I photographed the book's contents. I printed off a set of prints, put them in a red card-board binder, and the following week had Ray Karmin get them, by very circuitous route, into the hands of Mr. Zaretsky, at the synagogue in Fornier Street. By which time, of course, I not only had those negatives, but also the ones I'd made of the Windsor letters from NOB HQ, all locked away in a very, very safe place far, far out of the Smoke. I'm not daft.

As ever, Ray had been my guiding light and North Star through much of the caper. And, certainly, his advice early on had helped me keep my head on straight. So the very first Monday evening after I'd got myself sorted, I'd visited him with a bottle of The Glenlivet that'd fallen off the back of a lorry and two elegantly battered suitcases full of jewellery and trinkets I'd acquired at Vashfield Hall. And perfect fence that he was, he disposed of everything in time-honoured fashion, very slowly, and very, very carefully. We held back the two rings set with red jasper; the ones with the octopus engraved on them; Ray had the one, I had the other. "You never know, they might come in handy," he said. But as for the gold chain of the Order of the Garter that'd belonged to Vashfield, and that Belfold had covet-ed so much, Ray suggested we simply melt it down, cackling in that way of his, "It's the only fitting end I can think of." And I'd laughed until I saw him rifling through his collection of records looking for Gustav Holst's "Mars," so as to put me into the proper frame of mind for my inevitable defeat in our coming game of chess. I pleaded with him to be merciful and he put on "Saturn, the Bringer of Old Age and Wisdom," instead. "I'll still run rings around you," he said, grinning like a bandit.

I gave the Red Book to Walsingham as it was the right thing to do. He had the original, anyway, but not its carbon copy. So, I became the old taxi-driver again and waited outside Boodles, having tracked him much as I did before; the devil in me wanting to see the look on his face when "Jethro" popped out from behind the old cabbie's spectacles. And I'm tickled to say he had to do a double take, even though I know he'd never admit it. Of course, it might've just been the sight of yet another Red Book.

"I had a hunch and acted upon it," I told him, by way of explanation. "Felicity Larsen was always so thick with Trent Tyler and all the rest of them, so when I saw she had the exact same black-leather valise, and the way she was acting, I just had to take a look."

"I'm very glad you did," Walsingham said. "My people missed it entirely. Her maid must've hidden it for her. Extraordinary, how easily one can miss the obvious." He patted the Red Book, now safely in his possession, then pointed in the direction of Boodles. "Won't you come in, for a glass of sherry or perhaps even a single malt?"

"Er, no thanks," I said, "it wouldn't be the same, me dressed as I am. I best get on. Where to, Guv'nor?"

As to the aftermath of the botched Heath Row job: six of Spottsy's hand-picked team got caught; only Tommy Nutkins, me, and two others managed to escape. No one admitted to anything, though, and no one grassed Spottsy. And the judge, his wig all but flapping in the breeze, had a field day playing the outraged defender of the public's morals. He said that a raid on such a scale profoundly shocked society. "You were prepared for violence and you got it," he said. "Your actions sought to rock the very foundations of trust upon which this country has been built, and to damage the country's efforts to rebuild itself anew after the lamentable conflagration of recent years." The sentences he then handed down were tailor-made for the headlines. Five of the gang got eight, nine, ten, eleven, and twelve years' penal servitude, respectively, proving if nothing else that the judge could count to twelve. The youngest got given five years; the judge no doubt moved to mercy because of the lad's baby face.

The real kicker to it all, though, was that the million quids worth of gold bullion had never even arrived at Heath Row. Not from any lack of planning by Spottsy or forethought by the Flying Squad, but because of bad fog across the Channel. So the aeroplane set to deliver the gold didn't even arrive until the following day. Unbelievable, but true.

But the million-pound question still remained. Who'd betrayed us? It'd been a good firm, all respectable faces. But someone, somewhere, had whispered into someone's ear. The police could never prove Spottsy was the raid's organiser, despite their suspicions. (Very similar to what happened with Lord Vashfield, now I come to think of it.) But, over time, every business Spottsy was known to have a hand in, was leaned on very hard by the boys in blue, and in the end, even his gambling club in St. Botolph's Row was forced to close. He fought back, but sometimes a single battle lost shapes the future in untold ways. And far more than can ever be comprehended by anyone at the time. Old friends became new enemies. Old enemies found ever-new ways to become even more of a threat.

The eternal law of unintended consequences, Ray called it.

Talking of which, having gone through all the palaver of staging the Olympics in London, we only ended up getting three gold medals for our troubles; two for rowing, one for yachting; but then with us being an island race, what do you expect? (The Yanks walked off with thirty-eight gold medals, if you must know.) Then after all I'd done for Clement Attlee and his Labour Government, not that he knew me from a hole in the wall mind you, they put up the price of cigarettes and watered down the beer again. Bread did come off ration at the end of May, though. And come October—everyone's idea of the perfect month for a spin—people were allowed a few measly pints of petrol for private motoring. It wasn't much, but it was a start.

Elsewhere, for something to do, the Russians blockaded Berlin. And so the people there didn't all starve to death, the Yanks and us Brits had to airlift in hundreds and thousands of tons of foodstuffs and supplies, daily; one cargo plane landing every two minutes, so the linens said. Meanwhile, the Arabs and the Jews were still battling one another; various cease-fires, truces, and even an armistice, having all been shot to pieces. The United States and the Soviet Union had both recognised the new State of Israel almost as soon as the Jews in Palestine had proclaimed their independence, back in May, but for whatever reasons Britain still hadn't done so as December drew to a close. Just the sort of game that goes on, I suppose, when countries play chess with life-size pieces on a board the size of the world.

Then as a finishing touch, when at last it seemed the dust was settling back over London, I got a postcard from America: a picture of a New York city skyscraper, the Rockefeller Center; a magnificent building, like something from another world.

There was no name, no initials, but it'd been written in red ink. *Watch the gimbals, Jeffrey; see the whole game,* was all it said. Though, in truth, *Jeffrey* had been crossed out and *Jethro* written in above it, in the same hand. I wondered how the bugger had found me. Then I remembered he really was a secret bloody agent. So, of course, he had ways of finding things out. I reached for my tea and gazed at the postcard; it'd have pride of place on the mantelpiece, upstairs.

So there I was, in the Victory, after a morning reading the linens; the postcard propped up against the sauce bottle. It was one of those rare moments when I was alone and sitting not in my usual place at the back of the cafe, but by the window at the front. Alone, that is, but for the new girl, Mary. And I tell you she was that eager to please, I only had to put my cup down and she'd have it whipped away and back within seconds, topped up and steaming hot. "Ta, love," I said, umpteen times. Then that last time, for some reason, I added, "It's a grand life, if you don't weaken," and she'd beamed and said that's what her gran had always said to her. And it struck me then, that who and what you believe in; what you hold to; is all you really are, and the only thing you have to guide you through life. And if we go on anywhere, afterwards, I suppose it's all we take with us, too. And fair do's, I reckon.

I reached for the sugar bowl and stopped, perfectly still, caught by how the sunlight reflecting in a shop window across the road could make even Church Street seem jolly, which in itself promised a balmy London night and dry rooftops. And with me now free as a bird, too. No longer dangling from anyone's strings. No more, a shadowy reflection in someone else's looking-glass. And there I was, my thoughts and feelings and imaginings caught in midair, my finger as if pointing to some unknown future, realising there were times when life really was sweet enough as it was. And at that exact moment the telephone rang and I jumped a mile and Mary picked up the receiver and held it gingerly to her ear as if it might bite her, and she listened and nodded several times. Then she gave a funny little cough, and in a posh voice that wasn't her, she said, "There's a gentleman on the blower for you, Mr. Jethro. He won't give his name, but he says, it's awfully important he has a word with you."